BOLD AND BRAZEN
THEY HAD THE COURAGE TO
FOLLOW THEIR DREAMS
DOWN STEEL RAILS
AND GOLDEN BYWAYS

LLOYD MILES—This capitalist's limitless ambition was matched by his brilliance and ruthlessness in finance. Now betraying a friend would get him into the inner circle of America's richest men, where he could grab the shiniest gold ring of all.

LEAH MILES—The lovely young woman not once but twice had allowed her brother to destroy her chances for marriage. Her third proposal offered one final hope . . . or a heartbreaking deception.

ABBY KERSHAW—The high-society beauty thought her family's wealth and position gave her the right to snub an Erie Railroad executive named Lloyd Miles. Then he ruined her family and blackmailed her into his bed.

PHILIP TRENT—The young congressman fought to stop the robber barons from sending Wall Street to a disastrous crash and plunging the entire nation into a depression. But he couldn't stop himself from coveting another man's wife.

TENNESSEE CLAFLIN—A self-styled psychic, she was mistress to Commodore Vanderbilt. Then her visions swept her and her flamboyant sister into a lawless fight to free women from the chains that kept them powerless.

Don't miss the first book in the Robber Barons
series, also available from Dell:

POWER AND GLORY

THE ROBBER BARONS Volume II

WEALTH
AND PASSION

Gerald Canfield

BCI Created by the producers of
The First Americans, The White Indian,
and **The Holts: An American Dynasty.**

Book Creations Inc., Canaan, NY • Lyle Kenyon Engel, Founder

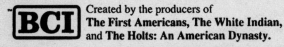

A DELL BOOK

Published by
Dell Publishing
a division of
Bantam Doubleday Dell Publishing Group, Inc.
1540 Broadway
New York, New York 10036

Produced by Book Creations, Inc.
Lyle Kenyon Engel, Founder

ISBN: 0-440-20546-8

Printed in the United States of America

Published simultaneously in Canada

May 1993

10 9 8 7 6 5 4 3 2 1

OPM

CHAPTER 1

Lloyd Miles handed the cabdriver a greenback and stepped down onto the curb in front of the Grand Central Hotel. A closed carriage drawn by a team of splendid roans took the place vacated by his cab. The coachman sprang down, opened the door, and extended his gloved hand to assist a lady swathed in a gleamingly white cloud of ruffled Lyons silk accented by yards of St. Etienne ribbon. With one glance of her pale eyes she swept past on the arm of her formally clad escort. The hotel doorman bowed and with a flourish admitted the couple. His greeting of Lloyd was less energetic, but Lloyd took no offense, even though he was a guest of the hotel. It was just human nature and economics: single gentlemen did not tip as well as those who were in the company of lovely ladies.

The swooping strains of a waltz came to Lloyd as he surrendered his silk top hat to the cloakroom attendant. A trumpeter was exhibiting his skill at triple-tonguing a brazen melody that soared over the sounds of violins, a string bass, a guitar, and a piano. Even before Lloyd stepped into the ballroom he could smell the perfumes and could hear the soft buzz of talk underlying the music. He planted his feet firmly on the glass-smooth floor and let himself be mesmerized by the graceful flow of movement as the dancers swung past him.

Gas jets in formidable crystal chandeliers burned brightly, the better to sparkle in the facets of a king's ransom of gems adorning slim, pale feminine necks, arms, and fingers. The women of New York society swirled around the floor, looking like glittering birds of paradise adorned by silks and taffetas and fine lace, in the arms of men of wealth and power. The men gathered in the ballroom of the Grand Central Hotel were those whose business and financial endeavors made the bustling city the most exciting place in the world.

The American elite had come together to celebrate the completion of the transcontinental railroad. The rails of the Union Pacific and the Central Pacific had been joined by the driving of a golden spike on May 10, 1869; and there wasn't a man in the room who failed to see opportunity for bettering himself in a nation that was now linked east to west.

Lloyd Miles, having had a part in the events that led to the completion of the Pacific Railroad, was well aware that the transcontinental had opened new and promising avenues of entrepreneurism. To him the use of the golden spike to join the two converging rails was symbolic—but not in the way intended by the dignitaries and politicians who took part in the completion ceremony.

Gold was very much on the mind of Lloyd Miles—Civil War ex-major in Ben Butler's Army of the James, holder of the Distinguished Service Medal, and onetime right-hand man of Thomas Durant of the Union Pacific Railroad— for, in spite of the wartime flood of greenbacks issued by the government, that precious metal was the official monetary standard of the United States.

Gold was the only true money, as witness the fact that during the greenback issue of 1862, it took between $130 and $140 in the late Mr. Lincoln's paper money to buy $100 in gold coins. Only twice before in the nation's history had paper currency been printed that was not immediately redeemable into gold. Both those times had come during war—the War of the Revolution and the War of 1812—and each time fiscal chaos had been the result, with the paper money becoming almost worthless. In 1869, however, the fiat money—paper currency not convertible into coin of equivalent value—was backed by a far richer and more powerful government, thus making for a more stable financial situation. Barring some totally unforeseen disaster, greenbacks would be around for some time, even though the man who sat in the White House, General Ulysses S. Grant, was on record as being in favor of "hard" money.

As long as the inflated greenbacks were in circulation, they would fluctuate in value when compared to gold, giving opportunity for profit to the speculators who gathered daily in the Gold Room on New Street. Following the lead of his new employer, Jay Gould of the Erie Railroad, Lloyd Miles had a new passion, speculating in gold, and he was doing quite well.

It was not Jay Gould who had invited Miles to the celebration in the ballroom of the Grand Central Hotel. Gould was a loner, a family man who—even if he had been accepted by New York society—disdained any activity not directly connected with making money. Neither Gould nor Jim Fisk, his flamboyant partner in the Erie Railroad, had been invited to the ball in the Grand Central, for this was a gathering of the "Four Hundred," the old rich. Parvenus such as Gould, Fisk, and a few dozen others who had made their money during and because of the Civil War had definitely not earned their way into such company.

For that matter, neither had Lloyd Miles. His presence was the result of having run into Abel Corbin, an old friend from Washington who had said, "Come along, Miles. I think you'll find it amusing. The aristocracy will be putting all their nubile daughters on show, my boy. Perhaps you can snare one for yourself." This last comment was delivered with a little laugh, for Lloyd, being a mere employee of the Erie Railroad, was not one of those men for whom the flowers of New York society were on display.

Lloyd Miles accepted the invitation because he was ambitious and sincerely believed that someday he would be counted among the giants of American finance and business. He had been fired by Thomas Durant, but one day, he vowed, he would have the pleasure of standing toe-to-toe with Durant on an equal financial footing. One day the name Lloyd Miles would be mentioned in the same breath as Andrew Carnegie, John D. Rockefeller, Philip Armour, Jay Cooke, and Commodore Vanderbilt.

Lloyd spotted the tall, slender man who had given him his invitation to the ball. He dodged his way across the dance floor to join Abel Corbin, who was standing beside his seated wife, Virginia Grant Corbin. He was twenty-five years older than his golden-haired Jennie. His shoulders were slightly stooped, and his hair was gray.

"Well, Miles," Corbin said pleasantly, his brown eyes twinkling, "I see that you have decided to join us, after all."

Lloyd bowed to Mrs. Corbin, who smiled up at him. She was an attractive woman with flawless skin and calm, dark eyes. She seemed truly devoted to her articulate husband in spite of the difference in their ages. There were those who speculated that Jennie Grant had married Corbin not so much for his wealth, his intelligence, and his urbane sophistication as to get away from her father's house in rural Illinois.

Cynics were even less kind in analyzing Corbin's reasons for marrying Virginia Grant. Corbin, a newspaper publisher, writer, financier, and avid politico, had been adviser to both Abraham Lincoln and Andrew Johnson. His marriage to the sister of the new President once again gave him access to the halls of power. That he had left Washington under a cloud, accused of attempted bribery in an effort to ease the passage of a textile tariff reduction bill through Congress, seemed to have been ignored by both Jennie Grant and her family.

"Mr. Miles, at the risk of seeming forward," Jennie said, "I claim one dance with you."

"My pleasure, Mrs. Corbin," Lloyd said, smiling, as the band began a new waltz. "There is no time better than now." Lloyd extended his hand.

Although Jennie Corbin was not invited to intimate teas

in the most exclusive New York houses, she was an accepted member of, if not the Four Hundred, at least the auxiliary echelon of society. She knew all the extravagantly bejeweled women and stiffly dressed men. She named names and passed along little items of gossip as Lloyd swirled her around the floor.

Lloyd noticed a black-haired, shapely, regally erect girl whose icy, unblinking eyes returned his gaze. "And that one?" he asked.

"Ah," Jennie said with a happy little laugh. "Abby Kershaw. Isn't she a beauty?"

"Lovely," Lloyd agreed.

"Would you like to meet her?" Jennie asked.

"Not likely," Lloyd said.

"Nonsense," Jennie told him.

When next they swirled near the impressive dark-haired beauty, Jennie pulled Lloyd off the floor. Abby Kershaw watched them approach. She was standing alone, her back to a small conversation group of other girls her age.

"Miss Kershaw," Jennie said.

"Mrs. Corbin." The voice was low, vibrant. To Lloyd's great surprise it sent shivers down his spine. "How do you do?"

"May I present Miss Abby Kershaw?" Jennie said formally. "Miss Kershaw, Mr. Lloyd Miles, of Washington."

Lloyd touched Abby's white-gloved hand with his fingers and bowed over it to bring his lips close.

"Lloyd isn't really shy," Jennie said. "He's just struck dumb by how beautiful you are tonight."

A cold smile twitched at the corners of Abby's full mouth. "Do I thank you, Mrs. Corbin, or Mr. Miles for the compliment?"

Lloyd smiled. "Please save your thanks for the moment when I can overcome my awe and think of some appropriate response."

Abby nodded. Jennie took Lloyd's hand. "I will lend him to you for one dance, Abby, after he has delivered me back to Abel."

"Charmed," Abby said in a flat tone.

The waltz ended just as Lloyd guided Jennie past Abel Corbin. "Go to her quickly," Jennie urged Lloyd, "before some other young swain beats you to it."

"What's this?" Abel asked.

"Mrs. Corbin is playing matchmaker," Lloyd answered.

"Abby Kershaw," Jennie explained.

"Ah," Corbin said, nodding. "She would make a splendid match for a young man on the way up. Old Psaleh Kershaw is an associate of Andrew Carnegie's."

Jennie said, "The comment once made by Mrs. Stuyvesant Fish could be applied to Kershaw. He is not rich. He has only a few millions."

Lloyd laughed. "A few millions are more than I have."

"A temporary condition, I'm sure," Corbin said. "I happen to know that you sold Crédit Mobilier short at its peak, young man."

Lloyd smiled and nodded. He had come out of his service with Thomas Durant with a sizable holding in the company that had fleeced all of the profit from the Union Pacific Railroad while charging double prices for materials and easing the pathway for the Pacific rails with widespread bribery in Washington. He would not deny Corbin's intimation that he was not exactly poor, but neither would he claim superior intelligence for having sold his Crédit Mobilier stock. He knew that sooner or later his onetime friend Congressman Philip Trent was going to blow the lid off Thomas Durant's bribery of politicians in Washington. When that happened, Crédit Mobilier stock would plummet. In the meantime he was safely out of the stock. Moreover, thanks to Durant's decision that the services of one Lloyd Miles were no longer needed by either Durant or the Union Pacific, the young man found himself at a comfortable distance from the growing scandal.

"Go dance with her," Jennie encouraged. "I don't believe she bites."

He walked toward the slender, regal girl and caught her green eyes. She did not look away. He bowed. "May I have the pleasure?"

"I feared that you would send Mrs. Corbin to ask," Abby said.

For a moment Lloyd was confused by the conflicting signals emanating from Abby. The way her green eyes studied him indicated that she was not displeased by what she saw; but her tone of voice seemed to convey hostility. Miles held himself in high esteem, however, so it took only a few moments for him to decide that Miss Kershaw's coolness was the result of shyness.

"I will always owe Mrs. Corbin a debt for introducing me to you," Lloyd said. He had known many interesting women, but never had one of them caused his pulse to pound as did this tall, remote, icily beautiful girl who came into his arms and pressed a hard, warm thigh against his as he swung her onto the dance floor.

"You're new in New York," she said.

"I work in Washington."

"Work?" Her low, vibrant voice made the word sound profane.

"I'm associated with the Erie Railroad."

"Oh, Lord, you don't work for that horrible Jay Gould?"

"Guilty," he said. "I represent the Erie in Washington. I have built up a few contacts there since the war." Actually, he was Jay Gould's number-two man in Washington. He owed his new job to the chap who was number one, Harold Berman, a friend and fellow member of a four-man investment club.

"Do you bribe congressmen?"

"On occasion," he said, smiling down into her upturned face.

"I've never danced with a crook before."

"I'm hardly that," he protested, off guard for a moment.

"What then? Jay Gould's errand boy?"

He flushed. There was a little smile on her full lips but a challenging look in her eyes. She was not shy at all, he realized. Perhaps she was one of the new breed of woman, the sort who fancied herself to be in competition with men. If so, that wouldn't bother him; he enjoyed a challenge.

"Would you care to walk into the solarium?" he asked. "I would like the roses to see you."

She beamed at him. "Nice try," she said. "Thank you. Not original, perhaps, but colorful."

"Miss Kershaw," he began, and suddenly he felt as breathless and fearful as when he had faced Rebel guns on a lonely stretch of the Wilmington and Weldon Railroad during the war. "Give me the opportunity, and I will think of something more original. At the moment I can only say that you are the most beautiful girl I've ever seen. May I call on you?"

"No," she said flatly. "I'm afraid not."

He was speechless for a few seconds. "That is a very definite answer. May I inquire why not? Am I that uncouth? Are you engaged?"

"Neither," she said. "I think it best not to pursue the subject."

He had been thinking that even though the Kershaws were not rich—not by the standards set by men like Rockefeller, Morgan, Gould, or Fisk—her social standing would admit her husband to any house in New York or, for that matter, the world.

"I respect your wishes," he said.

The music ended. He put his hand under Abby's elbow and guided her back to the wall. The group of young girls who had been standing together eyed him with curiosity.

"No luck here, ladies," Abby Kershaw announced in a loud voice. "Don't waste your time. He's only an Erie Railroad hired hand."

Lloyd's face burned. He bowed, then let his eyes move upward to the cold green fire of Abby's gaze. "I accept your rejection of my invitation," he said softly. "To say no is your right. But one day you will be terribly sorry you chose to insult me."

Abby's laugh was a full-throated contralto. The sound of it followed him as he gave her his back to rejoin the Corbins.

He found them at a refreshment table. Jennie offered

him a plate. He shook his head. "Abel, I appreciate your inviting me tonight."

"Not leaving, old boy?"

"Early appointment," Lloyd said.

"Romance was not favored, I take it?" Jennie asked.

Lloyd smiled ruefully. "Even the not-truly-wealthy Miss Kershaw is too rich for my blood." He was bumped from behind.

"I beg your pardon," a feminine voice said.

He turned. The woman looking up at him was rather short, her head coming only to his breast. Her smiling face was round and pert. She was fashionably voluptuous, a sweet little dumpling of a girl whose eyes radiated interest and warmth.

"I'm sorry I pushed you," she apologized. "It's just that I'm famished."

"Here, allow me," Lloyd said, taking a plate from the stack.

"Oh, I don't want to bother you," she said.

"No bother. Compensation for having blocked your way to the food, that's all."

"Well, fair's fair," she said, laughing.

Jennie Corbin caught Abel's eye. She was frowning a question that she didn't voice until Lloyd and the woman had moved off down the table, Lloyd placing tidbits on the young woman's plate. "What on earth is that creature doing here?" she asked.

"Well, you know Cornele," Corbin said, shrugging.

"Good Lord, is Vanderbilt here?"

"I wouldn't think so," Corbin said. "But I suppose he just likes to rub everyone's nose in the fact that at the age of seventy-five he can still handle a young thing like Tennessee Claflin."

"I'd wager you'll find her sister if you look around."

Jennie made a project of it, examining faces until, across the room, she saw the imposing figure of Victoria Claflin Woodhull, a woman who in a very short time had become more notorious than her younger sister.

Tennessee Claflin had seated herself and was taking the laden plate from the hand of Lloyd Miles.

Tennessee Claflin had been married, but in New York she used her maiden name. She had the plush figure favored by many men, a face given to extremes of expression, and an openly flirtatious manner that charmed Lloyd into forgetting the rebuff he had suffered at the hands of the frigid Abby Kershaw.

"You naughty man," Tennessee chided good-naturedly.

"I beg your pardon?"

"Naughty, naughty."

"What have I done?" Lloyd asked, laughing, spreading his hands.

"It's not what you've done," she said. "It's what you want to do."

"Eh?"

"I am a mind reader," she whispered, leaning forward, displaying her ample cleavage, and smiling as she stuffed a sweet into her mouth. "You want to make love to me."

Lloyd laughed uneasily, then thought, *Well, what the hell?*

"Don't you?"

"I do," he confessed.

"First help me finish," she said, thrusting the plate toward him. "Then one dance."

He was not hungry. "My name is Lloyd Miles."

"Ummm, such a nice name."

"And yours, my dear?"

"I have a nice name too."

"May I have the honor of knowing it?"

"I'm hurt that you don't recognize me by sight."

"I'm a stranger in New York. Up from Washington City."

"Oh, well, then. I'm Tennessee."

"Tennessee Claflin?"

"You see? You do know me."

"I know of you."

"It's all the same," she said. She licked her fingers suggestively while gazing into his eyes. "Must we dance before we go?"

"Miss Tennessee, the dance was your idea."

"Well, I guess we should, at least once. After all, Victoria made me buy a new gown especially for this affair, so I suppose I mustn't waste it."

"Dancing with you will be a delight," Lloyd said.

Tennessee Claflin was a weight in his arms, not at all like the feathery, light-footed Abby Kershaw. But when she smiled up at him and pressed close to him, he could feel the warmth of her body and see the willingness in her eyes. The dance seemed to last forever, and twice he whirled his partner past Abby Kershaw.

"Should you tell someone that you're going?" he asked as he led Tennessee toward the cloakroom.

"No one at all," she said.

He told the doorman to summon a cab, lifted Tennessee in, and climbed in beside her. Soft and warm, she snuggled to him. The cab pulled away into darkness, and she offered her lips. There was a sweet demand in her kiss, a fire that was contagious.

"Do you have a place?" he whispered.

"Too much family," she answered. "Where are you staying?"

"The Grand Central. We're driving away from it right now."

"Then tell the driver to turn around."

"And walk through the hotel lobby . . . not at all discreet," he said.

She laughed. "Are you afraid for your reputation?"

He laughed with her. "May I have a moment to think about that before I answer?"

"Coward."

"I was thinking of *your* reputation," he said.

"Let my concerns be my concerns," she told him. "The right to choose one's own course is not exclusively reserved for men."

"Don't tell me!" he said. "You're one of those."

He liked the way she laughed, tinklingly, wholesomely, liked the teasing tone of her voice as she recited,

"Gibbery, gibbery gab,
The women had a confab,
And demanded the rights
To wear the tights,
Gibbery, gibbery gab."

"Heaven protect me," he beseeched, looking skyward.

"Don't fret, darling. I won't try to fit into your breeches. I only want to help you remove them."

Victoria Woodhull and Tennessee Claflin had hit Manhattan with all the power displayed by the whirling, violent storms that swept across the open spaces of their native Ohio. Anyone who knew anything about what went on in New York City knew that the sisters—accompanied by various and sordid family members, including a cantankerous old father and a rather strange mother—had set up shop as spiritualists and magnetic healers in a brownstone at 17 Great Jones Street, that segment of Third Street between the Bowery and Broadway. Since their stated specialties appealed to the eccentricities of one of the most powerful men in America, Commodore Cornelius Vanderbilt, it had been almost inevitable that they should come into contact with him. It was common knowledge that Tennessee was the commodore's mistress.

So it was not fear for his reputation that gave Lloyd Miles pause. Adultery did not go unnoticed in New York society, although the peccadillos of a bachelor were largely overlooked. The thing that made Lloyd feel trepidation was being seen crossing a hotel lobby toward the stairs and his room with the mistress of one of the most powerful men in the world—a man who already had good reason to hate everything associated with the Erie Railroad. His decision was made, however, by the warmth of Tennessee's hand in his, by the memory of her kiss hot on his lips, and by the rankling memory of Abby Kershaw's laugh in his soul.

Lloyd escorted the juicy little woman across the lobby to the stairs, watched her jiggle her way to the second floor, then opened the door of his room to her.

She hardly gave him time to close the door behind him before she was in his arms, her mouth wet, hot, and demanding. He was momentarily alienated by her boldness as her hands pushed their way under his clothing; but when he explored her soft contours, when his kiss answered hers, his blood reached white heat. He was soon romping with the most wanton woman of his experience. Her desire matched his; her needs were equal in insistence to his own passions. Her hair smelled of a perfumed soap, her body of a light, pleasant perfume and the healthy secretions of a young woman. Time and again as the night went on they came together, laughing, panting, and heaving in the throes of an equal exchange of passions, in mutual need.

It was dawn when they dressed, went down to the hotel dining room, and ate ravenously. He delivered her to the house on Great Jones Street, and in broad daylight, with passersby gawking into the open windows of the hansom cab, he kissed her.

"I will call for you at eight tonight," he said.

"No, old dear," Tennessee said. "Sorry. Previous engagement."

"Break it."

"Shall I tell Cornele that you said so?"

"I'll be damned," he muttered.

"I most likely am," she agreed, smiling brightly. "It's been wonderful."

"Don't say that as if it's over between us."

"Well, I fear that it must be, old dear. Unless, of course, you'd care to sign up for a series of magnetic healing treatments."

"Which are?"

"Ummm," she said. She put her hands on his cheeks, and her palms seemed to emit heat and healing. "In my right hand I have magnetism and force. In my left I have tickles, squeezes, and tiny little slaps."

"When can we start?" he asked.

"Later, old dear. Right now we are very involved with my old boy."

"What does he call you?" Lloyd asked, wavering between a feeling of loss and plain curiosity.

She giggled. "He calls me his little sparrow."

"Ha!" he said.

She waved her arms like wings. *"Peep, peep."*

"Can't I see you again? Soon?"

"No, old dear, no. It was so good last night. Let's keep the memory that way."

Then she was gone, and for the second time in a span of less than twelve hours Lloyd had been rejected.

CHAPTER 2

The New York offices of the Erie Railroad occupied the upper floors of the newly constructed Pike's Opera House at West Twenty-third and Eighth Avenue.

Lloyd Miles walked into a splendor of marble and black walnut wood inlaid with gold shortly after ten o'clock on a lovely May morning.

A visitor had only to mount the spectacular stairway to the second floor of the building to understand why the press had begun to call Jim Fisk the Prince of Erie, for after his purchase of the Opera House, Gould's flashy partner had set about building himself a palace. At the top of the stairs beautifully carved oak doors opened into a marbled entry made elaborate with crystal chandeliers; rich stained-glass partitions; frescoes and objects of art; and gilded balustrades. In a prominent spot, under a bust of William Shakespeare, was a plaque engraved with the date *1869*, commemorating the year in which Gould and Fisk had wrested Erie away from old Uncle Dan'l Drew. The ceilings were filled with neoclassical designs in the Pompeiian manner. The walls were covered with paintings of nude cupids and scantily dressed nymphs cavorting among blue, carmine, gold, and lilac flowers.

Only female visitors saw the private suite where Jim Fisk, in his role as impresario of the Opera House, interviewed the company's aspiring young stars. On the other hand, Fisk was always pleased to show off his office, where a walnut desk sat on a raised dais and his chair was studded with golden nails. The ceiling in that room was decorated with red ovals on fawn and light blue. Inside the ovals *Erie* was lettered in solid gold.

Interestingly enough, the names of Gould and Fisk were on the deed for the property, although Erie money had purchased it; and the offices were leased back to Erie for the sum of seventy-five thousand dollars per month.

The anteroom where Lloyd was told to wait was decorated by colorful frescoes by the Italian Giribaldi, who had gained fame by painting the interiors of the Academy of Music and Booth's Theater. The sound of a soprano voice running scales came to him through the walls. "Ah-A-O-E-Ah-A-O-E-Ahhhhhh."

Lloyd had never seen his new employer. When he was ushered into Jay Gould's office he did not immediately notice that it was the most splendid business office he'd ever seen, for he had eyes only for the frail, undersized man who rose from his desk and walked forward to shake his hand. Gould had the look of a frustrated poet. His sad, deep eyes complemented his delicate, melancholy face. Although he was a young man—only thirty-three—his heavy beard was shot through with gray. His thick, dark hair had receded from his forehead.

"Mr. Miles," Gould said. His handshake was cool, almost limp. He turned away and sat down behind his desk. He did not invite Lloyd to be seated. Nor was he a man given to idle talk. "I like to meet all the men who work for me."

"The pleasure is mine, sir."

"I don't like empty words, Miles. You're as curious about me as I am about you."

Lloyd grinned. "Guilty."

"You sold Crédit Mobilier at the top," Gould said, his soulful eyes glued to Lloyd's face.

"Yes."

"Accident?"

"No." The interview had taken an odd turn, but Lloyd remained calm.

"I thought not," Gould said. "Now you're buying gold. May I ask why?"

Lloyd was becoming apprehensive. He had not expected Gould to begin interrogating him immediately about his private financial transactions. He decided to be frank. "I'm buying gold because you're buying gold, sir."

Gould's expression did not change. "And how do you know that I'm buying gold?"

This was getting touchy. Lloyd had a decision to make. He had the distinct impression that Gould was irritated. Perhaps it wasn't that serious, but Lloyd saw his choice as being between loyalty to a friend and his own self-interests. Seen in those terms, however, it was no contest. "Harold Berman told me," he answered.

Gould's eyes shifted away for just a moment, then he chuckled. "Berman told me you had a head on you."

"I will make it a point to thank Harold for the compliment," Lloyd said.

Gould wrote something on a notepad. Lloyd supposed it had to do with finding out just who had told Harold Berman he was buying gold. Jay Gould did his trading in the Gold Room through Henry Smith, his brokerage partner in Smith, Gould, Martin, & Company. He would certainly want tighter security in the future.

He turned back to Lloyd and tented his long, delicate fingers under his chin. "So, Miles, let me give you a belated welcome to our circle. I think you'll find that an ambitious young man has ample opportunity to advance himself."

"Thank you, sir. May I say, sir, that I will always stand ready to be of service to the company."

"Your job is to be of service to me. You can be useful to my organization. You have good contacts. You're an ex-staff officer and personal friend of General Benjamin Butler, now a congressman from Massachusetts. You hold a high military decoration, and during the years you worked for the Union Pacific, you made contacts with men of power in Washington."

"I understand," Lloyd said.

"I want you to arrange an introduction for me."

"Of course, if I can," Lloyd agreed.

"You can. I want to meet Mr. Abel Rathbone Corbin and his lovely wife."

"That I can do," Lloyd confirmed.

"Aren't you going to ask why?" Gould asked, raising one eyebrow.

"When I work for a man, I work for him," Lloyd said.

Gould nodded. "If I didn't believe that, if I didn't believe that you were loyal to Thomas Durant while you were his man, you wouldn't be here. All right. I'm going to tell you why anyhow, Miles, because I'm going to need your help in Washington. Perhaps you'd better sit down."

Lloyd sat in a comfortable leather chair and crossed his legs. He looked expectantly at Gould.

"Talk to me about gold," Gould said.

Lloyd swallowed. "Is this an oral examination in economic theory?"

"Exactly," Gould said, his face stern.

"Gold and greenbacks are the weights on opposite ends of a balance," Miles began. "When the price of one goes down, the other goes up. The economic welfare of the nation rides freely on the balance bar, sliding one way or the other as the bar tilts."

"Good, good," Gould said.

"The situation came about in 1861 when President Lincoln needed money to build an army. Congress suspended the gold standard and printed four hundred fifty million dollars in paper money that had only the word of the government behind it. It was not redeemable for gold. In addition, the government sold two billion dollars' worth of long-term bonds. Suddenly we had a dual-currency monetary system: greenbacks were legal tender for domestic debts; but gold coin—specie—was still the only currency for foreign trade, for tariffs, for customs duties. The value of the paper money fluctuated, influenced mostly by the tides of war. Each time Robert E. Lee whipped a Union general, the price of gold went up. It hit almost three hundred dollars of greenbacks for one hundred dollars in gold coins in 1864 while Grant was stalled outside Petersburg producing shocking casualty lists. But when Sherman took Atlanta, prices started down. And after Appomattox gold stood at a hundred and forty-four."

Gould was staring at the ornate painted ceiling.

After a moment of silence Lloyd added, "Jay Cooke called the New York gold traders General Lee's left flank."

Gould chuckled. "While counting the millions he made selling government bonds." He looked at Lloyd. "My family's original name was Gold. Did you know that?"

"No."

"Until about 1806. The first Golds came to this country in 1647. They became Connecticut jurists and Revolutionary War heroes. I was named Jason, after he who sought the golden fleece. Did you know that?"

"No, but it's fitting, I think."

Gould's eyes narrowed. "Why do you say that?"

"Because, sir, you've done quite well."

Gould smiled coldly behind his beard. "Miles, suppose Jim Fisk and I bull up gold prices and hold them at one forty-five to one fifty through the fall harvest season. What happens?"

Lloyd nodded. "I think I see what you're getting at, sir. The price for exported grain is set in London in gold, of course. If the price of gold is high in this country, the farmer would get larger amounts of paper money for his crop." He was gambling that Gould had not wanted him to say that by artificially tilting the gold market—by buying and holding huge amounts of gold—Gould would turn the international financial structure into a river of profits for the Erie Railroad . . . meaning for Jay Gould and Jim Fisk.

"I see that you have done your homework," Gould approved with his cold smile. "Bigger profits for the farmer can only be good for the country."

At that moment, as Gould touched one cheek with his

long fingers and stared at him as if in challenge, Lloyd decided to take a gamble. "And while you're increasing grain exports, you're selling gold at a profit."

For a moment Gould was silent. When he spoke his voice was soft. "But there's some fourteen million dollars' worth of gold specie circulating in New York banks alone."

Lloyd swallowed, knowing that he'd been asked another question. He plunged in. "I think, sir, that if I were trying to, uh, stabilize the price of gold in the one hundred forty-five-dollar range, I would buy as much as I could and immediately lend it out against greenbacks as security. I would then take the greenbacks and buy more gold—"

"Or the same gold," Gould said, a smile spreading on his face.

"The same gold could be lent and borrowed again and again." Lloyd laughed in appreciation of the concept. "It would be possible to own more gold than actually exists."

"And the advantage of that?" Gould asked.

"At any given time the gold loans could be called in, making prices rise drastically." Lloyd spread his hands. "To say the least, it could be highly profitable."

"Unless?" Gould asked, sounding like a schoolteacher.

Lloyd thought for a moment. He felt like saying, "Aha!" for now he knew why Gould wanted an introduction to Abel Corbin, whose wife was the sister of the man who had control over the United States Treasury, the President, General U. S. Grant. "Unless the federal Treasury opens its vaults and sells gold."

There was a flaw in Gould's reasoning, however. Lloyd's soaring hopes of riding Jay Gould's coattails to the point of being fabulously wealthy were cooled. "If there is one man in this country who cannot be influenced by the prospect of riches, it is Ulysses S. Grant."

"Exactly," Gould agreed. "You still have a lot to learn, Miles. Hide in the bushes and watch. Don't be too rash with what little money you have, for it is my experience that a broke man is a dangerous man. Don't be greedy." He rose, signaling that the meeting was over. "Please tell my secretary when it will be convenient for me to entertain Mr. and Mrs. Corbin."

Lloyd moved quickly. He knew from Corbin himself that the Erie Railroad wanted to lay track across a piece of land that Corbin owned in New Jersey. He gathered all the data and presented himself to Jay Gould's secretary.

"Mr. Gould is not available to see you," the secretary said. He was a very proper young man, solemn and dedicated to his job. "You may leave your message with me."

"That I can't do, friend." Lloyd leaned over the desk, put his face close to the secretary's, and said, "Now you get your well-tailored butt off that chair and tell Mr. Gould that I have something of importance for him."

"I will convey whatever message you have," the secretary said stiffly. "You may leave now."

Lloyd seized the young man by his collar, lifted him from the chair, and drew back one fist. "Your little nose is really too pretty to be smashed all over your face."

The secretary twisted from Lloyd's grasp and ran through the door to Gould's office. Lloyd could hear his nearly hysterical voice. He pushed open the door and entered. Gould glared at him but motioned the secretary out.

Lloyd spoke quickly. "Sir, we have an appointment with Abel Corbin."

"We?" Gould asked, raising one eyebrow.

"I thought that would be best for a first meeting," Lloyd explained. "Abel will be more comfortable with a friend on hand while he talks with the Erie Railroad about a right-of-way."

"I don't like high-handed underlings, Miles."

"And I, sir, don't enjoy dealing with fancy-boy flunkies like your secretary."

For a moment, as Gould glared at him, Lloyd thought it was over, that his employment with the Erie Railroad and Jay Gould would come to a quick end. Then Gould laughed. "Sebastian can be rather trying at times." He waved Lloyd to a chair. "Now tell me why Mr. Corbin wants to talk with the Erie."

* * *

The Corbin home was a five-story brownstone mansion on West Twenty-seventh Street. Imported French furniture made for an atmosphere of quiet elegance. Jennie Grant Corbin greeted Lloyd with genuine pleasure, accepted his introduction of Jay Gould, then led them into a large sitting room, where Abel Corbin rose to shake hands. Jennie served sherry. Gould sipped once, put the glass aside, and turned quickly to the business of a right-of-way across Corbin's New Jersey land.

Lloyd sat to one side with Jennie, listening as the boss of the Erie negotiated with a retired man of affairs. Lloyd hid a smile, for if the Erie had been as generous with all landowners as it was with Corbin, the railroad would have been bankrupt before ever laying a rail.

Hardly a quarter hour had passed before the deal was set and Gould turned the subject to personal matters, bringing Jennie Grant Corbin into the conversation by asking questions about her family in Illinois and her famous brother. Jennie spoke freely, for she felt comfortable with Lloyd, and she was coming to like his soft-spoken employer. She said she was excited about a prospective visit to New York by her brother and his wife.

"Poor Ulysses," she said, "he's had hardly a good night's rest since the war started. I've told him that he works much too hard, puts in far too many hours."

"Yes," Abel Corbin agreed, "the general needs a little rest and relaxation. Jennie and I have been insisting that they visit us."

"Perhaps," Gould suggested, "the President and his party would enjoy the use of my yacht?"

"How nice of you, Mr. Gould!" Jennie said. "I shall pass along that offer to Ulysses."

Gould, having done his homework, knew that in the 1850s Abel Corbin had tried to extract bribes from Massachusetts textile mills. Now he set about discovering whether the money bug's bite had lost its sting for the man. He smoothly turned the subject to the state of the economy. Corbin took the bait and exchanged views with Gould about the market and the desirability of paying off the wartime bonds in gold instead of with paper money.

With Corbin himself having introduced the subject of gold, Gould said, "Speaking of gold, what are the President's personal feelings in regard to the nation's monetary system?"

Lloyd stiffened, wondering if Gould had erred in asking Corbin so soon to talk about his brother-in-law.

"I can assure you, Mr. Gould, that the President is an advocate of hard money," Corbin said pompously.

"Excellent," Gould said. "I would have supposed so."

"He'll have no luck with this Congress, however," Corbin continued.

"Ah, but as President he has certain powers," Gould pointed out. "Through the secretary of the Treasury he controls the nation's gold reserve. If, for example, gold prices were to rise, farmers would sell their grain abroad in order to have a larger profit in greenbacks. There would be an export boom, and the entire economy of the country would benefit."

"Yes," Corbin said, his eyes gleaming. "But it has been government policy to keep gold prices stable."

"Well, that's it, don't you see?" Gould asked. "If the President could be shown that higher gold prices would greatly benefit farmers and factory workers—"

"As it happens," Abel Corbin interrupted, "the President values my advice in matters of the economy."

"Then, sir," Gould suggested, "you can do your country a great service."

"We must talk more of this," Corbin declared. "I must tell you that your crop theory—the view that high gold prices would stimulate farm exports—interests me very much. I believe that the President will be interested as well. As you might have guessed, this gold thing is a major problem for Ulysses. He thinks the Gold Room is nothing more than a bomb waiting to explode, and the results would be to the detriment of the economy."

* * *

Lloyd was awed by the ease with which Jay Gould had converted Corbin to his cause. When he returned to Washington, pleased by Gould's praise for a job well done, he began systematically to convert all his assets into cash, with which he purchased gold. He had a feeling that destiny was on his side. At last he would begin the rise to wealth and power that would make most men forget—and cause some men to remember—that he had been chosen as a scapegoat by Thomas Durant . . . fired because he had failed to prevent his onetime friend, Philip Trent, from working to expose the unbridled corruption that had been involved in the construction of the Pacific Railroad. Trent's investigation in Congress was still in progress.

Now Lloyd was an insider in a financial scheme that, if successful, would make the profits and booty garnered by the railroad builders and Crédit Mobilier seem like pocket change, for Jay Gould was moving toward establishing a corner in gold, and the men who controlled the price of gold would control the monetary system of the United States.

As Lloyd Miles converted all his holdings to gold, he did not question Gould's theory that the "little man," the farmer and the laborer, would benefit from cheaper paper money while a few men at the top reaped unimaginable wealth. It was a grab-and-hold world, a world of opportunity for the man willing to take the risk and make the effort. The gold market and, in fact, the capitalistic system were Darwinian devices. The man fit to survive seized opportunity, just as Lloyd was seizing his with both hands.

When he had at last borrowed to his personal limits and had his little hoard of gold working for him, he sold the jewelry that he had given to his sister, Leah, during the years when he was working for Thomas Durant. He didn't realize much from the sale, but each time he bought and loaned out one hundred dollars' worth of gold, he was guaranteeing himself a profit when Gould would push the price of gold to $145 and perhaps above.

Finally, as the price of gold began to rise, he sold shares of stock that were not really his—Crédit Mobilier stock, which he had promoted for his friends Paul Jennings, Geoffrey Lancaster, and Harold Berman when the Union Pacific Railroad was using Crédit Mobilier stock to buy allies in Washington. He had kept control of the stock while sharing earnings with the members of what once had been his Breakfast Club; but since he had left the employment of the Union Pacific, his contacts with Jennings and Lancaster had been limited. As for Berman . . . well, Lloyd rationalized, he'd make it up to Harold when he sold gold at its peak price.

During his career Phineas Headley had been on the staff of a half dozen of the nation's finest newspapers. He had started his journalistic training when he was twelve, as a copyboy on Horace Greeley's New York *Tribune*. By the time he reached his majority while covering the often bloody action on the western fronts for Alfred Guernsey's *Harper's Magazine*, he had become, in professional circles, one of the most respected of newsmen.

Headley was a spare fellow with a fortunate metabolism. He could eat his weight in the richest of foods but not add an ounce to his tall, wiry frame. He sported a shock of brick-red hair, which gave the appearance of a haystack in the wind. His dress was often frowsy.

After the war he had worked in both New York and Washington before taking a sabbatical to assist General Lafayette Baker in writing his memoirs. Working with Baker had been an eye-opening experience, even for a man who thought that he'd seen and heard just about everything. Turning Baker's often turgid prose into something at least halfway professional had proved both interesting and frustrating. The general fancied himself to have been the virtuoso spy master of all times and stated, to what Phineas was certain would be the confusion of future historians, that his organization under the auspices of the War Department had been the beginning of the United States Secret Service.

Phineas had argued with Baker about that, but Baker had maintained that it was idiotic to call the organization founded by Secretary of the Treasury Hugh McCulloch in 1865 *the* Secret Service, since McCulloch's group's sole assignment had been to maintain the integrity of greenback currency by halting the activity of counterfeiters.

Baker's organization, on the other hand, had dealt in the stuff of real secrets. The general himself had traveled through the wartime South and at one point had actually obtained an interview with Confederate President Jefferson Davis. He had sent spies into the Confederacy, and he had made a specialty of apprehending Southern spies in Washington.

During the months in which Phineas lived in close proximity with Lafe Baker, he had attempted to elicit from the general answers to questions that still plagued the journalist about the death of Lincoln's assassin. Baker good-naturedly brushed off any inquiry as to why he had allowed John Wilkes Booth's body to be burned beyond recognition before any formal identification had been made, or how he, of all people, happened to know just which farm and just which barn the assassin had chosen for his hideout. Moreover, Baker was adamant about not giving examples of the activities of the spies he had sent into the South. Such information, he had said, should not become common knowledge, lest in some future war the nation's intelligence-gathering network be hampered by too intimate public familiarity with spy methods.

Baker's book turned out to be rather self-serving, but it made money. Phineas Headley was paid well enough to eschew steady employment and pursue stories of his own choice, which he then sold to various newspapers and magazines.

Headley was in New York doing an analytical piece on the stock market's odd way of trading stocks and bonds when Jay Gould and his associates made their first tentative moves into gold. Lafe Baker had come down to Manhattan from his provincial hotel in Michigan to collect a royalty check. Over dinner Headley told Baker that some interesting activity was going on in the Gold Room and that what seemed to be Erie Railroad money was being shifted into gold coin.

"Gould and Fisk," Baker said.

"Apparently."

"Smart fellows," Baker said, and the curling of his lip indicated that he was using the word in its derogatory sense, meaning something just short of criminality.

"They don't like publicity," Headley said. "I've asked both Gould and Fisk to give me an interview on the subject. They are always conveniently busy. I've tried sniffing around the edges of the Erie organization, but the rank and file don't know or care what's going on in the Gold Room."

"What you need to do is contact some middle-level fellow, some man who fancies himself to be important because he has some access to the top management and knows just enough to make him want to see his name in the paper."

Headley nodded. "I've tried that too. I talked with a young man from the Erie's Washington office, name of Miles."

"Lloyd Miles?" Baker asked.

"Yes. Do you know him?"

"He used to work for Thomas Durant and the Union Pacific," Baker replied. He fell silent, remembering the tangled web that had finally snarled him in Washington where he, too, had been working for Thomas Durant. "If I were you I'd keep an eye on Lloyd Miles. He's not top level —at least not yet—but he'll be close to those who are at the top. He might just be the key to what you're looking for."

"Well, he's a cool one," Phineas remarked. "I asked him point-blank if there wasn't some unusually brisk trading going on in the Gold Room, and he just shrugged and said that almost everything that went on there was unusual."

"Let me see. . . ." Baker said, compelled by his own image of himself to try to impress Headley with his command of information. "Miles was associated with three other young fellows. One of them was named Bergman, or something like that."

"Berman. Harold Berman."

"That's it. And Miles had a sister."

"Leah Miles," Headley said.

"Talked with her?"

"I don't think it would be worthwhile. She's the stay-at-home type."

"Well, you never know, Headley," Baker said. "You never know who is going to have the one little nugget of information that leads you to the mother lode, and you'll never find out if you don't pursue all your leads."

"Thanks a hell of a lot," Headley said with a chuckle. "You sound like one of my old editors."

Headley hadn't been to Washington for some time. He boarded a train and settled in with the morning papers. In his pocket was a small notebook into which he'd entered the names of those he wanted to question in Washington. Harold Berman's name led the list. Then there were the names of Leah Miles and an old acquaintance of his, Congressman Philip Trent.

CHAPTER 3

Harold Berman was a gentle man, well-read and soft-spoken. He had a mass of heavy, kinky black hair, which he wore close cropped. Like Lloyd Miles, whom Harold had brought into his office after Lloyd was dismissed by Thomas Durant, he disdained joining the hirsute majority. His clean-shaven face was a pleasant one. His smile, when Leah Miles opened the door to his knock, was warm and open.

"Mr. Berman!" Leah said. "How nice to see you."

"My dear Leah," Harold responded, "you can always be depended upon to ease one's feelings with the harmless little white lie. I apologize for dropping by unannounced."

"No apology needed," Leah said. "Please come in."

The apartment that Leah Miles shared with her brother was spacious and well furnished. She had opened the windows to a warming May morning. A smell of spring freshness was in the air and, because the house was on a moderately busy thoroughfare, the ammoniacal scent of horse manure.

"I'm sure you know," Leah said, "that Lloyd has not yet returned from New York."

"Yes, I know," Berman said. He was standing uneasily,

his hat in hand, gazing at Leah with such evident longing that the feeling was almost tangible.

At twenty-seven Leah Miles gave the impression of being mature and self-assured. Although her figure was a bit too thin for popular taste, she curvaceously filled the bodice of her calico gown. A modest bustle accented the round flow of her hips. Her thick golden-brown hair was ideal for the top-heavy styles of the day. She had a full mouth that smiled easily. Her intense blue eyes were a startling surprise to those meeting her for the first time and a delight to the man who stood awkwardly before her.

Head tilted downward, he looked at her with a quizzical smile. "I didn't come to see Lloyd," Berman admitted.

"Well, then, I am flattered," Leah said. "Please sit down, Mr. Berman. I was about to have my second cup of coffee. Do you prefer yours black or white?"

"White, please." He sat in a delicately constructed occasional chair, placed his hat on the floor beside him, and watched her bustle sway toward the kitchen. She was back quickly with a tray on which a coffeepot steamed aromatically.

"Lovely weather," Leah said after she had poured. Berman's distress was evident to her. It was not the first time that a man had become inarticulate in her presence. She found herself wanting to help him.

"Yes, isn't it?" Berman said. He took a gulp of hot coffee, swallowed wrong, then gave a little cough.

"Days like this make me want to be outside," she continued. "I do love walking."

"Ah, yes," Berman said. "Where do you walk?"

"Along the river, mostly."

"Would you, I mean do you fancy—uh, well, as it happens I have nothing pressing—"

"More coffee?" she asked.

"What I'm trying to say is would you do me the honor of walking out with me?"

"Yes, thank you," she said.

The motivation behind Leah's ready answer to Berman's invitation had its root in years past. Had she been asked—

and had she thought deeply and objectively—she might have said that her quick, unhesitating affirmative was one minor result of the Civil War—the most deadly conflict that had ever been fought. It had taken the cream of young manhood and, thus, was producing a generation of maiden ladies.

Leah would not have admitted that the heartbreak of having broken off her engagement to Philip Trent influenced her reply, but her greatest fear was that she might live out her days as an unmarried spinster. That fear had been reinforced when, at her brother's insistence, she had made a European tour with friends who had small children. She had offered to help with the young ones and had become "Aunt Leah."

To be a courtesy aunt to someone else's children was, to her, the great abyss. She had happily looked forward to being Mrs. Philip Trent, but because her brother had given her an impossible ultimatum, forcing her to choose between him and the man she loved, her life had been altered fearfully.

So it was that she accepted Harold Berman's invitation with alacrity, strolled with him along the Potomac, put her hand on his arm, and encouraged his hesitating conversation. The best way to avoid being "Aunt Leah," to escape being Lloyd Miles's spinster sister for the rest of her life, and to be delivered from living with Lloyd and cooking his meals and washing his clothing and keeping his house, was to become Mrs. Somebody. She knew Harold Berman as a considerate man, a man of culture and quietness. If he proposed, she would be a good wife to him, with or without love. Perhaps, in time, love would come to her.

She had watched Harold's fascination with her grow from the time when Lloyd went to work in the Erie's Washington office. Berman was a frequent guest at the Miles table. He always brought a gift for the house—a bottle of wine, a wheel of expensive cheese, a specially baked loaf of bread. Because he was Lloyd's friend and business associate—and his superior—and because Leah was an innately gracious person, she had made him feel at home.

The three of them had engaged in spirited discussions on just about everything under the sun, with Harold being articulate and obviously well educated.

Now, as they walked beside the river, Harold was red faced, tongue-tied, and shy. He was obviously trying to say something but was having the devil's own time of it.

She actually hurt for him because of his discomfort. She looked up at him and willed him to come out with it. Finally she said, "Harold, for heaven's sake, what is the matter? If you want to say something to me, please feel free to say it."

He flushed even more, turned his head away, and said, "Miss Miles . . ."

"Now, you stop that this instant!" she said with mock severity. "Since when did I cease to be Leah to you?"

He gave her a weak smile and in a rush of words said, "Leah, I think you must realize that I have fallen very deeply in love with you, and although I know that I'm not much of a catch and I'm probably being overtly inane, I cannot rest until I ask you if it would be possible for you to entertain a formal courtship from me directed toward the hope that someday you might become my wife." He had run out of breath.

She laughed as he inhaled deeply.

"I can see why you'd think that amusing," he said, crestfallen.

"Harold Berman, don't be silly," she said gently. "Aside from the fact that you almost choked yourself, you spoke beautifully." She squeezed his arm. "Now, a girl doesn't get such a proposal every day, you know. I wonder if you could start again and say those lovely things slowly enough so that I can savor them."

He stopped walking, and she turned to face him.

"Do you mean that there is a chance for me?" he asked.

She smiled. Those startling blue eyes fixed his. "I would say much more than a mere chance."

"Ah, Leah . . ."

"I'll bet you don't even remember what you said," she teased.

He laughed, a bit more at ease. "Actually, you're right. I said that I love you. And, oh, how I do love you, dear Leah. You're smiling at me, and that is enough encouragement to last me for years."

"Oh, no, you don't," she said. "I'm not going to wait years."

"Leah?"

"All right," she said. "I think I remember that somewhere in that cascade of words you said something about my becoming your wife?"

"Would you?"

"Yes," she said, and her heart sank, weighted with memories of Philip Trent. Overwhelmed, she could not prevent tears from overflowing her eyes.

Harold was deeply touched. "Oh, my dear," he whispered. "Tears? Do I dare think that they indicate happiness?"

She pushed the old pain into its dark little closet in the back of her mind and smiled. "As I said, it isn't every day that a woman gets such a beautiful proposal of marriage."

It was three days before Harold kissed her. Each night while Lloyd was away in New York, Harold came for her and they dined in quiet little restaurants. He could not get enough information about her. She found herself reliving her childhood in answer to his questions. Each night, after he had delivered her to the apartment, she realized that they'd talked about nothing but her. She knew little about him.

On the evening before Lloyd was due to return to Washington, she persistently turned the talk to Harold. He was the son of immigrants from Germany. He was Jewish but not, as he expressed it, rabid about it. His father, who had worked himself to death in the mines in Pennsylvania, had vehemently opposed Harold's joining him there even when money was short. He insisted that his only son remain in school.

When his mother had died shortly after his father, Harold had gone to New York, where he worked his way up

from messenger boy to a junior partnership in a brokerage
house. Like many men who could afford it, he had bought
a replacement when he was about to be drafted. He had
come to the attention of Jay Gould by pushing Erie Railroad stock during one of the periodic railroad wars between the Erie and Commodore Vanderbilt's New York
Central and had leapt at the chance to hitch his wagon to a
rising financial star.

"I may never be rich," he told Leah, "but I promise
you'll never want for anything."

To Leah, being a member of the American royalty was
not important. True, she could remember times when
money had been a concern. When Lloyd came for her and
rescued her from a dreary, unpleasant, often painful existence with a guardian aunt, he had been quite young and
just beginning to find out that making a living is a man's
job. There were times when they had to skimp, when, in
order to pay the rent, they made an evening meal of corn
bread and milk.

When she considered her background, Harold Berman
was rich enough. He had a town house, a matched team of
blacks to pull his carriage, and he dressed well. When she
visited his home—at her own insistence because he questioned, justifiably, the propriety of being alone with her
there—she saw that his taste in furnishings was sophisticated. She hungered for the chance to pore over the large
selection of books in his library.

Out of curiosity she tried to read some Jewish religious
literature but found it heavy going. She asked Harold if
their differences in belief would be a problem.

"We won't be married by a rabbi in a synagogue," he
said, "but that doesn't matter."

"Because they would not accept me?" she asked.

"I accept you," he said. He smiled and held her close. "I
will make you a proposition: if you won't try to convert me
to be a Methodist, I won't try to get you to become Jewish."

Since the matter seemed to be settled to her satisfaction,
Leah gave it no more thought.

* * *

Upon his arrival at the Washington station Lloyd Miles went straight to the office. After Harold Berman had greeted him warmly and asked about the trip, Lloyd launched into an account of his activities in New York. Berman was impressed when he heard that Lloyd had arranged a meeting between the President's brother-in-law and Jay Gould.

"My God, Corbin and the President's sister?" Berman said with a little laugh. "Gould thinks he can bribe General Grant through his sister?"

Lloyd felt irritated. From the time that he'd revealed to Jay Gould that it had been Berman who told him about Gould's purchases of gold, his attitude toward Berman had begun to change. He still felt gratitude, for Harold had arranged a position for him when he was unemployed and in disfavor in certain quarters because of his dispute with Thomas Durant. But he had analyzed the situation in the Washington office of the Erie and had come to the conclusion that Berman was not the right man to be in charge. Harold tended to be more interested in the day-to-day details, keeping records and accounting for every penny spent, than in doing what he was supposed to do, which was making contact with the politicians who were in power and advancing the cause of the Erie Railroad through dealing smoothly with people and, occasionally, passing along sums of money.

Even before Lloyd had been called to New York, ostensibly to meet his boss but, surely, to be the instrument of bringing Jay Gould into contact with Abel Corbin, he had begun to take on more and more of the real work of the Washington office. Berman, always easygoing, had willingly stepped aside, leaving Lloyd to be the outside man, the man-about-town, the high-rolling, heavy-tipping host of intimate dinners in expensive restaurants for congressmen and senators.

After hearing Lloyd's full account—with only a few things left out, such as Lloyd's revelation to Gould that

Berman had been somewhat loose of tongue—Harold asked, "Can he do it? Do you think he can actually corner the market in gold?"

"It all depends on what the federal Treasury does," Lloyd answered. "If Mr. Gould and Corbin can convince the President that high gold prices will be good for the farmer and for the country, then Mr. Gould just might be able to do it. The test will come when prices start to rise steadily."

"It'll be a risky situation," Berman warned. "I believe I'm going to stay out of it, Lloyd, and I'd advise you to do the same. If Mr. Gould and his friends attempt this, they'll be putting up millions."

"But if they're willing to risk millions, wouldn't you be willing to risk a smaller amount?" Lloyd challenged, feeling contempt for Berman.

"Well, you see," Harold explained, "if the Treasury should step in and stabilize the price of gold, Mr. Gould might lose a few million dollars. That sounds impressive, but when you consider that he'll be risking only a fraction of his fortune, things fall into perspective. If you or I invest —what? a couple of hundred thousand? If we put what we have into gold and lose it—or even a significant portion of it—we'd be hurt far worse than Gould."

Lloyd's contempt changed to pity. He knew that he was looking at a small man, a man doomed to remain insignificant. He resolved at that moment to begin to sever all connections with Harold Berman. And at that moment, even though the man had not the least suspicion, Harold Berman had ceased to be the boss in the Erie's Washington office. It was only a matter of time.

"Well, Harold," Lloyd said affably, "I hope you won't be disappointed if I decide not to accept your advice."

It was not Lloyd but Leah who invited Harold to dinner that night. She had donned a smart little town dress and had taken a cab to the office to see if her brother had returned from New York. She accepted a shy kiss on the cheek from her fiancé, heard from him that Lloyd was in-

deed back from meeting Jay Gould and, eager to get back
to work, had gone to do business on Capitol Hill.

"My dear," Harold said, "I wanted to speak to him
about us, but I admit that I couldn't muster up the courage.
I had no reason to think that Lloyd would be anything but
pleased—he is my best friend. And yet I could not bring
myself to speak. Isn't that odd?"

"Men," Leah said. "What if I had an old bear of a father
instead of a rather nice brother?"

"I'd probably commit suicide," Berman joked.

"Don't worry. We'll tell Lloyd together. You come to the
apartment at seven, and we'll tell him during dinner."

"All right," Berman agreed.

"We're having lamb chops," she said. "You do like them,
as I remember."

"I do indeed." He leaned to her—kissed her with a hint
of wetness for the first time. "I do love you, my dear girl."

She patted his hand and smiled up at him.

Lloyd Miles was not a man to squander his attention and
efforts on the feelings of others, not even his sister. It was
not that he didn't love Leah. She was, in fact, a dear and
necessary fixture in his life. He remembered when he had
pushed his way into the home of their aunt and declared
emphatically that he was not going to leave his sister to be
treated as a poor relation any longer, that Leah was not a
slave or a bond servant. The tiny slip of a girl had flown
into his arms and wept in happiness. He had watched her
become a woman.

From the first day that they had made a home together
she had done her share and more. She was his housekeeper, his hostess, a sounding board for his opinions, a
companion who demanded nothing of him. Without question he accepted her gratitude and love. He was generous.
He had spent many hours with her in fine shops, purchasing elaborate gowns in the latest fashion and all the acces-
sories to go with them. She had her own household account, and he never questioned her expenditures.

Once, when it appeared that Leah was going to leave

him to marry Philip Trent, he had felt concern, for living without Leah to manage his home would require certain adjustments; but it was not his dependence on her that had been the strongest motivation for his ultimatum to her regarding Philip Trent. Trent had proved to be a self-righteous prig, a hypocrite who pretended to look down on Lloyd because he used what were nothing more than good business practices to promote the interests of his employer, the Union Pacific Railroad.

After he had forced Leah to break her engagement to Philip Trent, she moped a bit. But as if to prove that he'd been correct in assuring her that her attachment to Trent would soon pass, she had recovered, at least in his estimation.

And now the feckless little wench was at it again.

"Lloyd," she announced at dinner, "Harold has asked me to marry him."

Lloyd gasped and had to cough half-chewed food into his napkin. Leah leapt to her feet, ran around the table, pounded him on the back, and gave him a drink of water. When he could breathe again she asked, "Was it that much of a shock?"

"Unexpected," he said.

She seated herself and looked at him with concern. "I said yes, Lloyd."

"Yes, I expect you would have," he said.

Her eyes pleaded with him.

His face was set and his mouth firm, but then he smiled and turned to Harold. "Old friend, you surprise me."

"Not unpleasantly, I hope," Berman said.

Lloyd remained coldly silent.

"Lloyd?" Leah asked, her face pale.

He smiled and reached across the table to pat her hand. "You would make a lovely bride," he said.

Berman visibly relaxed, sinking down into his chair.

Leah smiled. "We thought to have a rather small wedding. And we see no reason to go through a long engagement." She laughed. "After all, neither of us is getting any younger."

"That's true," Lloyd said. "Well." He rose. "Harold, let's leave the galley slave to clean up while we have a cigar."

In the room that he used as his library-study, Lloyd studied Harold Berman as if seeing him for the first time. Berman's olive skin alienated him; Berman's black, tightly curled hair was a cause for revulsion. Lloyd had been vaguely aware that Harold Berman was a Jew and, therefore, different. Now that difference rose up to smite him. He thought of Leah married to Berman, and an unreasoning anger grew in him.

"Harold," he said, "I think you're being hasty."

"Do you?" Berman asked anxiously. "Actually it is Leah who wants to be married quickly."

"I see," Lloyd said with ill-concealed irony. "Of course." He snipped the end of a cigar, rolled it in his mouth, and lit it. "Harold, it just won't do, you know."

Berman flushed. "I don't quite understand. Are you objecting?"

"Just talking sense," Lloyd said. "You're very much different, you and my sister. I just don't think you two are suited."

"I'm sorry to hear you say that," Berman said. "I had hoped that you would be pleased."

"Oh, it's not that I'm displeased," Lloyd said, holding a close rein on his rage. "You're a fine man, Harold." After all, he was going to have to work with Berman for a while longer, until he found a way to eliminate him, and there was no sense in making his own life difficult. "Leah could certainly do worse. But I'm doing you a favor by talking to you like this. I know my sister, you see, and I know that she's not ready for marriage."

"Good Lord," Berman said. "She's certainly old enough to know her own mind."

Lloyd could be pleasant no longer. "And I know mine, Berman," he grated. "Since you won't listen to reason, let me say this: You are no longer welcome in this house. You will stay away from my sister. There will be no marriage."

"But why?" Berman asked, truly puzzled.

"All right, if you want me to be specific, I would never allow my sister to enter into an interracial union."

"Interracial? My God." Berman was pale, aghast. "That's how you feel?"

"I'm afraid so."

Berman rose. He was shaking. He turned and walked slowly from the room. Lloyd followed, then handed him his hat.

"I want to speak with Leah before I go," Berman said.

"No," Lloyd said firmly.

Harold seated his hat on his head, nodded to Lloyd, and left quietly.

Leah emerged from the kitchen shortly afterward and looked around. "Where's Harold?"

"He remembered a pressing engagement," Lloyd said.

"What?" she asked incredulously.

"Leah, he had to go."

"Without giving a reason?"

"He had reason."

"Well, I'd like to know what it was," she said. Suddenly she felt apprehension. "You two didn't have an argument?"

"No argument," he said.

She came to him, put her hands on his arms, and looked up into his stern face. "Lloyd, I can see that something's definitely wrong. You must tell me."

"You would actually marry him?"

"You *have* had a falling out," she said. "What was it? Business?"

"Damn it, Leah, he's not like us."

She shook her head. "I don't understand. What do you mean?"

"Don't be stupid," he said angrily.

She stepped back two paces, her hand flying to her mouth. "Because he's Jewish?" She inhaled sharply. "Not that, Lloyd, surely not that. Why, he doesn't even go to church—to synagogue. We've talked about all that. It isn't going to make any difference."

"My sister will not marry a Jew," Lloyd said, jaws clenching.

"I can't believe this," Leah said softly. Then her voice rose, and her face flushed. "If you said horrible things to that gentle, loving man, I will never forgive you."

"I told that gentle, loving man to get out of my house and stay out."

"But you have to work with him," she protested.

"Not for long."

"Oh, may God forgive you," she said, her own anger taking hold. "For the second time you have interfered in my life. You asked me to give up the only man I ever really loved—"

"I don't want to hear about that," Lloyd said, turning away.

"Oh, but I want to say it!" Leah shouted. "You made me choose between Philip and you, and I, out of loyalty, chose you. He was your friend. But because he wouldn't enter into your questionable activities, you came to hate him. You thought only of yourself, not of me. And now you're trying to come between me and another man."

"For your own good, Leah," he said, trying to soothe her.

"No! I don't accept that. I don't think you are capable of deciding what's good for me. You think only of yourself. You're free to marry anyone you choose—"

He laughed ironically and felt again the anger and shame he'd known when Abby Kershaw belittled him.

"—but you would deny me another chance to have a good man as my husband. Oh, Lloyd, be fair."

"Can you stand there and tell me, in all honesty, that you love Harold Berman?" he demanded.

"Not as I loved Philip, no. But I respect him, and I want to be his wife."

"Respect?" He laughed harshly. "I'd have more respect for you if you became a woman of the streets."

"Like the women you favor?" she shot back.

"Enough," he said. "I've heard enough. Berman is not welcome in this house. Now, if you're so dead set on marrying him, go to your room, pack your things, and go to him. I don't give a damn. If you want to become the wife of—" He paused. She was weeping. He went to her and took her in his arms. "No, little sister, I don't mean that. I wouldn't let you go."

She pushed away from him, wiping tears from her eyes. "Will you think about it further?"

"No need."

"For me, will you please consider it?"

He relented. "All right. I will consider it."

The Erie Railroad office in Washington was a three-man operation: Lloyd, Harold Berman, and a male secretary. When Lloyd entered the next morning the secretary rose from his desk and left the outer office quickly. Harold Berman was standing in the doorway to his own office looking with unblinking eyes at Lloyd.

"Morning, Berman," Lloyd said.

"I have posted a letter asking Mr. Gould to assign you to duties elsewhere," Berman said.

"Yes, I expected something like that. Can't blame you, Harold."

The soft answer obviously surprised Berman.

"But I wonder if he'll do it?" Lloyd asked. "Harold, how long has it been since you were head-to-head with a congressman?"

"Don't concern yourself," Berman said coldly. "I handled the office alone before I asked Mr. Gould to hire you. I can do it again."

"But not half as well, Harold," Lloyd pointed out. "You know, I might just write Mr. Gould a letter myself."

"I can't prevent that," Berman said.

Lloyd smiled. "Well, we'll see, Harold."

"Surely you can't expect things in the office to continue as if nothing had happened."

"Why not? I don't let personal matters interfere with business." He sat on the corner of the secretary's desk and grinned at Berman. "Just so we understand each other, Harold, I hold no animosity toward you. I am grateful to you for giving me the opportunity to work for the Erie and for Jay Gould. I won't have you as a brother-in-law, but if you can stand it, I won't object to working with you."

Berman was shaking his head in puzzlement.

"I imagine Leah will be here to see you sometime today," Lloyd said.

"I would have thought that you would not allow that," Berman said.

"She can be a foolish girl at times, Harold," Lloyd said genially. "However, you and I understand each other, don't we?"

Harold nodded numbly.

"And I don't think you want to get into a fight with me," Lloyd continued.

Berman's head jerked up.

"So you might consider sending along another letter to Mr. Gould, saying that you were in error in asking him to fire me."

"No, I don't think so," Berman said.

"As you will, then," Lloyd said, his plans solidifying quickly. "I'll be away for a day or two."

"Yes, that's a good idea," Berman said.

Harold Berman had been awake most of the night. At first he had been resolved to meet with Leah and insist that she marry him, that she leave her brother to his prejudice if that was the only way.

But as the slow night hours passed, purity was, by proximity, tainted to rot, as often happens in life. It became difficult for him to think of Leah except in connection with her brother. Perhaps he rationalized away his love for her in an effort to avoid the ultimate hurt—outright rejection by her—but before morning he had decided to have done with both members of the Miles family, to put his pain behind him.

Now he wavered. He spent the day listening for Leah's voice, waiting for her to come in the front door. Lloyd had said that she would probably come to see him. He wanted to beg her to marry him. He dreamed of holding her in his arms, of hearing her say that she loved him and would marry him in spite of her brother's opposition.

But the next minute he felt the self-protective urge to say, "A plague on both of you."

He finally realized that no forethought could prepare him for Leah's visit. He would wait until she came and allow the course of their future to rest upon her behavior toward him.

Leah went so far as to get dressed for the street before she changed her mind about going to Harold's office. Her decision was the result of a variety of factors, but the underlying reason was growing disappointment. It had bothered her that Harold had left the apartment on the previous evening without saying good night to her. In her heart she expected him to fight for her. So it was that she, too, spent most of the day waiting and watching.

Twice a knock came at the door. The first time it was a messenger with a note from Lloyd telling her that he'd been called to New York. When she hurried to the door again she opened it to face a tall redheaded man who smiled at her and asked, "Leah Miles?"

"Yes, may I help you?"

"I was hoping to find your brother here," said the man.

"I'm sorry, he is not here," she said.

"Miss Miles, I'm Phineas Headley. If you are a magazine or a newspaper reader, you might recognize my name."

Leah shook her head.

"Well, such is fame," Headley said pleasantly. "I'm a newsman, Miss Miles. I wonder if I might ask you some questions."

She blushed in confusion. She did not know this person. He had no right to ask her anything, and yet she was reluctant to be rude.

"Miss Miles, is your brother investing in gold?" Headley asked.

Leah's face flamed, for a touch of anger was added to her confusion. "I don't pry into my brother's business affairs. And if I knew the answer to your question, I would still tell you that the proper person to ask would be my brother."

"I understand that Lloyd Miles works for, or with, Mr. Jay Gould and Mr. Jim Fisk."

"What you understand, sir, is your affair," Leah said. Her natural desire to be considerate had been overcome by resentment toward Headley's intrusion. "I must bid you good day." She closed the door in his face.

The day ended with her sitting alone in the quiet apartment. During the long evening there was no knock on the door. Philip had fought for her, had tried to see her, and had written letter after letter to her. But Harold Berman apparently valued her so little that he did not even come to her to tell her why he was disappearing from her life.

Lloyd had taken a midmorning train to New York. He had decided that all ties between Harold Berman and him had to be dissolved. There wasn't a place for both of them in the Washington office, and he was not willing to leave Berman in charge without a fight.

There was no assurance that he would win, but there was too much at stake not to try. First of all, he needed the salary. He was not yet a rich man, and at the moment every dollar he owned or could borrow he had invested in gold. Second, if he continued his association with Berman, meaning if he allowed Berman to remain in Washington, in the employ of Jay Gould, the Jew might gain enough courage to defy him and pursue Leah. Leah, being a woman and, therefore, foolish and weak, might just decide to marry him. Lloyd was banking on Jay Gould's business sense. Gould had not become the financial power that he was by being stupid. Only an unobservant man could have failed to notice that Lloyd was far more effective than Berman in his contacts with the powers in Washington.

As it happened, the course of Lloyd's future was influenced by a chance encounter on the train. He had taken his seat as the engine puffed and jerked prior to departing. He caught sight of a well-dressed man running across the platform just as the train began to move. Seconds later the latecomer was entering the car.

Lloyd got to his feet and waved. "Over here, General," he called.

General Dan Butterfield lifted a hand in greeting and smiled from behind his huge black mustache. He shook Lloyd's hand and sat down facing him as the train jerked once more, then began to accelerate smoothly.

"Almost missed it," Butterfield said.

Daniel Butterfield was a tall man. His receding black, wavy hair emphasized his domed forehead. His father, John Butterfield, had organized the American Express Company. Daniel himself was not unsuccessful. He had emerged from the Civil War a hero, after commanding a division at Fredericksburg, serving as army chief of staff at Chancellorsville and Gettysburg, and accompanying Sherman on his march to Atlanta.

Lloyd knew Butterfield through Abel Corbin, for Corbin and Daniel's father had been friends, and after the war Dan Butterfield had joined Corbin in investing in a St. Louis-to-San Francisco stage route.

"Well, Miles," Butterfield said, "we're well met. Nothing like a friendly face to make a boring journey pass more quickly."

"Well, sir, I've traveled under less comfortable circumstances," Lloyd said.

Butterfield laughed at the reference to the war. "Good times and bad, eh, Major?"

"Sometimes I miss it," Lloyd admitted. He laughed. "But, in all frankness, not a helluva lot."

"Oh, I don't know," Butterfield said. "If you could have a war without an enemy and without getting shot at, it would be a wonderful adventure—good companions, a good horse under you, the long road into country you've never seen before, and the campfires at night."

For a moment Lloyd was taken back in time to an autumn evening in wartime, with the scent of wood smoke, and the lingering rays of a red sun reflecting on the James River, and the distant sound of a bugle playing "Butterfield's Lullaby." The melody lingered, dying slowly as twilight edged down on the camp. Now people were calling the melody "Taps," that bugle call written by the man who sat opposite him.

Lloyd shook his head. No, he didn't really miss the war. He pulled a flask from his inside coat pocket and poured brandy into twin small silver cups. "Here's to friends who are gone," he toasted.

"Hear, hear," Butterfield said, lifting his cup.

"What takes you to New York, General?" Lloyd asked.

Butterfield looked toward the ceiling of the car for a moment and watched a lamp sway. "Well, I suppose it won't be a secret for long," he said. "As a matter of fact, I've been asked by President Grant to be subtreasurer in New York. Of course I said yes."

"Congratulations, sir!" Lloyd concealed a quick rush of elation. He was on his way to New York to try to get Jay Gould to put him in charge of the Washington office, and here, like a gift from the gods, was the means of assuring that Gould would grant him his wish. "So you'll be living in New York?"

"Indeed."

"It would be my pleasure, sir, to introduce you to friends of mine."

"Well, Miles, that's a very nice offer. Of course I do know a few people myself."

"Yes, sir, I'm sure you do."

"Hear you're working for the Erie Railroad," Butterfield said. "What sort of a fellow is Jay Gould?"

"A gentleman," Lloyd answered. "You haven't met Mr. Gould, then?"

"Haven't had the pleasure."

"May I have your permission to remedy that situation?"

"Don't mind if you do," Butterfield agreed.

"As it happens, General, Mr. Gould and a few associates are embarking on a very exciting project. Perhaps you might be interested."

"Always interested in making an honest dollar," Butterfield said. "Tell me about it."

"If it's all the same to you, I'll leave that to Mr. Gould."

Lloyd knew that Butterfield was no exception to the rule that everyone looked for advancement. And Butterfield was a Grant man, in spades. In 1866, when it was hinted that General Ulysses S. Grant would not be averse to accepting a pecuniary prize for winning the war, Butterfield, who at that time was commander of New York Harbor, raised $150,000 from businessmen for General Grant. Only recently—Lloyd knew of it from Corbin—Butterfield had advanced five thousand dollars each to generals Orville Babcock and Horace Porter, ex-aides to General Grant now on the White House staff, to buy choice lots on 185th Street in New York.

In short, Dan Butterfield knew how business was conducted. Lloyd did not doubt for a minute that Butterfield would be interested in an offer from Jay Gould to participate in the gold scheme, and he thanked his lucky stars that Butterfield had taken the same train and had boarded the same car.

Jay Gould was with his Erie partner, Jim Fisk, when Sebastian, Gould's secretary, told him that Lloyd Miles was in the waiting room.

"Your young man from Washington?" Fisk asked, smoothing his mustache. "I'd like to meet him."

Fisk was a big, jolly man whose outgoing nature belied his financial shrewdness. He was in uniform on that day. He styled himself as admiral of the Narragansett Steamship Company, of which he owned a controlling interest, and liked to wear the blue uniform with its big brass buttons, gold-trimmed hat, and a huge, circular diamond pin on his right lapel.

Fisk and Gould had been through some interesting times together. They had bested shrewd old Uncle Dan'l Drew at his own game when he tried to take over the Erie, and they had gotten away with tweaking the beard of the old lion Commodore Vanderbilt. In spite of those successes Jim Fisk was dubious about Jay's scheme to corner the gold market. It wasn't that Jim was afraid to take a risk—he'd proven his courage during the war by buying contraband cotton from warehouses in the Confederacy and smuggling it past Union troops to the textile mills where Jordan Marsh wove it into uniforms for Mr. Lincoln's army. It was just that Jim wasn't positive that his partner could keep the government from halting a price rise in gold by dumping coin onto the market from the huge federal hoard in the U.S. Treasury.

When the young man from Washington was escorted into Jay Gould's office, Fisk examined him with outright curiosity and tried to squeeze Lloyd's hand, only to find that the smaller, thinner man matched his grip. Then Fisk stood back to learn what was what.

"I don't recall summoning you, Mr. Miles," Jay Gould said mildly.

"No, sir, you didn't." Lloyd fell silent and matched Gould's unblinking gaze.

Finally, with a shrug of irritation, it was Gould who spoke. "Since you seem reluctant to tell me why you're here, I will ask."

"I'm here to make a personnel recommendation, sir."

Fisk chuckled because Gould was a fanatic when it came to handling details; he was obsessed by neatness and order. For a newly hired man to suggest a change in Gould's smooth-running organization was to court disaster.

"I recommend, sir, that you release Harold Berman from his position in Washington."

"I see," Gould said.

Fisk played with his mustache and waited for the detonation. Again there was silence, and again it was Gould who broke it.

"And I suppose you are to take Mr. Berman's place."

"For the time being, yes, sir," Lloyd replied, "until it's time for me to come to New York."

"You have this all thought out, I see," Gould said.

Fisk recognized the deadly softness of his partner's voice. Gould was like a poised snake, motionless before the strike.

"I will need to be in New York, sir, to keep in close

touch with my good friend General Dan Butterfield, who has just been put in charge of the New York subtreasury."

Fisk's hand froze as he stroked his mustache. Gould's face became animated.

"I rode up with General Butterfield on the train," Lloyd said. "As you know, he's a very good friend of both Mr. Corbin and of the President." He smiled. "And," the young man added modestly, "of one Lloyd Miles."

For a moment Fisk thought that he'd gone too far in being flippant, but then he roared with laughter. "He's got you, Jay," Jim said.

"I have arranged for you to meet with General Butterfield at your convenience," Lloyd added.

Fisk could see that it had taken Gould only seconds to realize the advantages of having a contact in the New York subtreasury. In the event of government intervention the Treasury gold to be sold would be in the New York vaults. A contact there would provide early warning of a change in government policy.

"If I am 'got,' as you say, Jim," Gould said, chuckling, "then this is certainly the way I prefer to be had." He turned to Lloyd. "Now, what's this about Berman?"

"He's not the right man for the job," Lloyd said.

"And you want him out?"

Lloyd nodded. "For the good of the company."

"Of course," Gould said. "And it doesn't bother you to put a knife in the back of the man who got you the job with Erie?"

Lloyd had prepared himself for that question, although he now felt exposed to enemy fire. "I think, sir, that you will see that my concern is for the good of the company. As I understand it, you were once in the same position, presented with a choice between efficiency in business and friendship."

Gould's eyes narrowed dangerously, then he relaxed. "Then we must hope, Miles, that Mr. Berman is made of stronger stuff than the man to whom you refer and will not shoot himself in the temple."

Jim Fisk looked with new respect at Lloyd Miles. The

young man had put his head into the lion's mouth and emerged not only unscathed but strengthened. Without putting it into words Miles had informed Jay Gould that he knew the story of Gould's first business venture, when he convinced Charles Leupp to invest sixty thousand dollars in a tannery. The story—true or not—was that Jay had managed to bleed all the money from the business, leaving Leupp to bankruptcy and suicide.

Fisk was looking back and forth from Lloyd's calm face to the face of his partner. Fisk smiled, having decided that he rather liked the brash young upstart from Washington. Fisk was pleased, therefore, when Gould said, "By the time you get back to Washington, you will be in charge. We will speak about your replacement there at a later date, when it is time for you to move to New York."

"At the risk of seeming arrogant, sir, I would like to say that there will be no need for a replacement—only a secretary. I will be able to handle the Washington business from here."

Once again Jim Fisk was amazed. "Miles," he said, "my partner here doesn't like public places, so how about you and me going to have a drink."

"If Mr. Gould has no further need of me, it would be my pleasure, sir," Lloyd replied.

CHAPTER 4

Harold Berman was alone in the office when the telegram from Jay Gould was delivered. He flipped the messenger a silver dime, then with shaking fingers opened the envelope. There was no way Gould could have received his request to remove Lloyd Miles from the Washington office, so he wondered why Gould had sent him a telegram. His eyes took in the black words in a rush, assimilating the message as a whole. Gould did not believe in saving a penny by using telegraphese.

MR. HAROLD BERMAN

CONSIDER THIS TO BE FORMAL NOTICE THAT MR. LLOYD MILES IS NOW MANAGER OF THE ERIE RAILROAD'S WASHINGTON OFFICE. AS OF THIS DATE YOUR SERVICES ARE TERMINATED. THANK YOU FOR YOUR PAST EFFORTS. SEVERANCE PAY, WHICH I BELIEVE YOU WILL FIND GENEROUS, WILL BE FORWARDED TO YOUR HOME ADDRESS FROM THIS OFFICE.

JASON GOULD

Berman sat motionless for a long time, his hands no longer shaking. It was difficult for him to accept the finality of the telegram. He had served Jay Gould and the Erie to the best of his ability. He had been loyal, and he had believed that his employer was loyal to him in return. Now it was ended. He had taken a cowbird's egg into his nest, and the chick had outgrown him and had pushed him out.

For a long time he sat as if paralyzed. He had no prospects. He had believed that his future rested with the Erie Railroad. He had entertained hopes of being promoted to the New York office, perhaps as office manager, or of being assigned to the records department of the railroad, where his talent for handling detail would be of maximum benefit. That was not to be. His career with the Erie was at an end because he had fallen in love with Leah Miles.

The pain of losing Leah was equally as devastating as the knowledge that Jay Gould had valued him so little that one request from Lloyd Miles had been enough to oust him.

As he rose, the telegram dropped from his nerveless fingers. Leah Miles. Lloyd Miles. Brother and sister. A working unit. One his friend, the other the woman he loved. They had delivered a one-two punch that left him reeling. He brushed his hand over his thick, curly hair and closed his eyes, and his anger began to build a defensive wall between the Miles siblings and his own sensitive inner core. If Leah had really loved him, she would have come to him after the humiliating scene with Lloyd in the Miles apartment. And it was clear that Lloyd Miles had never been a true friend. He remembered that both Geoffrey Lancaster and Paul Jennings had expressed doubts about Lloyd's loyalty to his so-called friends of the Breakfast Club when Lloyd presented them with shares of Crédit Mobilier but kept title and control.

Thinking of Lancaster and Jennings was comforting. Perhaps they would have something for him to do. After all, he had come to the rescue of Lloyd Miles when Miles was unemployed. The world wouldn't come to an end just because he'd been betrayed by Miles and Jay Gould.

A light came into his eyes. He was one of the very few people who knew Gould's plans, knew that Gould was going to try for a corner in gold. True, he had advised Miles to stay out of the gold market, but if a man was careful . . . He had inside information, the knowledge that powerful interests would be buying gold and driving up the price. If he bought in early, while prices were still low, and if he didn't get greedy and sold well before the top, settling for a moderate profit, he could very well make up for the fact that he'd been fired. He would ride Gould's financial coattails to independence. That would be sweet. The scholar Hillel, a rabbi who had lived in the time of Jesus, had said: *Live well, that is the best revenge.* Well, he decided, he would use Gould's own strategy to do just that.

And in the end he just might do something else. In order for Gould and his ring to succeed in cornering the market in gold, it would be vital that the U.S. Government do nothing. If the Treasury should decide to sell its huge hoard of gold, the scheme would be doomed to defeat, so those who had purchased gold at inflated prices, expecting it to go still higher, would face financial ruin. Perhaps, just perhaps, the man who had been so wronged would have the last laugh.

He was preparing to leave the Erie office for the last time when a tall redheaded man in rumpled dark clothing came in and said, "Hello, Mr. Berman, may I have a moment of your time, please?" At first Berman was cold, wary. For a dismal moment he wondered if the newsman was going to run a story on some obscure financial page about a change of command in the Erie office. When Phineas Headley's questions indicated an interest in the gold market, Berman became calmer but much more wary.

"Mr. Berman, as an employee of the Erie Railroad, are you aware that large sums of Erie money are being diverted into the gold market?"

"I'm sorry," Berman said, "I'm afraid I can't help you there. I don't see the company's books, you know."

"But if Erie and its managers, Mr. Jay Gould and Mr. Jim Fisk, were investing heavily in gold, wouldn't you have some inkling of it?"

"Why should I?"

"Well, you look like a pretty smart man to me, Mr. Berman."

"Yes, I'm so smart that I've just been fired."

Headley shook his head in sympathy. "Tough," he said. "Sorry to hear it. Have you any plans?"

Berman laughed. "I thought I'd go to New York and do some speculating in gold."

"As it happens, I'll be going back to New York very soon, Mr. Berman. May I give you my card?"

Berman accepted the business card and put it into a pocket of his coat.

"If you ever decide you'd like to have a chat with me about the gold market or anything else of interest, you'll have my address," Headley said. "Maybe we could get together for lunch someday. Do you have a New York address?"

"Not yet," Berman replied. "Thank you, Mr. Headley. If I have anything that I think might interest you, I'll drop you a note." His mind was running in two directions. By using Jay Gould's own scheme he planned to exact revenge and make more money than he'd ever had before. He felt an urge, however, to make things happen in a much more certain and rapid way. All he had to do was tell this newsman that Jay Gould and Jim Fisk had plans to devastate the economy of the United States by taking a corner in gold. Forewarned, financial interests and the federal government could stop Gould cold.

He looked at the redheaded man and began to speak, but all he said was "Good day, Mr. Headley," because now was not the time to reveal Gould's plans. If the speculators were stopped now, they wouldn't be hurt badly. It would be best to wait until Gould, Fisk, and Lloyd Miles were committed heavily in the gold market. A crash in gold prices at that time would be painful to Gould and Fisk and destructive for Lloyd Miles.

Harold Berman felt much better when he left the Erie Railroad office. He was in control. The way was open to him to make money, and if he played it just right, he could very well become rich and ruin Gould and Miles forever.

* * *

Harold Berman was not the only one to receive a telegram from the New York office of the Erie Railroad that
day. Leah Miles was informed by wire that her brother
would be delayed in New York and that she should prepare
for a celebration of his promotion to Washington office
manager upon his return. If the message had been intended by Lloyd to please her, he had miscalculated.

She went pale. A dreadful certainty that Lloyd had succeeded in ousting Harold not only from her life but from
his job made her weep, and her tears were followed by
anger. Lloyd had no right to ruin Harold simply because he
had asked her to marry him. Determination to right the
matter sent her to her bedroom, where she freshened herself, changed into street clothes, and took her jewelry box
from under her intimate garments in a dresser drawer.

She gasped when she opened the box, for it contained
nothing but costume jewelry. The lovely diamond-studded
cameo that had been Lloyd's Christmas present to her was
gone, along with her pearls, jeweled hatpins, gold neck-
laces—everything that he had given her over the years. She
sifted frantically through the costume jewelry and did not
find what she sought—the diamond solitaire that Philip
Trent had given her upon their engagement.

Her first thought was to send for the police to report that
she had been robbed, but then she noticed that a piece of
paper was pinned to the quilted satin lining of the jewelry
box. The note read: *Sister Dear, I have borrowed your baubles. It is a temporary thing, and I will make it up to you. L.*

With a moan of helpless anger and disgust she slammed
the box closed and tossed it into the drawer. Had he asked,
she would have given the jewelry to him. But he had not
asked, and he had taken something that had meant a lot to
her, although she had not realized it until she had discovered that it was missing—Philip's ring.

It was the ring that took on special significance. The loss
of the ring was, actually, meaningless in comparison to
other things that Lloyd had done, such as forcing her to

break off her engagement to Philip and driving Harold Berman out of her life and out of his job. But it was this last, bitter blow that sent her into the street with a resolve to show Lloyd that she was not going to submit to his dictatorial wishes any longer.

She took a cab to the Erie offices to find the secretary there alone. Mr. Berman, she was told, had cleaned out his desk and left abruptly. No, he did not know where Mr. Berman had gone. No, he had not heard from Mr. Miles, who was in New York.

Outside, she told the cabdriver to take her to Harold's town house. There was no answer to her knock. The building's custodian told her that he had helped Mr. Berman carry some luggage down to his carriage. No, Mr. Berman had not mentioned where he was going.

"Harold," she whispered to herself as she walked back toward the cab, "you could have given me a chance. If you really loved me, you could have asked me how I felt about all this."

Leah could not bear the thought of going back to the quiet apartment. She did not want to be alone. She asked the cabdriver to stop near the White House. After she paid him, she walked idly down the busy sidewalk. Ahead of her a young couple strolled arm in arm to halt in front of the President's home. The young woman looked up at the man, and the tenderness in that stranger's eyes caused a pang of intense loneliness to stab Leah. She was helpless under a great weight of melancholia. Alone, totally isolated in spite of the crowds, she walked aimlessly, her mind dulled.

"Aunt Martha . . . Aunt Martha," a young voice was saying.

Startled into awareness, Leah looked around. She was walking near the Capitol Building. A spinsterish woman in rumpled calico was standing with three children ranging in age from two years to five. The two smaller children clung to the woman's hands. "Aunt Martha," asked the larger one, a boy, "when are we going to eat? I'm hungry."

"Aunt Martha," piped the two-year-old, "Aunt Martha, Aunt Martha."

The little voice became, in Leah's mind, a plaintive liturgy: *"Aunt Leah, Aunt Leah, Aunt Leah—"*

She felt faint and knew she had to find a place to sit down. She walked up the stairs. The House of Representatives was in session. She found herself in the spectators' balcony. It was crowded, for the House was in the midst of an investigation into corruption in the building of the transcontinental railroad. She found a seat beside an elderly man who leaned forward, hand cupped to his ear, to hear the words of a conservatively dressed young man who held the floor.

Her heart leapt. "Philip," she whispered, for it was Philip Trent who was addressing the membership.

He spoke so well, so clearly, so convincingly, about several congressmen who had accepted bribes from the holding company that controlled the Union Pacific Railroad, that for a long time Leah's attention was on his words, not on what might have been. When he finished and took his seat, her eyes followed him. He leaned forward to whisper to a colleague, then exchanged notes with another.

Vain hopes buoyed her, and then she sank back into deep depression. It was too late to dream of the way things had been with Philip. She had made her choice. In spite of what Lloyd had done, she had not been able to think of deserting her brother. She had known in her heart that Lloyd's attitude, not Philip's actions, had poisoned the friendship between the two wartime comrades. Furthermore, events in the House were vindicating Philip completely and making it clear that Lloyd had been involved in the growing scandal.

Leah had never spoken with Lloyd about his role in the Crédit Mobilier affair, but she knew enough from following the exposé in the newspapers and from little things that Lloyd had said in the past that her brother had been the contact between the men in Congress who accepted Crédit Mobilier's bribes and the moguls of the Union Pacific, specifically Thomas Durant. Lloyd clearly believed that the investigation spurred along by Representative Philip Trent was a witch-hunt. As far as Lloyd was concerned, it was just

good business practice to involve members of the House
and the Senate in Crédit Mobilier. The whole point of selling Crédit Mobilier stock to the lawmakers at give-away
prices had been to make them put their own necks on the
line. A man who has a financial interest in an affair will
protect himself. To Lloyd, Philip Trent was a do-gooder, a
hypocrite, a pretender.

The words of the congressman who now held the floor
buzzed off into a meaningless mumble as Leah sank down
within herself, hearing those small, piping voices, *"Aunt
Leah, Aunt Leah."* She uttered a small startled cry when
she felt a hand on her shoulder. She looked up to see the
smiling face of Gus Trent, Philip's father.

"I didn't mean to frighten you," Gus whispered.

"I'm afraid I was daydreaming," she whispered back.

"Let's get out of here," Gus suggested.

She followed him. In the open area under the great ro-
tunda Gus took her arm. "What a pleasure it is to see you,
my dear," he said.

"And you," Leah agreed, smiling. This man was to have
been her father-in-law, and a bond had existed between
them. She had looked on Gus as the father she'd never
known, and she had been more than willing to grant Gus
his fondest wish, to have grandchildren.

As for Gus, he had been extremely fond of Leah from
their first introduction and mourned the unfortunate circumstances, of which he knew only a part by guess and
intuition, that had caused Philip and her to part. "I am so
pleased to have run into you," he said. "I thought that I
was going to have to eat lunch alone."

Leah was not hungry, but she allowed Gus to guide her
into the open air and down the great steps.

Gus Trent, the consummate politician who was content
to be a member of the Maryland State Legislature and to
manage his home precincts, was a master at reading the
character and emotions of others.

It was not until Leah and he were seated opposite each
other in a cozy little restaurant, however, that the man got

the full impact of the emptiness in her eyes. He wanted to reach out and touch her, wanted to take Leah in his arms and comfort her. He felt a small rush of anger at his son for having thrown away this valuable young woman without a real knock-down-drag-out fight. Ah, how beautiful she was! And through it all she had maintained her dignity.

He was saddened. That combination of beauty and the hint of melancholy in her eyes would intrigue men, and that worried him, for only as long as Leah was unmarried could he have hope that she might become his daughter after all.

Gus had not missed subtle evidence of a growing attraction between his son and Mrs. Julia Grey, who worked in Philip's office, although perhaps without the actual awareness of either of them. He foresaw potential tragedy there. Adam Grey, Julia's husband, was a candidate for an early death because of his terrible war wounds, which included the loss of both legs.

Aside from Gus's concern that someone would be hurt and hurt badly by the mutual affinity that was growing between Philip and Julia, the older man was being selfish about the matter. After several years of marriage Julia was still childless. So although Julia was a fine, vibrant, vividly pretty, and intelligent woman, even without the complication of her having an invalid husband, Gus would have preferred Leah as his son's wife because of her glowing health and fondness for children.

Leah found that under the pleasant stimulation of being with Gus, she was a bit hungry, after all. Gus ordered bay oysters on the half shell as an appetizer, followed by roasted beef and mashed potatoes, asparagus and hollandaise sauce. Leah and Gus talked about the weather and the usual inefficiency of Congress but made no mention of Philip. Gus politely inquired about Lloyd. When the meal was finished they lingered over coffee.

"My dear," Gus said sincerely, "I do miss you. Perhaps you could be kind to an old man and make lunch with me a regular event when I am in Washington."

"I'd love to," she said quickly, then laughed. "Although

you must promise to help me exercise willpower so I won't
eat as much as I did today."

"I'll ration it out to you, bite by bite," he vowed.

After lunch they walked together. Gus had a midafternoon appointment, then he was going to spend the night
in Philip's apartment before returning to Baltimore. Leah
had no plans. He walked her all the way to her apartment
and at the door took both her hands in his. "At the risk of
being too personal, dear, I want to say that if I were the age
of a certain young man whose name I will not mention—"

She smiled, hiding the sudden pain. "I know," she said.
"Please do let me know when you're going to be in town
again."

Lloyd Miles could almost smell money as he walked with
Jay Gould past the marble columns of the Federal Building
where George Washington had taken the oath of office.
The building now housed the subtreasury and the offices of
General Dan Butterfield. Just across the street the New
York Stock Exchange thrust one hundred feet of marbled
splendor into the sky.

Gould led the way past the stock exchange and through a
doorway opening on to New Street. Among the hallways
inside was a back entrance to the stock exchange, but
Gould's destination took the pair past several doors and to
an entryway guarded by a uniformed attendant. Recogniz-
ing Gould, the guard admitted them into a high-ceilinged,
expensively decorated, spacious room. In the center of the
room a wrought-iron railing circled a bronze fountain de-
picting Cupid and a dolphin. Water poured into a basin in
which schools of goldfish cavorted.

From this central railing the room rose in circular ter-
races to the outer walls. The trading pit at the center was
well lit by ornate chandeliers and natural light coming in
through high windows. The chairman of the Gold Exchange sat at his desk on an elevated platform at the New
Street end of the chamber. Above the trading pit were
galleries for spectators and the telegraph operators who

relayed news of price changes to far-flung parts of the nation and the world.

Next door, in the stock exchange, the newly invented stock-ticker machine kept traders apprised of price changes. In the Gold Room a twenty-two-year-old lad named Thomas Alva Edison operated a variation on the ticker machine. The electronic indicator instantly flashed gold prices onto a large board high in the rafters and to a gilded indicator outside on New Street, where men gathered to pass the time and to bet small change on whether the next price change would be up or down.

The Gold Exchange had 485 members, and at first it seemed to Lloyd that all of them were crowded onto the floor, calling out bids and acceptances of offers. There was an air of excitement in the room, an electric tension that caused Lloyd's pulse to pound faster.

Jay Gould took a chair and motioned Lloyd to sit beside him. He pointed out the man he had chosen to act as his agent, an independent trader named Henry Enos. Enos was buying.

Gould motioned to Lloyd, and he leaned close. "He's buying one and one-half million today," Gould said.

Lloyd nodded. Daily volume usually ranged from seventy to ninety million in gold traded. On that afternoon, with Gould's agent buying heavily, it was evident that the volume would double.

"For the account of our friend Mr. Corbin." Lloyd calculated quickly. The gold deposited into Corbin's account would not be turned over to Corbin; only the profit would be. For every dollar rise in the price of gold, Corbin would gain fifteen thousand dollars. Lloyd nodded. Jay Gould was giving Corbin quite a handsome gift. His employer understood how to do business.

Gould motioned again, and Lloyd leaned close, putting his ear near Gould's mouth. "I think it would be a friendly thing," he said, "to do the same for General Butterfield. Sort of like throwing an anchor to windward."

Lloyd nodded.

"See to it, please. We would not want it to come as a total surprise to the general."

Lloyd was reluctant to leave the electric excitement of the Gold Room. When Gould rose to leave, however, Lloyd accompanied him, then parted company with him at the street and watched Gould walk away.

The sky had darkened. The smell of impending rain scented the air. Lloyd walked slowly toward the Federal Building and almost bumped into a shapely woman wearing a fashionable wine-red velvet gown. He'd been thinking about what he was going to say to Dan Butterfield and didn't recognize his old friend Rosanna Pulliam until she said, "Hello, Lloyd."

He stopped in his tracks. She had allowed her hair to return to its original blond. She seemed just a bit less plush than he remembered.

"Rose!" he said. "What an unexpected pleasure."

"It is a pleasure," she said with a smile that caused Lloyd's blood to race. "I'd say it's a good omen that I should meet you today. I've been lonely, Lloyd, and very, very bored. You're usually a good one to provide me with some excitement."

Lloyd had used Rose as an industrial spy. She was, he remembered as he stood looking down into her ebullient smile, the second most exciting woman he'd ever known. In fact, as she moistened her full lower lip with her tongue, his opinion changed. He decided he'd been judging Tennessee Claflin as the most exciting woman simply because he'd made love to Tennessee since he'd seen Rose. Now, though, as he looked into her face, there was no doubt in his mind that Rosanna was the most stimulating woman of his experience.

"We must talk," he said.

"Yes."

"Dinner?"

"Isn't it a little early for that?" she asked. "Are you free for the rest of the day?"

The talk with Dan Butterfield could wait. "I am yours to command."

They spoke of inconsequential things during the cab ride to Rosanna's apartment. Lloyd brought her up to date on his life, including his change of employment. When she learned that he was working for Jay Gould, she nodded approvingly.

Rose was guarded in what she told him, and then she was escorting him into her retreat, a place she owned under an assumed name, a place safe from the reach of even such powerful men as the Ames brothers.

For the rest of the afternoon there was little talk. Like Tennessee Claflin, Rosanna approached sex with a male attitude, insisting on receiving as well as giving. The result of that philosophy provided a consummation pleasing to Lloyd.

Later, they sat at the dining room table. Lloyd had dressed and ventured forth to bring back sacks of food. Rosanna's appetite matched his. They laughed a lot, made bawdy references to the afternoon's activity, then fell to reminiscing.

"You were determined to get rich," Rosanna said. "Have you done so?"

"Not yet," he admitted with a grin. "But soon."

"Well, share the secret with a working girl."

"To start," he said, "do you still hold Crédit Mobilier or Pacific Railroad stock?"

"Sold out several months ago."

"Smart girl," he said. Already, because of Philip Trent's investigation in Congress, Crédit Mobilier stock had fallen.

"Doesn't take much intelligence to know that your friend was going to blow the lid off," Rosanna said.

"If you have any loose assets, buy gold."

"Risky," she said.

"Not if you check with me as to when to sell."

She came around the table and pressed one warm breast against his shoulder. "You're not telling Rose everything," she teased.

Like most men Lloyd still had some characteristics of the small boy in him, and a boy wants to brag of his doings, his feats, his victories, his plans. If the listener is a beloved woman—and to some men any sexual partner is beloved for a time after the event—he is apt to be unguarded in his remarks. But Lloyd had good reason to trust Rosanna—he knew too much about her and she about him for either of them to break confidence. Otherwise he would not have told her everything.

"But gold is like air," she protested. "It can be transferred by telegraph from San Francisco or London to New York. It can be brought into the city by the hundreds of thousands of dollars in little streams from banks all over the United States. And if the Treasury should decide to sell, it would be like a dam breaking, a flood of gold."

Lloyd listened, impressed.

"How much gold has been mined since the California rush of 1849?" she asked.

"About fifty million ounces," he said. "That translates into one billion dollars' worth. But most of it was purchased by Europeans. There's probably about sixty-two million in minted gold coins in circulation in the United States, and another thirty million in gold certificates. Then there are the millions on store in the U.S. Treasury. I've heard it said that trying to corner gold would be like trying to drain New York Harbor with a hand pump."

"So?" she asked.

"In 1863 J. P. Morgan shipped off over two million dollars' worth of gold to Europe. The price jumped from one forty-six to one fifty-six in four days. Nobody was paying attention because they were still reading the casualty lists from Vicksburg and Gettysburg; but those who sold at the top made a profit of ten dollars on the hundred."

"Surely there are people watching more closely now."

"The only law on the street is the size of a man's bankroll," Lloyd said. "No one keeps records. The deed will be half done before anyone realizes what's going on. Then it will be too late. It's also interesting to note that the market makes sheep out of intelligent men. A man who is as staunch as the Rock of Gibraltar becomes jelly when rumors sweep the street. Let some adverse rumor break out, and otherwise sensible men panic and send out orders to sell."

"But there's so *much* gold."

"Little Rose, a man with five hundred dollars in his pocket can buy and sell a million dollars' worth of gold in a day as long as he comes out ahead or breaks even by the end of that day."

She mused for a few moments. "And you're in?"

"I'm buying, yes."

"And you'll tell me when it's time to sell?"

"Absolutely."

"I think I've just become a gold bull," she said, smiling. "Whatever that means."

"I think I liked you better as a soft-eyed heifer."

"I'm not sure that's flattering."

"But practical, if there's a bull around," he said, laughing, as he pulled her down into his lap.

In the dawn hours, after a bull market of talk, love, wine, and simply lying together, arms and legs entwined, he noticed the faint scars on her face, her neck, shoulders, and breasts. He traced one scar with his fingertip and asked, "What happened?"

"You don't really want to know," she whispered.

"All right," he said. "Accident?"

"No."

There was a scar in one eyebrow where her skin had been split. "It's almost as if—" He stopped abruptly. "Rose, someone hurt you! Someone hurt you very badly."

To Rose's surprise hot tears rolled freely down her cheeks. For months she had been keeping to the privacy of her small but pleasant flat in Brooklyn. At first her semi-seclusion had been a necessity, to allow for the healing of the terrible physical battering she had suffered at the hands of Oliver Ames, lover, employer, and the man who, along with his brother, Congressman Oakes Ames, had been deeply involved in the rape of the U.S. Treasury by Crédit Mobilier.

Although she had been alone for a long time, tonight she

had been thoroughly loved by a man for whom she felt genuine fondness. And Lloyd was right: she had been hurt . . . for the first time in her life. For weeks after the beating she'd ached every time she moved. Worse, she had been forced to accept the fact that she was not invulnerable after all. She could feel pain. She was human.

As she healed slowly in solitude, she came to realize that she was but frail flesh, that she could bleed, in spite of the fact that she had lived through the war without even a close call. She hadn't even cried that night years before, when it had become necessary for her to end her husband's life by pressing a pillow over his face as he lay wounded in his bed in Richmond. She had not wept when Ames was beating her. Instead she had thought only of a way to murder him. Wartime spy, killer for hire, as deadly as a black-widow spider, Rose was still a woman. She sobbed into Lloyd's shoulder and told him about Oliver Ames. Rose knew he was shocked to learn that she'd been deceiving him all the time he had thought that she was solely his employee. And yet she had not been false to him, for she'd done what he had hired her to do.

She left out any hint that she could have been involved in the Washington murders that had thrown Philip Trent under suspicion. And Lloyd was so astounded to find out that Philip Trent's entire exposé of bribery in Congress depended on names and figures sent to him anonymously by Rose Pulliam that he did not take the leap in logic to connect her to the murders. Men who had been involved indirectly with Thomas Durant had died by violence, and their deaths were still a mystery; but while she lay in Lloyd's arms, soft, weeping, and clinging, Rose knew he would never imagine that she could have been capable of those unsolved murders . . . even though she was an accomplished assassin.

It pleased him, he told her, to think that Rose was the instrument of the downfall of such powerful men as Oakes Ames. He laughed heartily. "Rose," he said, gasping, "we do make a terrific team."

"In bed?" she teased, drying her tears.

"And elsewhere. Look, start converting your holdings into cash, and I'll have my man buy gold for you."

"It'll take a few days."

"There's time. I'll have to go back to Washington, so I'll introduce you to my broker."

"I'll use my own."

"Is he a member of the Gold Exchange?"

"I don't know. I'll find out." She snuggled close. "Tell me again how Gould is going to prevent the Treasury from selling gold to keep the prices down."

He told her again about Corbin and Dan Butterfield and the President's sister. He explained Gould's crop theory again. "All right. Gold's at one-thirty. It goes up to one-fifty. Wheat is priced in gold, on the London market. For one hundred dollars in gold a farmer gets one hundred thirty dollars in greenbacks now. At one-fifty he'll get one hundred and fifty in greenbacks for the same amount of grain."

"And you think this will favorably impress the President?"

"I do," he replied.

"And in Butterfield you have insurance," she mused. "Plus, if you should be wrong and Grant decides to order the Treasury to sell gold, Butterfield will give you warning in time for you to sell your gold holdings at a profit."

"Correct," he said.

"I think," she said, "that we could use another little insurance policy."

"Such as?"

"Perhaps you could introduce me to General Butterfield," she suggested, wiggling her rump meaningfully under his hand.

"He's a married man."

"So are they all," she said, "except you—and that is only because no decent woman would have you."

He laughed, but his heart wasn't in it. Rose wondered if Lloyd had suffered a recent rebuff.

"Perhaps you and I should be married, Rose."

"Not a chance in hell," she said quickly. Then she

squeezed him, kissed him, and said, "It's sleepy time, dear. I must be bright and starry-eyed when I meet the general."

Harold Berman had visited Geoffrey Lancaster and Paul Jennings, the other two members besides Lloyd Miles of the Breakfast Club, shortly after his dismissal from the Washington office of the Erie Railroad. Both his friends had expressed shock and sympathy, but neither had been able to offer any encouragement about a position with their respective employers.

With no immediate opportunity for employment in the offing, Berman became more determined to exact revenge by benefiting from the same situation that had brought about his downfall, Gould's scheme to corner gold. He began to buy. Like Lloyd Miles he sold all his stocks, borrowed as much as he could borrow, and compounded his purchases by lending the gold he purchased for greenback security, using the greenbacks to buy more gold.

Berman had worked for Gould since before Gould had taken control of the Erie. He believed that he knew his former employer well enough to gauge when Gould would begin dumping gold to take his profits. For the sake of safety Berman, settling for a solid but lesser profit, decided he would begin selling before the big holders began to unload.

In order to watch the market closely he traveled to New York and took a room in a small boarding hotel on the East Side. With a hat pulled low over his face so that he would not be recognized by Jay Gould, he sat in the visitors' balcony at the Gold Room and observed the frenzied action.

Harold was not the first man to fall victim to gold fever in one of its many forms. The fever held enough force to be the driving power behind a wave of westward immigration, as it had been in 1849, or to cause dozens of perspiring, half-hysterical men to wave their arms, yell out buy-and-sell orders, and scribble frantically on little slips of paper. As Berman watched the action confined to the smoke-filled splendor of the Gold Room, where not a single yellow coin was on display, he felt his blood pressure rising as the price edged inexorably upward.

He knew to the exact dollar the amount of gold he controlled. He could add his profits without the aid of pencil and paper. He sweated. He squirmed. He dreamed of grandeur and long-term financial independence. He imagined himself at Leah's door: he would knock, and when she answered she would smile at him.

"What your brother thinks doesn't matter now, Leah, for I am a very rich man. Come. I will give you everything you have ever desired."

He determined that he would start selling when the price hit $148. In that he would be acting with more daring than he had originally planned, for he believed that there was an invisible price barrier in the vicinity of $150 beyond which gold could not pass.

CHAPTER 5

Rosanna Pulliam knew New York City well. As a young girl in Brooklyn she had crossed the river onto Manhattan Island and was determined to become a famous actress. She had failed to conquer New York, but she had been taken on by a touring company of players, who taught her enough about acting to be able to play life-and-death parts in the drama of the Civil War.

For years, from the time she was a girl, she had lived dangerously. She had worked for and with men such as the wartime spy master Lafayette Baker and Secretary of War Edwin Stanton. She had served the Union well, but her reward had been dismissal. Not in so many words, but in actions, Stanton had told her, "Sorry, Rose, we don't need you anymore."

Baker, too, had been driven out of Washington. He was in the hotel business somewhere in the Midwest, and he'd written a book about his contributions to the Civil War. Rosanna had read the book with interest, and she had found it to be inaccurate—perhaps deliberately so, in order to make Lafe Baker look better—and extremely self-serving. To her relief Baker had kept his last promise to her: he had not mentioned her name. In fact, there was nothing at all about the female spy who had spent the war years in Richmond.

Perversely, although she wanted to remain anonymous in order to pursue her chosen career, it did irritate her to think that Lafe had valued her services so little that he had not even alluded to her. It would have been perfectly safe, and it would have added interest to a rather dull book if he had told the story about a young actress who, for four years, had played the role of wife to a Confederate officer on Jefferson Davis's staff in Richmond. After the war she had been forced to find employment outside government. Because of the competition between the Union Pacific and the Central Pacific as they vied for public lands and federal subsidies during the construction of the transcontinental, Rose had found a place for her talents in the employ of Lloyd Miles, then Thomas Durant, and finally Oliver Ames. For a while she became first a double agent and then a triple, with three men thinking that she worked solely for him. Intrigue fulfilled her, made her feel alive.

Like most young people Rose had dreamed of returning in triumph to her place of birth—rich, successful, famous. Instead she had returned to Brooklyn incognito to purchase a pleasant little flat for which she paid cash and used false credentials so that her own name would not be on record. It was from there, her retreat, her place of safety, that she renewed her acquaintance with the burgeoning, audacious, vibrant city where ostentatious riches were on display adjacent to the most abject poverty.

For some time after taking refuge in her cozy flat, safe from discovery among Brooklyn's four hundred thousand people and Manhattan's nine hundred thousand, she contented herself with becoming reacquainted with her immediate surroundings. She was financially secure, although she was not rich. She knew that sooner or later she would have to return to the world and find a way to put her peculiar talents to work in exchange for money, but she was in no hurry. First she wanted to savor the fall of Oliver Ames.

Shortly after her beating, she had believed that it would

be a simple and quick matter to slip into Washington and kill Ames; but she soon realized that there was a difference in degree between the murder of little men and that of a financial titan. She was not afraid, nor did she doubt that she could accomplish the deed, but after thinking about it she always returned to her original purpose: She knew Oliver Ames well enough to understand that the cruelest revenge she could have of him was to expose him to shame and to hit him hard in the pocketbook.

Thus as Rose healed in mind and body, she exacted her pound of flesh from the man who had beaten her: she slowly furnished Representative Philip Trent with the names of the congressmen who had taken Crédit Mobilier bribes, thereby implicating Oliver Ames in the scandal.

Furthermore, Philip Trent was sure to have Oliver's brother, Oakes Ames, ousted from the House of Representatives. The growing scandal was driving down the price of the stocks in which the Ames brothers were most involved, Crédit Mobilier and the Union Pacific Railroad. She was hurting Ames, but to her surprise she was growing bored with the whole thing.

To assuage her boredom she ventured farther from her flat in Brooklyn, to explore Manhattan's Broadway and Fifth Avenue, proud streets dense with people, horses, and wheeled vehicles. She visited P. T. Barnum's museum and, after her bruises had healed, had her photograph made at Matthew Brady's studio. She walked the two-mile stretch of newly developed Central Park, then strolled to watch steamships and graceful sailing vessels come and go in the harbor.

She was not, of course, invited to the society affairs at the Grand Central Hotel or the Astors' house, but twice she attended concerts at the Academy of Music. Although her main purpose in life was not philanthropic concern for her fellow man, she was not blind to the contrast between the expensively dressed men and women who strolled into the glittering academy and the people in and around the dance halls, saloons, and whorehouses in the Bowery and on Canal and Greene streets. Even she, who had killed, who had lived as a Union spy in the heart of the Confederacy, was wary when she ventured into the Five Points area, where streets were named Murderer's Alley and Cow Bay. There, only blocks from prosperous Broadway, she had to walk carefully to keep from stepping in filth. There she saw homeless children begging in the streets and heard the babble of foreign tongues, for Europe's poor were streaming into the city.

Although sightseeing helped to cheer her somewhat while she continued to manipulate events in Washington with her carefully supplied information, she still felt stale. Once, she looked for cheap excitement in the dance halls and found the men there to be common and odious. She never went back. Through the newspapers she followed the escapades of the slum gangs, the Bowery Boys and the Dead Rabbits, and participated vicariously in their violent clashes. Nothing held her interest for long. She was frustrated, and she longed to be at the center of the action.

In New York the action centered around William Marcy Tweed, grand sachem of the executive committee of the Democratic party of New York, known as Tammany Hall. Tweed, Rose felt, was her kind of man—big, swaggering, and energetic; he was a doer, not a talker. Unfortunately, she did not know New York's "Boss," and it would have been a bit presumptuous, not to mention dangerous, to walk into the office of a man she didn't know and say, "Mr. Tweed, I'd like a job. I'm an expert at espionage, whether in wartime or in business areas, and I know more than a few ways to kill a man."

Thus it was that when she encountered Lloyd Miles on Wall Street, she seized upon the opportunity. Once before she had used Lloyd for her own purposes. Now, in her moment of need, he offered opportunity again. A man who worked closely with Jay Gould would be of use to her. Gould and the Erie Railroad represented huge money, and in peacetime what excitement there was revolved around money. She quickly agreed to do a service for Lloyd because his employer was associated with William Tweed in several areas of business. For example, Jay Gould and

Tweed had bought a bank, the Tenth National Bank on Wall Street, and Tweed sat on the board of directors of the Erie Railroad. Through Lloyd she would move to the heart of the action, to Gould and to Bill Tweed.

The target of Rose's attentions was to be General Daniel Butterfield. Lloyd felt that it was overkill to hire Rose to insinuate herself into Dan Butterfield's life; but as Rose pointed out to him, there was a lot at stake. In a matter that would either make or break him, he could not be too careful. It was possible, she allowed, that his friendship with Butterfield, coupled with the general's interest in increasing his fortune, would be enough to assure Butterfield's cooperation. But with Rose on the scene, Lloyd could be doubly sure that any word concerning the possible sale of government gold would be passed to him immediately.

Rosanna prepared herself for duty by dressing in one of her most flattering outfits. She applied makeup lightly but expertly. Ready to go into action, she clung to Lloyd's arm and smiled up at him pleasantly as they emerged from her flat in Brooklyn. She was fond of Lloyd. If all she had wanted in life was a good bed partner, she would have chosen him. Lloyd was a clean man, and he could be incredibly sensuous.

Lloyd had arranged for them to have lunch with Butterfield, and when they arrived at the appointed place, the general was already there, seated. Butterfield waved to them, and his eyes did not leave Rose, who was on Lloyd's arm as he escorted her to the table.

After introductions Butterfield touched his lips to the back of her hand. "And I thought it was to be just the usual masculine talk at lunch," he said. "How pleasant to have your company, Miss Pulliam."

Rose smiled confidently. There was simply no challenge involved here, she thought. Men were always too damned easy.

Toward the end of the meal Lloyd excused himself, as had been prearranged, and went to the men's lavatory, where he lingered for a good five minutes. When he returned to the table Rose surreptitiously winked at him to let him know that he had been gone long enough. The defenses of the wartime brigade commander had fallen with ease.

After being told by Rose that Butterfield was definitely interested in "doing business," Lloyd arranged a meeting between Gould and the general. He learned another lesson from his employer when the sad-eyed financier smoothly passed a check for ten thousand dollars to Butterfield as a real-estate loan. The amount represented two thousand dollars more than Butterfield would earn in a year as sub-treasurer. Not one of the three men present mentioned that Butterfield had not asked for a loan or that Gould did not require either interest or a repayment schedule.

Jay Gould had a new friend, but Lloyd was confident that his own ties to Dan Butterfield were closer, through the sense of comradeship that had carried over from the war. Moreover, he had the confidence of the general's new lady friend, Rose Pulliam. Now Lloyd was more certain than ever that he could ride the rising price of gold to a small fortune and have plenty of warning if something should go wrong. He began to invest Rose's capital in gold as she slowly sold off her other holdings.

He performed one more service for his employer before going back to Washington: He delivered a twenty-five-thousand-dollar check to Abel Corbin. The amount represented the paper profit accrued on the gold that Gould had bought for Corbin's account.

In the meantime Jay Gould had done for Dan Butterfield what he'd done for Corbin. Now Butterfield had an account at Gould's brokerage house from which he would earn the increase on one and a half million dollars' worth of gold specie.

Abel Corbin's association with the Ulysses S. Grant family had begun in the early 1830s when, as a schoolteacher in St. Louis, he had enjoyed an especially friendly relationship with young Julia Dent, who was to become Mrs.

Ulysses S. Grant. During the exciting time of balls and receptions following Grant's election to the presidency, Julia Dent Grant's friendship with Corbin was renewed, and the sixty-one-year-old politico courted Miss Virginia Paine Grant, the President's younger sister.

It did not take the articulate Corbin long to gain the President's respect as an unofficial adviser. In spite of Grant's long absences from home during his army service prior to the war and, of course, during the bloody conflict, U. S. Grant was a family man. Regardless of the fact that Jennie's husband had been touched by scandal in the past, Abel Corbin was fully accepted as a member of the presidential household.

It was inevitable, then, that Ulysses S. Grant, President of the United States, should eventually make the acquaintance of one of Corbin's friends, Mr. Jay Gould, in the drawing room of the Corbins' New York brownstone.

The Grants were traveling. The President was on his way to the Peace Jubilee in Boston. Julia and the children planned to stay with Jennie in New York. Conveniently for Corbin and Gould, Grant had accepted an invitation to ride the *Providence*, flagship of Jim Fisk's Narragansett Line, to Boston. The trip would take twelve hours, more than enough time for Jay Gould to explain his crop theory and the desirability of scarce gold.

The pudgy "admiral" of the Narragansett, Fisk, had ordered the *Providence* to be freshly painted. The ship and her owner were equally splendid looking. Jim was bedecked in a military tunic with three silver stars on the sleeve, a golden braid on his hat, and a diamond pin on his breast. The ship sported gay streamers from stem to stern. A military band played "See the Conquering Hero Comes."

Until he saw it with his own eyes, Lloyd would have said that the idea of Ulysses S. Grant allowing himself to be put on public display with Gould and Fisk was preposterous. First of all, it was common knowledge that the Erie partners were political cronies of the Democratic boss, William Tweed. Secondly, less than one year previously Gould and

Fisk had been renegades, temporarily on the losing side of a fight with Commodore Vanderbilt, and threatened with jail if they entered New York State. A New York State legislative committee was still investigating Gould's bribery of Albany lawmakers during his takeover of the Erie Railroad.

Lloyd Miles, also on board the *Providence*, was bemused by the resemblance between Grant and Gould. Grant was taller, but they both had dense black beards, both dressed soberly, and to Lloyd, looked quite ordinary. Grant's erect, proud military stance had deteriorated by the end of the war. Now his shoulders were stooped, and the quiet assurance with which he had commanded the largest army ever assembled was gone. He seemed to have to strain to make small talk, and the crowds of admirers that lined the streets and the docks made the President nervous.

Oddly, Lloyd felt as if he were being besmirched along with Grant, for they had both been soldiers, and a strong bond connected all the men who had survived the four years of destruction. Grant had agreed to the transportation arrangements only because Corbin had advised him to do so and the President trusted his family member. For a moment Lloyd resented Abel Corbin, because Lloyd knew that Corbin's motive was self-serving. Then the moment passed. The resentment and guilt engendered by his feeling of wartime companionship for the President were submerged by thoughts of the money that he himself would make. And of course Abel Corbin hoped to benefit. So did they all. Perhaps, although Lloyd could not bring himself to believe it fully, the nation as a whole would benefit through the prosperity of its farmers. Then he rationalized the guilt away, telling himself that Grant would benefit from a higher price for gold; a President who brings good times to the country is a popular man.

Lloyd was not included at Grant's private table that night at dinner, but he sat close enough to hear the words of such distinguished guests as Cyrus Field and William Marston. Gould's intention was to remain silent about his crop theory until the President had enjoyed a drink or two.

Then, when Grant was feeling relaxed, while he was surrounded by congenial Republicans who happened to be very, very rich, Gould would make his pitch. Grant, however, surprised them all by abstaining from alcoholic beverages.

Gould was the youngest man at the table, fourteen years the President's junior. After he quietly introduced the subject of gold, he fell silent and allowed the older capitalists to express their opinions. Finally it was time for him to take the floor.

Gould spoke politely, softly, persuasively. "I'm sure you see, Mr. President, that your administration can help the producers of the nation, the farmers, become more prosperous while at the same time increasing our exports. It's a simple matter. It's a natural state of affairs for the price of gold to rise and the value of greenbacks to fall."

President Grant's position on the economy was well known. He had spoken often of the desirability of hard money, of a return to the gold standard. Making paper money even more worthless did not fit into his philosophy. He showed little reaction to Gould's attempts at persuasion. He puffed on his cigar and said nothing.

"Actually, Mr. President," Gould continued, "it would be good politics for the government to allow the price of gold to rise. Not only would farmers and factory workers benefit by cheap greenbacks, but business would as well. The railroads, for example." Gould smiled and spread his hands. "And I admit readily that I am not unconcerned in that area. The Erie and other roads would carry the increased exports to the ports." He laughed. "I'm sure that I don't have to point out that most businessmen are Republicans."

Grant merely nodded.

Jim Fisk, not having Gould's polish and patience, broke in. "Well, sir," he asked directly, "what do you think of Jay's idea?"

Grant appeared reluctant to give the men surrounding him what they obviously wanted: definite knowledge of the administration's policy toward selling gold in the event of rising gold prices. "There is a certain amount of fictitiousness about the prosperity of the country," he remarked. "The bubble might as well be tapped in one way as another."

Fisk looked helplessly at Gould. At his table Lloyd Miles hid a snicker by covering his mouth with his napkin. As commander of the army Grant had learned that talk often gets a man into trouble. He had given the Wall Street sharks at his table a dose of political dodging. Each man could take his own meaning from the statement.

Then, possibly because Grant did not want a misunderstanding lest some of them think that he was agreeing to do nothing about a rise in gold prices and set out to profit from what they thought was inside knowledge, the President spoke. His voice was firm, his look that of a commander of men. "Gentlemen, paper money is too cheap now, with all due respect to the farmer. I'm afraid I don't buy your argument, Mr. Gould."

Lloyd, watching Gould, saw the color rise in his face. He held his breath as the diminutive financier challenged the President of the United States.

"Mr. President, if the price of gold should be allowed to diminish there would be great distress."

"I am quite familiar with the financial panics that seem to grip you Wall Street gentlemen with some regularity," Grant declared. "That does not change my opinion that the nation needs hard money. In short, I have no intention of having any part in propping up the price of gold."

Gould leaned forward. "But, Mr. President, therein lies ruin. Why, any attempt to bring the price of gold into line with the value of paper money could lead to civil war."

Lloyd was startled. He couldn't believe that even Jay Gould would have the nerve to threaten U. S. Grant with civil war.

Gould continued. "Such a policy would produce strikes. Workshops and factories would close. Production would cease."

"General," Jim Fisk said, "Jay and I are responsible for running the Erie Railroad. We've got about forty thousand families to look after, and we can't feed those families if all of our rolling stock is on sidetracks, empty."

Grant did not put his opinions into definite words, but at the end of the three hours of conversation, no man there doubted that he was a contractionist, that he wanted to shrink the supply of paper money, not increase it, that he wanted to return to a time when the only money was gold or gold certificates. As he smoked his cigar and rubbed his beard, he didn't say that he was unmoved by Fisk's hungry Erie Railroad families or that he was against helping the farmers; he just sat silently and let the storm of words flow past him.

When the *Providence* docked the next morning Lloyd Miles sent one telegram to his broker from Fall River. Another telegram went to Rose Pulliam. The message on both was short and simple. Sell gold. He was not the only one to give his broker sell orders that morning, and as a result the gold market halted its steady advance, and prices tumbled.

Harold Berman left his room in an East Side boarding-house and, after stopping to have breakfast, made his way to the financial district in a leisurely manner. When he arrived on New Street, he glanced up at the indicator that displayed the current price of gold. He halted with a jerk. His face went pale. He had invested in the gold market every dollar he could raise. He had spent every day at or near the market, watching the price indicators. This was the only morning he had slept late, and in the first two hours of trading, he had been ruined.

He grunted as if in pain, then rushed into the spectators' gallery to witness the madness on the trading floor. A panic had seized the traders, and the orders were to sell, sell, sell. He, like many others, had used his small fortune as a lever to control gold in multiples of his net worth. With each fall of one dollar in the price of gold coins, he lost what was to him a staggering amount. If he gave his broker sell orders, he might be able to cut his losses; but if he could sell all his gold at the current price, he would be rendered penniless and in debt. He did not wait to see what developed on the trading floor. He dashed from the building and ran to the offices of the Erie Railroad, where he asked for Lloyd Miles.

"I'm sorry," said Sebastian, Jay Gould's secretary, "Mr. Miles is traveling with the presidential party."

"Then I'll talk to Mr. Gould," Harold said. He was feeling desperate. Beads of perspiration formed on his forehead, and his lower lip trembled.

Sebastian had frequently handled disgruntled men seeking to speak to his employer. Working for Mr. Jay Gould, he had found, was not without its moments of excitement.

"I fear that Mr. Gould, also, is away from the city."

"When will they be back?" Already it was too late. He felt sure that gold prices were still falling.

"I expect Mr. Gould later in the day. I believe that Mr. Miles will be with him."

Berman snatched paper and a pen from Sebastian's desk, bent, then scribbled for a few moments. He folded the paper and handed it to Sebastian. "Please give this to Lloyd Miles the moment he returns."

Sebastian held the folded sheet of paper gingerly with thumb and forefinger as Berman rushed out of the office. He unfolded the paper and placed it on his desk. The hasty words were almost illegible, but he was finally able to decipher the scrawl.

Miles
I don't know what you and your masters did to cause this debacle on the gold market, but you will make good my losses, or I will divulge the entire scheme to the newspapers.

H. Berman

CHAPTER 6

When Rose Pulliam opened the door of her flat to Lloyd Miles she sensed immediately that something was bothering him. His embrace was perfunctory, and Rosanna was not a woman to inspire dutiful kisses. She pushed him away and looked up into his face questioningly.

"Thank you for telling me to sell my gold holdings," she said, "but I decided to wait and take my chances. Do you want to tell me what went wrong?"

He explained to her about the day aboard Jim Fisk's flagship, about the dinner and Grant's flat statement that he would do nothing to prop up the price of gold. She served coffee while he talked.

"But did he say that he would work to bring down the price of gold?" Rose asked. "Did he actually state that he would not allow high gold prices?"

Lloyd frowned as he reviewed the conversation he'd overheard from the President's table. "He made it clear that he thinks paper money should be equal in value to gold, that our currency should be guaranteed for equal exchange into gold specie. He left no doubt that he favors hard money." He grinned. "You seem to be searching for hidden meaning in his words. In your last incarnation were you a diplomat?"

"I think I was Messalina," she said with a smile.

"He didn't say one hell of a lot, Rose. He was mostly silent. The others did the bulk of the talking. He made his feelings clear, then he clammed up. Not once during the entire three hours did he state definitely that he would order the Treasury to sell gold if the price went up too high in New York."

"Then I think I will hold off from sending that sell order," Rose decided.

"That's unwise. You stand to lose everything. The price has stabilized—at least for the moment—but in my opinion there's very little chance it will go up again."

Her eyes seemed to cut into him. "Lloyd, you assured me that I would gain."

"I have gotten a bloody nose myself, Rose."

She shook her head slowly. "I still think you're giving up too soon. Give it one more try. The President is coming back to New York after his visit to Boston, isn't he?"

"Yes. Mrs. Grant and the children are staying with the Corbins. The plans are for the President to join them and have three days of private family togetherness."

"And so, enter young Lloyd," she said.

"No, I don't think that would be wise," Lloyd said. "I guess Corbin would cooperate, but Ulysses Grant is not the kind of man who'd take kindly to having his family time spoiled by the presence of company."

"You'll think of a way," Rosanna said. "We've arranged things too well to have it all go to waste now."

Lloyd was handed Harold Berman's note when he stopped by the Erie offices just before the end of the business day. He read the scribbled words and felt the heat of anger creep up his neck. He crumpled the note and flung it into the wastebasket beside Sebastian's desk. His first reaction was to ignore Berman's threat. After all, Harold was a weakling. Let him go to the newspapers with his story. He had no proof, and the events of the day, with the price of gold falling toward normal levels, would be the best evidence that Berman was nothing more than a whining loser, trying to make good his losses on the market by blackmail.

Lloyd looked at Sebastian, who had been studying him closely. "You read that note?"

Sebastian nodded.

"There is no reason for Mr. Gould to know about this," Lloyd said. "I'll handle it."

"The note was not addressed to Mr. Gould," Sebastian said.

"Thank you," Lloyd said.

"But since it does imply a threat to Mr. Gould I think I shall tell him about it," Sebastian said with a sweet smile.

"You are a temple of charm and consideration, Sebastian," Lloyd said with open sarcasm. "I told you I could handle it. Berman's a fool."

"If I were you, I *would* handle it," the secretary said, and his usually insipid expression toughened into something that Lloyd had not seen before. "And quickly, before Mr. Gould and Mr. Fisk get back to the office."

Lloyd made no answer. He retrieved the note from the wastebasket, then smoothed the paper so that he could read the scribbled address. He took a cab to the boardinghouse on the East Side and found Harold Berman in his room.

"I didn't expect you quite so soon," Berman said.

Lloyd pushed past, then turned to face him. "You always were a fool, Berman."

"I put two hundred and thirty thousand into the gold market," Berman said. "I want it back."

Lloyd ached to put his fist into Berman's face. "Damn it, Berman, today's drop was just temporary. The price will go back up tomorrow."

"If so, you will lose nothing," Berman said. "You buy my obligations for two hundred and thirty thousand and you're welcome to any profit the money earns as the price goes up."

"You know that I don't have that kind of money," Lloyd

said. "I'm in the same boat. I'm as deep into the market as you."

Berman laughed raggedly. "You're a good liar. If I didn't know that your broker started selling gold for you early this morning, I would believe you." He stepped forward and put his face close to Lloyd's. "I'll give you twenty-four hours. If you can't raise the money, go to your master. He stands to lose more than you do. A scandal won't bother you, Miles, because you are just a hireling. But when Phineas Headley reveals in the newspaper that Gould and Jim Fisk have used Erie Railroad money in an attempt to corner the gold market, the resulting outcry won't help Mr. Gould any, will it?"

"Berman, if you'll just wait—"

"No!" Berman yelled, his voice rising. "I want out! You and Gould owe me, Miles. You engineered my ouster from my position in Washington, and Gould listened to your poison. You both owe me, and you have just twenty-four hours to make it right."

Lloyd nodded. "All right," he said with a calm that caused Berman to look at him in question. "We will make it right, Harold. I promise you that."

Rosanna returned to her flat in Brooklyn shortly after midnight. She was pleasantly tired. A fine wine served by Dan Butterfield in his pied-à-terre in Manhattan had relaxed her and made her eager for bed. She fished in her handbag for the key, and as her fingers closed around it she noted that the straw she always positioned so carefully before leaving home had fallen to the floor. That meant her door had been opened. She glanced around her and checked the stairs at her back. The building was quiet. Her hand went once more to her bag, but this time it closed around the butt of her Williamson derringer. It was a small gun of the type that John Wilkes Booth had used to kill Abraham Lincoln. At close range the .41 caliber bullet could be deadly, and Rose always carried it.

As she opened the door slowly she saw that a gas jet was burning in the sitting room. She moved silently, staying in shadows, until she saw Lloyd Miles stretched out on the sofa, his eyes closed. In a moment of weakness she had given him a key to her sanctuary. More angry at herself than at Lloyd, her pulse rate lowered, and she glided across the room to place the muzzle of the derringer at Lloyd's forehead. He opened his eyes with a start.

"Give me my key," she whispered in a hiss of pure menace.

He sensed that she was deadly serious. Without protest or question he moved slowly, brought the key from his pocket, and holding it between thumb and forefinger, extended it toward her.

"You gave it to me," he reminded, because the pressure of the cold gun metal was still at his temple.

He could feel her relaxing, and he breathed deeply as she took the derringer from his head.

"What the hell, Rose?"

She turned her back. "Sorry."

"A bit nervous, are we?"

"I don't like surprises," she said. The derringer had disappeared into her handbag. "I'll fix you a drink."

"They're ready," he said.

"Thank you."

He examined her face as they sat quietly, sipping a sweet drink made of rye and maple syrup, a concoction she liked very much.

"Rose, who was that woman holding a gun at my head?" Lloyd asked.

She laughed. "It's just that I've been a little jumpy since the affair with Ames." She came to kneel before him and put her arms around his waist. "I'm sorry I frightened you."

"Woman," he said, "I was frightened when I saw a hundred Reb cavalrymen riding hell-for-leather toward me with their carbines blazing. What I experienced when I woke up and felt the cold muzzle of a gun at my temple was sheer terror." He laughed with her and pulled her up and into his lap. "How was your evening with the good general?"

"Hmmm," she said.

"That good?"

"Do you really want to know?"

"Call me curious." A huskiness had come to his voice.

"I call you perverted," she whispered, for his hands were caressing her. She had come to his bed directly from that of another man before, and she knew that it excited him.

"And if I am perverted, what does that make you?" he asked as he began to unbutton her dress.

Lloyd awoke to nagging worry. Rose slept beside him, the sheet bundled at her waist, her beautiful torso exposed. As if she sensed that he was looking at her she stirred and opened her eyes.

"Time is it?" she mumbled.

"Early. Want some breakfast?"

"Umm."

He'd learned long before that Rose wasn't much of a cook. He went into the small kitchen and set bacon to frying and coffee to brewing. She joined him, a silken peignoir accentuating more than concealing her breasts and the definite outthrust of hip.

"You've lost weight," he said.

"Yes."

"I liked you better soft and curvy."

"What is the date?"

"Why?"

"I want to mark this day on my calendar. Yours is the first complaint I've ever had."

"No complaint," he said, laughing. "One egg?"

"Please." She poured coffee. He sat across the small table from her and ate with serious intensity.

"Something's bothering you," she said.

"Several things are bothering me," he admitted.

"Anything I can do?"

"No." He looked at her. She had cleansed her face of all traces of makeup. She looked younger—not at all like the woman whose eyes had burned into his as she held a derringer to his temple. Her look of freshness gave him an idea. "Well, maybe. You remember Harold Berman?"

She nodded.

"He put everything he had into gold, and yesterday after the price fell, he panicked. He threatened to reveal the whole scheme to the newspapers."

"That would be the end of it, I take it."

"Absolutely. There'd be a public outcry. If gold happened to be increasing, the public would demand that the government sell gold to stabilize the price."

"We can't have that, can we?" she asked.

"He wants me to make good his losses. He was greedy. He bought long and went heavily into debt, well past his ability to pay. Yesterday's price drop wiped him out."

"Do you have the money to buy his holdings? When the price goes up again, that would put you in a good position."

"If the price goes up."

"It will. I think that Jay Gould will see to that."

"In the meantime I've got less than twenty-four hours to settle this thing with Berman."

"What do you have in mind?"

He spoke softly. "It would be very convenient if Mr. Harold Berman, made desperate by his losses, took a dive out a fourth-story window."

Rose poked at her egg with her fork and was silent for a long time. "I might be able to help, after all."

The same look that had chilled him the previous evening came into her eyes. She noticed his stare and smiled, her face softening.

"I know the city," she said. "I just might know someone who could teach Mr. Berman how to dive."

Lloyd stirred uneasily. In his memory he was suddenly transported back to Thomas Durant's office, and Durant was giving him orders couched in careful, nondefinitive words to kill Philip Trent. In that situation he had tried, and failed, to have Trent meet with an accident. It was ironic, he thought, that his position was now different, and he was giving nonspecific orders to Rosanna Pulliam to hire a man to kill Harold Berman.

"Rose, I don't think I could be a part of that. . . ."

"Of what?" she asked, smiling sweetly. "Don't pay any attention to what I say, Lloyd. I was just trying to show off, that's all, trying to make you think that I'm a knowledge-able woman-about-town. I don't know any hoodlums or toughs." She thought for a moment. "Would Gould give you money to give to Berman to keep him quiet?"

"He would give me the money for Berman along with my walking papers," Lloyd said ruefully. "And we need to re-main in Gould's confidence until we sell all our gold hold-ings."

Rose sighed. "Well, you say you have a few hours? Let's just wait. The situation might solve itself. Perhaps the mar-ket will rise today. If it does, Berman will forget his threat."

Lloyd shrugged. He almost wished that Rose had known someone who could have solved the problem with Berman permanently. "I suppose that's the only way," he agreed. "I'll go to the market and see how things are progressing."

She rose and kissed him. "And put that brain of yours to work," she said, "thinking of a way to undo the damage done by President Grant's statements aboard the *Provi-dence*."

"I don't see how—"

"Now, now, never give up." She kissed him again. "That's my boy."

If there were just some way to give the public the im-pression that the President approved of Gould and Fisk . . . Lloyd pondered. A theater poster on Jim Fisk's desk in the Erie offices provided Lloyd with an answer as to how to undo the damage done by Grant's statements aboard the *Providence*. That night the Morlacchi Ballet Troupe would dance the scandalous French cancan at the Fifth Avenue Theater, which was owned by Jim Fisk, and in the accompanying light opera, Mlles. Desclauzas and Irma were to sing *La Périchole*.

While the President rode in Central Park with Edwards

Pierrepont and Julia Grant shopped at A. T. Stewart's fine store on Broadway, Lloyd, after a consultation with Fisk, sought out Abel Corbin and delivered a handwritten invitation for the presidential party to join Fisk in his excellent box in the theater.

Abel urged the Grant family to accept the invitation, saying that he thought they would enjoy the performance.

That night the President was greeted with a standing ovation as his party entered the box, where he sat with the Corbins, Jay Gould, and the Barnum of Wall Street, Jim Fisk.

And while the President of the United States sat in the darkened theater, Harold Berman received a visitor in his small room at the boarding hotel on the East Side. When a knock sounded at the door, he leapt to answer it, thinking that it would be Lloyd Miles. He didn't recognize the attractive blond woman at first, and he was in no frame of mind to appreciate her lovely curves or flashing smile.

"Hello, Harold," she said. "May I come in?"

"Why?" he asked, confused. Then he remembered her, and his face brightened. The woman had worked for Lloyd when he was employed by Thomas Durant in Washington. "You're Rosanna Pulliam."

"Yes." She swept past, holding her handbag in front of her.

Berman closed the door. "Miles sent you?"

Rosanna sat on a hard black leather chair and smiled.

"Well, did Miles send you?" Berman demanded.

"As a matter of fact, no," she replied. "I heard you were in town, Harold, and wanted to see you. I have always admired your financial knowledge, and I thought you might give me some advice. I'm thinking of going into the gold market and—"

Berman's face turned deathly pale. "You're joking."

"Joking?" She rose and walked to stand near him, her smile warm, open. "Are you in the gold market, Harold?"

"If Miles sent you here to taunt me, he's a bigger fool than I thought."

"Is there something wrong?" she asked. "Have I upset you in some way? I assure you that Lloyd has nothing to do with my being here. I came to ask your opinion on the gold market."

She was a beautiful, soft-looking woman. He shook his head and ran his fingers through his hair. The color returned to his face. "Then you've come to the right place," he said. "Stay away from the gold market, or you'll be ruined."

"But there's word on the street that very powerful interests are buying gold."

"They're ruthless," Berman said. "They manipulate the market to squash small investors. They drive the price up by buying, then they cause it to fall by selling heavily, wiping out men like me"—his throat constricted, and he had trouble speaking—"in the process."

"You are in the gold market?"

"I was," he admitted, then coughed and cleared his throat. "Yesterday and today I lost everything I had—and all because of Lloyd Miles and his boss."

"You poor, poor man," Rose sympathized. "Whatever are you going to do?"

"Do?" His eyes were wide, his lower lip trembled. "Do? I'm going to take them down with me. I'm going to tell the world that Gould and his ring are conspiring to corner the gold market."

"Good for you!" she approved, patting him on the arm. "And have you done anything about it yet?"

"Not yet. Miles still has a few hours to get me my money back."

"And then?"

"I have made an appointment with a newspaperman," he said.

"Not just any newspaperman, I hope," she said, her soft hand still on his arm, her face expressing concern. "I'd hate to think that such a story as you have to tell would be lost through unskillful handling by some little hack reporter."

"Not just any newspaperman," Berman reassured her.

"I'm going to meet with Phineas Headley. He can get the story out."

"Yes," Rosanna agreed, "I think he could." She took Berman's arm and led him to the sofa, then seated him and took her place beside him. "You look tense, Harold. Your upset is quite understandable, but I want you to try to relax. I'm going to fix you something to eat."

"I'm not hungry."

"Something to drink, then."

"All right. There's brandy in the left cabinet in the bath." He pointed.

She disappeared, taking her purse, and brought back one small glass of brandy. She talked soothingly as he sipped it.

"I'm so sleepy," he mumbled. "I'm terribly sorry to be so rude after all your kindness, but I don't think I can keep my eyes open."

"Put your head on my shoulder and rest," she said. She pulled his head down, patted his cheek, and ran her fingers through his tightly curled hair.

It was probably his being so overwrought, Rose decided, that weakened his defenses and enabled the drug she had put in his brandy to take such quick effect.

The lodging house was only a three-story building, but there was a brick sidewalk directly below Berman's window. It took her a few minutes to drag him to the window. She waited until there was no traffic on the street. He was unconscious as he fell, and he struck the sidewalk headfirst.

The next day a happy Lloyd Miles was buying gold. The apparent suicide of a resident of an East Side boarding-house had been noted by only a small paragraph on the inside pages of the morning papers. He had not seen Rosanna to confirm her role, but he thought it very odd that Harold had died in exactly the way he had described to Rose as being desirable. He felt that it was a remarkable coincidence and resolved to say as much when next he saw Rosanna.

Small price fluctuations had made his sell transactions profitable. A few days later he ended up with more gold than he had previously owned. Following Gould's example he loaned the specie to banks and used the greenbacks he received in return as collateral to buy more gold. He was into speculating in gold as deeply as his resources would allow; regardless of Ulysses S. Grant's feelings about hard money, whether or not Grant would order the Treasury to sell gold, huge sums were to be made in trading in gold as long as Jay Gould and Jim Fisk continued with their buying . . . and there was no indication that Gould was going to slow his purchases.

Lloyd knew that Gould felt confident that his scheme would work, for the President, by allowing himself to be put on display with Gould and Fisk in Fisk's box at the Fifth Avenue Theater, had given New York a message. Whether true or not, New York financial circles would think that Gould's move on gold had the support of the man in the White House. The small fry, the hangers-on who had been following Gould's lead in buying gold, no longer feared disaster. Their small panic had passed, and their orders to their brokers were to buy.

Spending one August in the nation's capital was enough to make even the most patriotic resident wonder why George Washington had chosen a southern swamp as the site for this important function. Heavy rains made quagmires of unpaved streets, and horse manure mixed with the mud, cooked in the sun, and became pungent. Steamy heat and ubiquitous insects limited Leah's walks along the river. When Lloyd came home from New York, he gave her a small hug and complained of the heat. Their apartment was open to the muggy air.

Lloyd found the Erie's capital-city offices to be running in good order. The male secretary greeted him respectfully and began to bring him up to date on callers, inquiries, important mail. But the August doldrums extended into all facets of Washington life: Congress was marking time until the fall recess; Philip Trent's committee was still grinding away at the Crédit Mobilier affair, but nothing spectacular had emerged during recent hearings; the President and his family were traveling again. Lloyd had a few contacts to make with congressmen who were on the Erie's payroll, and then there was nothing for him to do but watch the slow, inexorable rise of the price of gold on the New York Gold Exchange.

He missed the intensity of New York, and he missed Rosanna Pulliam. He lived for the telegrams and letters from New York and from Kentucky, where Abel and Jennie Corbin were spending two weeks with fractious old Jesse Grant, father of Jennie and Ulysses. By the time Lloyd reached his apartment at night, he had more often than not numbed the edge of his frustration at being exiled from the arena of real action with a few ounces of alcohol. So involved was he with events in New York that he failed to notice that his sister was treating him with unaccustomed coldness.

Corbin, Lloyd was pleased to learn from their correspondence, was doing his best to be gracious and pleasing to the Grant family. He even took old Jesse back to New York for a stay.

"My Dear Friend," Abel Corbin wrote to Lloyd. "Certain events in Saratoga, where Jennie and I have been holidaying with my brother-in-law and his family, are worthy of report. I have, of course, passed this information along to our mutual friend Mr. Gould. I'm not sure whether you know Mr. A. T. Stewart of New York. You may remember that he was President Grant's initial choice for secretary of the Treasury, but his appointment was opposed by the Radicals. The President has always valued Mr. Stewart's advice. As it happens, I was present when the President entered into an extended conversation with Mr. Stewart on the subject of the economy and the gold question in particular.

"Mr. Stewart told the President flatly that it was a mistake to have the secretary of the Treasury, Mr. Boutwell, selling gold on the market. It was Mr. Stewart's opinion that any action taken by Washington would favor one group of speculators over the other. The President was advised to steer clear of the entire matter and to keep the government's gold where it belonged, in the Treasury."

Lloyd's expectations soared. Now things would really move. He telegraphed Rosanna: VITAL STAY IN TOUCH MUSICMAN. STAND READY SELL ON HIS SIGNAL.

Musicman was the agreed-upon designation for General Dan Butterfield, who was to give early warning of any change in government attitude toward selling gold from the Treasury.

After that it was only a matter of waiting. Volume at the Gold Room swelled as Gould and Fisk poured millions of dollars into gold. Four days after Grant's talk with Stewart, gold had risen four and a half dollars. For each one-dollar increase Jay Gould was a minimum of $180,000 richer, at least on paper.

Lloyd Miles sometimes awoke in the night, his palms sweaty, his heart pounding, for he, too, gained in paper riches with each advance in the price of gold. But to make the gain permanent, he had to sell at the right time.

Slowly the bids of buyers in the Gold Room went higher. In New York the eccentric newspaper editor Horace Greeley used the New York *Tribune*'s editorial columns to exhort the U.S. Treasury to sell its gold. Although there had been no danger signal at all from Dan Butterfield at the New York subtreasury, Greeley's editorial made Lloyd nervous. If he still held gold if and when the Treasury brought prices back to normal through the sale of huge quantities of specie, he would not be the man most hurt—he owned only a fraction of Jay Gould's holdings of over forty millions in gold; but his loss, in proportion to his entire net worth, would be far greater than Gould's.

Finally he decided not to wait for a warning from Butterfield. When gold closed at one hundred and forty-four paper dollars for one hundred dollars' worth of coins, he began selling and advised Rosanna to do the same. Their brokers sold only small amounts each day and took advantage of the prices that would, just as Lloyd and Rosanna closed out their gold accounts, touch $150.

* * *

Leah Miles was discovering a universal truth: One of the most frustrating experiences a woman can suffer is to be ignored when she is genuinely angry with a man and is evincing her displeasure by speaking only when she is spoken to and by answering questions in as few words as possible through pursed, unsmiling lips.

Ever since her brother's return from New York, he had been preoccupied. He made no effort to conduct conversation at the dining room table. He had not once tried to join her on the balcony where she sat in the evenings to catch a breath of air. She knew Lloyd well enough to understand that he was concerned about some affair of business, and it made her even more angry to think that her very silence was serving his needs.

She decided to make her brother aware of her unhappiness with him at supper on an evening when September had become well enough established to break the sticky hold of summer on Washington. For once he was on time for dinner and he had not been drinking. She waited until he had finished the meal and was savoring one of her special treats, lemon pie.

"There is something we must discuss," she began.

"Ummm?" He did not look up.

"I have given you every opportunity and, I think, ample time to tell me of your own accord what you have done with my jewelry."

He looked up at her and grinned, and her resolve was softened momentarily, for he looked so young, so sheepish. "I wondered when you were going to miss the stuff."

"I missed it some time ago," she said.

"Well."

There was a long silence. "Must I ask you again?" she asked angrily.

"Well, Leah," he said, "the time is not far away when I will replace every one of your baubles with something far nicer."

"There is one thing you can't replace," she said.

"Oh?" He was puzzled.

"Did you have to take the ring that Philip gave me?"

"Goddamn. So that's it."

"Please do not use that language before me."

"That's why you've been moping around here like the heroine of a cheap drama? The blasted ring that Trent gave you?"

"It was mine," she said. "Since you gave me the other things, I suppose you had the right to take them back—"

"I didn't take them back," he protested. "I borrowed them."

"But you had no right to steal my ring."

He threw down his fork with a clatter and leapt to his feet. "You featherbrained little get," he said. "Here I am risking everything I have—"

"I did not ask you to risk anything," she said.

"Putting up everything I own—"

"And some of mine."

"To better our financial position—"

"*Our* financial position?"

"You live here, don't you? It is my money that pays the rent, isn't it? It is my money that buys the food that goes on the table and the clothes on your back. So isn't it ours?"

"If you consider me to be a burden—"

"Don't be any more absurd than your continued mourning for your precious Philip Trent has already rendered you," he said.

"—I am sure that I can make my own way."

"Don't talk nonsense," he growled. He turned away and paced the room. "Damn it, Leah, I've got too much on my mind—there's too much at stake for me to be distracted with this petty bickering. I'm sorry about your goddamned ring. Perhaps I can buy it back. I can afford to do that now. I'll see to it tomorrow."

"Thank you," she said with elaborate gratitude.

He came to her and put his hands on her arms. "Look, Leah, I really am sorry. It didn't occur to me that the little diamond was the one Trent gave you or that you'd be sentimental about it." He smiled. "Only weeks ago you were ready to marry Berman."

She pulled away. She had not heard of Harold Berman's death until Lloyd came home from New York and told her, almost as an afterthought, about the suicide. She could mourn for Berman's immortal soul and pray that he had made himself right with God, but she could not find it in her heart to mourn. As wrong as Lloyd had been about Philip Trent, he had been right about Berman. Harold had not been man enough to fight for her hand, and in the end he had exhibited the ultimate weakness—the inability to cope with life—by leaping to his death.

"Come on, now," he teased. "Hey, it's you and me against the world, remember?"

It was an old appeal, one she could not ignore, for when she was a child and Lloyd no more than an overgrown boy, they had been very much alone. In those early days, after he had freed her from the tyranny of living with their aunt, there had been nights when there was inadequate food on the table. But they had been together, and that was what had sustained her.

"One day, little sister, we'll have oysters and beefsteak every night. We'll have a big house and a fine carriage and team of black horses, and—"

No, she could not forget his confident promises to her of a comfortable future. And yet there were times when she felt as if she were fading away, like a page of newsprint left in the sun . . . when she could not find an existence beyond being Lloyd's sister, cook, housekeeper, and home companion—on his own terms.

"Us against the world," she said, wanly smiling in spite of herself.

"You haven't asked what I'm doing these days or why I took your jewelry."

"I think I know. You're with Mr. Gould in this gold speculation, aren't you?"

"Pretty smart," he approved.

"Pretty obvious. The first thing you check in the paper is

the market page, and you told me you had sold all your stock and gone liquid."

"Can't keep secrets from you, eh, Leah?"

She laughed.

"I put everything we own into gold at one thirty-one," he said. "I started selling at one forty-four."

He took her hand, led her to a velvet-covered love seat in the parlor, and sat beside her. "Leah, I've made a pot of money. I'm not rich—not by a long shot—but I can buy you a diamond that'll make Philip Trent's look like a grain of sand. We'll be moving to New York soon, I expect, and we'll lease a lovely brownstone in a good neighborhood. You can go to concerts and visit the museums, walk in Central Park and shop at the finest emporiums in the world."

She nodded, her anger dissipating. He had not realized what he was doing in selling Philip's ring. He was her big brother, her best friend, and she could do nothing but forgive him.

"Sound good?"

"It sounds very exciting," she said. "Perhaps in New York I might go to work. Find a respectable job."

"Whatever for?" he asked. "I've just told you that we're fairly well-off. We'll be in an even more favorable position when my broker sells off what's left of my gold holdings."

"Well, I just thought that I might help out," she said.

"Nonsense," he said. "You've helped me immensely over the years by just being my sister, by feeding me well, and making sure that my clothes match."

"I'd like to do more," she said in a soft voice. "I'd like to feel . . ."

"What?"

"Well, I guess I'd like to have the world know that I'm here. I'd like to have people say, 'Look, there's Leah Miles. *These* are the things that *she* has accomplished.' And I don't think that cooking, mending your socks, washing, and cleaning would make a very impressive list of achievements."

"All right," he said. "We'll talk about it again later. Okay?"

She nodded.

"Really," he said. "We will talk." He laughed. "After all, old man Vanderbilt has set up his spiritualist and his magnetic healer as female brokers on Wall Street. Perhaps we can find you a position in some prestigious firm where you can give financial advice to rich men, in the same way that Victoria Woodhull and Tennessee Claflin do for the commodore."

"Now you're teasing me," she said. "Besides, from what I've heard, what Tennessee Claflin gives the commodore is not merely monetary advice."

"Why, sister," he said in mock surprise, "would you suspect one of the pillars of New York society of hanky-panky with the delectable Tennessee?"

Congressman Philip Trent, along with all of Washington, had welcomed the break in the weather. But as the middle of September approached, summer mounted one final assault with muggy heat and a horde of mosquitoes from the Potomac marshes.

Miss Mercy, the ancient despot who managed Philip's congressional office, actually had to wipe perspiration off her forehead. Miss Mercy was so old, so dried up, that seeing her sweat was an event. Julia Grey, Philip's indispensable researcher, writer, and right-hand "man," winked at Philip and whispered, "Do you suppose that she has blood in her veins too?"

"Hush," Philip said.

Julia was wearing a smart tan outfit without hoops in the skirts. Hoopskirts were difficult to manage, although they looked incomparably beautiful on a lady standing in the shade of a magnolia tree and holding a silk fan. Young ladies donning their first hoopskirt had to be shown how to sit down without upsetting themselves or, as the case might be, decency. A hoopskirt in the office was impractical. Julia's skirts were full, and they draped nicely as she moved. She was a petite woman, small of waist, slim of neck, and long of leg. Her eyes were the color of summer seas and as changeable, being now greenish-blue, now bluish-green. They were animated eyes, playful most of the time. But they could be brooding at others, as when she was looking at her husband, Adam, without his knowledge. Her hair was dark with auburn highlights. She was the most vividly alive person Philip Trent had ever known.

Adam Grey was a Virginian who had fought for the Union, thus cutting himself off forever from home and family. He had lost his legs during one of the last significant actions of the war, the taking of Fort Fisher, the key to the port at Wilmington, North Carolina. Adam's terrible wounds had drained him of everything but his courage. The artillery shell that had shattered his legs had also sent small pieces of jagged metal into his stomach, and he had never fully healed. His face was rather handsome, but although he was only in his late twenties, his eyes were those of an old man, pale, gray, shrunken, lined in half-moon circles of darkness.

Of late, at the insistence of both Julia and Philip, he had been keeping fairly regular office hours as the congressman's chief researcher. It seemed to be good for him.

When Julia laughed at Philip's admonition to be quiet, Adam rolled into the room on his wheeled dolly. The stumps of his thighs stuck out in front of him. "What's all the hilarity and mirth?" he asked.

"You don't really want to know," Julia said, snickering.

"It would seem to me," Miss Mercy declared, "that if certain people stopped lollygagging and telling jokes there'd be more work done around here."

It was Miss Mercy's nature, and her self-claimed right, to reprimand the congressman equally with his employee.

"Yes, ma'am," Philip said, winking at Adam.

A bell tinkled, indicating that someone had entered the reception area. Julia hurried to do her duty. She was back in half a minute. "Mr. Trent, a gentleman of the press to see you, sir."

"Oh, Lord," Philip said, rolling his eyes. "Another one?"

"This one is from New York," Julia said, handing over a calling card that read simply, PHINEAS HEADLEY, JOURNALIST.

Philip went out to greet him. Headley stood in the outer office, hat in hand. He took Philip's outstretched hand with confidence and smiled into Philip's face. "Congressman, may I have a few minutes of your time?"

"Well, Mr. Headley, you certainly may, but I fear that I have nothing new for you," Philip said.

Headley laughed. "It would be an unexpected bonus for me if you had. But I'm not here to have you tell me anything, Mr. Trent."

"Then in observance of this very unusual occasion, let me offer you some coffee."

"I'd like that very much," Headley said. "Had a long train ride down from New York."

Philip stepped into the middle office and signaled to Julia by making cup-tipping motions with his hand. She nodded. He held up two fingers.

He led the journalist into his office, and they sat in deep leather chairs arranged to face each other.

"Mr. Trent, I have to get back to New York today," Headley began. "I have just an hour or so before my train, so let me get to it quickly. Do you follow the financial news, especially the gold market?"

"Not as closely as I should, I suppose," Philip replied.

"First of all, let me say that I'm coming to you with this information because I approve highly of what you're doing to expose those who took bribes from the railroads. If I had to make a guess, I'd peg you as a straight arrow."

"Thank you. I hope to hell so," Philip said.

"Gold is up to one forty-four," Headley explained, "and the best guess on the street is that it's going to at least one fifty. Now, sir, at the risk of making it seem as if I'm lecturing you on matters of the economy—"

Philip held up a hand. "Mr. Headley, if you have no objections, I'd like to have my aide join us. As it happens, he knows more about economics than do I."

"My pleasure," Headley agreed, and to his great credit he showed no surprise when Adam Grey wheeled into the room and swung himself up into a chair by using his over-developed arms.

Philip made the introductions. "Now, Mr. Headley, if you'll continue . . ."

"As I was telling the congressmen, Mr. Grey, there's something askew in the Gold Room," Headley said.

"Up to one forty-six today," Adam said, nodding, his lifeless eyes straying from Headley's face to the ceiling.

"I don't have any proof of this—at least not in the form of documents," Headley said, "—but I think you're going to find that the Erie Railroad, or more precisely Erie money, is behind an attempt to do something that has never been done before."

"A corner in gold?" Adam guessed.

"Exactly," Headley said.

"What do you have to substantiate your suspicion?" Adam asked.

"Only the steady rise of prices," the newsman answered. "I had a source that had promised to give me chapter and verse on Gould's scheme, but he is dead."

"Dear me," Julia said. Carrying a tray of coffee, she had entered the office unnoticed.

Philip smiled. "Please don't be put off by the growing size of your audience, Mr. Headley. I have an extremely efficient but *nosy* staff."

"Delighted," Headley said, accepting a cup.

"Is it possible to corner the gold market?" Julia asked.

"Up until now I'd have thought it was impossible," Adam said. "Simply too much specie in circulation and available on short notice, not to mention the coin in the federal Treasury."

"It is estimated by reliable sources that Jay Gould and Jim Fisk control more gold than is immediately available in New York State," Headley said. "They could create a panic simply by calling in all the gold loans they have out on greenback collateral."

"Mr. Headley, just what concerns you about this affair?" Philip asked.

"If my sources are correct," Headley explained, "then

Gould, Fisk, and one or two others control over one hundred million dollars' worth of gold. The first adverse effect is already being felt. Normally it's simple to convert greenbacks into hard money for foreign exchange; but the bulls in the Gold Room have crippled the machinery by making gold very, very scarce. Imports and exports are grinding to a halt. I'm told that the waterfronts in port cities like Boston and Savannah are like abandoned towns. And there's more. It's happening slowly, and my friends in banking in New York say it's only the beginning. Even now farm prices are being affected. One after the other the prices of farm commodities are falling like a row of dominoes."

"All because the price of gold has gone up?" Philip asked.

Headley nodded. "Men are being laid off. Workers on docks, such as stevedores, sailors, and the draymen who carry goods to and from the ports, are out of work."

"Because of expensive gold," Philip said.

"Yes," Headley confirmed. "And this is what the bankers are saying, Mr. Trent. Wall Street has known for weeks that Gould and Fisk are working toward a corner. What everyone can't understand is why Washington is doing nothing."

"Well, this isn't exactly in my field of responsibility," Philip said, still not fully understanding the situation.

"Congressman," Headley said, "I don't think that the President and his men are crooks and thieves." He laughed. "Well, at least not all of them. But it is going to appear to the world that Ulysses S. Grant is either venal or stupid. Either way wouldn't be very flattering to the man who won the war. Do you agree?"

"I agree fully," Philip said. "What is it that you think I should do, Mr. Headley?"

"You're a friend of the general's, I understand."

"Not an intimate friend."

"But a man who holds the Congressional Medal of Honor can get U. S. Grant's ear at any time of the day or night," Headley said. He went on to explain Abel Corbin's supposed part in the machinations.

Adam Grey nodded. "And you want Mr. Trent to ask the

President why he has not yet intervened in the gold market?"

"No, I do not want that!" Headley said vehemently. "I want you to warn General Grant that he's allowing a pack of hyenas to pick the bones of this country. I want you to warn him that things are going to get worse. Tell him that I believe there's been at least one murder because of what's going on."

"Murder?" Philip asked.

"A man named Harold Berman."

"Berman? By God, I know him!" Philip said.

"He worked for the Erie in Washington. He had made an appointment with me to outline how Gould, Fisk, and a coworker named Lloyd Miles were planning to get a stranglehold on the nation's money supply. Berman fell to his death from the window of his room on the third story of a New York lodging house. I don't think it was a suicide."

"Why is it believed that he committed suicide?" Philip asked.

"He'd lost everything on the gold market," Phineas said. "But that's minor—to everyone but the late Mr. Berman—when compared to the harm that Gould and his ring can do. Or the harm Berman could have done to them. His meeting with me could have ruined their scheme. You must see the President, Mr. Trent. There are those who are saying that he's a part of it. I can't believe he is, but if he continues to do nothing, he might as well be. I don't know what it's going to take to wake up the government; a lot of men far more influential than I have already passed their concerns along to Washington. It seems that Treasury Secretary Boutwell is all for selling federal gold to keep things in balance, but no action is forthcoming."

"Thank you, Mr. Headley," Philip said. "I appreciate your coming all the way from New York to tell me these things."

"But was it an exercise in futility?" Headley asked.

"I will look into this matter," Philip said. "I can't promise you that I'll go to the President with it, but I will seek more information and the advice of economic experts."

"Don't take too long," Headley cautioned, rising, "or you'll wake up, and this country will be in the worst depression you've ever seen."

Alone with Adam and Julia Grey, Philip finished his coffee in one swallow. "Adam, what do you think?"

"I think we owe Mr. Phineas Headley a debt of gratitude," he said.

"His name seems familiar," Philip said.

"He was the actual writer of Lafayette Baker's book."

"Ah, I see. . . ."

"Don't sell Headley short," Adam said. "He's a professional. And having spent a few months picking Lafe Baker's brain, I'd imagine that he knows where a few bodies are buried."

"Then you believe him? You think that men like Jay Gould are out to ruin the nation's economy?"

"That's not their aim," Adam corrected. "I'd guess that the goal is to make more money than ordinary simpletons such as you or I can imagine. And if, in the process, a few million people get hurt, that wouldn't really matter to them."

Philip mused for a moment or two. "Well, it's getting late. There's not much I can do about it today."

His real reason for the delay was that his father was in Washington and planned to spend the night in Philip's apartment. Before Philip went running to Grant, he wanted to talk the situation over with Gus. In his mind there was nothing incongruous about a U.S. congressman seeking counsel from a lowly Maryland state senator. Gus Trent wasn't Golden Age rich; he was not powerful outside his own district in Baltimore and among the members of the Maryland Republican party. But he just happened to be one of the wisest men his son had ever known.

CHAPTER 7

Father and son enjoyed a leisurely dinner at their favorite little restaurant, where a hefty black woman produced miracles of Southern cooking on a wood-burning stove in the kitchen. Philip waited until Gus had finished the entrée, and then as they were served sweet-potato pie and coffee, he told his father about Phineas Headley's visit.

"Sometimes I think I'm too ignorant to hold this job, Dad," Philip said ruefully. "I still don't understand exactly why there *is* a difference in value between greenbacks and gold."

"I don't think you're quite that dumb," Gus soothed with a grin.

"Well, maybe not quite. But if what Headley says is true, don't you think President Grant would be aware of it without my calling it to his attention?"

"Maybe yes, maybe no," Gus said, leaning back to allow the waiter to place his dessert and coffee in front of him. "The general has a lot on his mind. Your investigation of the transcontinental probably causes him to lose sleep at night as he wonders which member of his party you're going to expose next as a bribe taker."

"Or in this case, if Headley is right, which member of his

108

family. Frankly, I'm reluctant to get mixed up in this affair," Philip said. "I don't relish telling General Ulysses S.
Grant that his brother-in-law may be involved in something
that could prove disastrous for the country."

"I can understand your reluctance," Gus agreed. "But
even though there is a good possibility that the President is
in control of the situation and is just waiting for what he
and his advisers consider to be the right time to dump
federal gold into the market, I think you're going to have
to talk with him." He cut a bite of sweet-potato pie with his
fork and said, *"Ummm,"* as he tasted it.

"Could someone get a corner in gold?" Philip asked.

"Well, it would take a sight more money than I've got,"
Gus said. "But I reckon if anyone could plan it and execute
the strategy, it would be someone like Jay Gould. He's a
smart fellow. He and old Jim Fisk not only cleaned Uncle
Dan'l Drew's plow, they got into Cornele Vanderbilt's
pocket for millions. That's playing with the big boys, when
you can go nose to nose with men such as Drew and Vanderbilt and come out ahead. Drew is the man who coined
the phrase *watered stock.* He used to go out into the hinter-
lands and buy cattle, then move them to the New York
market. Just before bringing them into the city he'd feed
them all the salt they would eat, and then let them loose at
water troughs. Since cattle sold by on-the-hoof weight, the
water the cows soaked up added a tidy little margin of
profit. And old Uncle Dan'l got the best of Vanderbilt a
couple of times when the commodore decided he wanted
to gobble up the Erie Railroad. After one of their battles
for control, when Drew came out ahead largely because of
the help of Jay Gould and Jim Fisk, Vanderbilt observed
that 'it don't pay to kick a skunk.' "

Philip had finished his pie. "Want to be sinful and have
another piece?" he asked.

"You talked me into it," Gus said.

Philip called the waiter and gave the order.

"It was right after that, right after Gould, Fisk, and Drew
ran off a few million dollars' worth of Erie Railroad stock
—watered stock—on a printing press and fleeced Vander-

bilt of several million dollars that Gould eased Daniel Drew out of Erie. That's the kind of man we're talking about. Gould knows his way around the financial battlegrounds."

"And if the Gold Ring succeeds in getting a corner?"

Gus shrugged. "I guess it could be as bad as Phineas Headley predicts. It's hard to say. The problem is, you see, that otherwise sensible men become dimwits when they get into the stock market. They become lemmings and commit financial suicide over some silly rumor that wouldn't have been believed by an eight-year-old. They draw absurd conclusions about the effect of external events on the market. What is happening to Pacific Railroad stock is a good example of what I'm talking about. You're letting the whole country know that a few congressmen and senators took bribes from the builders of the transcontinental, mostly in the form of stock in the Union Pacific's holding company, Crédit Mobilier. Now, does that make the transcontinental any less valuable? Of course not. But just because there's a scandal, men yell, 'Sell! Sell!' Others hear and follow suit, and the first thing you know the little people who invested their life savings into Pacific Railroad stock find that their certificates are worth only half what they paid for them. It's a damn stupid system, but what can you do? That's the American way. Under the Constitution a man is free to make a jackass of himself and lose his shirt; and in order to give him that privilege we also have to extend him the right to hurt other people with his foolishness. And it's also a part of the system that some few profit by the herd instincts of those who play the market. There's always someone around who understands the system a little better and, thus, benefits from the idiocy of the majority. What I'm getting at is that scarce gold would probably have a devastating effect on the stock market as a whole."

"The activity in the Gold Room is already causing price drops in the farm commodities markets," Philip said.

"So there you are. And it's all linked together: if the farmers can't spend for supplies, tools, and equipment, several industries are affected. Some speculator sees the price of corn go down, sees exports falling off, and he tells his broker to sell stock in Erie and New York Central because they won't have farm goods to carry to the ports. And then another says, 'Sell,' and the price goes down still more. Others try to cut their losses, and the first thing you know there are more sell offers than buy offers, and it spreads from railroads to steel and so on."

"I should have a talk with General Grant, then," Philip said, resigned.

"Couldn't hurt," Gus said, his mouth full of pie. "If he knows more about economics than you do, that's only fitting. After all, he's the President, and you're only a congressman from Maryland. But the main reason why you'll go to the White House is because you know and I know that U. S. Grant is an honest man. Maybe a bit too trusting, a little bit naive, but a man of honor. And neither one of us wants to see the tar generated by others rub off on him, do we?"

"That's one of the troubles with you, you old son of a gun," Philip said. "You know me sometimes better than I know myself."

In the early days of his presidency Ulysses S. Grant had been swarmed by office seekers. It had seemed that every Republican in America had promised federal jobs to at least half a dozen men. Thus it was that Grant had learned early that he could not have an open-door policy at the White House.

Philip Trent stated his identity to a man at the front entrance and was admitted to the reception rooms, where he was informed that the President was in New York. He was about to leave when Julia Grant walked through, saw him, waved, and smiled. He bowed. Mrs. Grant approached.

"How pleasant to see you, Mr. Trent," she said.

"You're looking very well, Mrs. Grant."

"Feeling well, thank you. I imagine you've come to see Ulysses?"

"I guess I should have read the newspapers this morning

to save myself a trip," Philip said. "Having had the pleasure of seeing you, Mrs. Grant, the walk wasn't wasted."

"Pshaw." She smiled. "Join me for a cup of coffee."

"My pleasure," he said.

She led the way into a private sitting room, where they were served by a young black boy in white livery.

"Mr. Grant's trip to New York was rather unexpected," Julia explained. "I'm sorry you missed him. If it's anything pressing, I'm sure that one of the President's aides would be glad to help you."

"Actually, I'm not sure I should bother the President with it," Philip said.

Julia Grant knew that her husband had high regard for the young war hero who was currently battling the powerful railroad interests. She, too, was fond of Philip, although she'd spoken with him only a few times. "I'm sure that the President will be interested in hearing anything you have to say."

Philip had been very reluctant to go with unfounded gossip and suspicions to Ulysses Grant. By the accident of Grant's absence he was being presented with a way of bringing the matter to the President's attention without putting it on top of the table.

"Being a somewhat nosy woman," Julia Grant said goodnaturedly, "I wonder what's on your mind." She held up one hand. "Although, mind you, I'm not asking. Heaven forbid that it be bandied around that I take a hand in running the White House other than seeing that meals are served on time."

"Given a choice," Philip said, "I'd rather pass along potentially disturbing rumors to you, Mrs. Grant, than to the general. He has a way of looking at a man that can be quite intimidating."

"Oh, don't you know it?" she agreed with a little laugh. "But he's a dear. He has a soft heart."

Philip could not imagine the man who had ordered the charge at Cold Harbor as being softhearted, but he didn't dispute Mrs. Grant.

"You have raised my curiosity," she said.

"Mrs. Grant, perhaps I am being cowardly in telling you this—"

"Now I *must* know."

"I have just had a visit from a New York newspaperman who gave me some information that, if true, could be damaging to the country and disturbing to both you and the President in a personal way. It is because the information —which, I admit, is not documented—touches on the Grant family personally that I am speaking to you in the President's absence."

"Oh, dear," Mrs. Grant said.

"When you were in New York, you, the President, and the President's sister and brother-in-law attended a theater performance with Jay Gould and Jim Fisk."

"Yes."

"There are those who interpreted that appearance in public with Gould and Fisk as being presidential approval of a scheme to drive the price of gold to artificial highs," Philip said. "And, although I hesitate to repeat gossip, it's being said in New York that your brother-in-law, Abel Corbin, is a part of the Gold Ring."

"I assure you that Ulysses has nothing to do with this," Julia said quickly.

"Of that I am sure," Philip responded.

"But there's talk?"

"I fear so."

"I am very grateful to you, Mr. Trent," Julia said. "Am I to take it that you want me to pass along what you've said to the President upon his return?"

"As you wish," Philip replied.

She escorted him from the family area of the house. "Thank you again for speaking frankly with me," she said, giving him her hand.

Julia Grant hurried to her private study. Her face set in a concerned frown, she picked up the first writing implement she saw—a pencil—and wrote rapidly.

"Dear Jennie," she wrote to her sister-in-law. "Rumors have reached me that Abel is connected with a certain group of speculators in New York. If this be so I wish that he would disengage himself from those men at once, for I am very much distressed by such rumors. If you have any influence with your husband, tell him not to have anything at all to do with the gold speculators. If he does, he will be ruined. Come what may, I can assure you that your brother will do his duty to the country and the trusts in his keeping."

She hesitated for a moment, decided not to sign her name, and wrote only, "Sis."

CHAPTER 8

Just before noon Lloyd Miles received a note by messenger from Jennie Grant Corbin. He was urgently requested to call at the Corbin home.

When he arrived and was admitted by a servant, Jennie Corbin, wearing a frilled hoopskirt that floated her toward him as smoothly and gracefully as a galleon on a calm sea, rushed to meet him. He touched her outstretched hand.

"Oh, Lloyd," she said, "thank you for coming. I didn't know where to turn."

"If there is anything I can do, dear lady . . ."

She dabbed at a tear as she handed him a sheet of paper. The penciled message was so dimly written that to read it he had to hold the letter to the light. He realized that what he was clutching in his hand was political dynamite. The missive from Julia Grant to her sister could be interpreted as a warning for Abel Corbin to get out of the gold market or "be ruined."

Julia Grant had acted very unwisely in sending the letter to the Corbin household. Whatever her motives, if the contents of her note became public knowledge, the net result of her actions would be to imply guilt not only for Corbin, her sister, and herself, but for the President as well.

All Lloyd had ever wanted from the President was for him to do nothing. He could not believe that Ulysses Grant was directly involved in the gold scheme, but in this acquisitive age there would be many who did not have the respect for the old warrior that was shared by every man who had worn Union blue.

"Jennie," he said, "I would advise you to destroy this letter and never to tell a soul that you received it."

"But I must tell Abel," she wailed.

He nodded. "Yes, I suppose you must." Lloyd was certain that if Corbin, a businessman and an opportunist, was pushed into a corner, he would have no hesitation in using Julia Grant's letter to his own advantage. But Lloyd could not imagine that Corbin would use the letter in an effort to prove that U. S. Grant had full knowledge of the gold scheme and that the President had considered high gold prices to be desirable government policy. He comforted Jennie Corbin, assuring her that her husband was indeed safe from any scandal or from ruin, since Abel himself had not invested in the gold market but was earning his money from profits made on gold purchased by Jay Gould.

After a long and trying day that included train rides to Washington and back and a hurried visit with the President's wife squeezed in between, Lloyd was in his nightdress and ready for bed when he heard a knock. He pulled on a dressing gown and opened the front door to see Rosanna Pulliam. She slipped into the foyer and said, "Sorry to be so late. I've been with General Butterfield."

"Something to drink?" Lloyd offered as he escorted her inside.

"Thank you, no." She removed her coat and slung it over a chair. "Are we out of the gold market?"

"Not entirely," Lloyd answered. "The brokers are selling off our holdings a little bit at a time. We don't want to shock the market by putting up large lots."

"I think you'd best tell them to accelerate the process," she suggested.

Lloyd, instantly alert, watched her lips for her next words.

"Butterfield started selling his gold bonds this afternoon," she said. "Day after tomorrow he's going to post notice at the subtreasury that Secretary George Boutwell has decided to prepay in gold the November interest on the national debt."

Lloyd knew from Rose that Butterfield, in addition to profiting from Jay Gould's purchases of gold in Butterfield's name, had bought a sizable amount of foreign gold bonds in his wife's name.

"Damn," Lloyd said under his breath. The news that the government would be releasing huge quantities of specie at a later date would have little immediate effect on the overheated gold market; but Lloyd chose to interpret the information as advance warning that the government was beginning to take an interest in what was happening in New York.

"I thought you'd want to get word to Mr. Gould," Rosanna said.

"Umm." He rubbed his chin, nodded. "I think tomorrow will be soon enough to inform Mr. Gould. Butterfield wouldn't contact Gould himself, would he?"

"I don't think so," she replied. "He said something else, Lloyd. He said that all hell was going to break out in Washington pretty soon."

"That's all he said?"

"He didn't explain, but in the context, he couldn't have been thinking about anything other than the gold situation. I don't know whether he meant that the Treasury would start selling gold or—"

Lloyd nodded. Butterfield had indeed kept his agreement to give advance warning of a change in federal policy. "Rose, I think I need a drink, and I'm afraid you'd better join me. And then we'll both need a good night's rest, for tomorrow is going to be quite a day."

It was September 22, a fair, bright day of pleasant temperatures. To the usual smells of the city was added a hint of wood smoke. Rosanna and Lloyd went uptown together and were waiting to transact business as soon as the brokerage offices opened. When trading began in the Gold Room, their respective brokers began to sell the last of their holdings in specie. Then Rose and Lloyd sat together in the spectators' balcony and watched the price of gold climb to $144. Lloyd's broker looked up, caught his eye, and nodded. Lloyd smiled and winked at Rosanna. He was a happy man. He could not yet be compared to the barons, but when he added up his worth he could think in terms of millions. He had built a small holding of just under three hundred thousand dollars into a sum of greenbacks that totaled almost seven times his original investment. Rosanna, by following Lloyd's advice, had also multiplied her nest egg, but she had started the run with much less money than had Lloyd.

His next task was to transfer over two million dollars in greenbacks from his brokerage account. Rose and he parted ways, and Lloyd went to deposit less than one million in his account at the Tenth National Bank. Since Jay Gould owned the bank, he could take a look at his employee's balance to see how well Miles had done during the great bull market in gold. Lloyd had to chuckle a little from the irony of the situation as he placed the remainder of his gains in other banks. Much of his profit was due to Gould and Fisk, who, by buying heavily during the time Lloyd was liquidating, most probably had purchased Lloyd's gold.

He didn't care to have Gould know exactly how well he had done. Although a couple of million dollars was an insignificant amount to Gould, he could be a dangerous man. Uncle Dan'l Drew had once said that Gould's touch was death, and Lloyd didn't want to risk alienating Gould by flaunting the fact that he had sold his gold early.

He would keep his holdings liquid for a time because it was beginning to look as if the prognosticators of doom might have been right in predicting that high-priced gold would have a deleterious effect not only on the market but on the nation's economy as a whole.

Shortly after midday Lloyd found Jay Gould in his office.

He told Gould of Butterfield's orders to post notice that the government would be releasing large amounts of gold in payment of interest. He did not mention the general's cryptic remark about trouble in Washington. He had done his job: a clear warning had come from the subtreasurer, and what Gould would do now was his own affair.

What Gould did was to start unloading forty millions in gold in a market that on September 23 reacted like a school of sharp-toothed fish in a feeding frenzy. Gould, to protect his own interests and to prevent a panicked selling that would cost him millions, did not bother to tell his partner, Jim Fisk, that he was doing a one-hundred-eighty-degree turn or that the lead bull was becoming a bear. As a result, Fisk, a shark among the small fry, bought millions of the very gold that Gould was selling.

Phineas Headley was a frustrated man. Time and time again in his efforts to document what was happening to the nation's money supply at the hands of Gould and Fisk, the journalist had had doors slammed in his face. Everyone on the street seemed to know that the Erie twins were behind the surge in gold prices, but by dealing through various brokers they covered their tracks well.

What aggravated Headley most profoundly was the fact that he had had proof in full detail at his fingertips, only to have it slip away with the death of Harold Berman. He had been hounding the homicide detective who'd investigated Berman's dive from a third-story window only to be told, and not too kindly, that the police were not about to make a mystery of a simple suicide.

"Go peddle your papers," he was told.

The problem was that he had no papers to peddle. He was about ready to abandon the entire story. After all, he was not a financial reporter. The sums of money that passed through the Gold Room numbed his brain and left him dizzy.

He was almost ready to admit defeat. But on September 23 the journalist visited the Gold Room for lack of any-thing else to do. There he saw Lloyd Miles seated with a striking blond woman in the spectators' balcony. Remembering Lafe Baker's advice to keep an eye on Lloyd Miles, Headley began to make his way around the balcony . . . only to see Miles leave. The blond woman, however, remained seated. Headley approached her, tipped his hat, and said, "Pardon me for intruding."

The woman gave him a polite smile.

"My name is Phineas Headley," he said. "I am a reporter."

She looked at him with new interest.

"I saw you sitting with Mr. Miles," Headley continued. "As it happens, I've been trying to get an interview with the gentleman. Perhaps you could help me."

"In what way?" she asked.

"I understand that Mr. Miles speculates in the gold market," Headley said. "Are you, too, an investor?"

"Only an interested spectator," Rosanna said.

"But Mr. Miles is buying gold?"

"I think that you'd have to ask him that question," she said smoothly.

Headley smiled. "Well, we know for sure that his employer, Mr. Gould, is buying gold, don't we?"

"Actually, I'm quite ignorant about such matters," she said. "Lloyd told me that I might find the antics of the traders on the floor amusing." She stood. "I was, in fact, just leaving."

"Perhaps, Miss—" He paused, looking at her inquiringly. She did not respond. "Perhaps you could put in a word for me with Mr. Miles? Would you ask him if he'll give me a few moments of his time? I merely want to get the details of the workings of the gold market from an expert, as background for a financial study I'm doing."

The woman was silent, a hint of a smile on her lips.

"Well, thank you, anyhow," Headley said. "I'm sorry I bothered you."

"Not at all," she said.

"Good day, then," he said, "Miss—?"

"I'm Rosanna Pulliam," she said, widening her smile.

He bowed. "My pleasure, Miss Pulliam."

"I think we have a mutual friend. Lafe Baker?"

"Ah, you know General Baker," Headley said. "An interesting man, indeed."

"Yes," Rosanna said. After an awkward silence, the reporter tipped his hat. "Well, then . . ."

"Good-bye," Miss Pulliam said.

On Friday morning, September 24, gold opened at $145, and there were no sell orders. Brokers seeking to buy for eager clients yelled out bids. Jim Fisk, still unaware that his partner was selling gold, ordered his brokers to send the price to $150. Fisk was confident, for the Gold Ring held the legal right to demand immediate delivery of six times the total amount of gold coin and gold certificates immediately available in New York. Fisk's holdings had topped sixty million. Gould's were in the area of fifty-five million. Other, lesser sharks brought the total of gold calls owned by the ring to over one hundred million. Each increase of one dollar in the price of gold meant a million dollars in profit for the ring.

By Friday the effect of the corner was being felt far beyond the gilded confines of the Gold Room. The stock market was in disarray. Even the most powerful of the barons was affected. Commodore Vanderbilt's railroads had suffered as a result of high-priced gold to the point where one bank had the gall to require interest payments of two percent per day on loans secured by New York Central stock. That equated to a yearly interest rate of seven hundred and thirty percent. Vanderbilt, of course, was furious, and he knew just where to place the blame for the panic dumping of his railroad stock.

Although Vanderbilt did not go into action immediately, other men were actively battling the gold bulls on the floor of the Gold Exchange. A cabal of bankers and financiers, wanting to halt the drive that seemed destined to push the price of gold to $200 and, in the process, smash the nation's economy, were represented on the floor by a banker named James Brown.

At eleven-thirty in the morning Jim Fisk gave orders to

raise the price to $160. His representative on the floor, one Albert Speyers, yelled out, "One hundred sixty for five million!"

This bid meant that the price had risen fifteen dollars in three hours.

"One hundred sixty for five million," Speyers repeated, his words signifying ruin for bankers and merchants all over the country, for the economy operated on borrowed gold, and if the bulls called in their loans, the gold would have to be purchased by the borrowers at current market prices.

"One hundred sixty-one for five million," Speyers shrilled. "One hundred sixty-two for five million."

No broker answered the bids.

Other members of the New York financial world were demanding that the federal government intercede. Fifty bankers and businessmen forced their way into Dan Butterfield's office at the subtreasury and demanded that Butterfield inform Washington that disaster was imminent unless the government took action. Many of the angry men accused Secretary of the Treasury George Boutwell of being a party to the conspiracy.

Butterfield sent a telegram to Boutwell telling him that the government was being accused of complicity in the Gold Ring and that it would be wise to sell Treasury gold. He himself, having sold all his gold certificates, would not be affected if the corner failed and the price of gold went back to normal. He considered his obligation to Miles and Gould to have been honored by his warnings.

In Washington, Ulysses S. Grant was playing croquet with his children on the White House lawn. It was a splendid day, and Grant was well rested after his latest travels. He looked up in exasperation as he was approached by Secretary of the Treasury George Boutwell and the young Republican congressman Philip Trent. He deliberately kept the men waiting. He didn't like intrusions into his time with his family. When he finally handed his mallet to one of his sons and turned toward the two men, his face was grim.

"Sorry to butt in, Mr. President," Boutwell said.

"I'm sure you have good reason, George," Grant allowed.

"I think so, Mr. President," Boutwell said.

"How've you been, Captain Trent?" Grant asked Philip.

"Well, sir," Philip said. "Thank you."

"Good, good," Grant said. "Well, gentlemen, out with it."

Boutwell bowed to Philip, giving him the floor.

"General, the business and financial community is in an agony," Philip began.

"Goddamn it!" Grant thundered. "Not that gold mess again."

"I'm afraid so, General," Philip said. "The stock market is in a panic. Prices are going through the floor, with railroad and industrial stocks hardest hit. I've had several hundred telegrams from responsible businessmen warning of depression, a stock-market crash, total chaos. And I agree with them, sir. When I left my office to meet Secretary Boutwell, the price of gold was at a hundred fifty-five and rising."

"It's a cyclone of disaster, Mr. President," Boutwell added. "There is nothing we can do but stop it. Congressman Trent is not the only one receiving telegrams. At the Treasury Department we're snowed under by requests, pleas, and demands to do something."

Grant put his hands behind his back. For a moment he looked very much as he had in a photograph taken after Cold Harbor. His eyes looked into distances; his mouth was firm.

"All right, George," he said. "Sell enough goddamned gold to give the bulls in the Gold Room a terminal case of auric poison."

Lloyd Miles entered the Gold Room just before noon. On the floor Jim Fisk's broker was screaming out in his shrill voice, "One hundred sixty-two for five million."

Lloyd grinned wryly. He'd sold the last of his and Rosanna's holdings at $150. He sat down to watch the show.

"One hundred sixty-two for five million," Albert Speyers kept repeating.

And then, suddenly, a deep voice answered. "Sold, one million at one sixty-two." The banker James Brown, representing the gold bears, had taken a serious step, offering to sell gold that he didn't have, gambling that promised relief for the shortage of specie in New York would arrive before the end of the day, or that the government would, at last, be forced to move. At that moment it was in the interest of Brown and the bears to drive the price to ridiculous heights. If gold went past $160, the government would be forced to act.

After Brown's words a hush came over the trading floor. Lloyd could hear the water tinkling in the fountain at the center of the room.

"One hundred sixty-one for four million," Speyers said, lowering his bid one dollar.

"Sold, one million at one sixty-one," Brown answered.

The shrilling of bids and acceptances grew in volume. In one corner of the trading floor the price hit $165.

Thomas Edison's price indicator was an ingenious piece of machinery, a series of wheels imprinted with numerals and fractions. The machine, however, was too slow for the frenzied action on the floor. One wheel made ten revolutions to change a full digit, marking the change in tenths. The electric signals that were going out to three hundred indicators throughout the city were minutes behind. Edison weighted the wheels to make them spin faster, but the machine could not match the pace of trading.

Dan Butterfield received twin telegrams from Secretary Boutwell through both Western Union and the Franklin Telegraph Company.

"SELL FOUR MILLION ($4,000,000) GOLD TOMORROW (SATURDAY), AND BUY FOUR MILLION ($4,000,000) BONDS."

Butterfield copied the information in longhand and told a clerk to post it: *Notice: By order of the secretary of the Treasury, the assistant treasurer will sell, at 12 o'clock noon tomorrow, four million gold and buy four million of bonds.*

The bankers and speculators who had been keeping vigil at the subtreasury burst into applause. Messengers dashed through the streets. Typically, the amount involved was inflated as the news passed from person to person until the Gold Room buzzed with the rumor that the federal Treasury was going to sell fifteen million in gold.

Nearby, the bells of Trinity Church pealed the hour of noon. Edison's price indicator stood at $160. As the sound of the bells faded a voice on the trading floor said, "I will buy at one hundred thirty-eight." And then, "Buy any amount at one hundred thirty-five."

Phineas Headley, in the spectators' gallery, mentally composed a lead line for his story of the great crash. *Over the pallid faces of speculators stole a deadly hue.*

CHAPTER 9

The September evening was cool enough to warrant lighting a fire. With draperies and curtains drawn and the gas lights turned low, the flat was cozy. After Lloyd came in, bringing with him the scent of the outdoors, he saw that Rosanna had set the dining room table for two. When she met him in the foyer, she carried two tall, stemmed flutes in her hands.

"For the conquering hero," she said with a tilt of her head and a saucy smile.

The champagne was a good one. Lloyd enjoyed a sip, then lowered his glass. He could not resist giving a whoop of jubilation.

"I think the lad is proud of himself," Rosanna said.

"Lord, Rose, you should have seen it!" Lloyd enthused. "They got into fistfights. For a while it looked as if there'd be a riot. There was talk of calling out the state militia."

"What about Gould and Fisk?" Rose asked as she took his coat.

"I don't know," Lloyd said, his eyes shining. "They disappeared. If I'd been in their place, I'd have done the same thing. There's more than one man in New York who'd gladly shoot both of them."

126

"I'd imagine that their finances emerged unscathed. . . ."

Lloyd shook his head. "Hard to say, Rose. The market collapsed completely. Sheer chaos. I heard it estimated that there were a thousand tons of gold in transactions today, and when business started this morning, the Gold Exchange hadn't even posted Thursday's trading."

"A thousand tons?" Rose asked in awe.

"It would take a caravan of wagons to rival General Grant's supply trains at Petersburg to carry it—even if there were that much gold in the world."

She took his hand and led him to the table. While she hung up his coat, he refilled their glasses, then lifted his in toast as she returned. "But we were out in good time, little Rose. We won't be caught up in the pandemonium. We have our money, and that's more than is assured for others. A lot of brokers are bankrupt. They won't be able to pay for the gold they promised to buy today at prices going up to one hundred sixty. The exchange operates on trust—if a trader reneges on either a buy or sell order, there just aren't any laws to punish him. A deal made on the trading floor isn't worth a penny unless everyone honors the trust. Since it's becoming obvious that several of the biggest traders can't meet their obligations, there's fear that the exchange itself will collapse. And if that happens . . ."

She served his plate. In all the excitement he hadn't felt hungry, but the smell of hot biscuits and rare roasted beef with gravy awoke his appetite. He looked down at the food. "Did you cook this?" he asked in disbelief.

"You've got to be kidding," she replied. "I paid the neighbor to do it."

Lloyd applied himself to the meal.

"When Washington and the rest of the country realize what has happened, they'll start looking for scapegoats," Rosanna said. "Wouldn't now be a good time for us to reward ourselves with a vacation, an ocean voyage, perhaps?"

"Not necessary. They'll have their scoundrels," Lloyd said. "The press is already calling Fisk the ring-tailed financial orangutan, and they're casting Gould as the devil himself."

"But, Lloyd"—Rose pouted—"all my riches are burning a hole in my purse. I have a desire to be foolish, to spend shocking amounts on frivolous little Paris hats and gowns."

"Maybe later," Lloyd said. "I wouldn't miss what's going to happen here for a million dollars."

"We can read about it in the newspapers."

"Now, Rose, aren't you interested in seeing how Dan Butterfield explains his part in the affair?"

She laughed. "Oh, he'll explain it. He's already doing so. I stopped by to see the general before coming home. He was rather agitated. I think the suddenness of the crash and the totality of it has him running scared. When a newspaperman asked him how word got to the market so quickly that the Treasury was planning to sell gold, he said that someone must have tapped the telegraph lines from Washington."

"There's another reason for staying here in New York," Lloyd said. "The gold clearinghouse is going to be in confusion for a while, and as long as there's a possibility that the Gold Exchange Bank might fail, the market for stocks and bonds is going to be extremely volatile. You say your money is clamoring to you to buy a new gown? Well, mine is saying, 'Opportunity knocks, Lloyd. Keep your eyes open.' There'll be some good investments to be had cheaply, Rose. Want me to take a flyer or two for you?"

"Thanks just the same, sir," she said, laughing. "I'm pleased to be just moderately rich. I've tried it both ways—poor and not so poor—and I like the latter much better. I still think you should consider leaving the country for a while. What if someone like Phineas Headley decides to investigate what role one Mr. Lloyd Miles had in the gold corner?"

He lifted his eyebrows in shock. "Who? Me? Why, sir, I'm only a salaried employee in the Erie Railroad's Washington office. What would I, a mere wage slave, know about such rarefied things as the gold market?" He looked at her closely. "Why would you bring up Headley's name?"

"Because the man introduced himself to me after you left the Gold Room. He asked about you."

"And?"

"And nothing. I played Mickey the Dunce." Her eyes took on an angry light. "Can't understand why Lafe would have chosen Headley as his biographer. He certainly wasn't very impressive."

Lloyd chuckled. "You're still upset you weren't mentioned in Lafe's book. Listen, Rose, the man simply kept his word to you. You can't fault him for that."

"I suppose not, but when I told Headley my name, he had no reaction whatsoever. Either he's a very good actor, or Lafe never told him about me." She blew out a sigh. "I can't help the way I feel, Lloyd, and for some stupid reason I'm as angry with Phineas Headley as I am with Lafe Baker. That reporter had better stay out of my way, that's all I have to say."

Panic selling, triggered by fears that a prolonged crisis in gold would keep the cost of credit at impossible heights, hit the New York Stock Exchange on Tuesday. Among the stocks hit hardest was that of Cornelius Vanderbilt's New York Central, which fell from $177 to $150. On Wednesday a flood of business failures began to swamp the financial world. To add to Vanderbilt's worries his broker, LeGrand Lockwood, owner of Lockwood and Company, a Wall Street fixture for a quarter of a century, went into insolvency because of the stock market's woes and began to sell stock in total desperation.

New York Central stock then fell to $147. To save the Central, which was the centerpiece of his financial empire, Vanderbilt began to muster his reserves, draining all his cash accounts and selling off his interests in hosts of subsidiary operations, including one small western railroad known to only a few people outside its limited web of rails in southern Kansas.

Lloyd Miles was fascinated, watching the financial circus. Jay Gould's connection with Tammany Hall was paying off, for Gould had used his political influence to get favorable rulings from judges regarding the muddled situation at the Gold Exchange. Abel Corbin was showing signs of panic, just as Lloyd had feared at the time when he saw the letter that Julia Grant had written to her sister-in-law.

Lloyd paid a visit to the Erie offices in the opera house, where Gould and Fisk were holed up, hiding from the wrath of men who had been ruined on Black Friday. Fisk owed money to many of them. There Lloyd learned that Gould had sent a man to Dan Butterfield and demanded that Butterfield come up with the money to pay for the $150 million worth of gold that Gould had bought in his name. Jim Fisk, meanwhile, was claiming that he had not given orders to pay $160 for gold while the market was crashing or while prices were falling to normal levels. As a result the brokers who had been doing Fisk's trading were ruined.

But in all of the cacophony and hysteria Lloyd noticed an interesting pattern. He shook his head in admiration, for there was one man fighting a momentous battle, and the stakes were nothing less than the financial well-being of the United States. Cornelius Vanderbilt was the one bulwark that was keeping the financial world from falling into the abyss of depression. He was refused credit by bank after bank, even while he risked everything he had built over the years. Finally he reached across the Atlantic and borrowed ten million in cash from British interests. On Wednesday he poured his new capital into the market.

Lloyd watched in awe and with no little admiration as Vanderbilt alone stopped the debacle. He had a feeling that if it hadn't been for the efforts of the old man, Black Friday on the Gold Exchange would have paled in comparison to a stock market crash on Wednesday. But by the end of the day the panic was over. Bargain hunters were placing buy orders.

One of the speculators following a dictum as old as trading itself—buy at the bottom—was Lloyd Miles. He had watched the action closely as Vanderbilt took advantage of the misfortunes of others by buying a controlling interest in the Lake Shore Railroad, a gateway to the West. At first Lloyd was tempted to ride Vanderbilt's coattails and to buy into Lake Shore. Then he hesitated, realizing that he would be only a minority stockholder, with his interest at the mercy of any whim of Vanderbilt—or even Jay Gould, who, although he'd been in no position to battle Vanderbilt for the Lake Shore, had coveted the railroad for a long time. Gould and Vanderbilt would certainly go toe-to-toe again in the future, and Lloyd was not powerful enough to keep pace in such company. For now he was willing to take the leavings of the financial giants, and in the pandemonium of the near crash, Vanderbilt had left a tasty crumb.

Lloyd put his gold market profits into a small spur line in the Midwest, a railroad called the Kansas City and Southwest, or the KC&S. He bought the company quietly, in relatively small blocks of stock, knowing that it was on the market only because Vanderbilt had needed money and had considered the KC&S to be unimportant. The small railroad was running smoothly, hauling grain and cattle from the southern Kansas plains to the railheads in Kansas City. Lloyd did not plan to become an active force in running the KC&S until, perhaps, the market had normalized. He decided to stay in the background and let the line continue to haul cows and wheat.

Since he now owned over fifty percent of KC&S stock, only a few shares would change hands on the market, and then only occasionally, not enough to bring attention to the railroad until he was ready to announce to the world that a small, unknown line in the Midwest had suddenly become a highly desirable property.

For weeks Lloyd was content to remain with the Washington office of the Erie Railroad. His salary continued to be paid, although he had no contact with Gould or Fisk, who were still in the New York office. He took Leah on a shopping binge to replace the jewelry that he had sold in order to increase his profits in gold trading. Earlier, he had succeeded in buying back the small diamond solitaire that had been given to her by Philip Trent. To Lloyd's relief his sister seemed to be pacified.

The gold affair was going the way of past political scandals in the United States. Public anger, having a short life, soon changed into an attitude of bemused unconcern or, at most, interest only in the entertainment aspects of having rogues and worthies roasted in the newspapers. Quite often the villains became celebrities.

Lloyd was not surprised when Jim Fisk, in an exclusive interview with Phineas Headley, tried to take the heat off himself by implicating the presidential family. In a carefully written report Headley quoted Fisk as saying that Abel Corbin, the President's brother-in-law, had been the Gold Ring's contact with Ulysses S. Grant. Although no direct accusation was made, it was clear that Fisk was trying to convict Grant himself of complicity. Somehow Fisk knew about Julia Grant's letter, and although a few readers decried dragging a lady's name through such a cesspool of venality, the nation was shocked to learn that the President's wife had warned her brother-in-law to get out of the gold market lest he lose his fortune.

"How can they say such things about the hero of Appomattox?" Leah asked Lloyd.

"Little people ache to pull their betters down to their own level," Lloyd said. He pointed out that one newspaper, the Albany *Morning Express,* stated flatly that the charges against Grant were "base calumnies." The *Express* gave Grant credit for crushing the Gold Ring by selling government coin. But it was the only newspaper in which the President was the hero and not a villain.

"I think Jim Fisk is a blatant coward," Leah said, "trying to hide his own guilt behind the skirts of a woman."

"Yes, it's a shame that he had to bring the name of the President's wife into the affair," Lloyd agreed. "But it's a greater shame, isn't it, that the President's wife would put herself into a position so exposed that she could be made the butt of scandal?"

"Well, I think that their only sin—the President's and Mrs. Grant's—is of having corrupt relatives," Leah said.

* * *

By the clever use of the law and lawyers Jay Gould had arranged to have the Gold Exchange Bank put into receivership. The receiver was a Boss Tweed man and, thus, a Gould man. Once again Gould, called by the New York *Herald* "the great gorilla of Wall Street, the gold-gobbling Gould," was in full control. Not one penny could be released by the Gold Exchange without a word from the opera house.

Dan Butterfield refused to pay for the losses Gould had suffered on the gold he had purchased in the general's name. Butterfield granted an interview to Phineas Headley, in which he stated that the blackness and criminality of Jim Fisk and Jay Gould had brought on Black Friday and that their accusations against himself, the President, and Abel Corbin were groundless, worthless trash.

Following this publication Gould produced the canceled ten-thousand-dollar check he'd given Butterfield. Butterfield resigned from the New York subtreasury and went abroad.

In late autumn the hubbub in the press abated. In Washington, Lloyd watched and waited. He was not surprised to see both Gould and Fisk show signs of emerging unscathed from the debacle, while others, including U. S. Grant, had suffered irreparable damage to fortune or reputation.

While making his rounds in Washington, keeping up his contacts, Lloyd learned that when Congress convened in the new year, there would be a congressional investigation into the scandal and crash. He was not impressed, however. There was always one investigative committee or another at work in Washington, and nothing much ever came of them. For example, Philip Trent's group was still probing and poking at the Crédit Mobilier affair, and that was ancient history.

In November, Lloyd was summoned to New York by his employer. He left Washington willingly, eager to get back to the focal point of the nation's financial action. He was not yet ready to make the KC&S Railroad a household name, but in New York he could more efficiently keep his fingers on the pulse of the stock market. He took rooms in a moderately priced hotel. He didn't want to draw attention to his new—and, to him, exalted—financial status by staying in a first-class place. He did allow himself one luxury: He dined in the finest restaurants and tipped generously. Soon his arrival at any one of a dozen places produced instant activity on the part of headwaiters.

He tried to contact Rose, but she had closed up her flat and disappeared, leaving no messages.

At work he found himself acting as errand boy for Gould and Fisk. In spite of the multiple investigations getting under way into the gold market crash, life on the Erie Railroad went on. There was business to be conducted—men were to be seen, and messages needed to be sent. The communications were so sensitive that they could not be trusted to paper and had to be delivered orally.

Lloyd decided that it was not a good time to talk about the possibility of his moving permanently to New York. Gould was still too preoccupied with the failed gold corner. In addition, since his money was tied up in gold, Gould had lost the chance to obtain the Lake Shore Railroad during the stock-market panic.

At the end of his workday Lloyd found himself left to his own devices. For the first few days he was content to go to bed early. Soon, however, he was adjusted to New York's faster pace and was not content to spend his evenings with a book or to end them an hour or two after dark. He began thinking about the time when he would make a home in the city and have Leah with him. He wanted his sister to enjoy all the benefits of his small fortune and of the larger one that he was certain he would have in the not-too-distant future.

His social contacts in New York were limited. Jennie Corbin and her husband were in seclusion. Corbin's health, it was said, had been ruined by the recent events. Jay Gould had never been a social animal, and Jim Fisk's idea of high society was to have a tumble with one of the ladies from the opera company or to spend the evening seeing a show with his live-in mistress, Josie Mansfield.

Lloyd made constant efforts to gain an entry into the social life of New York. When his business for the Erie put him into contact with men of means, he never failed to extend an invitation to lunch. Occasionally the offer was accepted, and he would spend an hour or two inspiring some lesser member of New York's Four Hundred to talk about himself, for he had learned long ago that a good listener was a scarce commodity valued by everyone—even a man who counted his millions on the fingers of two hands and his toes. Once or twice his lunch invitations were reciprocated, but never in the form of a bid to join the pillars of society in their own little world of banquets and galas.

Meanwhile, as messenger boy because of Gould's enforced immobility, he was learning interesting things about the business of the Erie twins and, in the process, about Tammany Hall. He had occasionally been sent to the chambers of Judge Albert Cardozo. Cardozo had helped Gould with the tremendous coup that put the Gold Exchange Bank into the hands of a receiver friendly to William Tweed and, therefore, to Gould. During each visit Judge Cardozo had been cordial to Lloyd. Cardozo was only forty. He had met Boss Bill Tweed years before, when they were members of a lodge that admitted both Jews (Cardozo) and struggling young firemen (Tweed). The two had remained loyal friends. Tweed's Tammany had made Cardozo first a judge, then a member of the state supreme court.

Shortly before Christmas Lloyd delivered a sealed envelope to Albert Cardozo in his court chambers. He didn't have to guess twice what was in the packet, for it had the size and heft of greenbacks. On that day the judge was exceptionally friendly. He greeted Lloyd pleasantly and offered a holiday drink, which was immediately accepted.

"By the way, Miles," the judge said as Lloyd rose to leave, "we're having a little pre-Christmas gathering at my house Saturday night. It would please me if you joined us."

"Thank you, sir," Lloyd said, "but I'm afraid . . ." He

paused. His first inclination had been to refuse. Cardozo was a friendly fellow and an ally of Tweed's and Gould's, but Lloyd wasn't interested in becoming a part of a social circle that was centered around Jewish people. Then he reconsidered. "On second thought, sir," he said, "I would love to join you. I have a previous engagement, but I've just decided to break it."

"Good, good." Cardozo smiled broadly. "And don't worry about having to eat exotic food, my boy. We're not an ethnic household."

It was evident that it paid to be a judge friendly to the Tammany. Albert Cardozo lived in a brownstone just off Fifth Avenue. Winter was being kind to the city, so Lloyd had walked from his hotel. The house was ablaze with light. The sound of merry voices and music came through the closed windows. He was admitted by a servant in livery. Cardozo greeted him, then presented him to Mrs. Cardozo.

"Well, Miles, I imagine you'll see people you know, so just circulate," Cardozo encouraged. "There's food laid out in the dining room. You'll find the bar by seeking out the biggest crowd of people."

Lloyd saw a lawyer he'd come to know through Erie business, nodded, shook hands, and exchanged small talk. He made his way to the bar, filled one hand with a glass of heavily watered whiskey, and stood with his back to a wall to assess the smiling, chattering, milling people. He turned to find Abby Kershaw, slim, regal, her black hair swirled atop her head, coming toward him from only feet away. He felt an electric shock of recognition as he looked into her large green eyes. He nodded.

She halted in front of him. "You do have a way of turning up, don't you?" she asked.

He remembered their last meeting, the softness of her, the heat he'd experienced when she pushed her strong, hard thigh tightly against his as they danced. But he could also remember how she'd told her friends that they needn't bother with him, since he was only an employee of the Erie Railroad.

"Well, if it isn't beautiful Miss Kershaw," he said. "The epitome of politeness and consideration."

"And you, you're the railroad worker, aren't you?" she asked.

"They call us gandy dancers," he said.

"Oh, hardly," she said. She had a splendid, deep laugh, an unabashed outburst of pleasure. "But since you've mentioned dancing—"

"I don't recall that I did," Lloyd said.

"What brings a stiff-necked goy like you to a fine Yiddish household like this?" she asked.

"Invitation." He couldn't understand how he could hate the cold-eyed, imposing girl and ache for her at the same time.

"Not mine."

"No."

"Are you now in politics?"

"I have the Tammany Hall opium concession," he said with a straight face.

"How exciting."

"Look, do you want to dance or not?"

"I would like to dance," she said.

The floor was crowded. She was constantly being pressed against him. She made no attempt to prevent body contact, and when his manly nature caused a certain intimate portion of his anatomy to change, she pressed against him more tightly. When the dance ended he kept her with him by holding her hand, and when the band started playing again she came back into his arms.

He was flushed. His breathing was indicative of the desire he felt for her. She smiled up into his face. Her green eyes shone, and her full lips were invitingly glossy. The way she clung to him, dragged her thighs against his, and brushed past that engorged mound at his groin made him forget that once she had insulted him.

"I must see you again," he told her.

"Oh, must you?"

"Please."

"Don't beg. I don't like men who whimper and beg."

"I was merely being polite. When can I see you again?"

"Perhaps Judge Cardozo will invite you to his party again next year. I'll probably be here."

"Damn it, Abby—"

"Miss Kershaw, if you don't mind."

He thrust his loins at her. She pushed back, smiling mockingly. "Miss Kershaw, may I call on you one day next week?"

"You asked a similar question once before," she said. "The answer is still no." She jerked away from him and left him standing in the middle of the dance floor. Although the lights were dim and the floor was crowded, he was sure that everyone would notice the bulge below his waist. He pulled his coat together and edged his way into the dining room. Abby Kershaw was standing at the table, selecting tidbits of food for a tall, elegant, white-haired man to whom she showed a definite resemblance.

"There he is now, Father," Abby said, inclining her head toward Lloyd.

Psaleh Kershaw examined Lloyd with critical eyes, lifted one hand, and called out in a deep baritone voice, "You. Miles."

Lloyd was still seething. He walked to the table and looked across it into Kershaw's eyes. "*Mister* Miles," he said.

"Well then, *Mister* Miles," Kershaw said, "I want you to stop pestering my daughter."

"To my knowledge," Lloyd said coldly, "I never started such an activity."

"You're one of that scoundrel Gould's men, are you not?" Kershaw didn't give Lloyd a chance to answer. "And a damned social climber as well. Hear me, now. I mean this: You leave my daughter alone, or I'll see to it that you're horsewhipped and run out of town."

Lloyd's face flushed darkly. Abby was smiling at him, her green eyes twinkling. "Having fun?" he asked her, ignoring the old man.

"Loads of it," she said.

"Young man!" Kershaw thundered.

Lloyd returned his cold gaze to the old man. "For the moment," he said, "I'm going to ignore your rudeness and your daughter's also." He turned and left.

Kershaw's angry voice followed him out of the room. He found Albert Cardozo and expressed his appreciation for the invitation and his regrets at having to leave so early.

Once outside, he found that the temperature had dropped. He pulled his topcoat collar up around his throat and walked to Fifth Avenue to find a hansom cab. Once in the cab he gave the address of his hotel. He sank back in the seat and gave his simmering anger its head. Out of his silent fury, Abby Kershaw's face emerged, so beautiful, her eyes like green ice. He wished he could see Rosanna; she would have made him feel better.

He was almost at his hotel when another face came to mind. It was a softer visage than Abby's, and a less beautiful one than Rose's, but it belonged to a woman with no viciousness to her—Tennessee Claflin.

"Cabbie," he said, "do you know Great Jones Street?"

"Know it well, sir."

"Show it to me."

Although not as grand as its counterpart off Fifth Avenue, the brownstone on Great Jones Street was as well lit, and music was coming from within. Lloyd told the cabbie to wait. He knocked and, when the door pushed open at his touch, walked unnoticed into a milling group of dancers. He saw Victoria Woodhull immediately. She was holding court at the far end of the room and talking with animation. Tennessee was leaning on a baby grand piano, smiling down at the musician at the keyboard. Lloyd walked to stand at her shoulder and whispered hello into her ear.

She turned. Her smile was bland, polite. And then she remembered him, and her lips spread. She kissed him wetly and said, "Well, where have you been?"

"In Washington, yearning for you," Lloyd answered.

"I'm so pleased to see you," Tennessee said. "This affair was becoming such a bore."

"As a matter of fact, I've come to take you away from all this boredom."

"Wonderful," she whispered, leaning close, lifting her mouth toward his. "Dinner first. I'm famished."

"Where?"

"Delmonico's."

"My pleasure."

The cab was waiting. After Lloyd had helped Tennessee inside, the driver laughed and said, "I thought you didn't know Great Jones Street, sir."

"Just drive," Tennessee said, "and keep your mouth shut."

They made a handsome pair. Heads turned as the maître d' at Delmonico's ushered them to a choice table. A wine steward and waiter were there immediately, bowing and smiling. Lloyd ordered for Tennessee as well as for himself.

"My, my," she said in approval of his selections, "you have come up in the world, haven't you?"

"Well, we try, you know," Lloyd said with a modest smile.

"I think I'm going to allow you to spend a few days with me," Tennessee said.

"My pleasure."

"And nights."

"My *sincere* pleasure." He touched her hand. "I have missed you."

"My old boy is so busy these days," Tennessee explained, referring to Commodore Vanderbilt.

Lloyd laughed. "Charming," he protested. "First you make me think you're fond of me, and then you tell me that I'm second choice."

Tennessee gave him a beaming smile that dimpled her cheeks. "Oh, come now, darling. We are more sophisticated than that, aren't we?"

Lloyd was genuinely amused. He chuckled. "Whatever you say, Tennie."

"I do hope that you have become as prosperous as you look," she warned. "I have expensive tastes."

"Is this to be a straight business transaction?" Lloyd asked.

"Naughty boy," she said, frowning.

"If so, let's talk turkey."

"Why are you trying to insult me?" she asked, pouting.

He pressed her hand between his. "Sorry. I understand. I am just the fellow who knows how to cater to a lovely lady with expensive tastes."

"There now, you can be nice," she teased.

He used the time spent over the meal to satisfy some of his curiosity about Tennessee and her sister, although he was full of impatient need for her. Her perfume wafted to him from across the table to remind him that Tennessee Claflin, sweet little dumpling that she was, was the smoothest, most sensuous woman he had ever known— with the possible exception of Rosanna. But Rose was soft in flesh only, whereas Tennessee had a pliant disposition, a sweet, outgoing temperament, and a liking for men, which she did not try to hide. It would be possible, he felt, to become permanently involved with Tennessee Claflin. A long-term liaison with Rosanna Pulliam, however, would be like living in a cage with a tiger.

"Well, darling boy," Tennessee was saying, primed into talking of herself and her family, "both Victoria and I developed early, you know. At twelve Victoria had the men swooning over her." She pouted prettily. "I was always so jealous. She had those huge, wide eyes, and her mouth was so full and pretty."

"You caught up with her quickly," Lloyd said.

"Thank you, dear. It wasn't easy, being one of ten children, and when Papa left us—" She looked up at him through thick eyelashes. "It isn't true that he left town just ahead of a lynch mob."

Lloyd raised one eyebrow. "It sounds like an interesting story."

"The townspeople said he was a barn burner," Tennessee said. "An out-and-out lie."

"I understand," Lloyd sympathized.

"We had to leave our home in Homer—"

"Homer?"

"Homer, Ohio," she said. "We traveled like a bunch of Gypsies in a covered wagon. Victoria was old enough to help Mama."

"Help her to do what?"

"Demonstrations of spiritualism."

"Seances?"

Tennessee nodded. "Seances, table rapping, spirit contact . . . we're both clairvoyant, you know."

"So I've been told," Lloyd said.

"Mama talked with God," she said, quite serious. Suddenly she laughed. The soprano trill caused heads to turn toward them. She leaned forward. "She used to scare the devil out of me, dancing around like a crazy lady, talking in some gibberish that she called 'tongues.' She could mesmerize us. She used mesmerism to cure us of our ailments."

"She sounds like quite a woman."

"She's a horrible old crone," Tennessee said. "If it weren't for Victoria, I'd have left that house. I sometimes think that Mama never was really clairvoyant. But Victoria is. When she was only three years old she went into a trance, and a man who had died—a neighbor—took her to the other world. She saw angels and flowers and beauty. After that our dead little sister came and played with her. And once Victoria saw the devil."

"No!" Lloyd prompted in exaggerated disbelief.

"Yes! He was tall. He had cloven hoofs instead of feet, and he kept a red silk handkerchief over his face."

"I wonder why."

"So that if Victoria ever does anything really wrong and he comes for her, she won't recognize him."

"That's logical," Lloyd allowed.

"Did I tell you that our neighbors in Homer conducted a benefit to raise money for us?"

"That was nice of them."

"Yes and no." She giggled. "They were raising money to help us leave town."

Her laughter was contagious. He could not remember a time when he'd enjoyed a meal so much. He was sorry, in a way, to see it end. He knew that she would occupy his bed, and he was eager for that, but she was so flirtatious, so juicy in her youthful prettiness, that it was a genuine pleasure just being with her. Just before they left the restaurant, she decided to read his palm.

"Ah, my poor, darling boy," she whispered, after gazing at his hand for some time. "You didn't have it easy, either, did you? There was a time when you were hungry, and alone." She lifted her brown eyes to his. "You were always alone, weren't you, except for, ummm, a special someone. A woman. Not a lover. Mother? No. Ah, a sister. Am I right?"

"You are."

"Well, you're a fighter, aren't you? There's a great deal of stubbornness in you. You usually get what you want."

"Right now I want you," he said.

"You see? I'm always right." She purred at him. "I intend to see to it that you get what you want, and as quickly as possible."

In the cab he drew her to him. There was little talk. After he closed the door to his hotel room he found her to be as eager as she'd been on the night he first met her, and as skillful in pleasing him.

In the witching hours they lay side by side. She asked him about his childhood. He told her, speaking of Leah in tones of affection and respect.

"I envy your sister," she confessed. "My brothers like me, I suppose, in their own way. Even my papa likes me. But I've never had a brother love me the same way you love your sister."

He didn't want her mood to become somber. "Enough about me," he said. "When last we heard of the traveling Claflin family, they were headed cross-country in a covered wagon."

"Mama and Victoria told fortunes and gave spirit demonstrations," she said, always willing to talk about herself. "I developed a talent for magnetic healing."

"Whatever that is."

"I told you," she said, slapping him lightly on the belly. "I have magic in my hands—healing power, human magnetism. I did all right until Papa bought the recipe for some stuff called the Elixir of Life and had me sell it as a cure for everything. I'd been treating a woman with magnetic healing and the elixir, and she died of cancer in the breast. They charged me with manslaughter."

"Good Lord, I am consorting with a criminal," Lloyd teased.

"No, because I was acquitted."

"You smiled at the jury, and they were lost."

"No, I gave them a glimpse of ankle."

"You're the damnedest girl." He let his hand appreciate areas of soft warmth. "When did you get married?"

"Not until after Victoria married Canning Woodhull. She was fifteen. We were holding seances for rich women in Cincinnati and Chicago. I married John Bartels."

"But kept your own name?"

"Yes. Now, I ask you, what kind of a name is Tennessee Bartels? Victoria had divorced Woodhull and married Colonel James Blood. The colonel said that we were wasting our talents in the provinces—that's what he called Chicago and the Midwest—and so we all packed up and moved to New York, the whole family. Papa was with us too. It was real odd, the way it happened. Out there in Cincinnati we sometimes looked like the witches in *Macbeth*—you know, Shakespeare?"

"I have a smattering of knowledge about the Bard."

"Stirring a pot in the backyard and mixing up Papa's Elixir of Life." She sighed. "That was where I misplaced John Bartels."

"How do you misplace a man?"

"Well, I had ten dollars in my handbag, and he wanted to know how it got there. I told him it was none of his business, and it wasn't my fault if he had a nasty, suspicious mind."

Lloyd roared. "Where *did* you get the ten dollars?"

"I didn't tell John Bartels, so why should I tell you?"

"Because we're friends," he said. "Because I'm interested."

"Well, I had expensive tastes, even then," she said coyly.

"So you came to New York," he prompted.

"The spirits told us to."

"I thought it was Colonel Blood."

"Actually it was both," she said. "Victoria wasn't sure what to do, so she consulted the spirits, and they told her, yes, go to New York. Go to Seventeen Great Jones Street. There you will find a house that is ready and waiting for you and yours. And then a ghostly figure appeared and wrote on a piece of paper on the table in front of us one word: *Demosthenes.*"

"Very specific, these spirits, and educated, too. But why the name of an ancient Greek orator?"

"I don't know. And don't be skeptical," she said. "What I'm telling you is the truth. We came to Seventeen Great Jones Street, and there was this brownstone house, empty and plenty big enough for our large family. When we went in to look at it what do you think was lying on a table in the parlor?"

"I can't even begin to guess," Lloyd said.

"A book."

"Ummm."

"The Orations of Demosthenes!"

"Well, it was fate," Lloyd said, hiding his amusement. "Which bring us up to date and to your old boy. How did you meet Vanderbilt?"

"Through Papa."

"The senior Claflin moves in heady circles," Lloyd said.

"Don't sell Buck Claflin short," she cautioned. She giggled. "My papa has conned smarter men than the commodore, after all. He knew that the old boy believed in spiritualism and magnetic healing. He just took me to Vanderbilt's office, shouted his way past the secretaries, and told the commodore that his little girl had magnetism and force in her right hand and tickles, squeezes, and slaps in her left."

"Who convinced Vanderbilt to set you and your sister up in the brokerage business?"

"Oh, that was Victoria. The old boy admires her brains."

"But not yours?"

She laughed and reached for him. "I've never really needed brains," she said.

"And I was just going to ask what you know about stocks and bonds."

"Buy low, sell high," she said.

"Well, that's about as much as most brokers know."

"That's all I need to know," she said, putting her soft, sweet weight on him, "because I know men, you see."

CHAPTER 10

For a short time the snow blanketing Manhattan was a pure and pristine white before vehicular traffic turned the streets into gray slush darkened here and there by horse droppings. A cold wind blowing down from the Great Lakes drifted the snow, exposing buried trash and ugliness.

Lloyd Miles picked his way carefully along sidewalks that were sheathed in a thin layer of ice. The offices of New York's only female stockbrokers were his destination. Victoria Woodhull and Tennessee Claflin handled some of Commodore Vanderbilt's business—the old boy figuring, no doubt, that since he had to pay a broker's commission and since he told his brokers exactly what actions to take, he might as well use money that was to be paid out anyway to support his little sparrow.

The commodore hadn't stinted when he had set up his spiritual adviser and his magnetic healer in business. The offices were luxurious and roomy. In the reception area a neatly lettered sign read: ALL GENTLEMEN WILL STATE THEIR BUSINESS AND THEN RETIRE AT ONCE.

"I'm here on monkey business," Lloyd Miles told Tennessee when she greeted him. He put his cold hands on her cheeks, and she cried, "Oh!"

"Monkey business is no exception to the rule," she said. "You still must retire at once, but I'll go with you. Victoria is so stuffy about it all."

"Speaking of whom," Lloyd said as Victoria Woodhull came out of her office and looked at them questioningly. "I'd like to meet your sister."

Victoria Claflin Woodhull—she had retained the name of her first husband despite her divorce and subsequent marriage to Colonel James Blood—wore her silky, brown, naturally curling hair in a loose, feminine bun. Her blue eyes looked out from a pleasant, regular face that glowed with the health and softness of her rose-petal skin. She was in her early thirties, at the peak of her womanhood.

"So you're the sly rogue who has been keeping my sister from us of late," Victoria said as she gave Lloyd her hand in a soft-firm greeting. "I'm going to have to take you to task, sir, for depriving us of Tennie's company."

"Perhaps you'd like to join us for lunch," Lloyd said.

"Yes, do," Tennessee urged.

"Thank you," Victoria said. "Just let me get my wrap. Is it still frightfully cold outside?"

"Cold enough," Lloyd said.

From the beginning of time it has been pleasing for a man to escort pretty ladies and to be the envy of other men. Lloyd was no exception to the rule. He basked in the attentions of the sisters during the meal. They vied with each other in saying witty and often outrageous things but were equals in their ability to make Lloyd feel as if he were king of the universe and the object of all female desires. As it happened often with Tennessee, the subject turned to money.

"Lloyd became quite rich during the bull market on the Gold Exchange," Tennessee told Victoria.

"Good for Lloyd," Victoria said, eyeing him with new interest. "Perhaps you'd like to place some of your funds with Woodhull and Claflin for investment?"

"Perhaps I will," Lloyd said. "Although at the moment I'm into rails, and as you know, they're doing very well."

Tennessee laughed. "And I'm very glad they are. At least

the old boy is pleased for a change. You see? You do have something else in common with the commodore."

"I'm sorry to say that I'm not yet in Vanderbilt's class," Lloyd said ruefully. He grinned. "That's not to say that I won't be."

"I'm sure you will be," Tennessee said. "In all my life I've seen only two people whose financial future I could read without a shadow of a doubt. I know that you're going to be a very, very rich man, darling boy."

"And who was the other one?" Lloyd asked.

"Why, Victoria, of course," Tennessee replied. "When she was very young, a man in a Greek tunic appeared to her—"

"Demosthenes?" Lloyd asked, smiling at Victoria.

"She told you," Victoria said accusingly.

"—and told her," Tennessee continued, "that she would know wealth and power, that she would live in a mansion and be ruler of her people."

"Do you prefer to be queen or president?" Lloyd wanted to know.

Victoria's blue eyes went cold, telling him that she didn't appreciate his frivolity.

"There were times when I didn't believe," Tennessee said quite seriously. "Once when things were bad and I was little more than a baby, I was shipped off to relatives in Pennsylvania, away from Victoria and all my other sisters and brothers. I cried and cried because I thought that the Greek had lied. You see, I knew that if Victoria was going to be rich she'd take care of me."

Victoria seemed to have forgiven Lloyd. "And while she was in the bosom of our aunt's family, she frightened the young ones and mystified the old ones by reading minds. She told a farmer exactly where to find a lost calf."

"They were an ungrateful bunch, though," Tennessee said. "When I told them that there was going to be a fire at the seminary and sure enough there was, they accused me of setting it."

Victoria laughed. "Like father like daughter."

"Now, Victoria," Tennessee admonished, her eyes flashing, "that's a terrible thing to say. You know I didn't set the fire."

"Of course not, darling," Victoria said, patting her sister's soft, plump hand. She asked Lloyd, "How do plan to become as wealthy as my little sister's old boy?"

"As a matter of fact, I have something in mind," Lloyd said. "When everything is in place—quite soon, perhaps this summer—I'll let Tennie know. You might want to go along for the ride. It'll be profitable if you know when to get off."

"And you'll tell us that too?" Victoria asked.

"My pleasure."

"Vee," Tennessee said, "maybe there's something we can do to help Lloyd?"

Victoria smiled benignly. "We'll see." She reached for Lloyd's hand and held it tightly. Her eyes closed, and an intensity of thought emanated from her—an emotion, perhaps, or something else that created an almost tangible connection between them. "Yes," she whispered at last. "Yes, I think I understand."

"What is it?" Tennessee asked eagerly.

"Hush," Victoria said. She released Lloyd's hand. "What you plan will not take place soon," she said. "But in the meantime there will come an opportunity. It will come but once, and you will have to be ready."

"Thank you," Lloyd said. He wanted to laugh. What Victoria had said was fortune-teller talk, vague predictions that, in retrospect, could be made to fit almost any event. But he could not help feeling a bit unnerved by the intensity of the force that had flowed out from her. It was impossible for him to determine whether Victoria's mind had touched his or whether, since he was a normally healthy male with normal male appetites and reactions, he was merely reacting to her overt femaleness.

Although his family was constantly trying to wean Commodore Vanderbilt away from "those vixens," the notorious sisters, the old man made his way regularly to the brokerage offices near Wall Street. He appeared on a bright, sunny day in late winter, and both Tennessee and Victoria dropped everything, told the secretaries they did not want to be disturbed, and retired with Cornele to a room kept specifically for the purpose of contacting the spirits.

Vanderbilt took a chair at a round, solidly built oak table. Victoria sat across from him, Tennessee to his right.

"You girls know that I was skinned a little bit during that mess about gold, I reckon," the old man began.

"But you have recovered," Victoria said.

"Yes, I have," he agreed, "leastwise in the pocketbook. I hain't recovered yet from being goddamned unhappy with a few fellers that brought on the whole mess."

"I understand," Victoria said.

"Tory," the commodore said, "I want the goddamned Erie Railroad, and I want to skin that bastard Gould while I'm gittin' it."

"Shall we consult the spirits?" Victoria asked.

Tennessee drew heavy draperies over the two windows in the small room. In the gloom Victoria directed her sister and the commodore to place their hands on the heavy table. She closed her eyes. Her skin seemed to lighten, to pale. For some time they remained silent and motionless. Only the sound of the old man's raspy breathing could be heard.

"Yessss," Victoria slurred, and under their hands the solid oaken table quivered. It tilted, lifting three legs from the floor. "Yes, spirits!" she cried out sharply. "You know, yes, you know!"

The heavy table rocked, the legs thumping the floor loudly. One of the draperies' panels over a closed window billowed out for a moment, admitting a flash of brilliant daylight.

Tennessee moaned softly. "I hear them, Victoria," she whispered.

"They are saying—" Victoria halted, tilted her head, and listened intently. "You have a plan, Commodore," she whispered, "a plan to confound your enemies."

"I'm going to lower the freight rates on the New York

Central until I break the Erie," Vanderbilt said. "Ask 'em if that'll work."

"Oh, spirits," Victoria crooned, "you have heard. What is your answer?"

"Yesss," a bass voice rumbled, filling the room. "Yessss."

Vanderbilt was startled. He looked around, wide-eyed, but saw nothing. "I figure Gould's almost broke after his gold fiasco. I heard he got skinned real good. Are those spirits sayin' that I can finish him off by takin' away all of the Erie's business through low freight rates?"

Victoria started jerking violently. She went stiff. Her lids were open, but only the white of her eyes was visible. Her voice was low, odd. "Your desires will be granted so long as you are faithful to the spirits. That which you want is to be yours. Go forth and do not give up the struggle."

She sighed, then shook herself. The table fell to the floor with a crash.

Tennessee said, "Well, my goodness!"

"I am so very tired," Victoria said, slumping in her chair.

Tennessee leapt to her feet and took Victoria's arm. "Come with me, darling. You need rest." She pouted her lips at the commodore. "You just wait right here, Cornele. I'll be back before you know it."

As the door to the spirit room closed behind them, Victoria straightened. "Run on back, dear," she said. "He's waiting."

The only other furniture in the spirit room was a soft bed. It was time for the old boy's magnetic healing . . . among other things.

Vanderbilt began his campaign against his old enemy, the Erie Railroad, slowly. He cut freight rates on the New York Central only slightly, then nodded in satisfaction when Jay Gould followed suit immediately in order to keep the Erie's rates competitive. Now and then the old man would go back to the spirit room to be reassured and to feel the magnetic healing in the hands of the succulent Tennessee.

Meanwhile, the brownstone on Great Jones Street, the

sisters realized, had served its purpose. The Claflin family moved to 15 East Thirty-eighth Street, off Fifth Avenue, in the high-class Murray Hill district. The money that had made the move possible came from three sources: commissions on Vanderbilt's stock trading, putting their own money to work according to tips from the master of Wall Street shenanigans, and business that came to their brokerage firm from friends of the commodore's.

Delmonico's, near Wall Street, had opened an uptown branch at Fourteenth Street and Fifth Avenue. It featured Paris cuisine, and it quickly became, Tennessee knew, a favorite of Lloyd's. She hadn't been seeing much of him of late, for her old boy was demanding her time, much to the chagrin of the Vanderbilt family. She knew Lloyd would be pleased when she sent him a note to meet her for dinner at the new Delmonico's.

She arrived a quarter hour early, paid and tipped the cabdriver, then swayed into the foyer—only to be told politely that unescorted ladies were not served after six P.M.

She could have explained, of course, that she was meeting her escort there, but she was, after all, copublisher of a new voice for women, *Woodhull and Claflin's Weekly*. Actually, Victoria and Colonel Blood were the ones so all-fired interested in the matter of women's suffrage. But to be turned away from a restaurant because of her gender was a direct attack on her, and Tennessee rose to the challenge. She walked outside and called the cabdriver, who was still waiting for a fare, gave him a greenback of pleasing denomination, and thus escorted, took a table. It was there that Lloyd found them. The cabdriver, ill at ease, gladly made his escape from the crazy woman.

Tennessee had grown to be quite fond of Lloyd Miles— or as fond as she could be of one man. He pleased her. He bought her nice gifts. He was always polite and considerate, and he was a delightful scamp in bed. It was time, she had decided, to give him the help that Victoria had promised. Tennessee dropped her tidbit of information during their very pleasant dinner.

"So how are things at the railroad?" she inquired.

"You're suddenly interested in railroads?" he asked.

"I just wondered if you had noticed anything interesting happening lately."

He mused for a moment. "Nope, can't say that I have."

"Do you ever look at freight rates, darling boy?"

"Never. Should I?"

She let her eyes rove toward the ceiling, a tight little smile on her face. "Well, one never knows."

Lloyd took a look at freight rates the next day. He rubbed his chin in thought as he saw that there'd been three separate rate cuts in the past few weeks. It didn't take much time to find out that the Erie's rates had been lowered in response to cuts by the New York Central. The old man was up to something.

Before Lloyd could coax Tennessee into his bed again, there'd been another round of price cuts.

"Your old boy is going after the Erie, isn't he?" he asked Tennessee.

"I don't worry my head about such matters," she said.

"But you knew. That's why you asked me about freight rates. Is he going to try to break the Erie by taking away all the business with lower rates?"

"What does it look like to you?" she asked, a bit guilty.

"I'm not sure what good it will do me," Lloyd said, "but thank you for calling my attention to it."

"Call it sort of a farewell gift," she told him.

He lifted his head to look at her. "Farewell? I don't like the sound of that."

"I don't either, darling," she confided, nuzzling him, "but the old boy is a little restless now that he's doing battle with the Erie again, and he *needs* me."

"I need you too," Lloyd said with an intensity that surprised him. Having gone that far, he took the plunge. "Why don't you marry me, Tennie?"

She kissed him tenderly. "Thank you."

"Is that a yes?"

"That's no, darling boy." She pinched him playfully. "Good gracious, we'd make a terrible married couple."

"Would we? I think we go well together."

"In bed, Tiger," she said. "Picture this. You wake up in the morning and, knowing that you're going to have to go out into the cold to face the financial wars, you want some hot coffee and breakfast. But I just roll over and pull the blanket up to the tip of my nose."

He laughed. "We'll hire a maid and a cook."

"And you'll come home from work, but I won't be there because I'm out having dinner and with some nice young fellow."

He had no answer for that.

"Do you think, darling boy, that Vee and I are just trying to get attention when we write about equality for women?"

"I don't see what—"

"You have the right to go to bed with any woman you choose," she said. "I have that same right—with a man, of course."

"I thought—" He laughed. "Hell, I haven't heard any complaints from you."

She laughed with him. "But you see how impossible marriage would be, don't you? Free love is dignified only as long as its practitioners are, and I think you're the kind of fellow who'd punch some other chap in the nose for being free with your wife."

"Damn it, Tennie—"

"Now, come on, Lloyd. Admit it: you'd expect me to be the true-blue little woman, to stay at home and tend my oven and all that."

"I think we could work things out." But his voice carried no conviction. Her association with Vanderbilt hadn't bothered him, possibly because it was just too unbelievable to think of her in the arms of the old man; but to imagine her romping playfully and sensuously with a young man made him feel a bit desperate.

"Darling boy, keep in touch, won't you? Maybe, at some time in the future . . ."

"I will," he said.

But when she left his bed the next morning to go back to the house on East Thirty-eighth Street, he kissed her lingeringly and did not bother to say the words, but he thought, *Good-bye, little plum, good-bye.*

Congress had been in session for only days when Philip Trent returned to his office in midafternoon to find Miss Mercy and Adam and Julia Grey waiting for him in the reception room. A cake and coffee repast was arranged across Julia's desk.

"What's all this?" Philip asked.

"It's in the nature of congratulations," Adam Grey answered.

"For what, may I ask?" Philip inquired, raising his eyebrows.

"For being appointed a member of the Judiciary Committee, of course," Miss Mercy said primly.

Philip could see that the older woman had mixed emotions. She was genuinely happy for him, but she had worked for his predecessor for more than twenty years. J. T. Moverly had served a long apprenticeship before being named to such an influential committee. Philip Trent had served out J. T. Moverly's term after the old congressman died, and then had faced the Maryland electorate only once. He was just one degree better than a freshman representative, but already he was a mover and shaker on the committee investigating cost overrides on the Pacific Railroad. Now he was on one of the most important committees of all.

Philip rolled his eyes. "That's one of the problems with this town," he complained. "A man's staff knows more about what's going on than he does. How in the blazes did you get the news so fast? The majority leader told me about it less than a half hour ago."

"Naïveté is so becoming to you," Adam Grey said superciliously. "Who do you think told the majority leader?"

Miss Mercy giggled behind her hand.

"After all, Julia did arrange it," Adam said, trying to hide a grin.

"By gum, I don't doubt it," Philip said as Julia blushed under his gaze.

"I had a cup of coffee with the majority leader's private secretary this morning," Julia explained.

"Ah," Philip said. "I don't think I really want to know any more."

"Really, now," Julia protested. "She merely told me that it had been decided—I mean—oh, darn, you know that I couldn't arrange such an important thing."

"Naïveté does *not* become you, dear Julia," Adam said. He rolled his dolly to a chair and boosted himself up with his strong arms. "Now, if someone will serve the cake . . ."

Miss Mercy did the honors. Julia pulled up a chair next to her husband's. Philip sat on the end of her desk.

"It seems, Mr. Trent, that one of your first activities as a member of the Judiciary Committee will become a part of history," Julia said. "You will hear the first woman ever to testify before a congressional committee."

"That's splendid," Philip said sincerely. "Who is she, and what's the occasion?"

"Her name is Victoria Woodhull," Julia said.

"I don't think she'll be advocating free love, as she does in her magazine," Adam said.

Miss Mercy snorted. "Shocking."

"She'll be talking about the criminality of denying women the right to participate in the electoral process," Julia said.

"Hummmph!" Miss Mercy said. "J. T. Moverly didn't need women's votes to stay in office." She looked accusingly at Philip, who held up his hands defensively.

"Well, Miss Mercy," Adam said with a wink at Philip, "that's just it, you see. *Our* congressman is so handsome that he makes the common man jealous. We therefore would want to extend the franchise to women to be sure that we'll all have jobs when his term runs out."

"And that's how most of them would vote, too," Miss Mercy sniffed. "They'd vote for a handsome face and not the best man for the job."

"Mrs. Grey, would you please prepare a file on Mrs.

Woodhull for me before the time for her appearance?" Philip asked.

Julia nodded. "Yes, sir. It's already started."

"All this energy and efficiency makes me weary," Philip said after finishing his coffee. "I'm going into my office to have a nap. If anyone other than the President or a member of his cabinet wants me, tell him I'm in California."

He was not napping but going through transcripts of testimony before his investigating committee when Adam Grey knocked, then rolled into the room.

"Come in, Adam," Philip said, setting aside the paper he'd been reading. "I've been wanting to talk with you."

Adam swung up into a chair so he was on a level with Philip.

"I've been thinking about the Gold Ring scandal."

Adam nodded. Over the months since Adam had been coaxed into working in the office full-time, an easy relationship had developed between the two men. At first their friendship had been based on the strong tie that existed among all survivors of the four years of fratricidal mayhem that had been the war, but as they got to know each other something deeper developed. Philip respected Adam Grey's analytical-thinking abilities. Adam was pleased to find that his friend and employer was not only an honest man but an honorable one. Neither of them went around singing the other's praises in a loud voice, but they were aware of the strong elements of mutual admiration.

There was another bond between them that would have been more difficult to put into words. Adam Grey loved his wife. And although Philip Trent would have denied it and would have fought any man who intimated that he would be so dishonorable to his friend Adam, Philip also loved Julia Grey. Gus Trent was aware of it, and so was Adam Grey. To Adam's great credit he did not resent Philip's admiration of Julia. He knew in his heart that Philip would never make an improper overture to Julia. Besides, should the unthinkable happen and Philip lose his head, Julia would politely but firmly rebuff any advance.

Another aspect of Adam Grey's thinking that was never

voiced was related to his sure knowledge that his normal life span had been radically shortened. The wounds that he'd sustained on a sandy spit of beach in North Carolina near the end of the war had created chronic physical maladies. He would die, and worms would eat him, and Julia would be alone in the world. Because he had not been financially successful, Julia would be a young widow without means. Although Adam saved most of his salary, he was helpless to do anything substantial about providing for her future well-being. The most sensible solution would be for Julia to remarry.

Sometimes, when Adam lay in his bed and the unhealed ulcers in his stomach bubbled like molten lava, he thought of Julia's marrying another man. The emotional pain from that idea was as keen as the hurt in his belly; but pairing her in his imagination with Philip moderated the mental agony slightly. *I'll be gone,* he reminded himself. He'd either be strolling the golden streets of heaven or leaping about hot-footedly on the burning pavements of hell, but in either event he'd be too busy to worry about what was going on between one man and one woman left behind on earth. In his more lucid moments he told himself that after he was dead he could think of no man whom he'd prefer over Philip to take care of Julia.

Philip had been talking for some time, but the words had brushed past Adam's ears. Now he returned his full attention to the congressman, who was discussing Phineas Headley and the Gold Ring scandal. Adam caught up quickly.

"—sure that the ringleader was Jay Gould, but he's finding it difficult to get proof. He asked me if I had any ideas."

"It's over," Adam said. "The damage has been done. Why waste time looking up that dead dog's rump to see what made it die?"

"Well, I agree in principle," Philip said. "But wouldn't an investigation help to point out the weaknesses in a system that allows hundreds of millions of dollars' worth of gold to change hands on a man's word?"

Adam shrugged. "Want to change the stock market too?"

Philip nodded. "It could stand some changes."

"I think you're trying to talk yourself into biting off more than you can chew," Adam said.

Philip chuckled. "Well, if I do, I'll ask you to gnaw on it a little to help me. Wouldn't you like to know how Mr. Gould got a stranglehold on the money supply of the whole nation? Don't you think it might be a good idea to suggest the passage of a law or two to prevent its happening again?"

"I think, my friend, that you're more of a dreamer than I."

Philip shrugged. "Dreaming is thankless work, but someone has to do it."

"You're going to tackle it with your committee?"

"What do you think?"

"I think that if you do, you might do well to begin right here in Washington."

"Suggestions?"

"I'd call Lloyd Miles to be the first witness."

Philip grinned. "Are you way ahead of me on this?"

"I asked Phineas Headley to do some digging around in New York," Adam admitted, "just in case a certain congressman got a bee in his bonnet."

Philip looked surprised. "When did you do that? I didn't even know you were acquainted with Headley."

"I wasn't. At least not until after Headley wrote Lafe Baker's biography. Baker put Headley on Lloyd Miles's trail, and since you and Lloyd were friends, and since your committee was investigating Crédit Mobilier, I found Mr. Phineas Headley on my doorstep."

Philip thought for a moment. "Is Headley keeping you abreast of anything he learns?"

"Yes. I know, for example, that Lloyd Miles put a healthy pile of money into the gold market. Not nearly as much as some, but enough. He sold out before the crash. Headley couldn't get the exact amount, but he thinks that Miles became a millionaire. Interestingly enough, a man

who was once associated with Miles—Harold Berman—
also put a few hundred thousand dollars into the gold market but got stung. He went headfirst out a third-story window. The New York police said it was suicide."

"Right," Philip said skeptically. He turned his chair to
face the window, then looked down into the busy street.
"John O'Brian went out a window too." O'Brian, a congressman who had been involved in distributing Crédit
Mobilier stock to members of Congress, had landed on the
pointed spikes of a wrought-iron fence.

"I thought about O'Brian when I heard about this fellow
Berman," Adam said. "But during the course of a year
quite a few men and some women shuffle off this mortal
coil by bounding through a window."

"Miles went to work for the Erie Railroad," Philip said.

"He did."

"If we get into this thing," Philip said, "remind me that it
might be enlightening to have the committee ask a few
questions of my old friend Lloyd Miles."

"Will do," Adam promised.

The war had changed many things. Some changes were
as tenuous and as basic as adding words such as *shoddy* to
the language. This technical term for cloth made of re-
claimed wool and rags was transformed into a critical ad-
jective. Union soldiers had worn clothing made of shoddy
and had slept under shoddy blankets that tended to fall
apart . . . *shoddy*.

Other changes created by the war were more monumental. For example, because the war had eviscerated a generation of young men, it had altered forever the status of
women. Leah Miles was illustrative of the effect of the war
on many, for she was unmarried and fearful that she was
destined to remain so. Julia Grey was an example of another fundamental change affecting America—women in
the employment marketplace.

Since just after the war, when Philip had returned from a
Southern hospital to his home in Baltimore, he had been
fighting against the decay of ethics that many blamed on

the armed conflict. He had encountered the symptoms of moral rot while working for the Southern Pacific Railroad in California, and after being appointed to Congress he had been instrumental in exposing the corruption in the building of the Union Pacific. If asked, he would have said that he wasn't sure whether or not the war was directly responsible for the venality that had caught respected congressmen and the vice-president of the United States in its web.

Certainly the war had generated cynicism. While men died by the thousands, Philip Armour sold rotten pork to the army. Rifles that had been refused by the army in the East because they were likely to blow off the thumb of the soldier who fired them were sold at inflated prices to other army units in the West. It was true that the men who fought at Bull Run and Cold Harbor were fed beef from diseased cattle and that the cavalry rode nags that had been injected with stimulants so they might pass the casual inspection of government purchasing agents; but Philip would have said that as far as he could tell, there'd been corruption before the war and that the war had simply offered some pretty big business opportunities to greedy individuals. Thus there was only circumstantial evidence that the war had created dishonesty. In truth, the war had merely provided fertile ground for man's natural cupidity.

While he was working to expose the avarice of the men who, through Crédit Mobilier, had doubled the cost to the federal government of the Union Pacific Railroad, Philip had sometimes felt like John the Baptist, a lone voice crying in the wilderness. Now, however, he had been joined in righteous protest by the press and by preachers. One of the loudest and most eloquent voices was that of the Brooklyn minister Henry Ward Beecher, who warned that God's hand would smite down the evil that held the republic in its clutches.

Well, Philip thought, God hadn't smitten down the politicians who had led the nation into the bloodiest war in history, nor had He blasted U. S. Grant for feeding seven thousand young men to the ogre of war in ten minutes at

Cold Harbor. Robert E. Lee had ridden away from Gettysburg after ordering Pickett to lead a division to its death.

Philip believed that man was the result of Divine Creation and that God had a plan for the human race. A Being who could create a butterfly and a woman like Julia Grey wouldn't invent man, put him in dominion over a pretty nice world, and then just forget about him. But Philip had come to believe that if God had indeed defined a purpose for the race, the plan didn't include hands-on care for each individual during the obviously long and slow reachings for that God-given kismet.

"My, my, we're in deep thought this morning," Julia said cheerfully, coming into Philip's office.

"Sorry," Philip said, exchanging his musing expression for a smile. It was so easy to smile in Julia's presence.

"Bad case of the cain't-help-its?" she asked.

"Something like that."

"When Adam gets that look, he's thinking of the war," she said.

"I try to think of the war as little as possible," Philip told her.

"Did I hear someone call my name?" Adam asked, coming into the room.

The memories engendered by Julia's reference to Adam came back to Philip in a rush. The legless man's appearance strengthened them. Like Adam, Philip had been severely wounded. With people who knew him well, such as his father, he could joke about it. "I was shot in both legs so that I couldn't even limp. Didn't get any sympathy."

But thanks mostly to the fact that the Southern surgeons thought that he was going to die anyhow and didn't cut off his wounded legs, he, unlike Adam, was whole.

"I think we need to consider the war more often," Adam said.

"In what respect?" Philip asked.

"Think of what it did for industry," Adam responded. "Most obviously, if it hadn't been for the war we wouldn't be able to send a letter to California in a week on the transcontinental railroad. If it hadn't been vital to move troops and war materiel, the rail system in the North would still be rudimentary. The wastefulness of war caused massive expansion of our iron and steel industries; and hundreds of people in New England have jobs because the war created the need for shoe and boot factories."

"The new Industrial Revolution," Philip said with a cynical sneer. "I think the wives, mothers, and sweethearts of the men who died would trade all the industrial plants and rails for one day with their dead husbands, sons, and lovers."

"Your trouble, my friend, is that you're a romantic," Adam said. "You forget how easy it is to replace a mere man. A bit of fun under the blankets between man and woman, and *voilà!* In fourteen years you've got a young man tall enough to carry a rifle."

"Adam," Julia scolded.

"Whereas it takes thousands of workmen and millions of dollars to build a transcontinental railroad," Adam continued. His lips were smiling. His eyes, sunken behind dark circles, were not. "Anyone need more cheering up?"

"You're a little ray of sunshine," Julia said, smiling fondly. "I was just getting ready to tell the congressman all about Victoria Woodhull."

Adam curled his lip. "I'll leave you, then. Since millions of women are already superior to me in so many ways, I don't care to contemplate the consequences of Miss Woodhull's plans for dominant womanhood."

"He doesn't really feel that way," Julia said defensively after Adam had propelled himself from the room. "Actually he thinks it unfair that women don't have the vote."

"Well, thank God I don't have to commit myself on that question just yet," Philip said. "It's one of those damned-if-you-do-and-damned-if-you-don't propositions."

"Benjamin Butler is a strong backer of women's suffrage," Julia said.

Philip rolled his eyes and groaned. In his mind Ben Butler represented everything that was wrong with the democratic form of government, and Philip wondered what mysteries directed the political thinking of the people of

Massachusetts. They had a penchant for sending some eerie people to Washington. One of their congressman, Oakes Ames, would no doubt be ousted from his seat for his connivance in selling Crédit Mobilier stock to members of Congress at a fraction of its market value—an overt bribe thinly disguised as a purchase. Butler, the Beast of New Orleans, the man who had allowed the Army of the James to be bottled up by a far inferior force at Bermuda Hundred during a crucial period of the war, the blunderer who had muffed the first attempt to take Fort Fisher, the congressman who had narrowly failed in his effort to vote a huge, retroactive bonus for members of the House, would, Philip believed, sell his soul and his congressional vote at any opportunity. To have Butler on their side was, in Philip's opinion, a black eye for the women's suffrage forces.

"All right," Julia surrendered. "No more testimonials for a just cause." She settled into a chair. "Since the Claflin sisters began publication of *Woodhull and Claflin's Weekly* they've raised the ire of a good many people, including many leaders of the women's movement. I've read a few issues, and it's easy to understand why." She paused and cleared her throat. Philip waited.

"The problem is, you see," Julia continued, in a small voice, "they not only advocate equal rights for women in the voting booth—"

"Yes?" Philip prompted.

"—but in the bedroom," Julia said, blushing furiously. "Victoria is the most vocal, but it's said that many of the articles carrying her name are actually written by her husband, Colonel James Harvey Blood, or by Stephen Pearl Andrews."

"Good Lord," Philip said. "She keeps odd company." Andrews, an eccentric and wealthy idler, had voiced radical ideas ranging from anarchy to free love.

"I have here a typical issue of the *Weekly,*" Julia said. "The lead article is titled 'Law of Sexual Intercourse.'" Again she blushed. "Other titles from past issues include 'The Physiology of Menstruation and Impregnation.'"

It was evident to Philip that the mention of such intimate subjects was difficult for Julia. He wanted to reach out to her, to reassure her. Her being uncomfortable made him feel the same way. Neither of them recognized the real reason for the tension, or if either of them did, he or she would not admit that the consideration of sexual subjects intensified the hidden but powerful physical attraction that existed between them.

CHAPTER 11

Leah Miles was becoming an authority on the esoteric activities of the House of Representatives. Walking to the Capitol Building had become a daily ritual with her. Sometimes she was almost alone in the spectators' gallery. Her choice of seats allowed her to watch Philip Trent but made it nearly impossible for him to notice her. As the voices of the members droned on and on she passed the hours by knitting.

Philip did not take the floor often in the debates that ranged from inane trivialities to issues that were vital to the Republic; but when he did, she put down her knitting, leaned forward, and drank in every word. She learned through the newspaper that Philip had been appointed to the House Judiciary Committee. The sessions of that committee were open to the public, and she was tempted to watch him in action there too. Her hesitation was that the committee meetings were held in a room much smaller, of course, than the House chamber, and Philip could not miss seeing her in the audience. When it was announced, however, by Representative Ben Butler that the Judiciary Committee was to hear from Victoria Claflin Woodhull, Leah abandoned her fears and was determined to attend the session.

After Lloyd interfered with her plan to marry Harold Berman, Leah had begun to take a lukewarm interest in the suffrage movement. The women's radical stance both shocked and attracted her, and it took her mind off the fact that with each passing day she was closer to being a spinster forever. To that date Leah's involvement had been confined to reading the literature of the women's movement. She had subscribed to *Woodhull and Claflin's Weekly,* although the nature of the articles brought a flush to her cheeks. Lest she be ridiculed for reading what many men and not a few women called trash, she was careful to conceal the publication from Lloyd.

Since she was a maiden in every respect, Leah found it difficult to understand how the intelligent, attractive Victoria Woodhull could join the small but vocal minority of people in the United States who advocated free love. Victoria quoted the Reverend Erasmus Stone: "On Judgment Day unhappily married men and women will be soaring around, looking for the perfect mate. To avoid the search in the beyond, let us make delicate tests here on Earth."

Victoria wrote that since there would be no marriage in heaven, marriage was sinful on earth. Moreover, the Church had sinned by solemnizing matrimony. The ideal situation, according to Victoria, would be for everyone to mingle and love one another as brothers and sisters.

Leah giggled guiltily as she read that last statement, for she certainly understood sisterly love in a different light. She felt quite uncomfortable when she read the words of another so-called man of God, Reverend John Humphrey Noyes, who wrote: "There is no more reason to restrict sexual intercourse than eating or drinking."

Although Leah could not bring herself to agree with the Claflin sisters regarding the amount of freedom that women should be allowed in the bedroom, she was ardently supportive of the main thrust of the suffrage movement. She had acted as Lloyd's hostess while entertaining men of business, industry, and government, and from personal experience she knew without self-delusion that she was as capable of making an intelligent decision about the election of public servants as most of the men she had met. In fact, most of them voted their pocketbooks. She believed that she and other women would use other, more relevant criteria if and when they were allowed in the voting booth.

Although she secreted the bold *Weekly,* she did not hide other publications featuring the utterances of the Brooklyn minister Henry Ward Beecher, the president of the American Woman Suffrage Association, and Theodore Tilton, the head of the National Woman Suffrage Association. Now and then Lloyd would pick up one of the publications, glance at it, snort, and toss it aside, so she was very much surprised when he came home one night with a copy of *Woodhull and Claflin's Weekly* in his hand and a scowl on his face.

"I want you to read this claptrap," he said, tossing the paper at her. "And they're going to have that woman appear before a congressional committee!"

He explained exactly what article in the *Weekly* had aroused his ire. He pointed it out to her, furiously tapping the headline with his index finger. "And they brag about being the first American periodical to publish it!" he shouted.

"It" was called the *Communist Manifesto.* Leah had never heard of the man who wrote it, one Karl Marx. She listened, trying to understand, as Lloyd stormed on. She got the idea finally, after asking specific questions.

"The man is advocating revolution," Lloyd stormed. "Do you realize what that would mean to us? He would take my money—our money—and distribute it to anarchists and bums."

"Are the Claflin sisters advocating that we do what this Marx fellow suggests, or are they just printing his writings to inform us of what people in other countries are thinking?" Leah asked in a soft voice.

"Of course they're advocating it," Lloyd fumed. "Why else would they dignify it by putting it in print? What we should do is hang 'em all, all the anarchists and revolutionaries and the effete intellectuals who support their despicable philosophy by calling it free speech."

"It might be interesting to hear what Victoria Woodhull has to say to the Judiciary Committee," Leah suggested.

"I wouldn't waste my time," Lloyd said, but Leah could see that his conviction wasn't total.

"If she's advocating things that are against your interests, isn't it a good idea to know your enemy?"

He snorted. "I understand women like her. If she has a brain it's located in a spot just below her waist."

Leah blushed.

"Her mentality can be measured by her own words," he said. "She had the gall to stand up in public and shout that she is a free lover. That makes her no better than a woman of the streets."

"I think I'd like to hear what she has to say," Leah said. "I can't agree with her on the issue of women's morality, but she espouses other causes, too."

Lloyd shrugged. "If you want to poison your mind with such rubbish, I suppose you're old enough to know better," he allowed. "I think, if you're really interested in fighting for suffrage—God forbid—that you'd be better advised to attend the sessions of the convention being run by Susan B. Anthony."

"Yes," she agreed, "I had planned to attend. But I think I'll go to both. The timing of the convention doesn't interfere with my going to hear Mrs. Woodhull at the committee hearing."

Three days before Victoria Woodhull was to appear before the congressional committee, a cartoonist depicted her in a seductive pose luring a gnomelike, leering Representative Ben Butler into what was obviously going to be mischief. It had been Butler who invited Victoria to speak before the Judiciary Committee. The drawing appeared next to that week's chapter of a serial written by Harriet Beecher Stowe, who had roused the conscience of a nation with her poignant but highly inaccurate depiction of slavery

in *Uncle Tom's Cabin*. The serial featured a brazen hussy
named Audacia Dangyereyes, and the author made no pre-
tense of avoiding a distinct resemblance to Victoria Woodhull. The cheeky Audacia was to be the first woman to
appear before a congressional committee, and her remarks
were so outrageous that Leah had to laugh. She read the
chapter aloud to Lloyd, who laughed with her.

"I'd like to see Mrs. Stowe and Victoria debate toe to
toe," he said, his momentary anger over the publication of
the Karl Marx piece obviously forgotten. "I'll bet that
Woodhull would chew her up and spit her out."

"Do I detect in Mrs. Stowe's writing just a hint of hidden
admiration for Miss Audacia Dangyereyes?" Leah asked.

"No, no, I think not. She takes her morality from her
brother, from the stainless knight of Christ. Victoria and
Tennessee Claflin would be no better in her mind than the
dirt under her feet. Isn't it odd, though, that there's always
a Beecher rooting around in that dirt?" He laughed.
"Large family, the Beechers. And they all seem to have an
affinity for dirt."

"They say that the city has to schedule additional ferries
on Sundays when Henry Ward Beecher preaches," Leah
said. "One day I'd like to go to Brooklyn to hear him."

"I think we'll be moving to New York soon," Lloyd said.
"You might get your chance sooner than later."

When Victoria Woodhull first began to speak before the
House Judiciary Committee, Leah had to lean forward and
strain to hear her. Leah had chosen a seat so that she
could see Victoria's calm, pretty face beyond the committee members, who were sitting opposite her. As Victoria
became more at ease, her voice soared on the logic and
beauty of her ideals. Rather than shocking posturing about
free love in the Woodhull presentation to the committee,
her presentation held only calm reason, a polite and hum-
ble appeal to the congressmen to be fair to the women who
were their mothers, wives, sisters, and daughters.

And yet there was fire in Victoria's words. The woman's
eloquence moved Leah to tears and then to pride in the

fact that she was a woman. Before Victoria finished with a fervent plea that women be allowed to take their rightful place in society, she had fanned a tiny ember of interest in Leah Miles into a blaze of righteous indignation; and the symbol of her outrage became her brother, the man who had twice deprived her of love and marriage . . . the man who, in the guise of brotherly love and protection, wholly dominated her. Leah left the committee hearing room determined to claim her own life, to take charge of herself, and to become a part of what Victoria Woodhull represented.

To her surprise she saw Lloyd in the hallway. He stood with a group of people who were waiting for Victoria to emerge from the room. Seeing Leah, he waved to her. She excused her way through the crowd to stand beside him. He took her arm and winked.

"You heard?" she asked.

"She was in good form," he said. "Almost convinced me."

Leah was silent. Lloyd nodded, then pointed discreetly. "What did I say about there being a Beecher underfoot everywhere? There's another sister, Mrs. Isabella Beecher Hooker."

"Could it be that she's here to congratulate Mrs. Woodhull?" Leah asked.

At that moment Victoria swept through the door into the hallway, her rose-petal skin flushed with excitement, a pleased smile on her face. Isabella Beecher Hooker stepped forward. "I have never seen such a disgusting performance," Mrs. Hooker grated. "It makes me ashamed to be a woman. To think that respected congressmen would waste their time listening to a self-confessed wanton!"

Victoria, stunned, halted in her tracks. Her face flushed redder. She leaned forward, and for a moment Leah hoped that she would strike the rude woman. Instead Victoria spoke in a calm voice that carried well. "Isn't it odd that I am besmirched by a Beecher? I am reliably informed, Mrs. Hooker, that your brother preaches to at least twenty of his mistresses each Sunday morning."

Leah gasped, thinking that Victoria had gone too far by attacking the most popular and best known preacher in the United States. Isabella Beecher Hooker went pale and worked her lips to respond, but Victoria had already swept past to be surrounded by well-wishers.

Leah had a seat close to the front of the room at the convention session where Victoria sat next to Susan B. Anthony. When Victoria spoke to the gathering of suffragettes, Leah was thrilled anew. Victoria said things that became engraved on her mind and gave her purpose.

She wrote a note and had it delivered to Mrs. Woodhull. It was simple and direct: *I must meet you. I must work with you, for you have given my life new meaning with your words.*

The missive was effective. She found herself alone with Victoria in a small conference room. As she spoke, stating her admiration for Victoria's speech to the convention, her voice seemed lost in the empty room. Victoria's filled it.

"Miles . . ." Victoria said, "Miles. I know a Lloyd Miles from Washington."

"My brother," Leah said. "He didn't say he knew you."

"Well, he knows my sister better," Victoria said. "So you want to work for the cause?"

"I do. Yes." Her voice was full, sincere.

"The movement has a fine organization here in Washington. I can give you the names of those you should see."

"I want to work with you," Leah said. "My brother and I will be moving to New York soon."

"Ah? Wonderful. When you are settled in the city and are ready to become active in the movement, please visit me at the brokerage office."

"Thank you," Leah said.

"Can you spell?" Victoria asked.

"Fairly well."

"Good. If you can spell I might have a job for you at the *Weekly*. You live with your brother?"

"Yes."

"Wash his underwear and socks, clean up his house, cook his meals?"

"Yes," she said weakly.

"Then come back to New York with me," Victoria invited. "Declare your independence immediately."

"Thank you . . ."

"But?"

"My brother has been good to me."

"By his definition?" Victoria asked.

Leah nodded. "And, I suppose, I'm afraid."

Victoria smiled and put her hand on Leah's arm. "That I can understand. There have been times, my dear, when I was scared out of my pantalets. All right, then. Find me when you arrive in New York."

"Don't forget me," Leah said impulsively as Woodhull turned to go.

Victoria whirled back, took her into her arms, and hugged her tightly. "No," she promised. "No, I won't forget you."

Although Leah was eager to move to New York City to see Victoria again, to begin work in a cause that occupied her mind for most of her waking hours, she also experienced a feeling akin to desperation. Rightly or wrongly her heart told her that if she left Washington, she would never see Philip Trent again. Logic told her that would be for the best, but, as is often the case, logic and unrequited love were polar opposites.

Shortly after Victoria spoke before the Judiciary Committee, Gus Trent appeared at Leah's door to take her out for one of their periodic luncheons. She was, as always, pleased to see him. She kissed him fondly on the cheek and gave him a little hug. While they were enjoying his favorite dessert, sweet-potato pie, Leah told him that she was relocating with her brother to New York.

"I'll miss you," he said, genuinely moved.

"And I you," she said. "But Lloyd's career demands the move."

Gus had learned from Leah that a falling-out between his son and Lloyd had been responsible for dashing his hopes that Leah would be the mother of his grandchildren.

He often wished that he could get hold of them, Miles and Philip, and bash their heads together until some sense was pounded into them. "I don't want to lose touch with you, my dear," he said.

"Will you visit me in New York?"

"I will," he said.

There was a long silence. "Gus . . ."

When he saw the anguish in her eyes, he was deeply moved and took her hand between his.

"Gus, if there was anything I could do—"

"Are we thinking about the same thing?" he asked.

She flushed.

"I don't know," he said, remembering the way in which Philip looked at Julia Grey. He brightened. "Don't you think it would be in order, since you're going to move away, for you to say good-bye to an old friend?"

Tears flooded her eyes. "I don't think I could face him. After all, it was I who sent him away. It was I who refused him."

"Do this for me?" he requested.

She smiled, sniffed. He handed her his handkerchief.

"All right," she said reluctantly, "but if I make a total fool of myself, it will be on your head."

As she and Gus strolled toward Philip's office, her hand comfortably rested on his arm, and the sun felt warm and pleasant on her face. Nonetheless she told herself that she was allowing false hopes to build, that she was being shameless. *If he had loved you, he would not have given up so easily.*

But she had to admit the truth—that Philip had not accepted her rejection of him without trying to change her mind. He had been in an awkward position. Had he been more forceful in his attempts to see her, he would have had to confront Lloyd. Since her loyalty to her brother had forced her to obey Lloyd's ultimatum and had caused her to choose Lloyd over Philip, Philip must have known that for him to fight with Lloyd would only have deepened the chasm between himself and Leah. So she could not put any blame on Philip. She had made the choice.

Was she now ready to negate that decision, to deny her brother? As she matched the long strides of Gus Trent, her heart said, "Yes, yes, yes." She had no idea what she would say to Philip. She would rely on Gus to lead the way. And perhaps God in His heaven would allow Philip himself to recognize that her visit to his office was an offer of reconciliation. It would be wonderful if he would make the first move.

As it happened, Miss Mercy was away from the office when Gus opened the outer door and held it for Leah. She saw Philip immediately, leaning over the desk of a vividly pretty woman. She heard his voice, speaking in normal tones, the words having to do with a paper the woman was holding.

The way his eyes were locked with the woman's caused the breath to catch in Leah's throat, for she had once known and shared with Philip the obvious hunger that was passing now between him and the dark-haired beauty seated at the desk.

Too late, too late, she thought with a sinking feeling.

Gus cleared his throat.

Philip started, straightened. "Hello, Dad," he said. And then his eyes turned to Leah, and he became motionless, his smile freezing on his face. "Well, Leah . . ." he said.

Leah flicked a glance at Gus, who was obviously reprimanding himself for rank stupidity, for exposing her to this painful situation.

"Your father and I were having lunch," Leah said with a brightness that amazed her. "He said he was going to drop by your office, and I asked to come along. Lloyd and I will be leaving Washington very shortly, and I wanted to say good-bye before I left." She stepped forward and extended her hand.

Philip took it.

"You had better watch your p's and q's, Philip Trent," she said with a wide smile, "or you'll be minus one father, for I am trying desperately to steal him and take him with me."

"I'm not fighting very hard," Gus said, smiling gratefully at Leah for her aplomb.

"I wanted you to know, too, that I admire your work in the House very much," Leah said. "God knows we need more like you there."

"Thank you," Philip said. Silence settled. He filled it. "Forgive me for not making introductions. Miss Leah Miles, Mrs. Julia Grey. Mrs. Grey is an invaluable aide. She's secretary, research assistant, office manager—"

"Only when Miss Mercy is away," Julia said.

"Miss Miles is an old friend, Julia," Philip said. "Her brother and I once took an excursion behind Rebel lines together."

Leah's smile was forced, and the woman sizing her up from behind the desk obviously knew it. For a moment their eyes met, and it was Julia who looked away.

"It is Mrs. Grey?" Leah asked.

"Yes," Philip said quickly. "Her husband, Adam, is another of my aides."

"How convenient," Leah said. "I mean that husband and wife should be able to work together."

"Yes, it is, really," Julia said with a touch of defensiveness. She smiled at Gus. "Adam, by the way, is taking the afternoon off to cook one of your favorite meals, Mr. Trent. New England boiled dinner. Philip is joining us. Won't you please come?"

Leah knew that she had been put in her place as an outsider. She squeezed Gus's arm. "I must be getting home, Gus."

"Yes, yes," Gus said uncomfortably.

"You don't have to come," Leah said. "I'll take a cab."

"Wouldn't think of it," Gus told her. "Shall we continue our stroll?"

"It is a lovely day." Leah smiled at Julia. "A pleasure," she said. She stared unblinkingly into Philip's eyes. "Goodbye, Philip."

"I hope you enjoy living in New York City," he said.

"I'm sure I will," she said. She turned quickly and hurried down the corridor. She was weeping quietly as she and Gus gained the street.

"Oh, my dear girl," he said.

"It's all right," she told him, reaching for his handkerchief. "It's in the nature of a cleansing. It's time to forget him and get on with my life."

"Damn," Gus said.

"We were both dreaming, Gus. I should have known that a man like Philip would not be pining away, that there'd be someone else."

"That obvious, was it?" Gus asked.

"Only a fool would have missed the attraction between them."

He sighed. "I'm afraid so. In defense of my son, blast him, I don't think he even knows that he's in love with her. And I'd bet my last nickel that nothing dishonorable has passed between them."

"I believe you, Gus. But she's in love with him," Leah said. "That woman was ready to do combat with me."

"I fear you're right." He put his hand atop Leah's on his arm. "If there was only some way we could fight. . . ."

She smiled sadly. "Too late," she said. "The battle is over, and I was not even in the field."

Philip found Gus waiting in his apartment at the end of the day. Philip handed his father a small brandy to sip while he freshened himself and changed into comfortably casual clothing for the evening ahead. They walked to a main avenue and hailed a cab for the trip to the Grey home.

Once seated in the cab Gus immediately opened the subject that was on both their minds since Leah's quick departure earlier that afternoon. "I think it would be a good thing if you called on Leah before she leaves the city," he suggested.

Philip didn't answer immediately, but when he did, his voice was carefully neutral. "Now, Dad, you know that I won't do that."

"I know, but I don't understand why not," Gus said. "You loved the girl. Can you just turn love on and off?"

"She made the choice," Philip said.

"You know better than that," Gus said, his voice rising. "Lloyd Miles made the choice, and like children being reprimanded, both you and Leah knuckled under to him."

"Damn it, Dad, she's a grown woman," Philip said. "God knows I tried—"

"How hard?" Gus demanded. "Did you punch Lloyd Miles in the nose?"

"Dad—"

"All right, all right," Gus surrendered. "But damn, I'm sorry for you."

"If you'll just be patient," Philip said angrily, "I'll get you some grandchildren."

"When?" Gus shouted. "After Adam Grey dies, and you've observed a suitable period of mourning?"

"I resent that," Philip said forcefully. "You must know me better than to think that I'd do anything to hurt Adam Grey. I've never had a better friend. He—" He paused, for there was in him a sense of loss that stunned him. It was as if by voicing his loyalty for Adam he had given up forever any hope of—of what? "My God," he said.

Gus was quiet.

"Oh, my God . . ." Philip said. For a moment he felt an unreasoning anger toward his father. Gus had made him realize that he wanted Julia Grey more than he'd ever wanted anything in his life, and by prompting that epiphany, Gus had deprived him of Julia for all eternity. His guilt at loving Adam Grey's wife would prohibit his seeking Julia's hand when and if Adam died.

Philip could never soil the memory of their friendship by giving a name to the feelings he had for Julia while Adam still lived.

Not only was Adam Grey a true friend, he had become Philip's chief adviser. Adam had a knack for guessing the opinions of the average voter. Some of the most powerful men in Washington had come to respect Adam Grey and value his judgment. As informal chief of staff in the office,

Adam had proved his worth as researcher and idea man. He had taken on new duties when the press began to seek out Philip for information about the Crédit Mobilier scandal: taking the pressure off Philip, charming the newsmen out of their socks, and making them feel happy to get whatever tidbit of information Philip was ready to release.

It sometimes startled first-time visitors to Philip's office to see Adam on his dolly, propelling himself with the palms of his hand on the floor; but the war had created many similarly invalided veterans. To know that Adam was, in all probability, destined for an early death because of his war wounds was something that Philip did not want to think about. But as Gus made Philip realize that for months he had been finding every excuse to spend time with Julia, the young man faced reality. Adam would die, and because Philip had fallen in love with Adam's wife, he would deny that love out of respect for the memory of a friend.

The evening was a good one. Adam was pale, and he ate little. But the meal was splendid—boiled corned beef with rutabagas, onions, cabbage, potatoes, and carrots. Gus witnessed the beginning of a new phase of the relationship between Philip and Julia. As if to deny his attraction for her, Philip nearly ignored her. He spoke to her only when she addressed him directly. Otherwise the young man gave his attentions to Adam and Gus for the entire evening.

Gus made a special trip to Washington to congratulate his son when Philip's committee concluded its long investigation of Crédit Mobilier. The resultant report scorched even Washington's desensitized ears. As a by-product of Philip's work Oakes Ames, one of the nation's most powerful congressmen, was ejected from the House of Representatives. Another congressman, John O'Brian, was dead as a result of the scandal, and reputations had been damaged—some, like the vice-president's, irreparably. Others who were touched by the wrongdoing, such as Congressman James A. Garfield, would live down their participation.

The atmosphere of the office party was subdued; it was

as if everyone accepted the fact that nothing much had been changed by the work of the committee. Oh, sure, the nation was made aware of the shameful greed and the waste of public money in the building of the transcontinental railroad. But no one had been punished, not really, except John O'Brian. True, Oakes Ames had been kicked out of the House of Representatives, but he and his brother, Oliver, had kept the money they had made from the construction of the Union Pacific. The other men involved, the railroad barons of the East and the West, continued to live well and wield the power according to their own whims—a privilege that came with massive wealth.

There was little mention of the past as Julia served cake and coffee. Adam sat in a padded chair. He was wan and thin, and his eyes were mirrors of pain and exhaustion.

"Adam," Gus said, "I think you need a rest."

"I've tried to get him to stay home for a few days," Philip said.

"As if cleaning house, cooking, and gardening isn't work?" Adam asked. "Thank you all, but I get more rest here in the office."

"Well, if you're going to be hardheaded," Philip said facetiously, "you might as well get back to work. Don't think that just because the Crédit Mobilier investigation is over you're going to have it easy around here, any of you."

"Slave driver," Julia accused.

"The troops await orders, General," Adam said, saluting. "What is your pleasure?"

"Well, you know congressmen," Philip said. "The committee members like to see their names in the papers, so we're going after the men responsible for the crash on the gold market."

"Sounds like fun," Adam said in a flat voice.

"I'd like for you, Adam—since you were the one who suggested it—to dig up as much information as you can about the gold-trading habits of Mr. Lloyd Miles."

Gus looked up quickly. "Miles?"

"Sorry, Gus," Philip said. "I'm afraid it's necessary. Adam thinks that Miles might be the key to our learning about the whole affair. We can get at him a lot easier than we can get to men like Fisk and Gould."

Gus shook his head sadly, obviously concerned for Leah.

The party was winding down into almost morose silence when Adam gasped and clasped his middle. Julia leapt to his side. His face was contorted in pain.

"It's nothing." Adam gasped again.

"Oh, yes," Julia said. "That's why perspiration is popping out on your forehead." She turned to Philip. "Help me, please."

Together Julia and Philip carried Adam into the inner office, where there was a couch. Miss Mercy and Gus waited in the anteroom. The older woman made *tsk*ing sounds. "Ah, that poor, poor man."

"Yes, it's sad," Gus said.

"I think you realize what's going on in this office, Mr. Trent," Miss Mercy said.

"What do you mean?"

"It isn't Christian," Miss Mercy said through pursed lips.

"Now, Miss Mercy—"

"Oh, don't misunderstand me," she said. "Neither of them would do anything wrong. That's not it. It's the way that poor man deliberately throws them together."

"Philip and Mrs. Grey, you mean?"

"That poor man is trying to arrange his wife's remarriage before he is put into his coffin," Miss Mercy said. "It just isn't Christian, a husband trying to push his wife into another man's arms because he knows he is dying."

CHAPTER 12

Shortly after the committee that had spent years investigating cost overruns in the Pacific Railroad's construction issued its final report, the committee chairman died peacefully in his sleep. He had been a Washington fixture in his thirteenth term in the House. Because of Philip's leadership in exposing the criminal greed of the railroad builders, the House leadership bypassed seniority and named him the committee's new chairman.

"I don't know how many more honors like that I can stand," Philip complained to Julia and Adam. "So far my time as a congressman has been dominated by the Crédit Mobilier affair. I had hoped to spend some time now on affairs more directly related to the voters in my district."

"For better or for worse," Adam said, "you have been claimed by a nationwide constituency. People in every state perceive you as one of the positive influences in a city that they're beginning to call Clown Town." He forced a grin. Smiling was not always easy for him, since he was seldom free from the nagging pain in his stomach. "It was you, my friend, who decided to be a crusader, a reformer. Now duty calls again."

"Thanks a hell of a lot," Philip grumbled.

"I have sent two committee staff lawyers to New York," Adam said. He waved a hand. "On your authority, of course."

"Damn it, Adam, I was just named chairman this morning," Philip growled.

"Well, we peons knew it was going to happen," Adam said as Julia hid an amused smile behind her hand, "so we decided not to waste time waiting for the formalities. At any rate, it may take a while to dig out the information we want from the gold market bank. Mr. Gould's friends in City Hall and on the bench have, in effect, given him control of both the market and the bank. But sooner or later we'll be allowed to look at the records, and then we'll be able to get a listing of buy-and-sell orders."

"All right," Philip agreed. "I guess that's the place to start."

"And to allow us to get our foot in the door without alarming those most responsible," Adam added, "the staffers are going after the buy-and-sell records of Lloyd Miles first."

"On the theory," Julia explained, "that Gould and Fisk would think that to have us investigating Miles would be far preferable to having us examine their own financial dealings."

"Good thinking," Philip said. "Adam, have you heard anything from that journalist yet?"

"Headley, you mean? Not yet."

"Okay. I'm going into my office to take a nap."

Julia smiled at his joke. Philip never napped during the day. That was just his way of saying that he had things to do and didn't want to be interrupted.

He paused at the door. "By the way, my dad is going to be in town tomorrow. He wants to take us all out to dinner."

Adam frowned. He disliked going to public places because of people's reactions to his disability. "Think Gus would settle for a home-cooked meal at Chez Gris?"

"I guess he could be talked into it," Philip said.

"Let's see," Adam mused. "Gus likes good, solid food. I

think chicken and dumplings. And some of those fresh col-
lard greens, Julia."

"Candied yams," Philip suggested.

"Who's preparing this menu?" Adam asked.

"Just trying to help," Philip said.

"I guess we can make that little concession," Adam responded. "I'll have to take the day off."

"I knew there was a catch to it somewhere," Philip said.

Adam grinned. "Julia and Miss Mercy can keep you out
of mischief."

Gus was more than willing to have dinner at the Grey
house. He did his duty by the chicken and dumplings, then
leaned back in satisfaction. "Adam," he said, "if you ever
decide to open a restaurant, I'll invest in it."

"Nice to know that I've got something to fall back on if I
ever get fired from my low-paying job," Adam said.

"Dad, what do you do when one of your staff gets uppity?" Philip asked.

"If he cooks as well as Adam, I give him a raise," Gus
answered.

"Thanks a lot for your advice," Philip said.

Julia went to the stove, then came back with plates in
one hand and an apple pie in the other. "There's more
than one cook in the Grey family," she announced.

The pie was delicious. Gus had brought a bottle of aged
brandy. The three men agreed that they would, just this
once, allow a lady to join them for brandy and cigars.

"Thanks a lot," Julia said ruefully. She refused a cigar
but accepted a brandy.

The conversation covered a gamut of subjects ranging
from the gold scandal to the changing fashions in women's
clothing. When Julia began to clear the table Philip helped.
Gus, announcing that dining chairs in general were getting
harder and harder, took Adam off to the front room of the
house, leaving Julia and Philip to kitchen duty.

Adam hoisted himself into his chair, settled in, and
sighed. He had eaten more than usual, and he knew that he

was going to pay in severe pain for his indulgence. More and more often his stomach reminded him of his mortality.

Gus was in the midst of a tall tale about an appointed state official who had decided that he wanted to paint the Maryland state capitol building red, white, and blue when Adam's lips twitched and his wan face blanched.

"Can I get you something, Adam?" Gus asked.

"Some milk, if you don't mind," Adam said.

Gus found Julia and Philip side by side at the sink, Julia washing, Philip wiping. "Glass of milk," Gus said gruffly, remembering Miss Mercy's statement that Adam deliberately seemed to throw Julia and Philip together. "I'll get it."

Adam was still pale when Gus returned to the front room. He drank the milk slowly. "Adam, I've got a friend up in Baltimore, a doctor. I'd like for you to let him have a look at you."

"Lord, no," Adam said. "Not another doctor. I've had too many of them poking and probing as it is."

"Damn it, man, you worry me," Gus said.

"Well, I'm sorry for that."

"Wouldn't want to lose you, that's all."

"Given a choice, I'd linger awhile." He put one hand on his stomach and grimaced. "I'm afraid, however, that I don't have the choice." His sunken eyes burned. "At the risk of being morbid, Gus, it's going to be sooner rather than later."

"No," the older man said in denial. "You're a fighter, boy. You're going to be around a long, long time."

Adam shook his head. "But I'm glad the subject has reared its ugly head. I've been wanting to ask a favor of you."

"Anything I can do, you name it."

"You have noticed, I'm sure, that a . . . certain regard exists between your son and my wife."

Gus squirmed for a moment, but he relaxed when Adam smiled and continued.

"Don't feel uncomfortable. I approve of their friendship. Actually, I encourage it. I know Julia loves me, and I believe that Philip is genuinely as fond of me as I am of him. I know that there is nothing dishonorable between them. What I fear is that their honor, and their love and regard for me, will prevent what I want very much to happen after I'm dead."

Gus felt his eyes sting. He cleared his constricting throat.

"I can think of no man other than Philip I'd rather have taking care of my wife when I'm gone," Adam said. "It would ease my mind tremendously if I knew that their union was assured. That's the favor I want to ask. I want you, Gus, to tell them both after I'm gone how I feel. But my wish is for you to allow that attraction that they feel to grow naturally. I wouldn't want Julia or Philip to feel pushed at each other. Things like this take time. Give them that time to work it all through themselves. Intervene only as a last resort, if their sense of loyalty to me becomes convoluted somehow and stands in their way."

"Well . . ." Gus said, shifting in his seat.

"The one thing I regret most is that I'll leave her without means," Adam said. "Look around you. This is what I've been able to give her—a small house in a part of Washington avoided by most decent folks." He finished his milk. "I would give anything to be assured that she will be provided for, that she will be loved and cherished. If it were in my power I would arrange it so that I could say, right now, at this moment, that Philip Trent is taking my place with my wife. If I knew that, I could stop fighting for survival, for I am so tired, so very goddamned tired."

Gus was the only one who saw Julia appear in the doorway leading to the middle room of the house. She heard only a part of one sentence: "Philip Trent is taking my place with my wife." She turned and scurried away. Gus leaned forward and was about to call out to her; but Adam was in the midst of baring his soul, and the situation was so delicate that Gus was loath to interrupt.

"So, Gus, I ask you to promise me to play Cupid. Tell them at the appropriate time that they have my blessing."

"All right, Adam," Gus agreed. "But why haven't you talked with Julia about this?"

"Lord, man," Adam said. "She's so loyal, so true to me. It would hurt her deeply if I told her that I wanted her to start thinking about marrying another man. She'd end up running in the opposite direction. No, I think it best that we not mention the subject to either of them. Knowing them as I do, I think they'd feel guilty if they realized that I see the fondness they feel for each other."

To spare Adam worry, Gus did not tell him that Julia had overheard at least part of what he'd been saying. Gus attributed her coolness toward Philip for the balance of the evening to her concern about Adam.

When an official at the Gold Exchange Bank told Jay Gould that two congressional staff lawyers had asked for the buy-and-sell orders executed on behalf of Lloyd Miles for a period of six weeks before Black Friday, Gould mused for a few moments, then said, "Give them what they want."

Gould was accustomed to public disapproval. It didn't bother him if it didn't affect his pocketbook in a negative way. His first reaction to the news was curiosity. He knew that Miles had put some money into gold; the man had deposited almost a million dollars in Gould's bank. But, he wondered, was Miles smart enough to have made more and to have hidden it somewhere? "When you dig out the figures, send me a copy," he told the bank manager.

There was also another consideration. As the days passed the hue and cry was increasing in volume. A congressional committee—the one that had sent the two lawyers to New York—was beginning an investigation. Jim Fisk might well say, "Let each man drag out his own body," meaning let the guilt fall where it might; but Gould considered himself to be a bit more intelligent than his partner. For example, the flamboyant Fisk had been buying gold at high prices right up to the time of the crash, whereas Gould was selling as fast as he could without driving down the market.

Fisk tried to reduce the panic of Black Friday to a joke, saying, "A fellow can't have a little innocent fun without everybody raising a halloo and going wild." Gould, on the other hand, knew that it was no joke. The great American public, the so-called informed electorate that was supposed to make democracy work, wanted blood. Like the citizens of ancient Rome, they demanded their circus. Even those who had not been affected in the slightest by Black Friday and the subsequent stock market panic wanted to see heads roll—and the richer the heads, the greater the pleasure.

Fisk was playing a dangerous game by trying to draw the presidential family into the affair, all in an effort to take the heat off himself. He had already accused the President's brother-in-law in an interview given to the New York *Sun*, and now he was intimating that Grant himself had been financially involved in the attempt to corner gold. Gould wasn't particularly worried about Fisk; he had determined during the fiasco that followed Black Friday that Fisk was more of a liability than an asset. Gould liked the idea of taking away the attention of the newspapers—and, thus, the fickle public—from Fisk and himself. If the first speculator investigated by Representative Philip Trent's committee was a small fry, namely Lloyd Miles, that would be proof that Gould and Fisk were not totally responsible for upsetting the nation's economy.

It did not take the bank manager very long to send a copy of Lloyd's trading orders to his employer. When Gould saw the total of Lloyd's trading, he found that Miles had done much better than Gould had thought, with profits adding up to almost three million dollars. That would give the congressional committee something to chew on for a while; but it would not, in the long run, be damaging to Miles—his trading had been strictly legal, and he'd gotten out of the market before the crash.

Once again Gould had a change of mind about his employee. He sent a telegram telling Miles that the time had come for him to move, that a man of his talent was needed in the New York office.

Lloyd left the office in Washington immediately after receiving Gould's order to move to New York. He had formed his plans long ago and had been awaiting Gould's order to transfer to the main offices of the Erie Railroad.

He shouted out the good news to Leah as he entered their apartment. He was confident that he was ready to graze in richer financial pastures. The action was in New York. Tennessee Claflin and the delectable Victoria were in New York; and there, too, were Abby Kershaw and her father.

He decided to contact Tennessee immediately; she had said that their affair was over but that he should stay in touch. If she was still heavily involved with Commodore Vanderbilt, Lloyd was hopeful of becoming a bit more friendly with the luscious Victoria. Lloyd thought it was uselessly daring of Victoria to declare openly in her *Weekly*, which he had picked up because Tennessee had a hand in its publication, that she had sex with any man who pleased her. But rather than making her seem less desirable in his eyes, her admission made him wonder, with some warmth, what it would be like to have bedded both infamous sisters.

And he would find a way to make Abby Kershaw and her father wish that they'd never heard the name Lloyd Miles. Oddly enough, he still entertained thoughts of Abby as a suitable wife, but only after he had humiliated both the icy girl and her insulting father.

Leah felt relief on hearing Lloyd's news. After having seen the way Philip had looked at Julia Grey, her reason told her that there was no way she could force herself back into Philip's life. Now she wanted nothing more than to get away from Washington and any thought of Philip, to see Victoria Woodhull again, and to throw herself wholly into the righteous battle for woman's suffrage.

"How soon can you be packed?" Lloyd asked jubilantly. "Don't worry about the furniture. We'll sell it here, and when we find a place in New York you can decorate it completely."

"That's wasteful," she protested.

He laughed. "Little sister, I may not be really rich, but I

can afford to live in some style, which I intend to do. You'll have fun buying new furniture."

"Yes," she said. "All right, then. If you'll help me lift and carry I can be ready by noon tomorrow."

"That's my girl," Lloyd said, grabbing her and swinging her around playfully.

She found herself laughing. There were times when she could almost forgive him.

Leah was shocked when Lloyd agreed to pay four times the rent they'd been paying in Washington for an apartment in the Murray Hill district of Manhattan. He grinned at her and told her not to worry. "Honey," he said, "I could buy the building if I wanted to."

"Please don't," she said. "I'd work myself to death looking after it."

After checking in at the office Lloyd took a few days off and helped Leah shop for furniture. He spared no expense. Soon the apartment was carpeted and furnished and was, Lloyd said, "richly cozy." After they were settled in, he reported back to work. Leah had more shopping to do to buy the little extras that gave the apartment a lived-in look and made it seem less like a furniture-store showroom.

It was several days before Lloyd had a chance to stop by the new Claflin apartment on Thirty-eighth Street. The door was opened by Roxanna Claflin, the matriarch of the family. She had lost most of her teeth. Her hair was oily and stringy. She looked at Lloyd with open disapproval and demanded, "What in the hell do you want?"

"I've come to call on Miss Tennessee," Lloyd said. "I'm an old friend."

"I want you young hellions to leave my girls alone!" Roxanna screamed. "If you bastards would just leave them alone, they'd be good girls. Now, you git. Tennie's not here anyhow."

"Is Mrs. Woodhull in, then?" Lloyd asked.

"Not to you she ain't," the old woman said.

Victoria appeared behind Roxanna. "Who is it, Mother?"

"It's Lloyd Miles, Mrs. Woodhull."

"Mother, please go to your room," Victoria said.

"That's right," Roxanna fumed, "let the bastard in. There ain't no decency in this house anyhow. Let him in."

"Be quiet, Mother," Victoria said firmly, pushing the old woman away from the entry door. Roxanna, with a baleful glare at Lloyd, disappeared. "You'll have to forgive Mother," Victoria said. "She's quite senile."

"It's a pleasure to see you again, Mrs. Woodhull."

"Oh, come now," she said. "Only the gentlemen of the press call me Mrs. Woodhull."

"Among other things," Lloyd said, laughing.

"Among several other things," Victoria said. She led him into a pleasant sitting room. "May I offer you something?"

"No, no, thanks. I came by to tell Tennessee that I have moved to New York."

"Good for you," she said. "After experiencing what this city has to offer, life seems rather dull elsewhere, doesn't it?"

"No place would be dull if the Claflin sisters were around," Lloyd said.

"Flattery pleases me."

"You inspire compliments."

"I think I'm beginning to understand why Tennie liked you."

" 'Liked'?" he asked.

"Well, you know Tennie," Victoria said.

"I'm pleased that you are kind enough to receive me," Lloyd said. "It gives me a long-delayed opportunity to thank you for alerting me to certain aspects of the railway freight business."

"And have you had occasion to profit by your newly acquired knowledge?"

He shrugged. "I'm still waiting for that opportunity you told me would come." He lifted one finger. "But I'm alert. I'm very alert."

She laughed.

"I imagine Tennessee is still very much involved with her old boy."

"He's a dear," Victoria said. "And he's been so kind to us."

"It would be a pleasure to be kind to you."

"Why, Lloyd, are you flirting with me?"

"If I were, would you be offended?"

"Should I be?"

"I would be very pleased if you weren't."

"I am a very considerate person."

He smiled. "Have you had dinner?"

"What do you have in mind?"

"The new Delmonico's. I haven't had a decent meal since I was last in New York."

"Give me fifteen minutes to change my dress."

Three nights later, in a hotel room, Lloyd discovered that Victoria Claflin was not as active or as vocal as her sister during the act of love. Instead, she was the complete woman, soft, clinging, and intense. She was everything he had imagined. He was in love again, just as he had been in love with Tennessee when it was she who was in his bed, or with Rosanna under the same circumstances.

Having shared with Victoria what was, in his mind, the ultimate intimacy, he felt a new affinity for her, a kinship, a closeness that was, in fact, a weakness. In his mind sexual union was also union of purpose and trust. Like many men he assumed without expressing it in words that the giving of her body entailed loyalty from a woman.

With Victoria cuddling him, he believed that their lovemaking had estranged all others from her allegiance, made her his confidante, and made him her intimate friend. This line of thinking reminded him that she had pointed out that a freight rate war was beginning between the New York Central and the Erie. "Vee," he said, "is the commodore trying to break the Erie by taking losses on freight on the Central?"

For a moment Victoria didn't answer. But she, not unlike members of the opposite sex, had experienced the phenomenon that set tongues a-wagging in postcoital carelessness. "What does it seem to you?"

"A few weeks ago it cost one hundred twenty-five dollars to ship a carload of cattle from Buffalo to the New York City stockyards. Yesterday Gould cut his rates to fifty dollars a carload to match the New York Central."

"I would say that someone is up to something," Victoria said.

"I checked the going price on the hoof for beef cattle," Miles told her. "It's holding firm."

"Ummm?"

"I'm slow," Lloyd said, chuckling, "but I think I'm finally getting the idea that the opportunity you promised is at hand. The price of shipping cattle is down, but the purchase price hasn't dropped. If someone invested in cattle now, his expenses would be down, so his profits would be greater."

"Clever boy," Victoria said.

"Trouble is, I'm a bit low in ready cash," he said. "You remember that I told you I'd have something you might be interested in putting a few dollars into?"

"Yes."

"The time is not quite right," he said. "And all my available capital is tied up."

"Ummm," she said again.

"Now, if a certain lady broker I know had an investor in mind, I would be willing to do the legwork in cattle country upstate and out West," he offered.

"This lady broker could not afford, number one, to recommend investing in cattle to her clients and, number two, to make it appear that she was taking advantage of a certain old boy's financial dealings."

"I can see that."

"Don't be greedy, darling boy," she said, sounding very much like Tennessee. "Borrow the money from your boss and share the profits with him."

Jay Gould tented his fingers and stared through them at Lloyd Miles. Commodore Vanderbilt had just lowered the cost of transporting cattle from Buffalo to New York to twenty-five dollars a carload.

"What do you know about cattle?" Gould asked coldly.

"They have four legs. They eat hay and make mooing sounds, and their destiny is to be cut up, cooked, and eaten." He leaned forward. "And right now there's a built-in bonus profit in shipping a carload of them on the New York Central Railroad."

"It goes against the grain to hear you talk of shipping on the Central," Gould said.

Lloyd smiled confidently. "I merely thought, Mr. Gould, that it would sit easier with you to have Cornele take the loss than have it borne by the Erie. It makes no difference to me. The extra profit from the savings on shipping cost is there on either line. All I need is seed money. I think a couple of hundred thousand should do it."

"That's within your means," Gould said. "Why are you coming to me?"

"Well, I work for you," Lloyd said. "I'll admit that my loyalty is for sale, but right now you're buying it."

"Big of you," Gould said icily. "I'll let you know."

When Gould matched the Central's twenty-five-dollar-a-carload rate, Cornelius Vanderbilt, never noted for his even temper, slashed out in fury and lowered the freight rate on the New York Central to one dollar per carload of cattle. When Lloyd walked into Jay Gould's office the morning after Vanderbilt's last gambit, Gould handed him a checkbook.

"Just stop by the bank and sign the signature card," Gould said. "We split all profits fifty-fifty."

"That's a little steep," Lloyd said, "since I'm going to be the one living in country boardinghouses and wading around in cow pastures back in the sticks."

"The money man gets half," Gould said. "Take it or leave it. There are other men around who can buy cattle."

"Thank you," Lloyd said. He opened the checkbook. There was no balance indicated. He raised his eyebrows in question.

"The amount will depend upon how many head you can

buy and how many the Central is willing to transport at a dollar a carload," Gould told him.

Lloyd nodded. Getting a blank check from Jay Gould was, he found, rather satisfying. "I appreciate your trust," he said.

"It is more a delegation of authority than trust," Gould said. "I know where to find you, you see."

"You're all heart, Jay," Lloyd said, experimenting with familiarity. A smile was his answer. Emboldened, he said, "Mr. Gould, if it should be revealed later that you shipped a great many head of cattle on the Central at a dollar a carload, what would the effect be on Central stock?"

Gould touched one finger to his lower lip, pondered, then nodded. "After they stopped laughing at Cornele, I imagine they'd sell off a few shares."

"Enough to hurt?"

"One can only hope," Gould said.

For his part Lloyd hoped that New York Central stock would be sold with losses that would cut to the bone of large holders . . . for Abby's father, Psaleh Kershaw, had the bulk of his small fortune invested in Vanderbilt's railroad.

CHAPTER 13

Although Leah enjoyed her time with Lloyd furnishing the apartment in New York, she was relieved when he had had enough of the sibling togetherness and went off to his work. On her first free morning she took a cab to the office of Woodhull, Claflin, and Company. Victoria greeted her warmly. She was introduced to the generously proportioned Tennessee.

The *Woodhull and Claflin's Weekly* had no real home of its own. Most of the work, Leah found, was done at the house on Fifteenth Street by Victoria's two male advisers, Colonel James Harvey Blood, Victoria's husband, and Stephen Pearl Andrews.

Andrews, Leah decided, was an odd man. He was wealthy enough to be able to indulge in the promotion of a variety of radical causes, ranging from a form of socialism, through a group that he called Pantarchy, to women's suffrage and free love.

Leah was disillusioned when she learned that the majority of the articles that appeared in the *Weekly* under the names of Victoria and Tennessee were, in fact, written by Andrews or Blood. Both writers seemed to agree with

Thomas Jefferson, who stated that he had little respect for any man who could spell a word only one way.

Leah's job was to copyedit the material for the *Weekly*. She was given an office at Woodhull, Claflin, and Company. As she began work on the next week's edition of the *Weekly,* Victoria and Tennessee kept popping in to see how she was faring. Victoria's warmth was more than matched by that of her younger sister. Tennie was a tea drinker, and each time she brewed a new pot, she brought a cup to Leah. She took the opportunity to question Leah about her life, her past, and the way she thought about a variety of subjects.

Tennie's curiosity was friendly and companionable, and she was so very easy to talk to that within a week Leah had revealed almost all her secrets. When she told Tennessee that she had been deeply in love with a man of whom her brother disapproved, Tennie snorted.

"First of all," Tennie said, "it's foolish to fall in love with just one man. Secondly, I wish that Vee and I had been there when Lloyd told you that you were not to marry the man you loved." She frowned with indignation. "The very idea! Men are such pigheaded hypocrites. I don't know whether to be angry with that darling boy or with you for letting him run your life."

"Well, Tennie, we can't all be as strong as you and Victoria," Leah pointed out.

"Why not?" She giggled. "Let me confess something. It's not being strong, actually. It's being wily. Woman is physically weaker than man. Her two great advantages are here." She tapped her forehead. "And here." She indicated a spot below the waist. "I think I need to have a talk with our darling boy."

Now Leah was the curious one. "How well do you know Lloyd?"

Tennessee smiled. "Are you sure you want me to answer that question?"

Leah flushed.

"He asked me to marry him."

"What?"

"Ah, you see? You thought you knew your brother, didn't you?" She smiled fondly. "Let me tell you, Leah dear, that you can't really know a man until you've had him in your bed."

"He really wanted to marry you?" Leah asked.

"How would you like having me for a sister-in-law?"

"I'd love it," Leah said earnestly.

"Well, I wouldn't object to having you for a sister, but there's no likelihood of it. I tried marriage once. My goodness, men can be so possessive." She fell silent, sipped at her tea.

Leah, meanwhile, corrected the spelling of a word in the piece she'd been reading.

"Is that supposed to be my contribution for the week?" Tennie asked, peeking at the page.

"It has your name on it," Leah replied.

"Oh, my, do I detect disapprobation?"

Leah decided to be honest in expressing her opinions. "I will admit that I was surprised to learn that the very impressive writings of the Claflin sisters come from the pens of two men."

"Pshaw, little sister," Tennessee said. "If you can get men to do the work, it's best to let them do it—with the proper supervision, of course."

"Tennie, is it because of Colonel Blood and Mr. Andrews that so much is made of free love in the *Weekly*?" She wondered what the women of America would think if they knew that one of the basic planks in the Claflin sisters' platform for equal rights for women was being voiced by men.

"They write what Victoria and I tell them to write," Tennie said defensively.

"But if it became widely known that men write the arguments for free love, wouldn't some people say that it is all a male plot to destroy the modesty and morality of the American woman, so that men might more easily satisfy their own hungers?"

Tennie looked thoughtful. "I hadn't thought of it that way." Then she shook her head. "No, I think we've made it clear how we feel on the subject. It's on record. I think that every newspaper in the country printed Victoria's speech when she said, 'Yes! I am a free lover. I have an inalienable, constitutional, and natural right to love whom I may, to love as long or as short a period as I can, to change that love every day if I please.' "

Although Leah was not comfortable with the Woodhull-Claflin stand for unrestricted sexual activity for women, she became more committed with each passing day to what she considered the foundation plank for the women's movement, the right to vote. Other areas of freedom were attractive to her as well. After all, she told herself, she was an equal partner in her relationship with her brother. True, Lloyd's work produced the money that made their comfortable way of life possible, but she made an important contribution by seeing to it that he never had to concern himself with domestic affairs. His clothing was always ready for him; his bed was made; his apartment clean and neat; his meals were served on time; he did not have to bother with household bills. Yes, she had rights, and she promised herself that she would never again submit to Lloyd's idea of what was best for her.

It seemed incongruous to her that Lloyd had objected to both Philip and Harold Berman as prospective brothers-in-law, while he himself had proposed to a self-professed promiscuous woman. Leah could not understand the male double standard. She would have welcomed Tennessee as a sister-in-law, but why would any man want to marry a woman who was at the beck and call of an old man like Commodore Vanderbilt?

From the beginning of Leah's employment on the *Weekly,* Lloyd had been curious about her workdays. Before her talk with Tennessee, Leah felt flattered by his interest in her affairs. Afterward she understood why he asked so many questions. It was not that he was interested in her work; he merely wanted to hear about Tennie.

When next Tennessee brought her a cup of tea and sat down for a little chat Leah asked, "Why wouldn't you consider marrying my brother?"

Tennie laughed. "Well, he's not rich enough, for one thing."

"Really now, that's not a reason. Lloyd is going to be very rich, I'm sure."

"He's a darling boy. . . ." Tennie said.

"But?"

"Think of what he expects from you. You perform all the duties of a wife—housekeeping, cooking, cleaning. Don't you think he'd expect the same of me?"

"No, I think he'd hire as many servants as you would want."

Tennie laughed. "So you reject that reason, too. All right. How about this: I don't want to get married. If I did, I wouldn't marry your brother because he is more in love with Lloyd Miles than he could ever be with any woman."

Leah was stunned. But as Tennessee smiled at her to soften the impact of the criticism, Leah remembered with a sinking feeling that Lloyd had given no consideration to her feelings when he forced her to break her engagement to Philip or when he had driven away Harold Berman.

"Did that ring a little bell?" Tennie asked, still smiling. She covered Leah's hand with her own. "My dear, sooner or later you're going to have to make a stand. I think you've taken the first step by having a job—at least now you'll have a little money of your own. But mark my words, a time will come when you're going to be asked to make another choice as difficult as the one you made when you obeyed your brother's wishes about not marrying the man you loved. I only hope that next time you will have gained enough confidence and courage to do what's right for you."

Leah was disturbed, but she tried to hide it. After Tennie had left her little office she told herself that she had to consider the source of the warning. It had come from a woman who was guilty of the same self-centeredness of which she had accused Lloyd. For what was free love but a surrender to one's own selfish desires?

Lloyd had traveled by train through the rural vastness of states bordering the Great Lakes. He had seen so many cattle that he promised himself that he wouldn't eat a beef-steak for a year. He was distributing Jay Gould's money far and wide. Word had spread throughout Michigan, Wisconsin, Minnesota, Illinois, Indiana, Ohio, and western Pennsylvania that the market for beef cattle was good, that there was a ready buyer, paying cash, awaiting delivery in Buffalo. Transportation by water was relatively cheap, so cattle boats began landing at the Buffalo docks. From there a steady stream of New York Central cattle cars rolled toward the New York slaughterhouses—at one dollar per carload.

Lloyd understood that the key to the whole venture was the same as it had been during his speculation on the gold market: he had to know when to quit. But halting the cattle-buying operation wasn't as quick and simple as sending sell orders to one's broker. Although a broker could cease his activities immediately, boatloads of cattle on the lakes, steaming toward Buffalo, could not be abruptly interrupted. When Lloyd made his last purchase of cattle in markets across the lakes, it would be a matter of days or weeks before the last carload arrived in New York. If he got caught by rising freight rates while still in possession of large numbers of cattle, the profit would be bled out of the whole operation.

Victoria Claflin held Commodore Vanderbilt's hand and with one soft fingertip traced the lines in his palm. "You are concerned about something," she intoned. "Something to do with business. The railroad." She closed her eyes. "Things are booming, but that is not good?"

The old man sighed. "Hell, woman, the whole damned line's tied up with cattle cars. Hundreds of 'em. All of 'em being shipped at a dollar a carload."

"Ah," Victoria said. "I see. Business is good because of the war with the Erie, but you're losing money."

"'S'pected some of the cattle traders to take advantage of the war," he said. "But I didn't 's'pect 'em to buy and ship every gaddanged cow in the world."

Victoria finished her spiritual reading, then left the commodore in the tender care of Tennessee for magnetic healing of the outer and inner man. She went into Leah's office.

"How's your brother adjusting to life in New York?" Victoria asked.

"Very well," Leah said. "But he's out of town right now."

"Oh?"

"Business trip. Out West somewhere, and then to Buffalo."

"Well, it's good weather for traveling," Victoria said. *So, she was thinking, the darling boy has made his move.* She wondered how much money was being made at the expense of the New York Central and the commodore. She smiled because it gave her a sense of satisfaction to know that she had brought about the events that were pitting two of the richest men in America—Jay Gould and Cornelius Vanderbilt—against each other, with Lloyd Miles on the fringes picking up the loose change that scattered when megafortunes clashed. She was grateful to Vanderbilt for his help in getting Tennessee and her established in New York, but he was, after all, a man, and a very domineering man at that. He deserved a bit of comeuppance now and then. As for the Miles siblings, well, she rather liked Lloyd, and he'd been fun in bed; and Leah, a true sister, would benefit from the crumbs that Lloyd was gathering.

Victoria went next to her own office and was reviewing the accounts of one of her lesser clients when a fragile-looking young man with pale blond hair and watery blue eyes was escorted in by the secretary. The young man took a chair when Victoria offered it. He glanced around nervously.

"How may I help you?" Victoria asked, looking down at the slip of paper that the secretary had handed her. "Mr. Sebastian Garnade, is it?"

"Yes," he said. "I have come to you for help in locating Commodore Vanderbilt."

"What makes you think I know the whereabouts of the commodore?" Victoria asked coldly.

Sebastian Garnade squirmed in his seat. "Please, ma'am.

I'm taking a great risk in being here. Everyone knows that you're, ah, associated in business with the commodore. I must find him, and neither his office nor his family will help me." He pulled out a handkerchief and wiped his face. "Oh, God, I do hope he's not out of town. The information I have for him is urgent."

"As you obviously know," Victoria said, "Woodhull, Claflin, and Company often represents Commodore Vanderbilt. If you have any information for him, perhaps I can find a way to get it to him."

"I'm sorry, but what I have to say is for Vanderbilt's ears alone."

"Then I can't help you," Victoria said, standing to dismiss the agitated young man.

"Please," he implored. "If my employer knew that I was here—"

"Young man," Victoria said, "my time is valuable. I must ask you either to explain yourself fully or leave. Shall we start with your telling me just who your employer is and why he would be upset if he knew you were here?"

"I am Jay Gould's personal secretary," Sebastian said.

Victoria's eyes gleamed. A new aspect of the game was afoot. She sat down. "Mr. Garnade," she said, "if, as you say, you have information that would be valuable to the commodore, I advise you to trust me. I can only tell you that I will pass it along to Vanderbilt at my first opportunity." Sebastian started to protest, but Victoria raised one hand, palm out. "That is your only choice. One of my duties is to keep the commodore from being pestered by would-be confidence men with some scheme or the other to get their hands on some of the Vanderbilt money."

"No, it's not that," Sebastian protested.

"What is it, then? You intimate that you have information having to do with Jay Gould or the Erie Railroad. Of course you and I both know that the commodore and Mr. Gould are at odds again. Why would you be willing to betray your employer?"

Tears appeared in Sebastian's watery eyes. "I have worked for him for ten years, with never so much as a word of praise, with no advance in salary. I have endured all that. But I will not take revilement from him. I will not allow him to call me mean and cruel names."

"Which is what he has done?" Victoria asked.

The young man nodded miserably.

"What do you want from Vanderbilt?"

"A position, perhaps?" he suggested.

Victoria shook her head. "The commodore can't stand to have men like you around him."

Sebastian was weeping silently. "Money for information, then. Enough for me to get a fresh start somewhere else."

"That is possible. It depends on the importance of what you have to say."

Sebastian dug into his coat pocket and brought out a folded paper. "Here," he said, thrusting it forward. "Here is evidence that Gould and his people are making a fool out of the commodore." He leaned toward her. "What they're doing is shipping all the cattle they can buy on the New York Central at one dollar a carload. They're taking advantage of the rate war to fleece Vanderbilt and make him look stupid." He looked at her hopefully. "Do you think five thousand dollars would be too much to ask?"

"Oh, yes," she said. She opened a desk drawer, pulled out a stack of greenbacks, counted off one thousand dollars, and handed the bills to Sebastian.

"That's not enough," he whined. "I can't live on that for very long, and I'll have to leave New York."

"I'm sure that you can work out your problems," she said.

"But it's worth more than a thousand," he protested angrily as he jumped up from the chair.

"Little man," she said, also rising, "I want you to get your candy ass out of my office. If you don't, I will see to it that Jay Gould knows within the hour that you have betrayed his private business."

"You wouldn't!" Sebastian gasped. He wiped his eyes. "But what will I do?"

"Go back to work," she suggested. "Bring me tidbits about Mr. Gould's business from time to time. The compensation won't always be as good as today's, but since Gould won't give you a raise, we'll make it enough so that you can buy yourself a trinket or two and live a bit better."

He brightened, then looked doubtful. "But it's so dangerous."

"I thought you wanted to punish Gould for reviling you," Victoria said scornfully.

He nodded. "I do," he said.

"And the beauty of it is that he'll never know," Victoria said. "Will he?"

"No, of course not. He must never know. Oh, God, no. There's no telling what he'd do."

Victoria came around the desk and stood quite close to Sebastian. They were of a height. She put her face within inches of his and said, "Let me tell you what I will do to you if you ever betray me. As it happens, I, too, have certain contacts. With one message I can arrange to have your legs broken at the knees, to have your pretty face pulped. Did you ever have a broken nose?"

"Oh, God, no."

"Don't ever cross me, then," she said. "The men I know love smashing little pretty-boy noses."

Sebastian made a croaking sound, then found his voice enough to say as he made a rapid exit, "I won't betray you. I promise."

Sebastian Garnade was scarcely out the front door when Victoria took long strides down the hall to Leah's office. "Do you know how to get in touch with Lloyd?" she asked without preamble.

"Well, yes and no," Leah said. "I have the address of a hotel in Buffalo, but I'm not sure he's there yet."

"Damn," Victoria said. She leaned over Leah's desk and scribbled on a piece of paper. "I want you to go to the telegraph office and send this message just as it is, word for word. Sign your own name to it. Do you understand?"

"No," Leah said. "I'm sorry, I don't."

"It doesn't matter. Just go and send the telegram."

Leah read the words Victoria had written: "*Ancient Male*

Juvenile near discovery. Broker says stop stock buy orders. Sell quickly."

The wire, signed *Leah,* was waiting for Lloyd when he arrived in Buffalo at his hotel. He had ridden a cattle boat from Chicago, and the aroma that lingered around him was proof of the fact that he had been getting close to his current work. It took only a few seconds for him to understand the message. *Ancient Male Juvenile* was old Vanderbilt. So the commodore was about to find out that Lloyd and Gould were filling New York Central cattle cars and pocketing a hefty profit. The broker, Lloyd knew, would have to be Victoria or Tennessee. He hoped that the wire had come from Tennessee, for he still harbored desires for her. The rest was obvious if one read *livestock* for stock.

He sent wires to Chicago and Milwaukee in time to cancel large orders to buy beef on the hoof. There were only two cattle boats currently on the lakes, so he was in fairly good shape. He waited in Buffalo until the last two boats were unloaded and the cattle aboard New York Central cattle cars on the way to New York City.

Suddenly the New York Central's booming business in transporting cattle was cut to a trickle. The stockyards in the city were full to overflowing. The price of beef on the hoof dropped just after Lloyd Miles had sold his last carload. At meat counters throughout the city housewives were pleased to find that they could afford the better cuts of beef.

Cornelius Vanderbilt, still fuming about the intransigence of the owners of the Erie Railroad, watched his rail stocks tumble once more after earnings reports had been leaked to show the losses the New York Central had incurred since the freight rate war began. The commodore poured money into the market, trying to bolster prices, but a minor panic was under way, a selling frenzy that affected only a few stocks, the New York Central most of all.

Psaleh Kershaw knew Cornelius Vanderbilt only slightly. He had known Andrew Carnegie much better, and he considered calling on the wizard of steel to ask him for advice. But things happened too quickly for him to do even that. Suddenly a wave of concern washed over Wall Street, followed by sell orders that panicked Kershaw into dumping all of his New York Central Stock at a loss that was, for a man who was only a little bit rich, devastating.

The events leading to Kershaw's personal financial tragedy began when the last carload of Lloyd's cattle was unloaded and paid for. Lloyd went to Gould's office to make his final report and to write, in Gould's presence, a check for his half of the profits. There were only five zeros in the figure he wrote, but he was pleased, for the numeral in front of the five zeros was a four. He'd made over four hundred thousand dollars in a matter of a few weeks.

Gould was not ecstatic about his four hundred thousand; he'd risked more than that in an hour on the gold market. But he was mightily pleased to know that Vanderbilt had been bested once more. "Miles," he said, "I think we ought to give the old boy's tail another little twist by letting him know who did it to him."

Lloyd shrugged. "I'd prefer that you keep my name out of it."

"Not hungry for fame?" Gould asked, with a sardonic smile. "Or are you simply afraid of Vanderbilt?"

"Let's say that I have nothing to gain by making the commodore aware that Lloyd Miles exists."

"Suit yourself," Gould agreed. "But this story is too good to keep quiet."

And so it became known that Jay Gould had bought every head of cattle he could lay his hands on and had shipped them to market on his rival's railroad at one dollar per carload. The laughter on Wall Street was a mixture of pleasure at seeing the old lion of American finance have his tail twisted and begrudging admiration for Gould's "smart" maneuver.

Jim Fisk threw a gala at the opera house. The occasion was the birthday of his steady mistress, Josie Mansfield. Josie was resplendent in a new Paris creation. Looking as sleek as a seal, Jim was stuffed into evening formal wear. Lloyd Miles arrived alone. He had visited the Woodhull-Claflin house on Fifteenth Street, where he had been allowed a full five minutes with Tennessee.

Her words were still ringing in his ears as he walked into the hall to the strains of a full orchestra: *"You are becoming tiresome, darling boy. You're so unbecomingly persistent. I've told you and I've told you that I have no intention of ever getting married again, and certainly not to you. Now, will you please go?"*

And as he was walking out, she told him not to return until she issued him an invitation.

He had turned to face her then, and she was suddenly nothing more than a chubby little woman with a quite ordinary face. At that moment he wondered why he'd ever wasted his time on her. "If I come back, it will not be to see you," he said.

"My, my. Am I supposed to be shattered? Who will be the lucky recipient of your favors, darling boy, my mother?" She laughed.

"Good-bye, Tennie."

"If you're speaking of Victoria," Tennessee continued, "she has better things to do."

"Let Victoria speak for herself," Lloyd said. "She has the only set of brains in this family anyhow."

Victoria suddenly stepped into the room, her eyes blazing. She had been listening, standing out of sight in the hallway.

"Victoria," Lloyd said, smiling. "I didn't know you were here."

"Obviously," she said. "You have the nerve to belittle my sister?"

"Uh, I haven't had a chance to thank you."

"For what?" she asked in a frigid tone.

"For a certain communication," he said.

"Are you trying now to make my sister think that I've been going behind her back to take her leavings?" Victoria demanded.

"Not at all," Lloyd said, a bit shaken by Victoria's hostility. "I'm sorry."

"I should think that you owe the apology to Tennie," Victoria said.

What in the hell is going on? he wondered. *Why this sudden attack from Victoria?* Manhood asserted itself. "Tennie can go to hell for all I care."

"I think you had better leave," Victoria said.

"Perhaps I'd better," Lloyd said. "I'm sure that somewhere in this city there are women who make sense."

"Poor *little* man," Victoria crooned. "Look, Tennie, we've hurt his little feelings."

So now, as Lloyd looked around to see if he knew anyone in attendance at Fisk's party at the opera house, he was in a belligerent mood. His attitude improved, however, when he realized that the entire female cast of the opera house company was present, along with a fairly good representation of middle to lower upper-level New York society. He made his way to where the flamboyant Fisk was basking in the attentions of a group of brokers and businessmen.

"Well, here's the conquering hero!" Fisk crowed. "Here's the lad, gentlemen, who was the brains behind the latest fleecing of the great Commodore Vanderbilt."

"You do me too much credit, Jim," Lloyd said quickly. He shrugged and smiled modestly. "I ran a few errands for Jay, that's all."

"I guess you've heard, Lloyd, that the old boy wasn't the only one who got his fingers singed. That old walrus Psaleh Kershaw lost his nerve and sold out at the lowest point." Fisk roared with laughter. "I reckon he'll be shopping in earnest for a son-in-law now, one that can lend him money."

"How much did he drop?" Lloyd asked.

"Oh, couple of million, that's all," Fisk said.

Lloyd's grin was wolfish.

"If you're interested in being looked over," Fisk said with a wink, "Kershaw's daughter is here."

Lloyd found Abby standing as he'd seen her stand once before, with but aside from a group of young women. She was more regal than ever. She was wearing a magnificent black gown with black lace around her throat. Her green eyes shone like emeralds. He could not resist talking to her.

"I still work for the Erie Railroad," he said, moving in close, his eyes on hers.

"Indeed," she said flatly.

"But I understand that working for the Erie might be just slightly preferable, at the moment, to working for the New York Central. I hear that some of the Central's stockholders might not be able to come up with enough money to pay a good man his salary."

"They could pay much more than you'd be worth," Abby said.

"Now, how on earth can you make such a statement, Miss Kershaw, when you've done nothing to assess my worth?"

"One is able to put a value on you from a distance," Abby said. "Which would be the way I would prefer it."

He seized her arm. "You're going to dance with me, you frigid bitch. And you're going to like it."

She surprised him with a smile that opened up the heavens. Her green eyes sparkled, and then the smile was gone. "Why, of course I'll dance with you, Mr. Miles. As for liking it, well, you'll just have to guess about that, won't you?"

CHAPTER 14

The morning after Lloyd had forced himself on Abby Kershaw, he began the day with a headache brought on by too much drink and an attitude engendered by Abby's amused, slightly contemptuous acceptance of his attentions. He had danced with her only once and had found the temperature to be decidedly frigid. As a result he had left her so that he might find female company that was, if not totally satisfying, at least made cordial by the passing of a modest amount of cash.

He had proved himself in the competition that made New York the financial center of the nation, but in his personal life nothing had changed. He had once again been rejected by Tennessee Claflin. Even the more sophisticated Victoria had turned against him. Rosanna had not returned to the city from parts unknown. But Abby was the woman most in his thoughts. Her beauty and social standing captivated him, while her regal tolerance of his forcefulness rankled even more than her previous insults.

Leah was at the breakfast table when he emerged, dressed for the day, from his bedroom. Coffee steamed in an antique English sterling pot. Eggs and ham were being kept warm in silver servers. Leah poured his coffee and inquired as to his preferences.

"I want to have a talk with you," he said gruffly.

"At your service, sir," she said lightly.

Her sunny attitude exacerbated his bad mood. She was, he knew, pleased with the direction of her life. She loved her work and was meeting fascinating, powerful people. Only the day before she had told him that Victoria had introduced her to Theodore Tilton, head of one of the most powerful women's suffrage organizations and friend and confidant of the famous Reverend Henry Ward Beecher. She saw no clouds on the horizon.

"I'm serious," he said, putting down his fork without having taken a bite. "We might as well have it out now. You're to break off all contact with Victoria Woodhull and Tennessee Claflin."

Leah paled, and then high color rose to her face and throat.

"That means, of course, that you will have to resign your position with the *Weekly,*" Lloyd said. There. It was done. He had spoken. It was over. He picked up his fork and took a bite of ham and eggs, followed by a hot buttered biscuit.

He was startled when, after a pause, she said, "I'm sorry, Lloyd, I won't do that."

He wasn't sure he'd heard her correctly. His hand paused halfway to his mouth. "I beg your pardon?"

"For once in my life I am doing something that I consider worthwhile," she said. "I have made some very good friends. I will not quit my job. I will not insult Victoria and Tennessee."

He dropped his fork with a clatter. His voice grated. "You will do as I say as long as you live under my roof."

"Then consider my residence here a temporary condition," she shot back. She was clearly amazed at her own daring. "It will take me a day or two, I suspect, to find something that I can afford. Will you allow me that much time under your roof?"

"By God, Leah—"

She rose, looked down at him, and there was an expression of resolve on her face that he'd never seen before. "I'm sorry, Lloyd," she said calmly. "But what you demand is selfish and unreasonable. I won't even ask why you've so suddenly decided that your good friends Victoria and Tennessee are not worthy of my admiration and friendship. I suspect that it has something to do with the fact that Tennessee refuses to marry you. But that's your affair, not mine."

Lloyd sputtered, but he could not find words as she turned and marched off into her bedroom, her head high, her back stiff. "Goddamn it, Leah!" he bellowed after her.

She turned. "I will be out of your house as quickly as possible."

"All right, then!" he yelled. "All right, if that's the gratitude I get after all these years, then move out! It's your choice, not mine."

He did not feel like working. He decided he had earned a day off, so he didn't bother to report to the Erie offices. He walked the streets and burned with resentment for all women. In an Irish bar he drank straight whiskey flavored by Old World peat bogs and listened to the talk of the idlers who had nothing more to do than hang around a saloon before midday.

He lunched alone. He had a rare steak, which possibly, he thought, could have been cut from one of the steers he had bought in the Midwest and transported to New York. His hostility toward the women in his life was blunted by the glow of Irish whiskey and by the passing hours. The food sat well with him, and he left the restaurant to walk again.

The city's energy hummed and throbbed around him. A pretty girl smiled at him. He exchanged tips of the hat with well-dressed gentlemen whom he did not know. He walked through Times Square and was reminded that at one time the area had been a farm owned by a man named Eden.

John Jacob Astor had purchased the heavily mortgaged Eden Farm for almost nothing.

Thinking of Astor made Lloyd morose. He longed for a time when the pickings were easier and the competition less fierce. The Astor fortune had accumulated from the growth of real-estate values on Manhattan Island, and much of the Astor land holdings had resulted from foreclosing on farms and homes during the financial panic of 1837.

Things weren't as simple in the decade following the Civil War as they had been after the War of the Revolution, Lloyd thought regretfully, when Astor had come close to owning 51,012 acres—a full third of Putnam County—after he traveled to England to buy rights to the Tories' confiscated property. Since the heirs of the Loyalists who had owned the property prior to the Revolution had scant hope of regaining their lands, Astor got the rights for less than a hundred thousand dollars. To prevent Astor's ousting the farmers who occupied the land, the state of New York bought Astor's claims for half a million dollars, a respectable sum in the year 1827.

As Lloyd walked, his mood sank once more. Had there indeed been more opportunities in Astor's day? Jay Gould had built a fortune that, if the total sum were known, might not equal Astor's but would come close. During the railroad era several men had become very rich members of what some people called the American Royalty. And that trend, in reality, was just beginning. For some reason, he admitted as he strolled with his hands clasped behind his back, he had been delaying the venture of which he had spoken to Victoria Woodhull. Perhaps he was afraid to commit all of his small fortune.

Well, to hell with all of them, he thought, his spirits rising. He could get along very well without plump Tennessee, vivacious Victoria, the beautiful but deadly Rosanna, and regal Abby. He could even get along without his sister, if that was the way she wanted it. It was time to get on with the work. What was it Harold Berman used to say? Success is the greatest revenge.

Lloyd went back to his apartment. The place seemed sterile, empty. He seldom was there during the day, and when he came home in the evenings Leah was already there and good cooking aromas were emanating from the kitchen. He shrugged off the feeling, opened his personal books, took a pencil in hand, and began to lay out his strategy. His every instinct warned him to be cautious; but if the scheme was to be made to work, it would require everything he had and more.

The Kansas City and Southwest Railroad was a solid little operation under conservative management. Its limited service area had saved it from being gobbled up by the great financial sharks who swam in the oceans of money generated by the railroad boom. But then a small, inexperienced shark named Lloyd Miles had bought a controlling share of the KC&S during the stock market panic that followed Black Friday. Now that Cornelius Vanderbilt had given up on his latest attempt to gain control of the Erie, and now that freight rates were back to normal on both the Erie and the New York Central, the commonsense truth that railroads were the future of the nation had driven stock prices back up to respectable levels. KC&S stood at ninety-five on the day that Lloyd decided to take the plunge.

First he went to the bank—not the one owned by Gould and William Tweed—and put up his KC&S stock as collateral for a loan of three million dollars. Next a trip to Kansas was required, but before leaving he had something to do.

When he entered the apartment late in the evening, no aromatic cooking smells were coming from the kitchen. The lights were on, however, indicating that Leah was there. He found her in her bedroom, packing her clothing into a trunk. She hesitated when she saw him, then returned to her work with renewed dedication.

"Look, sis," Lloyd said.

She had been crying. He knew that by the redness of her nose, her swollen eyes. His heart went out to her.

"I don't think there's anything more to say," she said.

"Yes, there is," he said tenderly, moving toward her.

She backed away.

He stopped. "Leah, I am so sincerely sorry. I won't go into the reasons why I behaved so foolishly this morning."

Tears sprang into her eyes. He moved to her quickly and took her into his arms. "Leah," he said, "you're all I have, and I've kicked myself all day for making you unhappy. Forgive me?"

She sniffed back tears. "I can't give up my job."

"No, no. Keep it. It's all right." He lifted her face with one finger under her chin, then wiped tears from her cheeks. "I don't have to worry about you. You're the finest woman I have ever known. Rather than Victoria and Tennessee being a bad influence on you, you will uplift them. Right?"

She snuffled again and smiled wanly. "Well, I don't know about that."

"Let me help you put things back where they belong," he offered. "And if I ever, ever try to make you think that this is more my home than yours, I want you to come right up and give me a hard, swift kick in the seat."

"Well, you need it sometimes," she said.

"Forgiven?"

"Yes, you rounder," she said, giggling. "When you want to, you can charm the birds out of the trees. I don't understand how Tennie could refuse you."

"Ouch," he said. "Can we forget that?"

"If you want to. It's forgotten." She smiled mischievously. "But maybe I could put in a good word for you."

"No, thank you," he said. "I have other things on my mind."

"I'll go do something about supper," she volunteered.

"Just powder your nose and wash the red out of your eyes," he said. "I'm taking my best girl out to dinner."

The chairman of the board of the KC&S was also the president of the Liberal Bank, in the southwestern Kansas town that was the site of the KC&S roundhouse and offices. He was a man in his early sixties, bearded, smelling of bay rum and cigars. His name was Jackson Roundtree. He looked up in curiosity when Lloyd was escorted into his private office at the bank. He rose reluctantly, for the newcomer wore expensive Eastern clothing.

"I'm Miles," Lloyd said, not waiting for the flunky to introduce him. "Can we talk here?"

Roundtree sucked in his breath. He was not accustomed to being spoken to so abruptly, but he recognized the name of the majority stockholder of the KC&S. "We'll be quite secure here," he said.

Lloyd turned and stared until the young man who had escorted him in turned and hurried out of the office.

"Now, Mr. Miles," Roundtree began genially, "welcome to Liberal. Your first trip to Kansas?"

"And I trust my last," Lloyd said, pulling up a chair. "I won't waste your time and mine, Mr. Roundtree. I am here to take an active part in the management of the KC&S."

"Well, Mr. Miles—"

"Here is what I am going to do," Lloyd said. "I am carrying a cashier's check for three million dollars."

Roundtree's eyes opened wide.

"I'm putting that sum into the treasury of the KC&S."

"Good heavens, man, that's more than—" Roundtree had started to say that was more than the whole railroad was worth, but he caught himself in time. KC&S money was, of course, deposited in his bank.

"In exchange," Lloyd said, "I will take thirty thousand shares of stock—"

"I see no problem there—"

"And three million dollars in convertible bonds," Lloyd concluded.

Roundtree went white. For a moment or two he struggled mentally. He felt a burning desire to see three million dollars deposited in his bank, but he was a deacon in the church and the father of a fine family of six children. He had a dozen grandchildren and he was, perhaps, the most respected man in Liberal and, possibly, in southwestern Kansas. In addition to that, he was an aberration, a man out of his time, for he was not totally imbued with the philosophy of grab and hold. He cleared his throat. "Mr. Miles," he said, "I will not be a part of any scheme to strip the KC&S of its assets or to defraud the public."

Lloyd's face was grim. "You will call a meeting of stockholders as quickly as possible."

"That will take weeks. Our stockholders are so widely scattered—"

"I will give you three days," Lloyd said. "The meeting of the stockholders of the Kansas City and Southwest Railroad will take place at ten o'clock in the morning on Monday, three days from now."

"I can't possibly have a representative group there at such short notice," Roundtree protested.

"The majority of shares will be represented and voted," Lloyd said. "That is all that matters."

He stopped at the desk of the young man who had escorted him into Roundtree's office. "I'm Lloyd Miles," he said. "I own the KC&S Railroad."

"P-p-pleased to meet you sir," the young man said, leaping to his feet.

"And you?" Lloyd demanded.

"P-p-paul Boydston, sir. At your service."

"Paul, do you own any KC&S stock?"

"A f-f-few shares. That's all. M-most people in Liberal have a few shares."

"Paul, I'm going to need a friend here in Liberal, a man of some imagination and ambition. Do you have any suggestions?"

"I would be glad to be of service, if I may," Boydston said, standing straight.

"Where does the railroad have its printing done?"

"Kansas City, sir."

"All right. I want you to get up there, Paul. I need thirty thousand shares of KC&S stock printed. Think you can handle that?"

"But w-w-what about my j-job here at the bank?"

"As of now you're working for me." He put out his hand. "At twice what you're making in the bank. One thousand shares of stock, options on five thousand more. Deal?"

"Yes, sir!" Boydston said, taking Lloyd's hand.

"How soon can you leave for Kansas City?"

"On the next train."

"Good, good," Lloyd said. "There's one other thing I want you to do while you're there." He took a folded sheet of paper from his pocket. "I want you to take this into the office of the largest newspaper in town."

"M-may I read it?"

"Go ahead."

Boydston read quickly, then looked up, his eyes wide in astonishment. "But this can't be true, sir."

"I assure you that it is," Lloyd said. He had carefully composed the announcement on the train. Underneath flowery language was a simple fact that would make news: The Kansas City and Southwest Railroad would lay tracks across the western portion of Indian Territory to Texas. The KC&S would be the first direct rail link with the source of a major portion of the beef that was sold in huge sections of the nation. "What do you find unbelievable about it?"

"Sir, others have tried to negotiate a right-of-way through the Indian nations. The answer has always been no. Even the federal government hasn't been able to convince the various tribes that they should allow a railroad to go through to Texas."

"Paul, how many congressmen do you know?"

"Well, I've met the man who represents our district. . . ."

"I know a few dozen," Lloyd responded. "Look, Texas grows about thirteen percent of all the beef cattle in this country, and the only way to get those cattle to market is to make a long, dangerous, arduous cattle drive from the Texas grazing grounds to the railheads in Kansas. A railroad to Texas will not only lower the price of a steak in Kansas City and New York but will bring prosperity to vast areas of the Southwest."

"Then you've been assured by the people in Washington that we—uh, the KC&S can obtain a right-of-way through the territory?"

"Paul, Paul, haven't you ever heard the old adage that

the wish is father to the deed?" He grinned, patted Boydston on the shoulder. "Trust me," he said. "When does that train leave for Kansas City?"

"May I ask one question, sir?" Boydston said.

"Ask away."

"What about Mr. Roundtree?"

"What about him?"

"He was instrumental in getting the KC&S to build in southwestern Kansas, sir. He's been chairman of the board from the beginning. I don't think he'll like this." He looked a bit pale, and his stutter came back. "B-b-b-because I don't think Mr. Roundtree will accept adages in place of solid treaties with the Indian nations."

"Paul," Lloyd responded, "let me say this to you: I have no intention of letting the biggest minnow in this Kansas mudhole keep me from making the KC&S a household word throughout the United States. Now, you've got a decision to make. You're either with me, or you're not. What will it be?"

Boydston was pale, but he said, "I'm w-w-with you, Mr. Miles."

CHAPTER 15

Even as Philip Trent went through the motions of getting the investigation into the Gold Room scandal under way, he felt that his committee was like an overburdened locomotive on a steep grade, grinding its gears without making forward progress. Gus Trent had other analogies for the committee's functions.

"This investigation is about as useless as tits on a boar hog," Gus said. "It's about as foolish as a doctor doing an autopsy to determine the cause of death on a man with a bullet hole in his forehead. All you have to do is talk with any financial reporter or almost any trader on the stock market to know that Jay Gould was behind it all. And when you prove all that, what good will it do? The man broke no laws, and he's already held in low opinion by the press and the public. He and Fisk have been called foul hyenas and carrion eaters. Whatever you say about him in a committee hearing won't affect his life one bit. He'll still be a very rich man."

James Garfield was on the committee, having been appointed by the radical leadership in the Republican party. Philip had not been too happy about Garfield's becoming a member, but he was learning out of self-defense to be a politician. He had welcomed Garfield politely, in spite of his lack of respect for the man. His prickly relationship with the congressman from Ohio went back to a time when Lloyd Miles had asked Philip to place a bet on a horse race that later proved to be fixed. Garfield had made a slighting remark, implying superior morality on his part, without listening to Philip's explanation that he had been ignorant of the tampering and merely placing the bet for a friend and that he had given back the winnings when it became apparent that one of the horses had been drugged.

Philip's time to reciprocate for Garfield's gratuitous insult had come when Oakes Ames included Garfield's name on the list of congressmen who had been offered Crédit Mobilier stock at a fraction of its worth. With evident satisfaction Philip had reminded Garfield of the remark made long before on a cold winter day after a fine horse died of medications administered to slow it; he asked Garfield, in effect, what had happened to his elevated code of ethics when more money than could be bet on a horse race was involved.

Garfield had escaped censure in the Crédit Mobilier affair by claiming that he had refused Ames's offer and returned the stock. That Ames had delivered the stock in January of 1868 and Garfield had not "refused" the offer until two years later was overlooked by his colleagues in Washington but had not been forgotten by Philip Trent. In addition, at least in Philip's eyes, Garfield, an attorney, had difficulty in distinguishing between those clients who wanted his services because of his legitimate legal skill and those who were seeking political influence.

Adam Grey, who as Philip's top aide was coordinating the hearings, attracted good newspaper coverage even before the hearings opened by releasing the names of witnesses to be called. The list was a roll call of New York financiers, with the names of Jay Gould and Jim Fisk near the top.

Philip had hired a man to assist Adam with getting to and from the hearing room. The burly young man was strong enough to handle Adam easily and to hoist his wheelchair in and out of an open carriage. To get to the second-floor conference room Adam's man merely lifted chair, Adam, and all the folders of paperwork and, without so much as breathing hard, waddled up the stairs. The whole affair nettled Adam because it made him feel helpless; but he accepted it as being necessary, for he did want to take part in the action. He especially wanted to be present on the first day to hear Philip interrogate the first witnesses—the newsman Phineas Headley and Mr. Lloyd Miles.

Lloyd Miles was an angry man. He had just returned from Kansas, where he had set in motion a scenario that would either make or break him, to find that he'd been subpoenaed to testify before the Trent committee. He had consulted lawyers and had been warned that above all other concerns, he did not want to earn a contempt-of-Congress citation; his only alternative was to appear exactly when he'd been asked to appear, to be as polite and informative as he could possibly be, and to keep his mouth shut when he felt that it would not be possible to speak without departing from the absolute truth. Perjuring himself before a congressional committee would be even more serious than refusing to appear as summoned.

He strode from a cab to the steps of the Capitol Building on a clear, pleasant spring morning to see Phineas Headley standing on the sidewalk. Lloyd frowned. Headley had been pestering him since the gold-market crash, asking for appointments for an interview, and approaching him on the street.

"I have nothing to say to you," Lloyd told him angrily as Headley tipped his hat and smiled.

The journalist matched Lloyd's strides as they took the stairs two at a time. "Perhaps, Mr. Miles, the committee will get answers to the very questions I've been wanting to ask you," Headley suggested mildly.

"Whatever I say before the committee, Headley, you can print. But I retain the right to choose with whom I talk in my private life. I have not chosen you, nor will I at any

future date, so do your damnedest." He paused at the top
of the stairs. "Fortunately there will be other journalists
covering these hearings, so I can be assured that at least
some of them will report the proceedings without bias."

"What do you think Mr. Gould is going to tell the committee?" Headley, ever the newsman, asked, seeking just
one tidbit from the man who had avoided him so success-
fully for so long.

"Go to hell," Lloyd seethed.

Headley acquitted himself well as the first witness before
the Trent committee. He identified himself as a free-lance
journalist, coauthor of the book that bore General Lafayette Baker's name. Prompted by Adam Grey, he stated that
early in September of the previous year he had become
aware of unusual activity on the gold market and, thinking
that there might be a story there, had followed the action
that led to the price of gold rising to $162 before the mar-
ket crashed.

Philip asked a series of questions, which established that
Headley had been able to determine the identity of several
men actively buying gold during the period of rising prices.
The reporter named the brokers who had handled most of
the buying and stated that it was common knowledge in the
Gold Room that they represented Jim Fisk and Jay Gould.

"Aside from Mr. Gould and Mr. Fisk," Philip asked,
"were you able to identify any other men who, by purchasing gold, helped to elevate the price of that commodity?"

Headley named three of the small fry who had been
riding on the coattails of Fisk and Gould and added, "I was
able to trace specifically the buy-and-sell record of Mr.
Lloyd Miles."

"May I ask just how you accomplished this?" Philip
asked.

"In all respect, sir, for you and for the authority of this
committee, I do have an obligation as a journalist to protect my sources," Headley said. "I can only say that my
information is authentic and that I have placed a copy of

Mr. Miles's gold-trading activities during August and September of last year in the hands of your aide, Mr. Grey."

"I understand, Mr. Headley," Philip said, "that all your attempts to interview Mr. Gould and Mr. Fisk about their participation in this affair were rejected."

"Yes, sir, that is correct. I have been unable to obtain an interview with either of the men you have named."

"And was Mr. Miles cooperative when you asked him to speak with you about the gold market crisis?"

"He was not, sir." Headley looked at Lloyd and smiled. "In fact, his latest communication to me, just this morning, was to tell me he would like for me to take a long trip to a well-known locale where the temperature is very much above the level of comfort."

Other members of the committee, not wanting their names left off the official transcript for the day's proceedings, questioned Headley, but without plowing new ground. Then it was time for Lloyd Miles to take his place at the witness table.

"Would you please state your name, address, and occupation?" Adam requested.

"My name is Lloyd Miles. I live in Manhattan. I am employed by the Erie Railroad in its New York office."

"In what capacity, Mr. Miles?" Adam asked.

"Until recently I was manager of the Erie's Washington office," Lloyd said. "I am now a special assistant to the president of the Erie Railroad."

"And the president of the Erie is . . ."

"Mr. Jay Gould."

"As special assistant to Mr. Gould," Adam asked, "what are your duties?"

"It's difficult to be specific, Mr. Grey," Lloyd said. "And, in all respect I would hesitate to reveal the private business of my employer so long as it has nothing to do with the matter being inquired into by this committee."

"Mr. Miles," Philip said quietly.

Lloyd turned his eyes to Philip for the first time. His gaze was level, challenging. He smiled tightly. "Yes, Mr. Trent?"

"Perhaps you could give us, without breaching the confidence of your employer, an idea of just what sort of services you perform for the Erie and Mr. Gould."

"Yes, sir, I can," Lloyd said, still staring defiantly into Philip's eyes. "Just recently I made a trip into the Midwest to purchase cattle for Mr. Gould."

There was a burst of laughter from the audience, for the story of Jay Gould's tweaking of the tail of the commodore, the lion of Wall Street, had captured the imagination of the public.

"Yes, we have heard the results of that trip," Philip said. "You are, then, a sort of errand boy for Jay Gould?"

Lloyd's eyes flared, his lips twitched, but he regained his composure. "I prefer the word *assistant,* or perhaps even *executive assistant.*"

"Would you say that you are very close to Mr. Gould?"

"I think, Mr. Trent, that no man is very close to Mr. Gould."

"But you are a trusted associate?"

"I would hope so."

"Trusted enough to be told in advance that Gould and Jim Fisk intended to establish a corner in gold?" Philip asked.

Lloyd's facial expression was under iron control. "Mr. Chairman, I consider that an indirect accusation, and I reject it entirely. I was under the impression, sir, that I have been called to Washington to testify about my dealing in the gold market last fall. I am ready to answer any and all questions regarding my own business, for I have nothing to hide. I readily state that I speculated in gold during August and September. I state equally as quickly that in doing so I violated no state or federal legislation. I don't think I have to inform elected representatives of our Republic that in the United States of America if an individual's whim is to buy gold, that is his own affair and his right under the capitalistic system that has made our nation great. If, however, you have brought me to Washington in the hope that I will betray the confidence of my employer, then, sirs, you are to be disappointed."

"I remind you, Mr. Miles," Adam said, his voice rising, "that you are under oath and that there are federal laws requiring you not only to respect this committee but to answer its questions fully and truthfully."

"I am more than willing to do so, so long as those questions pertain to me and my affairs and not to those of others. I do not consider it my right nor my duty to reveal the business affairs of anyone other than myself, and indeed I am not qualified to do so, since I know only my own affairs."

"I will defer my last question for the moment," Philip said. "Mr. Miles, the record of your trading in gold, as submitted by Mr. Headley, shows that you began to purchase the commodity early in August and that you sold all your holdings of both specie and gold-redeemable bonds several days before what is now being called Black Friday."

"Is that a question?" Lloyd asked.

"Consider it so."

"Yes."

"Thank you," Philip said. "Are you to be congratulated on being a particularly astute observer of gold market trends, or did you have inside information that the federal government was preparing to step into the gold market and bring prices back to normal by selling coin from the federal Treasury?"

Lloyd reached for a glass of water and took a few sips before answering. He knew that he was on thin ice now. He hadn't expected the questions to get so quickly into that particularly sensitive area. "Actually, Mr. Trent, I can claim neither advantage." He laughed. "I think my net worth would show that I am not as astute as many. I'm not a rich man. Let me say, sir, that I got out of the gold market in time to preserve my modest profits either because my nerve failed me or because I am not basically a greedy man."

"You did not address yourself to the second part of my question," Philip said.

"Did I have inside information?" Lloyd shook his head.

"Privileged information, no. I had only the facts available to everyone."

Philip waited for long seconds. "Would you care to elaborate as to just what facts were in your possession when you decided to sell your gold holdings while the price of gold was still on the rise?"

"The information that came to me and convinced me that it was time to get out of the gold market was available to everyone interested enough to obtain it from the subtreasury in New York."

"From General Daniel Butterfield?" Philip asked.

"It was he, yes, who announced—*to the public*—that the secretary of the Treasury had decided to pay in gold interest on the nation's debt."

"Are you saying, Mr. Miles, that this announcement of future policy, of an action to be taken perhaps months in the future, was enough to make you think that the government would intervene in the gold market?"

"Well, I wasn't sure, of course," Lloyd replied. "There are times when successful trading is a guessing game, Mr. Chairman. Perhaps, as I said, I just lost my nerve."

James Garfield indicated to Philip that he had questions for the witness. Philip leaned back and listened closely as Garfield took over the questioning.

"I assume that you are aware of the conjecture that is being put forth in the nation's press regarding the events in the Gold Room last fall," Garfield said.

"I do read the papers."

"You have read, then, that in some way Mr. Abel Corbin was involved with those who wanted to corner the market in gold."

"Yes."

"I understand that you are a good friend of the Corbins."

"It is my pleasure to answer that in the affirmative," Lloyd said. "I am quite fond of both Mr. and Mrs. Corbin."

"And through Mrs. Corbin, who just happens to be the

sister-in-law of Mrs. Julia Grant, the wife of the President, you are on familiar terms with the Grant family."

"I wouldn't quite go that far," Miles said. "As an ex-officer in the Army of the Republic I am, of course, acquainted with the general."

"And not with Mrs. Grant?" Garfield asked. Before Lloyd could answer, the Ohio congressman added, "The visitors' log at the White House lists you as having called on Mrs. Julia Grant in September on a specific day, that happens nearly to coincide with the date on which Abel Corbin claims that his wife received a letter from his sister-in-law. That letter, incidentally, has a direct bearing on the matter before this committee. Do you deny that you visited Mrs. Julia Grant in September of last year?"

"I do not," Lloyd said. "I had dropped by the White House to have a purely social word with the President. As it happened, he was out of town. Mrs. Grant was kind enough to offer me lunch." He held up one hand to halt Garfield's next question. "I do not, however, have any knowledge of any letter written by Mrs. Grant, nor did any subject discussed between Mrs. Grant and me have any bearing on what was happening in the gold market."

As Lloyd lied, thus risking prosecution for perjury, his gaze was even more level, his eyes were more piercing. And he felt a giddy sense of unreality, for up to that very moment he had not decided just how he would answer questions, should they arise, about his contact with the President's wife. He was, in fact, a bit amazed by the strength of his aversion to Garfield's trying to drag Julia Grant into the mire of the investigation. If anyone had asked Lloyd Miles if he was gentleman enough to risk his freedom and reputation for the honor of a lady, he would have laughed. But there was more to it than that. His decision had been based in the years of cataclysm, the four years of war. Although his participation in battle had been limited to two raids behind Confederate lines—one with the navy daredevil William B. Cushing and one with his own command—he, like most veterans of that bloody time, felt kinship with every man who had worn blue; like most

of his countrymen he recognized Ulysses S. Grant as the
man who had won the war.

In those few moments that he had to consider his answer
to James Garfield's question, many images had crossed his
mind: Grant and Sherman posing together in the West
when both were just lesser generals exiled to what was then
considered to be a secondary front . . . Grant after Cold
Harbor, his eyes haunted . . . and Grant as President,
shoulders bent, no longer the proud, erect, farseeing warrior. He was a weary man, a man out of his element among
the sleazy denizens of Clown Town, a man whose only
faults were loyalty to his friends and too much trust for his
family members and associates.

Lloyd Miles had received a medal of commendation for
his attempt to cut the Wilmington and Weldon Railroad.
True, it was not the Congressional Medal of Honor, which
had been awarded to both William B. Cushing for sinking
the Confederate ram *Albemarle* and to Philip Trent for, it
was thought, having been killed on a railroad bridge just
inland from Wilmington. Still, Lloyd's was a fine medal and
well deserved, for he had performed courageously in the
failed effort to destroy the railroad that carried supplies
from the port of Wilmington to Lee's army at Petersburg.

But the deeds that had earned him the Distinguished
Service Medal did not represent Lloyd Miles's bravest moment. That came in a congressional hearing room in the
presence of fewer than a dozen members of the House of
Representatives, several interested spectators, and members of the press. There he risked not his life but a charge
of perjury because he would not be a part of the pack of
dogs howling and snipping at the heels of the greatest man
he'd ever known.

And when Lloyd held James Garfield's eyes and said
firmly that Julia Grant and he had not mentioned the gold
market or anything pertaining to it, Philip Trent looked at
Lloyd with grudging respect. Circumstantial evidence made
it almost certain that Lloyd was lying. Abel Corbin, in his
feeble attempt to clear his own name, had turned against
his in-laws and had revealed that Julia had written to her

sister-in-law warning Abel to get out of the gold market "lest he be ruined." Philip chose to believe that Julia might have been intimating that it was the reputation, not the money, of her brother-in-law that was in peril, but it was a delicate distinction. The letter was damning. And it had been written on the same day that Philip himself had visited Julia Grant in the White House. It seemed probable that after Philip had intimated to Julia Grant what was going on, Lloyd, as liaison to Gould and Corbin, would have been contacted by Jennie Corbin and then would have hustled to Washington. What possible reason could he have had for visiting the White House other than to reassure the President's wife and stomp out any possible emotional fires? That was what the rumors were saying. The taint of scandal was leaving a trail of questions through both houses of Congress and approaching the parlor of the White House.

"In the later part of the summer and in the early autumn of last year," James Garfield went on, "President and Mrs. Grant visited Abel and Jennie Corbin in New York. Were you, at any time, in the presence of the President, Mrs. Grant, or both during that visit?"

"I was," Lloyd answered. "As a friend of the Corbins I was invited to a small gathering of friends and relatives in the Corbin house."

"And was Mr. Jay Gould among those who hobnobbed with Mr. Grant in the Corbin house?"

"Hobnobbed? Not exactly. Mr. Gould was a guest, yes."

"And were you in the presidential party that traveled aboard a steamer owned by Jim Fisk?"

"I was," Lloyd said.

Garfield shuffled papers and looked sternly at Lloyd. "Mr. Miles, you recall that you are under oath?"

"I do."

"Upon your oath, and having been reminded that perjury before a congressional committee is a serious crime, did Ulysses S. Grant listen to, talk about, or address the subject of gold?"

"As a matter of fact, yes," Lloyd said smoothly. "There

was, both in the Corbin home and aboard the ship, considerable talk about gold. Mr. Grant had taken advantage of being in New York to call upon one of his most respected advisers. You might remember the man, Mr. Garfield, since you spoke in opposition to his appointment as secretary of the Treasury even though you were not a member of the body, which, under the Constitution, gives advice and consent to the President in such matters—"

"Mr. Miles!" Garfield thundered. "I need no lessons on government from the likes of you!"

"Mr. A. T. Stewart made the trip by water with the Grant party," Lloyd went on, smiling coldly. "I heard Mr. Grant discuss the subject of hard money versus greenbacks, plus other questions pertaining to gold and the gold standard. Several men joined in the conversation."

"Was Mr. Gould among them?"

"Yes, and others."

"Now I want you to consider this question carefully," Garfield said. "You seem to be a very observant man. You heard the conversations involving Mr. Grant?"

"I did."

"Then tell me, Mr. Miles, exactly what Ulysses S. Grant, President of the United States, said to Jay Gould and his cronies that assured them that the Treasury would do nothing to halt their nefarious scheme to get a stranglehold on this nation's money supply."

An immediate reaction swept through the gathering.

Philip Trent banged his gavel. "Mr. Garfield, you are out of order. Moreover, you are impertinent and insulting when you directly accuse the President of wrongdoing without a shred of evidence."

"Mr. Chairman," Garfield replied benignly, "I was merely asking a rhetorical question."

Philip banged his gavel once more. "This committee is in recess until"—he glanced up at the wall clock, then at the members of his committee—"one P.M. Mr. Garfield, gentlemen, I would like a word with all of you in the inner chamber."

* * *

The small room was crowded. There were not enough
chairs. Garfield stood near the door. Philip looked directly
at him when he spoke. "Gentlemen, I hesitated for a long
time before calling for this investigation, because I wanted
to avoid exactly what just happened in the committee
room. I feared that some member of the *opposition* party,
and I have to admit that we allow a few Democrats to sit
with us—"

The three Democrats on the committee chuckled.

"—I feared that our political adversaries would use this
forum as a means to launch an assault on a man who deserves all the loyalty we can give him. Instead this attack
comes from a member of my own party."

"Now I think you are out of order, Trent," Garfield re-
torted. "You may be chairman of this committee, but I
have seniority over you, and, I warrant, I have sources of
information equal or superior to yours."

"If you intend to accuse U. S. Grant of conniving with
the robber barons of Wall Street, Mr. Garfield, you'd better
damned well have your evidence and be ready to cite it and
prove it, because I'm not going to allow you to go on any
more fishing expeditions in an effort to blacken the name
of a national hero. Am I understood?"

Garfield bristled.

"James," another committee member said quietly, "he's
right. Lord knows there's talk enough about corruption in
the administration, and we've got an election coming up. If
Grant is implicated in this thing, you'll be in the minority
party, and Horace Greeley, God forbid, will end up in the
White House."

"I've been hoping," Garfield remarked, "that old Greeley would take his own advice and go West with the young
men."

"Not a chance," someone said.

"All right," Garfield surrendered. "All right. I will tiptoe
delicately around the questions that arise out of Julia
Grant's letter to her sister-in-law, and about Grant's hold-

ing hands with Jim Fisk and Jay Gould in an opera-house box in New York. If that's the way the majority of our party wants to play this, why don't we just cite young Miles with contempt so the committee can get a few headlines and then make an announcement that there was no conspiracy, that Black Friday was only a normal event on the gold market."

"I think we understand each other, Mr. Garfield," Philip said. "But let me go on record so there will be no question about where I stand. I will not allow unwarranted accusations against the presidential family, for as you well know, being senior to me in Washington, a reputation attacked in this town is a reputation damaged. If, however, you have one iota of evidence that there was a conspiracy that reached into official Washington or into the subtreasury in New York, I urge you to expose it."

"Thank you, Mr. Chairman," Garfield said with a mock bow.

Once again Lloyd Miles was the witness before the Trent committee.

"Mr. Jay Gould has stated in the press that he gave General Daniel Butterfield a check for ten thousand dollars as an unsecured real-estate loan," Philip said. "And Mr. Gould also has stated that General Butterfield owes him a great deal of money to cover the loss on a sum of gold purchased on General Butterfield's behalf. Do you have any personal knowledge of such transactions?"

"General Butterfield was—and is—a good friend of mine," Lloyd said. "After he was appointed to the subtreasury in New York, I introduced him to Mr. Gould and to others. This, I believe, is proper and normal. What I mean is this: Government officials whose policies can have drastic or beneficial effects on the nation's economy should be in touch with the businessmen of the financial community in order to share knowledge and information for the benefit of all. What occurred between General Butterfield and Mr. Gould in the way of business was, I sincerely feel, their affair and their affair alone. I was not invited to participate in any discussion or any business dealings involving the general and Mr. Gould."

Once again he was skirting the truth. He could sense the open antagonism emanating from some members of the committee. It was as if he were on a mission behind enemy lines, with snipers all around him. In such a situation he felt justified in using any means to preserve his safety.

"Did General Butterfield take a position in gold during the corner?" James Garfield asked.

"Sir, I was not asked to look at General Butterfield's personal accounts," Lloyd said.

Another member of the committee, unable to think of a pertinent question, asked, "Have you talked with General Butterfield since Black Friday?"

Lloyd smiled. "Sir, I am told that General Butterfield fled the field shortly after September twenty-fourth."

"In the company of a very handsome blond lady, I've been told," said James Garfield.

There was general laughter. "I've heard the same thing, sir," Lloyd said, smiling. He wondered if Rose Pulliam was the blond lady who had boarded ship for a passage to Europe with Dan Butterfield.

"I would like to get back to the time when General Grant was visiting the Corbins in New York," Philip said. "It has been intimated that undue pressure was put upon the President by Jay Gould and others. To your knowledge, Mr. Miles, did anyone ever ask the President directly about the policy of the government toward selling Treasury gold to control speculation on the market?"

Lloyd mused for a moment. "I was not privy to every minute of the President's conversations. I would think that the nearest thing to a direct question on that subject might have come from Mr. Gould when he told the President about his crop theory."

That required some explanation, and several of the congressmen had questions.

"In fact, Mr. Miles," Garfield said, "Mr. Gould was not only wrong but devastatingly wrong about the effect of high gold prices on farm products and the export trade, was he not?"

Lloyd, pleased to talk about anything other than the President and his family and his own affairs, expounded on the effects of the gold crash on farmers, workers, and foreign trade.

It was late in the day before Philip could return to questions about Lloyd's own gold trading and then it was time to adjourn. In the corridor Lloyd was cornered by members of the press, and for once he was willing to talk to them, for he was well satisfied with his performance.

"Listen, fellows," he finally said, "it's been a damned long day. These congressmen, Washington's finest, have just about picked my brain clean, and I'm exhausted. Let's save some questions for another day."

Philip Trent was also in the hallway waiting. Lloyd nodded. Philip fell in beside him as they walked rapidly down the hall to stay ahead of the reporters. "That was a good thing you did in there, Lloyd," Philip said.

Startled, Lloyd looked at Philip questioningly.

"You know and I know that the general is guilty of nothing more than carelessness in his associations; but then, too, we know that Mrs. Grant, whatever good she meant to accomplish, was pretty foolish to write that letter. I can't prove it, and I certainly won't try to, but as sure as hell, Lloyd, your visit to the White House wasn't merely a social call."

"I was under oath," Lloyd said with a sardonic smile. "Do you really think I'd lie to a congressional committee?" He laughed. "Never in a million years."

Philip halted. Lloyd took a couple of steps, then turned back to face his onetime friend. "Thank you," Philip said. "On behalf of the President and his wife."

"What makes you think that it's up to you to say that?" Lloyd demanded.

"Good night, Miles."

"Will there be much more of this comedy?" Lloyd asked.

"We'll probably dismiss you after an hour or so tomorrow morning. The vox populi is demanding meat—big fish instead of small fry."

"Watch it, Sir Shining Knight. You're letting this town turn you just a bit cynical."

Philip chuckled. "Yes, it has a tendency to do that, doesn't it? Good night again."

Lloyd nodded, shifted his case to his other hand, and walked rapidly away, leaving Philip to stare after him. It had been a good thing Lloyd had done, almost certainly lying to protect the President and his family. But then Miles had always been a man of contradictions.

CHAPTER 16

New York's financial district had some characteristics of a small town, including a tendency to gossip among those who spent their workdays there. The big topic of conversation was the Trent committee hearings in Washington, but other subjects were not neglected totally.

Since the stock market could be affected by what seemed to the uninvolved to be rather silly and insignificant events half a world away, sharp traders kept their ears open for any hint of data that might give them an advantage. When orders to buy and sell dealt in thousands of shares, a movement of an eighth of a point could mean significant profit or loss. Brokers and traders kept their eyes on certain players. When, for example, the commodore made a move, dozens of speculators would bet that he was right. Of course it was not always possible to know what men such as Cornelius Vanderbilt or Jay Gould were doing. Gould controlled his own brokerage firm, and thus, his trading could be kept hidden until, as it had been in the gold market before Black Friday, it became obvious that only such a large shark could be threshing the waters into foam.

There were enough leaks to fuel the gossip mill with juicy rumors at any given time. In theory a man's transactions with his brokers were strictly confidential, but insiders made it their business to learn which broker represented which investor. It was also possible to guess by the amount of the orders the source of the money being spent. Thus, when Lloyd Miles was ready to begin his Kansas City and Southwest venture, he worked through no fewer than four different brokers to keep his maneuvers secret.

The influx of capital that he had thrown into the KC&S had made a decided impact on the railroad's quarterly report. To the Wall Street sharks the little line in southwestern Kansas looked like a ripe plum ready for the picking. Its capital assets could be bled off after taking control of the company at what were, in effect, bargain prices. Under a steady demand KC&S stocks began a slow rise from $95.

Lloyd Miles, to the consternation of his four separate brokers, began to sell short in a rising market. On the surface it seemed an act of sheer madness. His sell offers were snapped up quickly.

Victoria Woodhull looked up in bemusement when her secretary announced that Mr. Lloyd Miles was in the reception room asking to see her on a business matter. After the scene at her home Lloyd was the last man she'd expected to see.

"Ask Mr. Miles to come in," she said. She patted her hair, arranged the lace on her bodice, and was smiling when Lloyd entered. He walked around the desk, took her hand, brought it to within a half inch of his lips.

"You're beautiful, as always," he said.

"Have a seat, Mr. Miles."

"Mr. Miles?" he asked, with a quizzical smile. "Why Mrs. Woodhull, are we going to be formal?"

Victoria laughed. "All right, Lloyd, get all the blarney out of your system, and keep in mind what the sign out front says."

" 'State your business and leave,' " Lloyd quoted. "I had hoped that we could talk about it over dinner tonight."

"You have a hard shell, Mr. Miles," she said, still smiling.

"Ah, but when the reward is so much to be desired, a few slings and arrows only make the seeking more interesting." Lloyd let his eyes fall to the line of her bosom, then he looked back into her face. "And I do know the worth of this particular sweet reward." He smiled winningly. "Friends?"

"I wouldn't preclude such a possibility forever," Victoria said. "But not tonight, Lloyd."

"At least you do not deprive me of all hope," he said. "Well, then, to business. I hope that you haven't forgotten that I promised to let you in on a rather profitable little deal when the time was right. Have you noticed that there's been quite a bit of activity in the stock of a certain small Kansas railroad?"

"Let's see," she said, searching among loose papers on her desk. "Yes, the Kansas City and Southwest." She looked at him and waited.

"Sell short," Lloyd told her.

She lifted her eyebrows. "But the price has gone from ninety-five dollars to one hundred five in a matter of days."

"Sell short, and be ready to make good your shorts when I give you the signal."

"Am I to take it that *you* are the Kansas City and Southwest?"

"Who was it that said I had something in common with Tennie's old boy?" he asked.

"And you're selling short?"

"As much as the market will bear."

"How long do I have?"

"Ten days, maybe two weeks." He put his hands on her desk and leaned toward her. "There is something I want you to do for me in exchange," he said.

"Yes?"

"KC&S stock is going to go through the roof in the next week or so because it's going to be announced that the railroad has right-of-way concessions through the Indian nations to the Texas cattle country."

"That would do it," Victoria agreed. "Why haven't I heard about that?"

"The news was printed in a Kansas City newspaper two weeks ago. It takes a while for the alert Eastern press to pick up on things like that. But you see the possibilities, I assume?"

"I would think that I should be buying, then, and not selling short."

"Well, the problem is this," he said, shaking his head. "It seems certain that the KC&S will have the right-of-way through Indian Territory, but there's always the possibility that something adverse might happen."

Victoria's eyes narrowed. "My God, Lloyd, you're taking a page from old Dan'l Drew's book. My guess is that the right-of-way to Texas exists only in your imagination."

Lloyd shrugged. "Well, one can only try."

"All right," she said, picking up a pen. "What do you want me to do?"

"You have occasionally represented Psaleh Kershaw."

"He's thrown us a few crumbs just to please Cornele."

"I want you to sell him on the future of the KC&S. I want him to think that he's fallen into the opportunity of a lifetime. Now, I happen to know that he got hurt by selling out at the bottom during the last Vanderbilt-Gould tussle, and he'll be looking for a way to recoup. I want him to buy into KC&S at the top and up to his chin."

"What do you have against Kershaw?"

"I'll tell you all about it one night over dinner."

"Check with me tomorrow afternoon," she said. "Yes. I think I can convince Mr. Kershaw that the KC&S is a very good buy." She rose and held out her hand. "You know, Lloyd, you can be one mean bastard."

"Who? Me?" He opened his eyes wide in aggrieved innocence.

The flow of information among the denizens of the financial district followed lines of self-interest. It was a you-scratch-my-back-and-I'll-scratch-yours world. An outsider, especially a member of the press such as Phineas Headley, had difficulty tapping into the gossip line.

Headley had been in Washington to testify before, then

to cover, the Trent committee hearings. When it became evident that, after Lloyd Miles, it was going to be weeks before the committee questioned anyone else of real interest, Headley returned to New York. He'd been spending a lot of time writing about the next presidential election, and he had gotten a very nice semihumorous piece out of the announcement that Victoria Woodhull was throwing her feminine hat into the race to become the first woman ever to run for president of the United States. It was rather amusing to think that a woman, who wasn't even allowed to vote, was a candidate for the highest office in the land.

To make the Woodhull candidacy even more interesting, she had chosen as her running mate the ex-slave Frederick Douglass, who had spent the war years using his gift of oratory to try to convince the world that first, the use of black troops in the Union Army would quickly end the conflict and second, that there was only *one* reason for the war: to free the slaves.

Phineas Headley gave free rein to his not insignificant writing talent and had a great deal of fun at the expense of one candidate whose platform included sexual freedom for everyone and of another who ignored questions about his stand on free love in order to concentrate on his attempt to convince the world that black troops had indeed won the war. Needless to say, when Headley put his size eleven boots inside the offices of Woodhull, Claflin, and Company and asked for an exclusive interview with the candidate Mrs. Woodhull, his reception was chilly. He refused to take no for an answer from the harried secretary in the reception area and was faced by a very attractive woman who told him politely but firmly that Mrs. Woodhull had no intention of ever talking to a journalist who tried to make a joke of a very serious effort to call attention to the dismal social status of American women.

Headley had the feeling that he'd met the brown-haired woman with the golden brown hair, the full, sensuous mouth, and the startling blue eyes. "And you are a spokesman for Mrs. Woodhull?"

"Not exactly," she said.

"May I quote you as saying that the purpose of Mrs. Woodhull's candidacy is to call attention to the fight for women's suffrage?"

"I don't see why you would want to quote me on anything."

"I know you from somewhere," Headley said.

"I think not."

"Your name, please?"

"I don't see why you need my name." She turned and retreated into the inner offices.

Headley sat on the edge of the secretary's desk. "I'm sure I've met that lady," he said. "What is her name?"

"I think your business here is finished," the secretary said.

"I'll leave if you'll tell me that blue-eyed lady's name," Phineas said, smiling disarmingly. "I won't put it in the paper. Why should I? All she did was tell me that Woodhull won't talk to me."

The secretary sighed. "I suppose it won't do any harm if it will get you out from underfoot. Her name is Leah Miles."

"Aha!" Phineas said. "She has a brother, Lloyd Miles?"

"Yes. Good day."

"And good day to you."

Phineas thought it was remarkable how he kept crossing the spoor of Lloyd Miles in everything he did. Miles had been pointed out to him by a man who had once known Washington as well as anyone, Lafayette Baker. Miles had been involved in the gold corner, and he'd been one of the first witnesses at the Trent hearings, where he'd come off rather well, even if it was evident to an old student of human nature like Phineas Headley that he wasn't telling all. And now he'd cut the trail of Lloyd Miles once more, in the form of a very attractive sister who worked for Victoria Woodhull and Tennessee Claflin.

At the moment, however, he saw nothing to be gained from that knowledge.

* * *

Leah Miles worked at a cluttered desk in the largest room in the suite of offices at Woodhull, Claflin, and Company. During the early part of the week she was mostly alone in the room, but as the deadline approached for the final laying out of the *Weekly*, the room became crowded with the comings and goings of Victoria, Tennessee, Colonel Blood, and Stephen Pearl Andrews. Things were often hectic. Leah had become an integral part of the team that put the *Weekly* together. The final copyediting and proofreading were among her duties. She found that Andrews was an easy man to work with, and she was intrigued by James Harvey Blood.

Often, when the week's work was done and the small staff could breathe once again—at least for a day—Blood would linger in the big room to chat with Leah. He was a handsome man, virile, the last man in the world, judging from his looks alone, who would be content while his wife practiced free love. But Blood was also a gentle soul, and he apparently believed fully that it was not normal for one man and one woman to adhere exclusively to each other for a lifetime.

"I fell madly in love with Vee the minute I saw her in St. Louis," he told Leah one day. "She was just a slip of a girl then, married to poor old Canning, rest his soul." Canning Woodhull had only recently died of a respiratory ailment. "I was told that I was crazy to give up a good job to go jaunting in a covered wagon with a clan like that." He laughed. "Victoria and Tennie were responsible for the well-being of the whole family, you know. And it was a big group."

Blood seemed to enjoy talking with Leah. She was, she knew, a good listener. She had come to accept the idiosyncrasies of the Claflin family. It no longer shocked her that no one really seemed to know whether or not Victoria had divorced Canning Woodhull before marrying Colonel Blood; furthermore, Leah was only mildly bemused by the fact that in New York Victoria had lived more or less happily with the colonel and Canning Woodhull in the same house along with the old barn burner and family patriarch,

Buckman, and the increasingly erratic mother, Roxanna. Other siblings and their spouses were in and out of the houses on Great Jones Street and then on Thirty-eighth Street. The only real problems that Leah had ever heard about in the Claflin family centered around jealousy of Tennessee and Victoria by one sister and on Roxanna Claflin's occasional attempts to introduce her wayward daughters to grace by chasing away the men who were leading them astray.

"I was the city auditor of St. Louis," Blood told Leah. He chuckled. "And then I was a barker for the Claflin sisters' traveling healing and medicine show." He held up one finger. "Not that I denigrate it, mind you. I've seen Tennie work her healing powers on people. I know that Victoria can see the future. I doubted that, the first time I met her, because she told me that she and I would be married. At that particular moment I had no intentions of leaving my job or my family."

Blood was not the only man who found that Leah Miles had a sympathetic ear and, apparently, no desire to make demands on any man. Theodore Tilton, head of the National Woman Suffrage Association and an intimate of the great Henry Ward Beecher's, had met Victoria and Tennessee while they were working for the movement, and he had become a great admirer of Victoria's. While Beecher was accusing Tennessee and Victoria of being painted women, whores, and Jezebels, Tilton was introducing Victoria to leaders of the women's movement and encouraging her to make more public-speaking engagements.

Tilton was a frequent visitor and an occasional contributor to the *Weekly*. He was a stickler for accuracy and spent hours with Leah, going over his articles to make certain there were no misspellings or typographical errors.

Leah was pleased to be associated with so influential a man, and she was impressed by his graciousness and his genteel manners. He was not reluctant to talk about the famous people he knew—Henry Ward Beecher among them—so through him Leah was able to satisfy some of her curiosity about the man she had heard and read so much about.

"I think, my dear, that the best way to form an opinion of Henry is to hear him in his pulpit. It would be my pleasure to take you to his church on a Sunday morning at your convenience," Tilton offered.

"Yes, perhaps one Sunday soon," Leah agreed, but the weeks continued to pass, and there was no further mention of the proposed excursion. She knew that it would be futile to ask Lloyd to take her all the way to Brooklyn by ferry to go to church, so the matter was put in abeyance.

It was a busy time. And, to Leah's complete surprise, the friendship between Theodore Tilton and Victoria Woodhull became more than friendship. Victoria, a true believer in her right to do exactly as she pleased, made no attempt to hide the fact that she and Tilton had become lovers. For some time Tilton was too preoccupied to visit the lowly copy editor in the *Weekly* room, and when he finally showed up one rainy afternoon, his face looked as gloomy as the weather.

"A brute of a day," Tilton said.

"There's hot coffee," Leah offered. "Shall I pour—"

"No, no, my dear, keep your seat," Tilton said. "I know where it is."

He served himself, then sat close to her desk. "I'm down to the last paragraph here," Leah said. "Just let me finish." When she looked up again, to her surprise huge tears were rolling down Tilton's cheeks.

She gasped. "Mr. Tilton, what on earth is the matter?"

"Forgive me, my dear," Tilton said. "I am unable to control myself. I have no right imposing my misery on civilized company."

Leah thought that Tilton had discovered, as had several men before him, that the affections of one of the Claflin sisters were based on the shifting sands of unbridled self-indulgence. She could not bring herself to pity him, for he had a wife, Elizabeth, at home. He had spoken often about her before he had been drawn into the Woodhull silken web.

"Can I get you some more coffee?" Leah asked, disturbed by the sight of male tears.

"No, no."

"If there's anything—"

"I just can't believe it," Tilton moaned.

"Well—"

"I just can't believe that either of them would do this to me." He shook his head and wiped the tears from his face. "And it's been going on for two years." His voice rose. *"Two years!* My wife and my best friend, the man I admired most in this world."

Leah felt a prickle of dread and shivered. There were times when she wondered what it was about her that made people spill their innermost secrets to her. She didn't know Theodore Tilton well enough for him to be telling her that his wife was committing adultery with another man, nor did she care to know such intimate and sordid facts.

"He married us, Miss Miles! The man stood there in the pulpit of his church and said the vows for us to repeat. He was our angel. He helped me to get my first job."

Leah was holding her breath. He could not be serious. He could not be speaking of—

"Henry Ward Beecher," Tilton said, spitting out the words like a curse. "And my Elizabeth."

"Perhaps you're wrong," Leah said. "You know how gossip is."

"But she told me herself," Tilton protested. "She said that she could no longer be the hypocrite. She told me all. For two years now they've been lovers. She has been a member of his church since she was ten years old, and he used his spiritual influence over her to get her into his bed. He told her, 'We share a divine and valid love, and a full expression of it is as proper as a handshake or a kiss.' He, who calls Victoria a whore, used the same rationalization that free lovers use to seduce my Elizabeth."

"What do you intend to do, Mr. Tilton?" Leah asked.

"Do? Why, I don't know, actually."

"Do you still love her?"

"Oh, my, yes," he said.

"Then I would think, Mr. Tilton, that she should not be made to suffer. It's easy to see how she, having looked up to him for so many years, would fall prey to his ugly desires."

"Oh, it's not her fault. Of course not." His face darkened. "But as for *him,* I will find a way to make him suffer. I will—" He paused, wiped his eyes. "What shall I do, Miss Miles?"

Leah didn't answer immediately, for she was lost in her own misery. She had just realized why people unburdened themselves to her. *Aunt* Leah was a good listener. *Aunt* Leah, the maiden, was a safe repository for their secrets.

"What shall I do?" Tilton repeated.

Leah tried to keep the anger out of her voice. "Well, first of all, if I were you I wouldn't go around telling the world about it."

"Oh, I haven't. I've told no one but you."

"And secondly, I would remove my wife from temptation."

He nodded. "Yes, I can see that. It will cause comment, but I can see that it's necessary." His face hardened. "What I should do is blazen the story across the front pages of every newspaper in America and let the whole world know that the knight of Christ has feet of clay."

"And let the whole world know that your wife is an adulteress?" Leah asked harshly. "You have worked hard for equal rights for women, Mr. Tilton. You are eloquent in the cause of womanhood. Would you really do that to the woman you love most?"

He put his face in his hands and wept.

"Perhaps you should go home, Mr. Tilton," Leah suggested gently. "I would imagine that your wife is quite upset too. Perhaps at this trying time it would be best if you two clung together?"

"Yes," he said. "Thank you."

After he had gone, Leah sat stiffly at her desk and stared unseeingly at the opposite wall. She had no desire to be a part of such a scandal. She did not appreciate Tilton's having shared such intimacies with her. She did not want the responsibility of knowing that the man who was the fore-most spokesman for Christian morality in the United States was a womanizer.

She remembered that in Washington, Victoria had told Beecher's sister that the reverend preached to at least twenty of his mistresses every Sunday. Leah had wondered then why the Beechers had not filed a libel suit against Victoria, for many had witnessed the remark. Could it be true that Beecher used his position as a trusted spiritual adviser to prey on foolish—or sensuous—women?

Well, it was none of her affair. Was it?

She had been working with the *Weekly* long enough to have experienced the satisfaction occasionally enjoyed by every person who works with the dispensing of information —the thrill of knowing that one has been instrumental in bringing something new, something previously totally un-known, to a great number of people. She had not origi-nated any of the stories that had made her feel that the *Weekly* served a purpose, but she'd felt admiration for those who had dug out facts that caused newspapers all over the country to quote, damn, or praise the Claflin pub-lication. Now she herself had the opportunity to put the *Weekly* in the position of dropping a bombshell on the na-tion. The revelation that Henry Ward Beecher had seduced a woman who had been in his church since childhood would make headlines from New York to San Francisco.

All she had to do was pass along Tilton's secret to Blood or Andrews or Victoria. All of them would chortle with glee, for there was nothing that an advocate of free love liked better than exposing the peccadilloes of self-righ-teous critics. Victoria, in particular, looked to fill the *Weekly* with arguments, pleadings, charges, indignations, and outrages on behalf of her right to have her chimes rung by any man who took her fancy.

But, no, Leah decided. She would not betray a trust. She would, however, satisfy her own curiosity and have a look at Mr. Henry Ward Beecher.

* * *

"Lloyd," she said after dinner that night, "I want to go to hear Reverend Beecher preach this Sunday."

"Uh-huh," Lloyd said. He was adding figures to a chart of the movement of KC&S stock and didn't really hear what Leah was saying.

"I'd feel better about going all the way to Brooklyn if you'd go with me," Leah said.

Lloyd looked up. "Go where?"

"To Henry Ward Beecher's church this Sunday morning."

"I never go to places of entertainment," Lloyd said.

Leah laughed. "I happen to know, dear, that that is what Park Benjamin told Mr. Beecher when he was asked why he never came to hear Beecher preach."

Lloyd chuckled. "You caught me. Have you heard the one about Henry Ward Beecher going to the stable to buy a horse? The stableman showed him a nice-looking animal and said that the horse was gentle and well behaved, that it stood anywhere without hitching, did anything asked of it, did not kick, and listened carefully to everything you had to say. To which Beecher responded, 'Ah, I shall make him a member of my congregation.'"

"You're terrible," she said.

A few minutes passed.

"Lloyd?" she said.

He looked up from his chart.

"I'm in somewhat of a dilemma."

Lloyd put down the paper and then folded his hands in front of him, indicating that he was ready to listen.

"I've been told something in confidence, something that would affect the reputation of a man in high places. In one way I think that it would be wrong of me not to make the, uh, indecencies of this man known. But on the other hand, I don't want to break a confidence."

"Since all of a sudden you want to go to Henry Ward Beecher's church, I take it that your information concerns him?"

She nodded.

"Look, I couldn't care less about what Beecher has

done," Lloyd said. "Your secret will be safe with me, and if I know what you're talking about, I'll be better able to advise you."

She told him, beginning with Victoria's remark to Beecher's sister in Washington, then giving him Tilton's account almost word for word.

"Well, I'll be damned," Lloyd muttered. "You do find yourself sitting on a stick of dynamite, don't you?"

"I feel so sorry for poor Mr. Tilton."

"Don't," he said. "If little Mrs. Tilton has been having her itch scratched by the reverend, Tilton doesn't have much to complain about. He's been doing some scratching himself with the lovely Victoria."

Leah blushed. "How—"

"How did I know that?" He grinned. He had spent the night with Victoria early that week, and she'd openly discussed the famous suffrage leader. "A little bird told me," he said. "No matter. Leah, I don't know what to tell you, really. I'd say that Beecher deserves a comeuppance. If he didn't get into the pulpit and damn all sinners—especially those whose sexual habits don't conform to Old Testament blood and thunder—I would say forget it. To avoid trouble, I think that would be the best thing to do. You really don't want to get mixed up in making accusations against a man like Beecher. He's very powerful. When little folks take aim at someone like that, the results can be more unpleasant for the accuser than for the man they accuse."

"You're probably correct," Leah agreed.

But it wasn't *right*. Lloyd had put his finger on it: Beecher laid down laws of behavior for everyone, calling his prerogative God's will. Thou shalt not commit adultery. Beecher and men like him equated that most human of sins with the most horrible of crimes—with murder, idolatry, stealing. It wasn't fair for him to go unpunished, without censure, when almost weekly he mentioned by name those foremost advocates of free love, Victoria Woodhull and Tennessee Claflin.

"Lloyd?"

He looked up with momentary irritation but smiled

when he saw that she was nibbling on her lower lip as she'd done while considering a puzzling problem when she was a little girl. "If Mr. Tilton and I both remain silent, won't we be, in effect, rewarding Beecher for his reprehensible behavior?"

Lloyd recited.

> *"To the hen said the eminent preacher,*
> *'My dear, you're an elegant creature.'*
> *The hen, just for that,*
> *Laid an egg in his hat.*
> *And thus did the hen reward Beecher."*

"You didn't make that up," she said.

"Nope."

"The hen is little Mrs. Tilton. She's a little bird of a woman, sweet and demure. It infuriates me to think of Beecher flattering her, telling her that she's elegant and beautiful and then—"

"Look, if you feel you must, reward the reverend. But don't ask me to go with you. And this time when the hen lays an egg in his hat, be sure it's very, very rotten."

"I just may," she said. "I just may."

The Reverend Henry Ward Beecher was a short, stocky, but compactly built man with a florid face and a leonine mane of silvery gray hair. His face was expressively mobile, and his eyes took on a light of joy as his voice soared over the congregation in the crowded Plymouth Church in Brooklyn.

On Sundays additional ferries were put on duty to handle the crowds crossing from Manhattan to hear from Beecher about a hell that was hotter and a heaven more blissful than those promised by most preachers. Beecher's oratory had built the largest church and the biggest congregation in the United States. To hear him tie evil and damnation to the devil on a Sunday morning gave a sinner enough grace to last him through a trying week.

In spite of herself Leah Miles nodded in agreement with

Beecher's fiery condemnation of the entire gamut of sins—war and killing, greed, selfishness, dishonesty; but when, his voice reaching for lofty heights, he attacked lust as the pièce de résistance of his moral repast of thundering words, Leah found herself looking at him in measurement. He was not a handsome man, nor was he young. He was approaching sixty. Leah decided that she herself would never have been tempted to accept his attentions, even if she had spent years listening to his spellbinding sermons.

Beecher burned all fornicators with his vocabulary and the strength of his voice and his powerful lungs, sang loudly with the choir, then made his way to the front entrance of the church to offer his loyal followers his hand and a few private words. Leah remained in her seat until the crowd had slowly dispersed. She sat with her head bowed, in communication with her God, asking for His guidance. When she heard businesslike footsteps approaching from the entrance she turned.

Beecher seemed larger when she stood at a level with him.

"You are Miss Miles?" the preacher asked with a beaming smile.

"Thank you for seeing me, Reverend Beecher."

"My dear, with one so lovely as you I am sincere when I say that it is my pleasure."

To the hen said the eminent preacher— She almost giggled at the thought. But Beecher was in total ignorance of the reason for Leah's presence and for her urgently worded request to have a private audience with him after the service. With his flattery, with his knowing eyes that seemed to be able—or so Leah thought—to penetrate several layers of her clothing to her naked and unprotected body underneath, and with his smarmy smile, the man had hardened Leah's resolve. From Theodore Tilton's description, Leah had spotted Elizabeth Tilton in the third row from the front, a pretty, birdlike woman whose eyes never left Beecher during the moderately long sermon. There had been something almost childlike in the worshipful look on Elizabeth Tilton's face; and, after Leah recovered from the hypnotic persuasion of Beecher's preaching style, she had wondered which of the other women in the congregation made up the balance of Beecher's score of mistresses.

But the combination of having seen the Tilton woman still mesmerized by the "eminent preacher," a little hen still ready to reward the smiling lecher with her "eggs," and of being face-to-face with a man who undressed her with his eyes only minutes after having the egotism to interpret the will of God for lesser mortals caused Leah to look Beecher full in the face and say, "Reverend Beecher, I have come to ask you if what Theodore Tilton has told me is true."

"I'm sure it is," Beecher said, still smiling, letting his eyes fall to Leah's small, tidy waist. "Theodore is a fine man."

"Then it's true that you have been committing adultery with Mr. Tilton's wife for two years?" Leah asked bluntly.

Beecher's eyes went wide, then blinked rapidly as he took a step backward. "My dear lady!" he said, gasping.

"Is it true?" She could hardly believe that it was she, Leah Miles, confronting one of the most famous men in the nation.

"Young woman," Beecher said, his voice going very, very hard, "I don't know who is putting you up to this, but I must warn you that you are on dangerous ground."

"Dangerous for me?" Leah inquired. "Or dangerous for you?"

"I must ask you, you child of Satan, to leave my church!" Beecher thundered.

"Listen to me," Leah said evenly. "I am a friend of Theodore Tilton's. He has told me that his wife has confessed to having a long-term affair with you. He has no reason to disbelieve her, for she is a sensitive, sensible, reasoning woman. I know that he believes it, and I have come to hear you confirm or deny it before I take any action. If, however, you do not wish to speak with me on the subject, I will leave your church."

Beecher, making a concerted effort to calm down, rubbed his chin thoughtfully. "I think, Miss Miles, that you had better come with me into my study." He led the way into a room of beautiful dark paneling, soft leather chairs, a couch large enough for purposes other than sitting, and a highly polished desk. He took his place behind the desk, then folded his hands.

"I have been concerned about Elizabeth for some time now," he confided. "The poor child has been quite disturbed about something, and I have been unable to determine the cause. You must realize, Miss Miles, that a man in my position—even a man of God such as I am, a man who is constantly before the eyes of the world, a man who does his best to give good advice and impart wisdom—can often, without any effort to do so, attract the affections of a certain sort of weak-willed woman."

He paused and looked at Leah appraisingly. "Now, you yourself, Miss Miles, would be too sensible to risk your marriage and your reputation in idle erotic dreams that are beyond your realization. But I have known Elizabeth since she was a child—a moody child, often taking refuge in daydreams. What you have told me answers a great number of questions that I have been asking myself about poor Elizabeth. I knew that she was troubled. I fear now that she has deluded herself into dreaming that she is in love with me, that her fantasy has, indeed, led her far astray into—"

"Why would she tell her husband that she's been having an affair with you, Reverend Beecher?"

Beecher was not accustomed to being interrupted. He glared at Leah. "I can see that you are not willing to listen."

"Oh, but I am."

"May I ask, then, what you intend doing if, in your private court where you are judge and jury, you convict me of this crime?"

"I will publish Mrs. Tilton's confession for the whole country to read."

"I see. You're a newspaperwoman."

"I work for *Woodhull and Claflin's Weekly*," she said.

Beecher's face went red. "So that's who is behind all this."

"Only I am behind this, so far," Leah said.

Beecher smiled and spread his hands. "Well, my goodness," he said, "there should be no difficulty in working this out between us. We are, in fact, of like mind, Miss Miles. Oh, I am not as free to state my own private views as, say, Mrs. Woodhull is; nor even am I as free as the most timid of her associates. All of us, however, share a divine and valid love, and a full expression of that love is as proper as a handshake or a kiss. I think, Miss Miles, that if you will have lunch with me we can find common ground."

Leah rose, her face aflame. With other men she had encountered the same reaction to the knowledge that she worked on the *Weekly* and was an associate of Victoria's and Tennie's. Men naturally assumed that she shared the Claflin sisters' morals and tastes. To have Beecher jump so deeply to the same conclusion, to have him turn away from a serious charge that would, she believed, if published, have a severe effect on his position as the most prominent minister in America, was almost incomprehensible. And yet he had used the same argument with Leah as Elizabeth Tilton said he had used with her.

"Such reasoning worked with Elizabeth Tilton," she said. "It only makes me want to vomit."

"Whore!" Beecher yelled after her as she moved swiftly out the study door and into the main auditorium of the church. "If you painted hussies think that you can threaten me, can intimidate me . . ."

He was still ranting when she ran out into the blessed sun.

CHAPTER 17

Partly because Jim Fisk didn't give a damn about what the newspapers said or what the public thought, the blame for Black Friday was being placed mainly on his well-padded shoulders. He was obviously a scoundrel, and he played the part when he took his turn before the Trent investigating committee. When it was over he said with a toothy smile, "Nothing is lost save honor." And that, to the Barnum of Wall Street, was a small matter.

James Garfield, like most congressmen eager to get his name in the papers, made an effort to inject a modicum of sexual titillation into the proceedings by asking big Jim what part Josie Mansfield had played in the schemes of the Gold Ring.

Jim bristled and shot back, "Mr. Garfield, I resent your intrusion into my private life. You called me here, using the power of the government of this country in an obvious attempt to smear my good name"—he laughed—"or what's left of it, to answer questions about my tradings in gold prior to Black Friday. Since I recognize and respect the legal power of this committee, I will answer questions on that matter truthfully, or to the best of my ability. I will not, however, allow you or anyone to drag innocents such as Miss Helen Josephine Mansfield into this circus arena."

Garfield sputtered and blustered and, finally, was silenced when Chairman Trent called a short recess, during which Garfield, with a smug smile, approached Philip. "I suppose you've heard, Trent, that I will not be attending further hearings of this committee."

"So I understand, Mr. Garfield. Congratulations are in order, I believe."

"Thank you. Yes, it will be made official tomorrow. I'm appointed chairman of the House Banking Committee. You know that I've developed the reputation of being a reformer."

Philip remained silent, but he was thinking wryly that, considering Garfield's shenanigans regarding his Crédit Mobilier stock, perhaps reform in Garfield's case should begin at home.

"In some respects, Trent, our investigation will parallel yours. If at any time you desire access to material gathered by our committee, please call on me."

"Thank you," Philip said. "But I guess we'll just muddle through on our own."

"If that's the way you want it," Garfield said.

One of the more interesting witnesses before the Trent Committee was Albert Speyers. The Wall Street broker spoke in a broken, quivering voice about Jim Fisk's wild instructions on Black Friday.

Next Abel Corbin was finally dragged out of the wilds of Kentucky, where he had fled, claiming to be ill. To Philip's relief Corbin whined his claims to innocence of skulduggery without trying to implicate the President or his family.

Later, it was Jim Fisk who once again claimed that Corbin, Butterfield, and Julia Grant were involved. After both he and Jay Gould had testified, they called an impromptu meeting with the press, over which Jim presided genially. He laughed and joked and recounted how Albert Speyers went pale and could only stutter when he was told to buy gold at $162. And he said to the newsmen, "I told the committee that I had a great desire that they should examine Mrs. Grant and Mrs. Corbin. In fact, I demanded it." He shrugged. "Will they call on those two ladies?" He laughed. "Ten to one they won't. The investigators have their scoundrels here in Jay and me."

Before the committee Jay Gould, pale, frail, and soft-spoken, had answered questions politely but firmly. Due, perhaps, to the tension of appearing before the committee, his consumption had flared up prior to his coming to Washington, and he often had to interrupt his testimony to cough quietly into a handkerchief. He wore the most expensive tailored three-piece suit that money could buy. His hair and his large black beard were trimmed perfectly. He chose his words with the care of a watchmaker replacing tiny precision parts. And his clever evasions infuriated Adam Grey.

Many people who heard Gould's testimony would remember only one highlight: the poetic-looking financier had looked Philip Trent directly in the eye to say, "I am satisfied that the President has never had any connection, directly or indirectly, with the bull market in gold, for Mr. Grant, fortunately for this country, is a very pure, high-minded man."

"That buffoon who likes to dress up in uniform," Adam said, meaning Jim Fisk, "doesn't have the brains to plan such a complicated program. You know and I know that the mastermind behind the gold corner was Jay Gould."

Adam, Julia, and Philip were in a private office near the chamber where the hearing was taking place. "So how do we go about proving it?" Julia asked.

"I think it will all come out in the end," Philip said. He was less concerned about distinguishing between Gould and Fisk as the principal villain than about what was going on in another committee hearing room, where the House Banking Committee was trying to answer one question and one question only: Were any officers of the national government directly or indirectly engaged in the conspiracy? In short, the pygmies were chittering and chattering around the ankles of the giant. What was meant by the question being asked by the banking committee was: What did the President know about the gold corner, and when did he know it?

Philip made it a point to meet with the press at the end of Gould's final testimony. He pointed out to them that the committee's investigation had been far-reaching and that there was not one shred of evidence to connect either Mrs. Grant or the President to the scandal.

Phineas Headley raised his hand, and Philip said, "Mr. Headley?"

"Congressman," Headley said, "are you not ignoring quite a mass of evidence? On the one hand it is documented that Grant and Jay Gould spent time with each other in New York. The House Banking Committee is calling these conferences 'secret meetings.' There is Abel Corbin's confessed complicity in the affair, and then there is the 'Dear Sis' letter from Julia Grant to Jennie Corbin, in which Abel Corbin is warned to disassociate himself from the Gold Ring or be ruined. Don't you think, in the face of such evidence, that this committee should dig a bit deeper?"

"Mr. Headley," Philip said, "you show me how to get more information out of any of our witnesses, and I'll gladly give it a try."

"Perhaps," Headley said, "you haven't called the right witnesses. Why doesn't the committee call Mrs. Grant and Mrs. Corbin, as Jim Fisk suggested?"

Philip cleared his throat. "First of all, Mr. Headley, I will not insult the wife of the President of the United States. Secondly, doesn't it seem a bit unfair to involve women in an affair like this when we don't even give them the right to vote?"

"Are you, like Ben Butler, coming out in favor of women's suffrage?" a reporter yelled out.

"When I'm ready to make a statement on that issue, you'll be the first to know," Philip said. "Today we're talking about an effort by the radicals on the Banking Committee to blacken the name of our President."

"Some people describe you as a radical," a man remarked.

"I am a radical only when it comes to ferreting out wrongdoing in government or business," Philip told him. "Were I a radical in other matters, such as the Reconstruction, I would hope that, unlike many, I could be a radical and not a fool; but that seems to be a matter of no small difficulty."

"Are you indicating, sir, that the House Banking Committee might be prejudiced?"

"I did not say that."

"Isn't it true, Congressman, that there is an eight to two Republican majority on the Banking Committee?"

"That is true," Philip confirmed.

"Don't you think that members of the President's own party are being fair in their investigation?" Headley asked.

"I would hope so," Philip said. "Now, gentlemen, if you're interested, the committee staff is at work on a summation of this group's findings. It may take them some time, for, as you know, we've questioned a lot of people. There have been fifty-seven witnesses. It's estimated that a printed transcript of the proceedings will top five hundred pages. And our people will have to try to reconcile inconsistencies, contradictions, and unavoidable gaps in the testimony. If you'll be patient I will see that you all have copies. When our final report is ready, people will be here to answer any questions you might have."

As the days passed it became evident that James Garfield was trying to milk the investigation of the banking committee for every headline in which his name would appear. While Julia and Adam joined other committee staffers in pounding out the Trent committee's final report, Philip attended several sessions of the banking committee to see the Ohio congressman in action.

Once again witnesses tried to implicate Dan Butterfield and Julia Grant. Since Butterfield was still abroad, that left only Julia as the target, and it appeared for a while as if

Grant's supporters on the committee would relent and agree to call Julia Grant to testify.

Gus Trent attended one of the banking committee's hearings with Philip and came away disturbed. "Men like that have already put one president on trial before the Senate," Gus grumbled. "Is that what Garfield is after?"

"The only thing Garfield is after is his name in the newspapers," Philip said.

"Far be it from me to give advice," Gus muttered. "I'm just a state-level politician."

"Ha!" Philip said.

"If we had something like this going on in the Maryland State Legislature, a couple of old pros and I would get together and have a little talk with the committee chairman."

"And what would you old pros tell the uppity chairman?" Philip asked.

"Well, obviously, if some whippersnapper were accusing a governor of our own party of misconduct, we'd tell him, 'Now, you look here, son, we just don't drag the governor before a dinky little legislative committee. If you want any testimony from the governor, you go to him. You ask him to tell you what he thinks about the whole thing. You don't demand; you ask.'"

Philip put Gus Trent's advice to work the next day. He gathered four senior members of the Republican delegation in the House of Representatives, including the Speaker, then beckoned to Garfield during a recess of the banking committee. Philip remained very quiet while four powerful men talked turkey to the congressman from Ohio. Garfield glared at Trent, but he did listen with respect. As an ambitious man Garfield knew that a maverick had little chance of advancement. If he didn't keep the backing of his party he would remain just a body filling a seat in the House chamber.

"Gentlemen," Garfield relented, "I will, of course, heed your advice."

"Good," said the Speaker. "Mr. Trent will arrange an appointment for you with the President."

"That's damned kind of Mr. Trent," Garfield said, unable to hide his bitterness.

Garfield carried copies of all the evidence against the Grant family when he and Philip Trent entered the White House.

Ulysses Grant was a tired man. He rose to shake hands when the two congressmen entered his office. He greeted Philip with noticeable warmth but dropped Garfield's hand quickly after saying gruffly, "Mr. Garfield."

Inside, the President was steaming. He listened, puffing on a cigar, as Garfield started going through the so-called evidence, stating that a number of witnesses had made "personal reference" not only to the President but to "members of his family."

"Mr. Garfield," Grant said, anger making his voice rough, "I have heard enough. I will not listen to any accusations aimed at my family. If, sir, my honor and my reputation are not enough for you, then you are quite free to continue this so-called investigation of yours until kingdom come. I will have no part in the name calling."

Outside, Garfield took Trent's arm and pulled him to a halt. "You have made a travesty of my investigation," Garfield accused.

"Well, Mr. Garfield," Philip replied easily, "there are those on my committee who say you organized the banking committee investigation just so that you could upstage ours before our final report had been submitted. Of course I don't make that charge, because our report will stand on its own; but others do."

"Good day, Mr. Trent," Garfield said curtly. "I imagine we will be seeing more of each other, if the voters of Maryland will it."

"And those of Ohio, Mr. Garfield," Philip said, tipping his hat.

The banking committee rushed its investigation to a conclusion and, not at all by coincidence, issued its final report

on the same day that Philip Trent called a press conference
to reveal the Trent committee's findings.

Phineas Headley filed one news story and then went to
work reconciling the findings of the two committees. He
was amused to find that both groups exonerated Julia
Grant and the President of, said the House Banking Committee's report, "groundless and wicked" charges of complicity. To support that conclusion both committees cited
the testimony of Jay Gould, who stated that Grant had had
nothing to do with the conspiracy. Both committees, however, blasted Abel Corbin. The banking committee report
said that to exploit one's family was "the worst form of
hypocrisy."

Julia Grey trailed an aroma of perfume as she entered
Philip's office, carrying a mug of coffee and a stack of
newspaper clippings.

Philip groaned when she set the clippings on his desk.
"Not more of them."

"There are two you should read," she said, pointing at
the pile. "This one and this one."

Henry Adams, the dean of American historians, grand-
son of a president, editor of the *North American Review,*
was reluctant to condone the findings of the committees.
He pointed out that two Democrats on the banking committee had refused to sign the final report because they
would not accept the finding that Grant was totally uninvolved, based as it was on "mysterious, unexplained, conflicting, and nebulous testimony" from witnesses who were
obviously unreliable. Adams took both committees to task
for not daring to probe and analyze the reams of evidence.

He wrote: "The trail always faded and died out at the
point where any member of the Administration became
visible. Everyone assured everyone else that the President
was the savior of the situation, and in private assured each
other that if the President had not been caught this time,
he was sure to be trapped the next, for the ways of Wall
Street were dark and double."

Adams was also astounded by the "incredible and inexplicable lapses of Grant's intelligence" in dealing with Fisk and Gould.

Even those who believed the President to be innocent of involvement were critical of Grant's bad judgment. The *Nation* said, in effect, that Grant had acted quite stupidly for "accepting the hospitality of, and entering into conversation with, such people as Gould."

Philip sighed and fingered the pile of clippings. "Well, at least the number is tapering off."

Julia waved the copy of Henry Adams's writing in front of Philip's face. "Is this all there is?" she asked, indignant. "Is this the end of what will happen?"

Philip shrugged.

"But these men created a financial panic. They almost pushed the United States into a depression. They caused suicides and business failures, and what has been done to them? Two congressmen gave them a little bit of a tongue-lashing before investigating committees. The newspapers call them names. Is that all?"

"There are no laws against what they did," Philip pointed out.

"Well, there should be."

"How do you make a law that forbids a man from buying gold if he has the money and the inclination?" Philip asked.

"I don't know," Julia admitted.

"Maybe we stung Gould a little bit," Philip said, "by putting the blame where it belongs, by letting everyone know that it was his idea, his plan, and that others, including his partner, Fisk, were just along for the ride. We've made him a public symbol of evil."

"But something more should be done," Julia insisted.

"As a matter of fact," Philip said, "I've drafted a memo to Adam to have a study made by a few reputable lawyers who deal in Wall Street finances, the object being to find ways to control wild fluctuations such as Black Friday not only on the gold market but on the stock exchange itself."

"Good for you," she approved.

He grinned. "Don't expect instant results, though. A relatively junior congressman from Maryland can't change the world by himself, not when he'd be going against a consortium of the richest and most powerful men in the country, men who would fight tooth and nail to prevent any change in their methods of doing business."

Julia sank into a chair. "I *am* glad it's over."

He felt quick concern for her. She looked pale. "Tired?"

"I am," she said, closing her eyes.

He gazed at her serene face. Her eyes opened, caught his, then widened in the shock of contact. For one breathless moment they were joined, their souls touching through their eyes. Then she sighed, rose, and left the office.

CHAPTER 18

Phineas Headley sat on a tall stool in a dimly lit Irish bar in Manhattan. The early afternoon crowd had departed, and the evening drinkers had not yet arrived. Headley was alone in the room save for the shamrock-tongued bartender and one besotted old man who slumped over at a table, mumbling to himself.

The bartender had directed his rich baritone toward Headley a couple of times, but at the moment the newsman wasn't interested in the Irishman's contention that the whole world was going to hell in a hand basket, and it was time for "day-sunt" folks to do something about it.

A copy of the newspaper to which the journalist had sold his final story on the Gold Ring conspiracy was spread on the bar in front of him. His half-empty glass had left a series of wet circles on words that seemed incomplete, ineffective.

It seemed to Headley that there should be more. He composed lead lines in his head. *We do not know the truth now, nor will we ever.* No. Too final. Maybe one day someone would talk. It might even be Fisk or Gould. Perhaps one of them would write the truth in his memoirs. Fisk would be the most likely to reveal facts and figures. The big, genial crook loved attention, and Headley wouldn't have put it past Fisk to seek posthumous attention by writing, "Jay Gould and I made a profit of . . ." or, "Jay Gould and I lost . . ."

If Jim Fisk had honored his buy orders on Black Friday, when, at his direction, his broker drove the price to $162, it would have cost the Erie partners millions. As it was, thanks to lawyers and to the fact that Boss Tweed's paid judge put the gold exchange into Gould's hands by appointing a powerless figurehead for a receiver, Gould and Fisk had, with impunity, reneged on their buy orders.

Enough of the scandal in the Gold Room had been leaked to give Headley an idea of what had happened, although many of the commitments made during the frenzied trading of Black Friday would never be honored. While Fisk was buying, Jay Gould was unloading most of his more than fifty million dollars in gold holdings. Exact figures were not available, but Headley could estimate a profit of between ten and twelve millions for Gould on gold alone—and that was just the beginning, for while Gould was selling gold, he was selling short on the stock market and feeling secure in the knowledge that stock prices would tumble along with gold once the crash came. Even after deducting a couple of million for Gould's lawyers and Bill Tweed's cut, Headley had to admit that Jay Gould had done a good week's work.

The fact that Jim Fisk was still Gould's friend puzzled the journalist. On the surface it would seem that Fisk had been betrayed. Gould had started selling gold while allowing his partner to buy at inflated prices. But Fisk and Gould were still as thick as the thieves they were, with Fisk chortling and chuckling and saying "Me and Jay this" and "Me and Jay that" outside the committee hearing room in Washington. Was Gould's apparent perfidy just another part of the scheme, a last-minute gambit designed to do exactly what it did, which was to assure high prices for the gold sold by Jay Gould and to muddy the waters so that Fisk was able to welsh on his buy orders?

"We'll probably never know," Headley said aloud.

"As we used to say back in Ireland . . ." the bartender began.

Headley remained immersed in his thoughts. If he could write one more story he would end it by paraphrasing something Jim Fisk had said in his jovial manner at the conclusion of one of his meeting with the press following the hearings in Washington.

"Jim," Headley had asked, "a mountain of money was thrown into the Gold Room by both the bulls and the bears. Now men like Henry Smith—of Smith, Gould, Martin, and Company—have to make good calls on gold running into the millions. What happened to all the money?"

"It has gone where the woodbine twines," Fisk had said with a huge belly laugh.

"Would you please explain that?" someone had asked.

"Well," Jim had said, "you'll usually see woodbine clinging to a downspout."

In retrospect it seemed to Headley that Jim Fisk had been too damned jovial, too relaxed, for a man who had lost millions. Headley could come to only one conclusion: that Gould had split his winnings with his partner. Ten or twelve million dollars divided in half was still a good week's work.

Phineas's calculations were disturbed when the old man at the table began to sing in a cracked, tuneless voice. The bartender yelled out, "Enough of that, Seamus!"

"Leave him alone," Headley urged. "He's the only man I've seen lately who is at peace with himself."

He left the bar and walked to the stock exchange. An interesting little drama was being played out there. Headley saw that the market in general was nervous, still looking over its shoulder at the shambles left by Black Friday and the near crash that had followed; but one stock was getting a lot of action: it was a rail stock, some small, previously unheard-of road out in the Midwest.

Victoria Woodhull could be self-contradictory. Since her arrival in New York she had been outspoken in the fight for women's suffrage. In the eyes of men who knew only what they read in the papers, Woodhull was an unsexed woman, a female who wanted to be a male. Men who knew her personally, however, wondered how a creature of such feminine grace could be a leader in the suffrage movement. In many people's minds any woman who wanted the vote was probably a hard-faced matron with a heavy chest and a broad bottom, not a smiling, flirtatious charmer who knew how to make a man feel like a man.

Victoria's charisma worked equally well on males just past majority and gruff, mature specimens such as Psaleh Kershaw. When Victoria sent a messenger to Kershaw suggesting that a private discussion might prove profitable to both of them, Kershaw sent an affirmative answer by the same messenger, suggesting lunch at a quiet Italian restaurant not far from Victoria's offices.

Kershaw was at the table when she arrived. He rose and watched her make her way swayingly toward him, kissed her hand, then expressed his pleasure at seeing her and his regret that so much time had passed since their last meeting.

"The manicotti is good here," he told her when she picked up a menu and began to examine it.

"I will put myself in your hands," she said with a demure smile.

Kershaw puffed out his cheeks and beckoned a waiter. "We have here, Luigi, a lady who likes Italian food. Tell the chef that Mr. Kershaw wants a sampling for two diners of his finest dishes."

He ordered an excellent Chianti and leaned back in satisfaction. Wine and antipasto were soon on the table. Victoria nibbled delicately, then wiped her lips on a crisp white linen napkin. "I have been led to believe, Mr. Kershaw, that you did not fare well in the wake of Black Friday."

Kerchaw bristled.

"There is a reason for my impertinence," Victoria said, reaching across to touch his hand. "I am here because of a mutual—shall we say—friend?"

She knew that Kershaw would immediately leap to the

conclusion that she was talking about Commodore Vanderbilt. And yet she had not lied. She had qualified the word *friend* by questioning the term.

"I must admit that I let my emotions carry me," Kershaw said.

"I am here to call your attention to what seems to be an excellent and rapid opportunity to recoup losses."

"I am always open to suggestions, Mrs. Woodhull, but at the moment I am putting my funds into blue-chip stocks."

"Which pay an honest but small return," Victoria noted. "The stock I am going to suggest to you may not be considered a blue chip, but if you'll give the matter consideration, I think you'll find it to be a little jewel."

The conversation was suspended while Luigi filled the table with steaming dishes. Victoria took small helpings from several, "*umm*ed" and "*ah*ed" over the taste, and commended Kershaw on his choices.

It was Kershaw who returned the subject to money matters. "This little jewel you've found . . ."

"Ah, yes," she said, dabbing daintily at the corners of her full lips with her napkin. "Very soon now, Mr. Kershaw, the Eastern newspapers are going to wake up to the significance of a certain little story that ran some weeks ago in a Kansas City newspaper." She opened her purse and handed him a folded clipping.

He read. When he looked up at her, his eyes were sparkling with interest. "If this is true . . ."

"Well, I know that one shouldn't believe half what one reads in the papers; but true or not, this story has caused some movement in the stock of the railroad, the KC&S. It's risen three points from where it has stood for months. The KC&S is such a solid little line that it didn't fluctuate as wildly as other railroad issues during the Black Friday panic."

"So you're suggesting that I buy KC&S," Kershaw said.

"I myself am interested in the KC&S," she replied. "I have a copy of the quarterly report here." She dug into her large bag again. "I think you'll see why."

He had forgotten his food. Victoria, however, ate with a

healthy appetite while he read the brochure. "By golly," he said, his eyes dancing, "they're grossly overcapitalized."

Victoria nodded, her mouth full.

"My dear lady," Kershaw said, "I do indeed see why you and our mutual friend are interested. You and he are buying, I assume."

"Indeed we are." Well, that was half-true. She and Lloyd were *promising* to buy at a later date to meet the calls on orders that they were currently selling short.

"I will need to think on this, Mrs. Woodhull, but I will give you my decision quickly."

"Of course Woodhull, Claflin, and Company will be glad to serve your needs," she said.

Psaleh Kershaw was in the offices' reception area and asking for Victoria before the close of business that same day. She took his arm and escorted him into her office.

"Mrs. Woodhull, I have told my regular broker to begin liquidation of my stock holdings and to enter the proceeds in a cash account with your firm." He chuckled. "There was some protest on his part, but he'll do his best in the hope that I will do business with him in the future."

"We would welcome you as a permanent client," Victoria said, "but I believe in being fair. Feel free, Mr. Kershaw, to continue to do business with your own broker."

"No, no. It is only right for me to give my purchase orders to you, after you so graciously called my attention to our little jewel. It would be safe, Mrs. Woodhull, for you to begin purchases of KC&S stock for my account. There is in excess of one hundred thousand dollars available at the moment, and that amount will grow considerably, as you might imagine, as I sell off my other holdings."

"Why, Mr. Kershaw," Victoria said sweetly, "you're not going to bet everything on KC&S?"

"Considering the source of my information, how could I not?" he asked.

"I never advise anyone to put all his eggs in one basket," Victoria said, laying a foundation for a future defense of her recommendation. Kershaw might not remember that she'd told him not to invest everything into the KC&S, but she would enter the remark into her daily business log, and before the end of the game she would make a point of giving Kershaw the same advice in the presence of witnesses.

"I would advise some diversification," she continued. "It's an odd world, Mr. Kershaw. I wouldn't want to see you hurt, as you were when you sold New York Central at the bottom."

Kershaw winced visibly at the reminder, and Victoria knew that she had hit him in his manly pride. That reference to his fiscal stupidity was the strongest appeal she could have made in favor of his doing what Lloyd wanted him to do—put his hat and ass into the KC&S. She was able to get in buy orders for some seventy thousand dollars' worth of KC&S for Kershaw's account before that day's closing bell.

Leah Miles knew that Victoria would react strongly if she learned that Elizabeth Tilton had confessed to having a two-year affair with the shining knight of Christ. Victoria might even get out an extra issue of the *Weekly,* not content to wait until regular publication time. She would never pass up an opportunity to call one of the most prominent spokesmen for anti-Woodhullism a sexual hypocrite, in her eyes the worst of all human scum.

Leah decided to talk the situation over with Stephen Pearl Andrews. Andrews had esoteric personal beliefs, but he was not a precipitous man. With Beecher's shouted insults fresh in her mind, Leah asked for a private talk with Andrews on the Monday following her excursion to the Plymouth Church.

Andrews listened with growing exhilaration.

"My, my, my," he gloated when she was finished. He leapt to his feet and actually rubbed his hands together in anticipation as he paced back and forth and said, "Oh, my. Yes. Oh, my, my, my."

"The reason why I came to you, Mr. Andrews, is that I'm not sure whether it would be in the best interest of the cause to confront Henry Ward Beecher. The man has powerful friends." She laughed. "But I don't have to tell you that."

Andrews threw himself down into his chair. "But my dear girl," he said, eyes flashing, "this is a perfectly splendid opportunity. We're going to toss a bombshell into the bedrooms of the nation. This is just what we've been waiting for." He jumped up, unable to contain his enthusiasm. "And it comes at such a perfect time, just when we're getting ready to run the Comstock story."

Leah raised her eyebrows in question.

"Oh, you don't know about that yet, do you? I'll have the draft for you later today, my dear, so that you can work your magic on it, smooth my clumsy prose, correct my spelling."

"You're speaking of Anthony Comstock, secretary of the Society for the Suppression of Vice?"

"Himself," Andrews confirmed. "And it's delicious, because what he's done is absolutely hedonistic."

"Do I want to hear this?" Leah asked with a wry smile.

Andrews laughed. It was an old joke with them, the fact that she, an unmarried girl, obviously not of the modern school, was the one who read, corrected, and put into final form a variety of writings that could, at times, be quite sensualistic. "But you must. We have incontrovertible proof that Mr. Anthony Comstock, man-about-town and self-appointed guardian of public morality, seduced two underage girls."

Leah blushed.

"Yes, isn't it hideous? Two of them. Innocents. We have their testimony, their affidavits. And to think that we're going to be able to blast Beecher himself in the same issue."

"You're going to tell Victoria and Tennie, then?" Leah asked.

"Why, no, *you're* going to tell them." He leaned forward. "Let's surprise them. You write the story—"

"Oh, not I."

"—just as it happened. After all, who is better qualified

to write it than the one who heard it all firsthand? And when it's finished, we'll show it to Vee and Tennie."

"There is one thing, Mr. Andrews. I am reluctant to betray a friend. Mr. Tilton told me in confidence what his wife had said."

"Just write the story," Andrews said. "And leave Tilton to Victoria."

With some remaining reservations Leah began writing. As she warmed to the task she found herself thinking, *So there. Take that, Henry Ward Beecher.* She was a quietly devout woman. She read her Bible often and prayed to her God each night and quite often during the day, especially when asked to edit some piece having to do with defiance of the commandment against adultery. But Leah had made her peace concerning her work with the *Weekly.* She prayed for the souls of those who believed in and practiced free love, and she rationalized her contribution to spreading their beliefs by telling herself that even though some of the methods employed by her workmates might be questionable—methods she neither condoned nor practiced—the overall goal of fair treatment for women was a just cause. She believed that God was in His Heaven and that Jesus Christ was His son and that both Father and son were in favor of women's suffrage.

She knew that it was the duty of a good Christian to follow the laws, and the duty of some who were called to spread the lovely promise of the New Covenant, "For God so loved the world, that he gave his only begotten Son, that whosoever believeth in him should not perish, but have everlasting life." And, like most laymen, she felt that those who answered God's call to spread His word should be above reproach. Men such as Henry Ward Beecher were not to be allowed human frailty. When a religious personage got caught with his human weakness showing, he disillusioned thousands—in Beecher's case, millions.

Although it was not logical for someone to say, "If that is being a Christian, deliver me," such things were indeed said, for it was inevitable that the Church and the basic credo of Christ would be judged by the actions of the men who spoke for the ideal.

In short, Beecher's adultery was not merely a sin of human weakness but a monolithic, phallic insult to God and to the Christian belief. In spite of the fact that his sin was the same as that of Victoria and Tennie and Colonel Blood and Stephen Pearl Andrews, it was more serious and, therefore, more deserving of punishment. Ironically, that punishment was to come because of the indignation felt by a woman who had never known a man in the carnal sense.

Leah showed the article to Victoria, who gave an unladylike whoop when she realized what she was reading. Tennie, a moment later, having reached the same point in Leah's writing, did a wild little dance.

"And he called us whores!" Victoria shouted.

"We've got him. Oh, by God, we've got him!" Tennie gloated.

Leah experienced a moment of doubt. When she had written the story of Elizabeth Tilton's confession, it had been done in a spirit of indignation and retribution. Now, seeing the glee of the Claflin sisters, she was reminded of another quote from the Bible: "Judge not lest ye be judged."

"Victoria, we must have Mr. Tilton's agreement before we publish this story," Leah pointed out.

"I can promise you that will be no problem," Victoria said, unable to stop laughing.

That promise was made good that very night in Victoria's bed.

The shocking revelation of Henry Ward Beecher's adultery was published in the November second issue of the *Weekly*. Those who were involved in the publication of the periodical felt that the Beecher affair far overshadowed the charges that Anthony Comstock had ruined two young virgins; and the immediate reaction by the press and the reading public supported that view.

Surprisingly, the reaction that had the most profound effect on all of those at the *Weekly* was Comstock's. The secretary of the Society for the Suppression of Vice used his political connections with stunning swiftness. A squad of policemen swarmed into the offices of Woodhull, Claflin, and Company and arrested both Victoria and Tennessee on a charge of transmitting obscene materials—the *Weekly*—through the mails.

CHAPTER 19

After Victoria and Tennessee were led away by armed, uniformed policemen, Leah was paralyzed by indecision and helplessness. She had protested to the officers, telling them that there had to be a mistake; but she'd been pushed rudely aside, then left alone, shocked and angry, in the outer office with the sisters' receptionist and secretary.

"They can't do that," Leah said to the woman. "They can't just burst into someone's office and make an unsupported accusation and haul someone away to jail."

"Looks as if they did," the secretary said. She was opening drawers, removing her personal belongings, and banging the drawers shut.

"What are you doing?" Leah asked as the older woman threw things hastily into a carpetbag.

"Getting out of here as fast as I can," the secretary answered. "Next they'll be coming after those who work here."

"Please, don't go," Leah begged. "I need you here. There'll be no one to speak with clients if you go."

The secretary laughed harshly. "Honey, haven't you noticed anything from that back room of yours? Clients? What clients? Since the old boy got himself engaged to a young society woman, you can count on one hand the clients this place has and still have fingers left over."

As the secretary opened the outer door Leah asked, "Will you at least stop in at the messenger service down the street and ask them to send a boy?"

"Sure," the secretary agreed with a sad little smile. "Look, Miss Miles, if you know what's good for you, you'll get out of here too. I always knew something like this was going to happen. You can't just defy God's will forever without His taking notice."

"Thank you for your concern," Leah said. "You won't forget to send the messenger?"

After the boy arrived, she sent notes to Colonel Blood and Stephen Pearl Andrews, both of whom showed up in the office within the hour. Blood, upon hearing the news, threw himself down into a chair and hid his face in his hands.

Andrews said, "Well, you two hold the fort while I pop down to Ludlow Street and see how much the gendarmes want for the ransom of our two lovely ladies."

"This could not have happened at a worse time," Blood moaned.

"Colonel," Leah said, "Victoria's secretary said that the firm has lost most of its clients."

He looked up. "Woodhull, Claflin, and Company is dead broke."

"But in an emergency such as this, wouldn't the old—I mean, wouldn't the commodore help?"

"Not likely," Blood said. "He's getting married, you know, and his family have finally convinced him to rid himself of the wicked Claflin sisters."

Andrews was back within the hour. Bail had been set by a judge. It would take fifty thousand dollars—twenty-five thousand dollars each—to get Victoria and Tennessee out of jail.

"Surely the firm can raise that much," Leah said. "Can't it be borrowed against assets?"

"What assets?" Blood asked gloomily. "Oh, we can sell the furniture. That'll raise a few hundred dollars."

"Mr. Andrews?" Leah looked at him expectantly. He was the idea man, the driving spirit behind the entire group centered around Victoria and Tennessee. And he was not poor.

"Leah, you know that I would gladly put up the bond if I could." He shrugged. "I fear, my dear, that my pose as a wealthy dilettante is nothing more than a charade. I have my little income—just enough to keep home and hearth together." He fidgeted uneasily. "I know that it will seem that I'm deserting in a time of troubles, but I simply must leave you. Sorry."

And he was gone.

"Are you just going to sit there and do nothing?" Leah demanded, turning on Blood.

He shrugged, spread his hands helplessly.

Anger brought intemperate words to Leah's lips. "Heaven help us," she said. "How long have you been living off the fruits of Victoria and Tennie's work? Ever since you joined them in St. Louis? How many years is that? And now that they're in trouble, what do you do? You shrug and weep a little bit and sit on your backside." She turned away, gathered her things, and hurried out into a crisp November day, leaving Blood sitting despondently in the empty office.

She found Lloyd, finally, at the stock exchange. He brightened when she sat down beside him in the spectators' gallery.

"I need your help," she said.

"Just a minute," he said, shushing her with his finger at his lips. On the floor his broker was offering to sell short five thousand shares of KC&S. Lloyd waited, breathless, until the calls of acceptance came from two jubilant brokers who were, most probably, thanking their lucky stars for the ignoramus who was selling short on the rising flood of interest in the small railroad.

Lloyd took Leah's hand. "Now. What can I do for you?"

"I need fifty thousand dollars."

"Whoa," Lloyd exploded, laughing in surprise.

"They've arrested Victoria and Tennessee, Lloyd. I need the money to meet their bonds so that they can get out of jail."

"I'll be damned," Lloyd said. He demanded the full story and chuckled appreciatively when he learned the reason for the sisters' arrest. He frowned, however, when Leah told him that the firm was broke. "No clients at all?" he asked. "What about a man named Kershaw?"

"I don't know," Leah replied. "All I know is that Blood and Andrews said that Vanderbilt has withdrawn his support and that as a result other clients have quit the firm."

"All right," Lloyd said, rising. "Let's get out of here and see what we can do." On the street he turned her to face him. "Go to the office and find Victoria's files. I want to know what actions have been taken on the account of Psaleh Kershaw. Can you do that?"

"What are you going to do about Victoria and Tennie?"

"I'm going to Ludlow Street now." He lifted Leah's chin. "Don't worry. I'll get your friends out of the jug."

She hugged him.

"Run along, now. You have the keys to the office?"

"Yes." She cocked her head. "I don't remember whether or not Victoria's desk has a lock."

"If it does, use a screwdriver or something," Lloyd said. "What I'm asking you to do is important."

When Lloyd arrived at the Ludlow Street jail and asked to see the sisters, he was shown into a room that did not look at all like a prison's. The horsehair stuffed leather chairs and couches showed wear but were comfortable. The hardwood floor was clean. A jailer stood in the doorway and smirked as Victoria and Tennie moved swiftly to kiss Lloyd on the cheek.

"I can't say that I admire your new parlor," Lloyd said.

"Don't be too critical, darling boy. After all, it's the best that the taxpayers of New York City can provide for us hardened criminals."

"You seem to be taking it fairly well," Lloyd said.

"Because of this obvious persecution of two women who are guilty of nothing but speaking out for the rights of their sex, we will"—she paused, smiled, and raised her voice so that the jailer could hear—"we will burn Mr. Anthony Comstock a new asshole."

Lloyd kept his face straight, knowing that Victoria was indulging in one of her favorite pastimes, shocking the staid members of the male establishment.

"Before we are finished with Mr. Comstock," she added, "he will be sorry he ever discovered what lurks under a woman's skirts."

"Well, I'm glad to see you in such high spirits," Lloyd said. "I have notified my attorney to arrange your bond."

Tennie, who had been striking a voluptuous pose on a black leather couch, lifted her head and smiled at Lloyd. "No, thank you."

Lloyd raised one eyebrow.

"We have been falsely imprisoned," Victoria said firmly. "We will stay here until the whole world knows that two innocent women have been persecuted for revealing the truth about the sexual appetites of men who claim to be honorable."

"Well," Lloyd said, "I wouldn't make that too final." He grinned. "Have you tried the food?"

"I'm told," Victoria said, "that it's adequate."

"I can imagine," Lloyd said. "At any rate you'll need a lawyer, so you will talk with mine when he shows up, won't you?"

"Yes, of course," Victoria replied. "And we're very grateful, darling boy."

"I imagine that Leah will be keeping in touch with you," he said. "She'll let me know if you change your mind about getting out." He moved close to Victoria. "What about Kershaw?"

"Oh, damn," Victoria said. "I'd forgotten that." She went pale. "And I've still got orders out to sell short."

"Don't worry. I'll take care of it and see that you meet

the calls when the time comes. I'll need your records and your power of attorney. How deep is Kershaw into it?"

"The dear man has delusions of grandeur," Victoria said. "He's dumped almost two million so far. I believe he has dreams of control, so that he can bleed off that beautiful three million of yours all by himself."

"All right. Good. That may be enough," Lloyd said.

"From the way he talked, I don't think he could come up with much more without mortgaging his home and other real-estate holdings."

"Leah can find your records, I assume."

"Yes."

"I'll keep in touch." He kissed her on the cheek, waved to Tennie, then almost collided with a beautifully dressed man with a mass of curly locks hanging down past the collar of an expensive suit coat.

"Excuse me," the newcomer said. "I've come to see Mrs. Woodhull and Miss Claflin?"

Lloyd bowed, introduced himself, and appraised the gentleman. The visitor had a face of Mephistophelian darkness, with piercing black eyes, a tightly trimmed beard, and tiny mustache. In spite of the almost sinister cast of his features he exuded genuine warmth.

"George Francis Train," the man said, extending his hand. He lifted his hat to Victoria and Tennie as Lloyd made the introductions.

"We have heard many wonderful things about you," Tennie said, forgetting her tiredness upon seeing the virile, interesting-looking stranger.

Since his days as a volunteer publicity agent and promoter for the Union Pacific Railroad and his adventures with Philip Trent, George Francis Train had been a busy man. Among his interests was publication of a paper called *The Train Ligue,* in which he praised the new philosophy of Karl Marx.

"I have come, dear lady," Train said, bending over Tennie's hand, "to see if you are in need of help."

"We will be grateful for all the support we can get," Victoria said.

"It will be my pleasure, then, to post your bond," Train said.

"You'll have to get in line," Lloyd said. "They want to become martyrs. They're going to stay in jail until—" He looked at Victoria. "Until when?"

"Until the city admits that it was wrong in arresting us and publishes a complete apology and exoneration," Victoria answered.

"Well, perhaps I can do something else in a very worthy cause," Train said.

Lloyd, delaying his departure, listened as Train questioned Victoria and Tennie about the charges filed against them. After he had heard the whole story—he had not yet read the edition of the *Weekly* that revealed Beecher's affair with Elizabeth Tilton and Comstock's dalliance with two young virgins—he laughed wholeheartedly.

Lloyd left when the conversation turned to the theories of governmental reform, which had been the work of Stephen Pearl Andrews in the *Weekly*. He felt that Victoria and Tennie were in good hands, for Train had purchased property along the right-of-way of the Union Pacific at pittance prices. The financial community estimated that he owned thirty million dollars' worth of real estate in Omaha alone. In addition, he had built a fleet of sailing ships, and he had been the promoter who introduced streetcars into Europe. If the sisters decided they wanted to post bond and go free, fifty thousand dollars would be pocket change to George Francis Train.

After leaving the Ludlow Street jail Lloyd went back to the stock exchange. KC&S was up three points on heavy buy offers. Later, at the offices of Woodhull, Claflin, and Company he went over papers that Leah had found in Victoria's desk and was pleased to see that Psaleh Kershaw had purchased shares in the KC&S totaling just over two million dollars.

The situation was approaching a critical point. As the price of stock in the small Kansas railroad rose past $100, and then $110, longtime stockholders had begun to take their profits. Now, with the price pushing $120, there was a small amount of profit taking by those who had bought in at the century mark or lower; but the availability of shares did not meet the demand. Soon there was going to be an explosion in the price of the stock—when it became clear to traders that something was very definitely afoot with the KC&S.

There remained only one task for Lloyd, and it lay in an area in which he would require help. When the stock market closed he went to the offices of the Erie Railroad.

Lloyd's position with the Erie was an ill-defined one. He had no regular duties. He was free to spend his time as he pleased, a fortunate state of affairs since his attentions were very much devoted to the stock market. He had to be ready to take the next step in his plan when the time was right.

As he had expected, Jay Gould and the office help had gone home. But he found Jim Fisk in the office that the amiable speculator had made so comfortable, a veritable home away from home. Carrying a bottle of the finest Scotch whiskey, he entered Fisk's ornate inner sanctum, went to a bar, took down two crystal glasses, and filled each almost to the brim.

"Miles," Fisk said, "if you ever get tired of working for Jay, you let me know."

"I'd be the most expensive damned bartender you ever had, Jim," Lloyd said.

Fisk roared with laughter, then downed his drink in three big gulps. "So, Miles, what's on your mind?"

"I need a little help, Jim," Lloyd said.

"Yep," Fisk said, "no one comes to see old Jim anymore unless they want something."

"Now, that's not true," Lloyd protested. "The pretty little girls who come up here from the opera's practice rooms are not expecting something from you."

Fisk roared again, rubbed his genitals, and said, "You're wrong there, boy. Dead wrong."

"I just need some help in getting something into the newspapers," Lloyd said.

"Hell, no problem." Fisk scribbled a note quickly. "Send this by messenger. We'll have a few drinks while we're waiting, and then you'll be fixed up nicely. I'm sending for Willis Reese." Fisk snorted. "His name used to be Resnick. Works for Horace Greeley's *Tribune*. He's been taking a little side money from me for years for planting items in the paper now and then."

Lloyd took the note and went to send off a messenger. He and Fisk were alone now in the suite, although Jim had a habit of leaving the lower door unlocked. He got some very interesting female visitors from his opera company that way. Reese would be able to get in without a problem.

Fisk wasn't looking well. He still was loud and genial, but his ruddy color had faded. There were rumors around the office that his love life with his steady mistress, Josie Mansfield, wasn't going as smoothly as it had in the past. That sort of gossip didn't interest Lloyd. When, after a few drinks from the bottle of aged Scotch, Jim began to complain about the duplicity of women and the ingratitude of their entire sex, Lloyd was only half listening; but suddenly his attention was riveted to Jim's face and his words.

"—bastards are blackmailing me, Miles," Jim was saying. "Can you imagine that? Bastards blackmailing Jim Fisk?"

"Well, Jim, it seems to me as if you could put a stop to that," Lloyd said, encouraging Fisk to keep talking.

"Trouble is, boy, they've got old Jim by the short hairs, and they know it."

"Are you talking about Josie?" Lloyd asked.

"After all I've done for her." The whiskey had hit Fisk heavily. He was on the point of tears. "Everything she wanted and then some. By damn, Miles, I've spent big money on that woman. And do you know what she was doing with it all the time?"

"No," Lloyd said.

"Been giving it to that pretty boy of hers," Jim spat out. "Taking money from me and spending it on that bastard Ned Stokes."

Lloyd filled Fisk's glass again.

"Hell, Jim, you can handle a couple of small-timers like them," Lloyd said.

"Yeah, but they're threatening to reveal everything they know about me and about Jay."

"What do they know? What could be worse than what's already public knowledge?"

Jim laughed. "Well, sonny boy, me and Jay, we ain't always been angels."

Jim Fisk, loudmouth though he was, was not the kind of man to reveal dangerous business secrets to a woman in bed. In spite of his public buffoonery Fisk was, Lloyd knew, one damned smart operator. A man didn't get to be half owner of a company like the Erie Railroad by being amusing. "It's more than just that, isn't it, Jim?" Lloyd asked.

Fisk was near tears again. "Goddamn it, she has letters from me."

"What do they say?"

"That I've been screwing her eyeballs out for years."

"For the love of God," Lloyd said, incredulous. "You're paying them off to prevent them from telling the public what it already knows?"

Fisk was weeping silently. The big, fat tears ran down his face into his grandiose mustache. "You've got me there, Miles."

Lloyd turned away to hide a smile. "Oh ho," he said, understanding at last. "What you don't want people to know is that you, the great lover, are being cuckolded by Ned Stokes."

"You go to hell," Fisk said angrily. He sat up straight. "One word of this, Miles, one word—"

"Hey, I'm on your side!" Miles protested. "Look, Jim." He hesitated. He wasn't sure how much longer Jim Fisk was going to last as partner to Jay Gould. It was obvious that Gould no longer considered the big, loud man an asset. And what Lloyd was about to offer was something not to be wasted on a man who might become powerless and, perhaps, penniless in the near future. Fisk's past record, however, convinced Lloyd that he would be making a good investment in future favors from Fisk with his offer. "Jim, if these two are really bothering you, I can have it arranged so that it will all cease."

Fisk looked up with interest.

"Abruptly," Lloyd said.

"You mean—"

Lloyd held up his hand. "Shush."

"Oh, my God no," Fisk said. "Not Josie."

"Well, it might not have worked anyhow," Lloyd said, covering his tracks quickly. "I was just going to have a policeman friend of mine throw a scare into them, tell them that the Comstock committee was after them for cohabitation or something, and get them out of town."

"Oh," Fisk said.

"I wonder where that reporter is," Lloyd said.

"Maybe you better go down and be sure the door is unlocked."

Lloyd started toward the door. A young newspaperman in a slightly soiled and wrinkled gray suit suddenly stood before him in the anteroom. His cheeks flamed, and his eyes guiltily looked away from making contact with Lloyd's.

How much has he overheard? Lloyd wondered uncomfortably.

The young man surged past him and entered the room.

"Hey, Will!" Fisk bellowed. "I've got a hot one for you."

"I appreciate it, Mr. Fisk," Reese said. "Glad to be of service."

"What is this hot one we've got for ole Will?" Fisk asked Lloyd.

Lloyd introduced himself, shook Reese's hand, gave him a copy of a news release on KC&S stationery. Reese read, then looked up, blinking. "This is on the level, Mr. Fisk?"

"If my boy says it is, it is," Fisk confirmed.

"Then this is one of your operations?" Reese asked.

"Let me see that," Fisk said. He stood, staggered, caught himself, took the paper, read, and then gave the paper back. "You see that my friend is fixed up, you hear?" he said to Reese.

"Sure. It's a good story," Reese said. "Anything else, Mr. Fisk?" He was looking at the almost empty whiskey bottle.

"Nope, that's it," Fisk said. He dug into his pocket and came out with a handful of crumpled greenbacks, which he handed to Reese, who made them disappear with amazing rapidity.

Fisk waited until the door had closed behind Reese. "What's all this, Miles? What's with the KC&S? You on the up-and-up when you say that they're going to lay track to Texas?"

"Well, Jim, that's what they tell me out in Kansas."

"How come you didn't cut me and Jay in on this? Sounds like something that might have interested us."

"It's small potatoes," Lloyd said. "Not enough gravy there to warrant you and Mr. Gould spending your time on it."

"But enough for you, eh?"

"Couple of million, that's all." He laughed. "I'm still not considered to be rich."

Fisk chuckled. "I think you're gonna get there, though. Couple of million, huh?"

"That's all. Small stuff. Not in the class with you and Jay."

The flattery put Fisk back into a jovial mood. Lloyd poured the last of the whiskey into Jim's glass. "My boy," Fisk said, "I want you to come to my party tonight."

"My pleasure," Lloyd said. "Where?"

"Hotel ballroom. Black tie and all that mess."

"Thank you. I'll be there."

Willis Reese had plenty of time to get back to the *Tribune*'s newspaper offices. He filed the story that a small Kansas railroad had obtained right-of-way through the Indian nations to the Texas cattle areas. Afterward, he stopped in at his favorite bar and ordered whiskey, knowing full well that it wouldn't be as smooth as that in the bottle on Jim Fisk's desk. The bastard, he thought bitterly, could at least have offered him a drink. Rich son of a bitch was too stingy even to offer a man a little drink.

Sure enough, the whiskey clawed its way down his throat like a tomcat sliding down a slate roof. Willis dulled the pain with another quick one, then nodded in greeting as Phineas Headley came into the bar and sat down beside him.

"How's it going?" Phineas asked. "Scooping the world?"

"Yep," Reese said.

"Anything you wanta share with your old uncle Phineas?"

"Har, har."

"Selfish boy."

"Come to think of it, maybe I do," Reese said, remembering that the story in his pocket was a plant bought and paid for by big Jim Fisk. If he could get Phineas to use it, he could hit Fisk for another bundle. "I do feel generous." He handed the sheet of paper to Phineas. "Have to make your own copy, though."

"Where'd you get this crap?" Phineas asked.

"You see the company name on the paper?"

"You check this out?"

"Haven't had time. Just got it from the source."

"Been out to Kansas, have you?" Phineas asked.

"No. But one of the Erie's big boys confirmed that it's true." Reese was beginning to feel a little doubtful about the wisdom of his action in taking the press release from Fisk's friend. "Think something's wrong with it?"

"Have you read anything in the papers about a new treaty with the Indian nations?"

"Hell, I don't read the papers; I just write for 'em."

"Who gave you this release?"

"Fellow named Lloyd Miles."

A loud bell rang in Headley's ears. Once more he was crossing the trail of Mr. Lloyd Miles, and he was beginning to believe that fate was trying to tell him something.

"How do you know Miles?"

"Didn't until tonight." Reese was young. He knew that Headley was a veteran of the newspaper business. "I already filed this. Should I go back to the office and pull the copy?"

"Naw. Why?" Headley asked with a shrug.

"You think it will be okay, then?" Reese asked.

"Why not? Hell, even if it's not true, it won't be the first time false information has been published. If it's false you can have yourself another story tomorrow, after you check it out with Washington."

Reese sighed with relief. "I heard another good one tonight. Too damned bad I can't print it."

"Why can't you?"

"Several reasons—best one being that Jim Fisk would kill me."

"Tell me," Headley said.

"Something I overheard. Seems that Fisk's steady girl's been two-timing him with some joker named Ned Stokes. They're blackmailing old Jim, and he's paying not because of what they have on him but because he doesn't want people to know that Josie's making a sucker out of him."

"Just where did you overhear this?" Headley asked. "Same place you picked up the news release from the KC&S?"

"I've told you all you need to know, Phineas," Reese complained. "Quit trying to dig more out of me."

"Fine. Buy you a drink?" Phineas tossed a dollar onto the counter and left.

Phineas smiled with satisfaction as he walked down the street. All of a sudden things were, at long last, breaking his way. If what Reese said was true, if Josie Mansfield and some fellow named Ned Stokes were blackmailing Jim Fisk, that made them very interesting people indeed.

And if Lloyd Miles was in the middle of some stock scheme involving the Kansas railroad, he, too, would be vulnerable to a bit of pressure. Lloyd Miles was up to something, of that Phineas was certain. It was a pretty good bet that no government agency had negotiated a rail right-of-way with the Five Civilized Tribes out there in Indian Territory. Therefore, the press release was a fraud.

Furthermore, Headley still had a lot of questions he wanted answers to about the events before and on Black Friday. He had decided that he was going to write the definitive history of the Gold Ring. He was still looking for a way to get inside, and if Lloyd Miles was up to something with a small Kansas railroad, that just might become the chink in the protective armor that had been thrown up around Fisk and Gould's activities on the gold market.

CHAPTER 20

If Jim Fisk's financial standing had been adversely affected by Black Friday, there was no evidence of it in the ballroom of the Grand Central Hotel. It was obvious to Lloyd—and to anyone else who knew New York prices—that the prince of Erie had spent lavishly in decorating the room. There were enough roses placed around in ornate vases to have denuded a thousand gardens. In one dining room five huge tables were laden with exotic and expensive foods; and the hotel had brought out its finest sterling flatware and servers. The tableware was paper thin, delicately hand-painted bone china from Prussia. The orchestra was larger than the one that played regularly in the opera house. A champagne fountain flowed sparklingly at one end of the large hall, and a fully stocked bar was quite popular with the almost three hundred people who had arrived before Lloyd.

Lloyd found Jim and paid his compliments. Josie Mansfield was clinging to Jim's arm. Her pudgy, sweet face was made up tastefully. She wore an ostrich feather in her wavy, dark brown hair. The huge diamond teardrops dangling from her earlobes spoke of Jim's lavish generosity toward her.

Josie and Jim made an impressive pair. Both had large

frames and carried a surplus of weight, but elegant clothing gave them dignity. Josie leaned toward delicate frills, which set off her chubby baby face. Her flawless complexion was accented by a black ribbon at her throat, from which hung an emerald the size of a man's thumbnail.

Jim didn't look too happy. He was curt with Lloyd, but that was not surprising. Lloyd knew from experience that one who opens himself to a friend or acquaintance and reveals deeply personal secrets often blames his confidant for his own weaknesses and wants nothing more to do with the person who is privy to his shame. Lloyd roamed the room, sampled the food, and sipped a glass of champagne from the fountain. He nodded and spoke to acquaintances, winked knowingly at the broker who was handling his business on the stock market, and had just decided that there was nothing for him at Jim's party when he spotted Jay Gould standing straight and alone against the wall. It was unusual for Gould to be at a public affair.

"Evening, Miles," Gould said on Lloyd's approach.

"Nice to see you, Mr. Gould," Lloyd said as Jim Fisk and Josie came wheeling ponderously by, at least four hundred pounds of waltzing couple.

"Healthy little devil, isn't she?" Gould asked in a dry voice.

"I suppose Jim likes everything to come in generous amounts," Lloyd said.

Gould chuckled, and it made him cough. "Isn't it interesting?" he asked. "They"—by a sweep of his hand he indicated the entire population of the ballroom—"condemn old Jim for having his Josie, for living with her while little Lucy Fisk waits loyally for her husband in Boston; but they will turn out to drink his booze and eat his food and hope desperately to be able to snap up a monetary crumb or two off Jim's financial table."

"Yes, I guess they laugh at him even while they're envying his knack for making money," Lloyd said.

"He had it once," Gould mused, something approaching sadness in his voice. "The Midas touch."

Lloyd remained silent, waiting.

"She's nothing more than an adventuress," Gould said. "Much like your friends the Claflin sisters."

Lloyd hid his surprise. He had no idea Gould had any knowledge of his private life.

"When Annie Wood introduced Josie to Jim—" He turned and let his soulful eyes study Lloyd's face for a moment. "You know Annie Wood, I assume."

"No, can't say that I do."

"She is quite well known. One of the most successful madams in the city."

"Ah," Lloyd said.

"Josie had one dress, no money, no home. Jim has given her a house, a stable, a carriage and horses, jewelry, and a private box at the opera house." Gould sighed deeply. "It is sad to see a good man ruined by something like *that.*"

The contempt that Gould put into the word referring to Josie was beyond measure. He lifted his head, put his hands behind his back, and swept his eyes around the room. "Miles, I can't abide affairs like this."

"It's not my favorite way to spend an evening, either," Lloyd confided.

Gould looked at him closely. "I understand you're in the railroad business."

Lloyd shrugged and laughed. "In a very small way, Mr. Gould."

"You have to start somewhere."

"Yes."

Another long pause ensued, and Gould appeared to be deep in thought. When Jim Fisk and Josie danced by again, his expression became even more brooding. His voice was so low that Lloyd could hardly hear the words "Be at my house tomorrow night at eight, Miles. Evening dress if you please." And then he was gone, weaving his way among the dancers, a small, neat man in dark clothing.

He left Lloyd with a lot of food for thought. Lloyd felt that he had been present at the end of an era, for Jay Gould never indulged in idle small talk. Knowing the man as he did, Lloyd concluded that there'd been purpose in Gould's comments about Jim and Josie, that Gould was saying a melancholy good-bye to his long-term partner. It was evident that Gould felt Jim to be an embarrassment to him. It would be fascinating to see how the partnership would end; but Lloyd was even more interested—because it involved him personally—to learn why Gould wanted him in evening clothing at the Gould house at eight o'clock on a Saturday night.

He was making his way across the dance floor and toward the front entry when he was bumped from behind by feminine softness. He turned to say, "I beg your pardon," and looked into the beautiful face of Abby Kershaw.

She pulled her dance partner to a halt and smiled at Lloyd.

"Sorry," she said.

The young man who held her in his arms glared at Lloyd in a decidedly unfriendly manner. "Yes, we're sorry," he said in a tone that showed he was not sorry in the least. He tugged at Abby, but she pushed his hand from her arm and continued to smile at Lloyd.

"You haven't claimed a dance with me," she told him.

His impulse was to laugh harshly at her and turn on his heels, but she looked especially beautiful in a sleek black silken gown, and her green eyes were smiling along with her lips. "Once again I beg your pardon. Shall we remedy that situation right now?" He reached for her hand.

"Now, look here, fella," her escort began.

"Is he with you?" Lloyd asked Abby.

"He was."

Lloyd stared through narrowed eyes at the young man. "She spoke in the past tense, 'fella.' Your presence here is no longer required, 'fella.'" He saw the young man winding up for an attack, saw him tense and begin to draw his right hand back and up in preparation for the blow. Lloyd stepped forward and quickly drove his fist into the softness of stomach at the solar plexus. The young man's breath exploded outward. Lloyd caught him before he fell and held him upright. "Be brave," he said into his adversary's ear.

Tears had formed in the young man's eyes. He was clasping his midsection and gasping for breath. Dancers were staring as they whirled past.

"He's all right," Lloyd said to one particularly nosy couple who momentarily paused beside them. "Just needs a little sit-down."

The fellow staggered away. Lloyd took the woman he had come to think of as the ice queen into his arms, but tonight there was nothing cold about her.

"You are a very decisive man," she remarked.

"I didn't plan to embarrass you with a scene in the middle of the dance floor."

"He was going to hit you."

"Yes." He looked down at her. Her raven hair smelled of a musky perfume. Her satin-smooth skin seemed to glow with health. She was showing even, white teeth in a radiant smile. "Was he your escort for the evening?"

"You're not going to tell me that it's the duty of a lady to leave with the man she came in with?"

"Not if you'll allow me to see you home."

"It would definitely be unladylike to be wandering the streets alone, wouldn't it?" she asked, her green eyes twinkling. As she looked him directly in the eyes, she pushed herself suggestively close, pressed a thigh against his. Within three minutes she had made him forget the way she had humiliated him.

Once, between dances, the man who had been her escort started to approach them as Abby and Lloyd stood beside a refreshment table. Lloyd took two steps to meet him, and the young man turned away and was not seen again. It was past midnight when Abby said that it was time to go home. He kissed her in the cab, immediately after the cabbie had closed the door.

Her lips warmed him as no other kiss had done. He felt weak when he pulled back to look at her. "Goddamn," he whispered, trying not to question this mercurial creature's sudden change of heart.

"Shall I take that as a compliment?" she breathed, leaning toward him until their lips met again.

The ride to the Kershaw house was far too short. He

escorted her to the door, then held both her hands in his. Her smooth olive skin was red around her mouth. He touched her there with one finger. He had not shaved since morning, and his stubble had irritated her. "I'm sorry."

"Not to worry," she said, leaning into him. "A bit of night cream and three or four weeks of healing, and it'll be all right." She lifted her face.

He kissed her, trying to be gentle, but she put her hands behind his head and pressed her lips forcefully into his mouth.

"When can I see you again?" he asked when their lips parted.

"Do you want to see me again?"

"Yes, very much."

She looked away. "It would probably be best if you didn't."

"Abby—"

"Oh, well. Yes, I'll see you again."

"When?"

"I'll send you a note."

"Abby, don't do this to me. Give me a time. Tomorrow night?"

"No," she said with no explanation.

"Sunday afternoon."

"No. Impossible."

"Damn it, Abby—"

"Look," she said, her voice rising, "you don't own me, Mr. Miles. I have said that I will contact you. If that isn't enough for you, you can go to hell."

She left him standing on the stoop, a mixture of need and anger making him feel helpless.

A butler admitted Lloyd to the Gould house precisely at eight o'clock and led him to a large sitting room, where a dozen people stood chatting, glasses in hand. Jim Fisk was conspicuous by his absence.

"Mr. Lloyd Miles," the butler announced, and all faces turned toward the doorway.

Lloyd saw Gould and smiled, then was stunned by the

regal beauty of Abby, in white. She stood beside her father. Resentment roiled within him at the sight of her. He made his way to his host.

"Pleased that you could come, Miles," Gould said. "Perhaps we can have a word later in the evening."

"My pleasure," Lloyd responded. He had a feeling that the world was about to open for him. Gould was certainly ready to dump Jim Fisk as a partner. Could it possibly be that Gould was going to ask Lloyd to join him in some affair of business? Gould's touch, as old Dan'l Drew had said, could be death, but it could also be golden. To share in one of Jay Gould's financial deals would seal his financial future and plant him firmly within Abby's social sphere.

The financier, meanwhile, introduced Lloyd to Mrs. Gould, then to others, all names that Lloyd knew, all names that conjured up dollar signs. Lloyd paused before the white-bearded Psaleh Kershaw.

Abby took Lloyd's hand and squeezed it. The aura of her smile made Jay Gould's parlor glow. Psaleh Kershaw shook hands politely but unenthusiastically, then moved away. He attempted to take Abby with him, but she would not go.

"I didn't think you were rich enough to be invited here," Abby whispered, smiling warmly to gentle his mood.

Dinner was announced. Lloyd found himself seated beside Abby, with an old half-deaf denizen of New York's "Gold Coast," upper Fifth Avenue, on the other side. The old man was not disposed to talk, which left Lloyd free to sneak looks at Abby as she ate, exchanged pleasantries with others at the table, and smiled at him. His anger receded.

The table talk was brittle, lacking in substance. At the dinner's end when Gould invited the gentlemen to join him in his study, Lloyd left Abby reluctantly. Cigars and brandy were distributed. Gould, after a few minutes of socializing, disappeared into another room with several of the men. Those left behind in the study formed another group, and Lloyd found himself seated next to Psaleh Kershaw.

Lloyd was surprised when Kershaw made light conversation in a pleasant, deep voice. Because of Abby's burning kisses on the way to her home in the hansom cab and Kershaw's own civility, Lloyd was feeling no enmity for the older man. Lloyd was even having difficulty remembering that the man had insulted him and was his enemy. The notion crept into his mind to include Kershaw in his scheme for the KC&S, giving him the opportunity to share in the profits instead of trapping him in a huge loss.

"I'm pleased to have this opportunity to get acquainted with you, Mr. Kershaw," he said. "I believe we have a lot in common."

"And what is that, Mr. Miles?" Kershaw asked.

Lloyd drew back, shrugged. "The market."

"Yes, that," Kershaw agreed. "It's a fine game, isn't it?"

"Keeps the blood circulating."

Kershaw laughed. "Sometimes too damned rapidly."

"I know what you mean," Lloyd said.

"Understand you've been seeing my Abby," Kershaw said.

Not knowing whether he had been enjoying the calm before the storm, Lloyd smiled tentatively. Still, he felt pleased that the man had opened the subject. "Not as much as I'd like to see her," he said.

"Willful girl, Abby," Kershaw said, shaking his head. "She often gives young men the wrong idea about her."

"I think she's a wonderful girl," Lloyd said.

"I suppose so, yes." He shifted uncomfortably. "Miles?"

"Yes, sir?"

"I trust that you're not getting any silly ideas about my daughter."

Lloyd went stiff inside. He turned his head to see Kershaw's expression. Through the white beard the man was smiling, apparently amused. Lloyd's guard came up clanging like iron gates. "And what, Mr. Kershaw, would you call silly ideas?"

Kershaw was still beaming. "Just because you are invited into the home of Jay Gould doesn't mean that you should get ideas about Abby."

"You're not making yourself clear, Kershaw," Lloyd said,

his voice low, icy. "Just for laughs, what would you say if I asked you for the hand of your daughter in marriage?"

"I'd try to be as kind as possible, Miles," Kershaw said, "but the gist of it would be to tell you that no goyisher parvenu will marry my daughter." He lifted one hand. "No hard feelings, Miles. It's just the way things are."

Lloyd's smile would have made a more astute man nervous, for it was the glacial, toothy leer of a predator. His pale blue eyes, which sometimes gave men a false impression of weakness, held an arctic chill. "That's how things are?"

"I fear so," Kershaw said. "Surely you understand. Differences of culture, background, religion, and all that. Of course I know you're just speaking hypothetically, Miles, for if my daughter had any interest in you, I'm sure she would have told me."

"Tells you everything, does she?"

"I don't see that it's any of your business, but yes."

"Then ask her to tell you about the cab ride home from Jim Fisk's party last night," Lloyd said, rising.

"Now, see here!" Kershaw blustered. "I won't have any insinuations about my daughter."

"None intended," Lloyd said. "No hard feelings, eh?"

He moved across the room, puffed on his cigar, and waited while Gould called other men into his private office for conference. Was he interviewing them as Fisk's possible replacement? Lloyd wondered. He hoped Gould wouldn't make any decisions until he, Lloyd, had had the opportunity to speak privately with his host.

There was plenty of time for Lloyd to seethe and to promise himself that one day he would amass more wealth than any of them. Then, with the power of money, he could do some slashing and cutting where it hurt the most, in the pocketbooks of those who had snubbed him. His personal revenge against one of them, Psaleh Kershaw, was already all but assured.

And still he thought of Abby. She had the power to change everything; she could even rescue her father from ruin. After Victoria and Tennessee had been taken away to jail and the *Tribune* had run the story saying that a right-of-way had been obtained through Indian Territory, Lloyd visited the broker whom Kershaw used. With a bit of persuasion in the form of hard cash, Lloyd had learned that Kershaw had invested another three-quarters of a million dollars into the KC&S. So the situation was right for Lloyd to make his final move, guaranteeing Kershaw's fall into deep trouble, into a financial hole from which only Abby could extricate him—if she acted quickly. If, without knowing anything about Lloyd's machinations but acting solely on her attraction to him, she defied her father, then, Lloyd decided, he would spare the old man and would advise him to sell his KC&S holdings as quickly as possible. He would even run additional risks: he would wait another week instead of putting his final plan into action Monday morning, and he would forgo his interview with Gould—if, in fact, that's what the man was doing in his private conferences—in order to see Abby and talk with her.

When Gould returned to the study, Lloyd stood and said, "Mr. Gould, I've enjoyed the evening, but—"

"Sit down, Miles," his host said distinctly. "You are not rich enough to be the first to leave."

Kershaw laughed louder than any of the others. He slapped his leg in glee and shouted, "And this is the young upstart who had the audacity to ask my permission for him to propose to Abby!"

"Well, Jay," Miles said, as calm as calm, "if you are that eager for my company, of course I'll stay." But his pale eyes stabbed the dark eyes of the financier. Gould stiffened, for he knew a challenge when he saw one. "You did say you might want a word with me, didn't you?"

"Did I?"

"My mistake, I suppose," Lloyd said. He poured himself a bit of brandy, sat down, and forced his way into a conversation group, daring the men to ignore him. He almost hoped that someone else would be rude to him. Psaleh Kershaw's slur had sealed that man's financial demise. And Jay Gould's insult had earned him an enemy. Lloyd looked across the room and was pleased to find that Gould was watching him. *You may not be too concerned about me at this moment, my friend,* he thought, *but don't forget to keep those cold eyes on me during the next few years. I will give you occasion to remember this night.*

When, just as if he was speaking a line from a play, Gould said, "Shall we join the ladies?" Lloyd sought out Abby immediately. She was conversing with two older women.

"Excuse me," Lloyd said, taking Abby's arm. "I need a word with Abby, if you don't mind."

One of the women sniffed. The other said, "Well!"

Abby was laughing as he pulled her into a corner. "You don't exactly have an advanced degree in manners, do you?" she admonished.

"I want to take you out to dinner tomorrow night. Sunday night," he said.

"I told you that I will be busy Sunday."

"This is important, Abby, to both of us."

"My, my."

"If not tomorrow, then you set a time."

"I'm sorry, I can't," she said. There was a hint of regret in her voice, which weakened his resolve for a moment.

"I had a talk with your father," Lloyd said. "He made it very clear what he thought of—and I quote—a 'goyisher parvenu' paying court to his daughter. Is that why you won't tell me when I can be with you?"

She turned away. "Don't be pushy, Miles. I don't like pushy men."

He seized her arm. "I told you that this is important to you as well as to me. Walk away from me now, and it will be the last time."

"Is that a promise?" she asked, her lips curling.

He bowed low and backed away, smiling grimly. He found Mrs. Gould and paid his respects. Jay, engaged in animated conversation, was in another room. Lloyd didn't bother to tell him good-night.

CHAPTER 21

On Monday morning Lloyd was waiting in the Erie offices when Jay Gould came in just after ten o'clock.

"An early bird, I see," Gould offered.

"Do you have anything in mind for me today?" Lloyd asked. He had flirted with the idea of going about his own business without checking in at his place of employment; but the world was a place of uncertainties, and his salary at the Erie was good. If things went wrong on the market, he could fall back on his pay and subsist.

"Nothing pressing," Gould said.

"In that case," Lloyd said, "I need some time for myself, if that's all right."

"Leave word with the secretary where you can be reached if we need you," Gould said over his shoulder as he disappeared into his office.

Lloyd gave the secretary his home address. He didn't want to be reached in the event of some sudden whim on the part of Jay Gould. He had, as the saying went, other fish to fry.

The market was off to a sluggish start on that Monday morning. Trading was slow except on one stock, that of the Kansas railroad the KC&S. When Lloyd saw the letters posted, and then the figure $120 beside KC&S, he felt a rush of elation. He took a seat in the spectators' gallery. The KC&S was pushing toward the threshold figure that Lloyd had set as a goal. It rose to $121, then to $122, and by noon jumped two points to $124.

At two o'clock a frenzied broker calling out a bid for KC&S stock spoke the magic words: "I'll buy five thousand shares of KC&S at one hundred twenty-five." It was some time before the offer was accepted. Lloyd leapt to his feet and ran down the stairs to find a clerk from the office of his broker.

"Tell him," Lloyd instructed, "to offer sixty thousand shares on the open market."

The clerk's face went pale. He, as would many men, cursed himself for being a stupid, cowardly, misbegotten schlemiel. Like all the others who were aware that some idiot was going short on KC&S in a rising market, he had laughed and called Lloyd Miles a lunatic. Now, too late, the clerk realized what he had heretofore failed to perceive.

The effect of dumping sixty thousand shares of KC&S stock on the market at 2:24 in the afternoon could have been compared with dropping a stone ten feet in diameter into a five-foot puddle. The effect was shattering, calamitous. A stock that had been in short supply was suddenly so plentiful that Lloyd's monumental sell order overwhelmed all demand. The price fell from $126 to $90, and then to $80; and with the closing bell still a half hour away, to $49. At that point, on Lloyd's orders, brokers began to buy to meet the short position taken by Lloyd on one hundred thousand shares for himself and twenty-five thousand shares for Victoria Woodhull.

At the closing bell, KC&S stock stood at $50.

Psaleh Kershaw was notified at four o'clock that the market had gone berserk. He hurried to the exchange to confer with his broker, only to learn that he had been wiped out, that what had been left of his small fortune was now gone, as Jim Fisk had said, where the woodbine grows. He had bought into KC&S at $95 and above, his last purchases having been made during the time that the stock was rising from $110 to its highest point at $126.

Kershaw's broker had followed his client's lead in buying KC&S, and he had also recommended the stock to all his best clients. As the closing bell sounded, he was near tears, and his hands were shaking.

Kershaw caught him coming off the floor.

"What in the hell happened?" he demanded.

The broker's hands were shaking. "I am ruined, Kershaw, ruined. And it's because of you!"

"You are ruined?" Kershaw felt the weight of the world on his shoulders. In his heart he knew what had happened, and he cursed himself for having fallen victim to a scheme that had been used with great success more than once by Dan'l Drew when that man was in command of the Erie.

"Who is behind it?" Kershaw demanded. "Who has ruined us?"

"Gould," the broker said, pronouncing the word as profanity. "Through his stooge, a fellow named Lloyd Miles."

"Miles," Kershaw breathed. *"Miles?"*

"Perhaps, Mr. Kershaw, now that Gould and his minions are finished with it, the KC&S will rise again. It's a good, solid little railroad. And, as you yourself pointed out to me, it was overcapitalized to the sum of some three million dollars."

Kershaw was numb. "I think, sir, that you will find that the three million in overcapitalization was secured by convertible bonds, and that those bonds have been called."

With the morning KC&S stock opened at $49 and dropped within an hour to $25 as stung speculators tried to cut their losses. Kershaw's "few millions" had been reduced by almost four-fifths. He had watched, helpless, as he became a poor man. To sell at $25 meant that there would not be enough money after brokerage fees to pay off the mortgages that he had taken on his home and his subsidiary real estate. His one forlorn hope was that KC&S stock would rise as time went on. That last wish was dashed with the next day's papers. A newsman named Phineas Headley had a bylined story in the *Tribune,* which quoted

Washington officials as saying any rumors to the effect that a right-of-way had been granted to a Kansas railroad were strictly false.

Lloyd Miles realized an average profit of fifty dollars per share on one hundred thousand shares, a net of five million dollars. By demanding that the KC&S redeem three million dollars in convertible bonds, he recouped his entire investment. The KC&S, having dipped into the tempting three million dollars in capitalization for modernization and some frills, was hard put to raise the money to buy back Lloyd's bonds. The control of the line was in doubt because of the sixty thousand shares that Lloyd had dumped onto the market. In short, what had once been a thriving but small company was crippled and badly in debt, and the authority of those men who had run it so well for a number of years was now in doubt.

Lloyd, after dispersing his winnings into the vaults of several banks, went home to the only person to whom he could boast of his victory. He had a bottle of fine champagne tucked under his arm and all intentions of celebrating. The apartment was empty, however. A note from Leah said: *Visiting Victoria and Tennessee.*

He crumpled the note in his hand and tossed it violently aside. He had pulled off his coup and had ruined the man who had laughed at him, Psaleh Kershaw. But there was only an empty feeling of need inside him. The apartment's thick walls shut out the sounds of the city, and he was alone in a silence broken only by the ticking of a clock. . . .

He was sitting in his chair, the empty champagne bottle beside him, when Leah returned from her trip to the Ludlow Street jail.

"Lloyd," she said. "Did you find the food I left in the icebox for you?"

"I was not hungry," he replied.

Leah saw the empty bottle and the sleepy look in her brother's pale blue eyes that indicated overindulgence in alcohol. "Can I fix you something? Coffee? Something to eat?"

"I wouldn't want to make any demands on you," Lloyd said sourly.

"All right," she said mildly. She knew his moods; he became testy when he drank. "I'm rather tired. I think I'll have a bath and go to bed early."

"Do what you damned well please," Lloyd said, reaching for the bottle. Finding it empty, he flung it forcefully to shatter on the marble hearth. He considered going out. He knew of several establishments where he could find someone who would listen to him . . . for money. For money they'd cling to his arm and say, "Oh, how clever." Then all desire for a woman left him. He closed his eyes and saw the faces of Rosanna Pulliam, Tennessee, Victoria, and finally the cool, distant smile of Abby Kershaw.

Phineas Headley was lying in wait for Lloyd when he came out of his building the next morning. Chill northwest winds were pushing dark clouds over the city. Lloyd, looking up at a sky that seemed to promise snow, didn't see Headley at first.

"Morning, Mr. Miles," Headley said.

"Mr. Headley, how are you?" The desolation of the previous evening was forgotten. The dark, threatening morning was not foreboding to Lloyd, only awesome and wildly, powerfully beautiful.

"I'd like for you to take a look at a story that I'm going to run today," Headley requested.

"Mr. Headley," Lloyd asked with a smile, "what have I done to deserve you?"

Headley grinned. "I guess you're just a lucky fellow, Mr. Miles."

Lloyd took the sheet of paper, read quickly, then frowned only for a moment. "I congratulate you on a good piece of reporting."

"You don't deny that the stories saying that the Kansas City and Southwest Railroad had a right-of-way to Texas were untrue?"

"Of course not," Lloyd said.

"Then it seems to me," Headley said, "that you won't

deny that you took advantage of these false stories to get people to invest heavily in the KC&S."

"Hold it right there," Lloyd said. "I can control only one man, Headley, and that man is Lloyd Miles. If other investors felt that KC&S stock was a good buy, that was their affair. I had not one goddamned thing to do with it."

"Miles—"

"Mister Miles."

"Mister Miles. I haven't quite pinned down who it was that dumped an impossible number of shares on the market. But I have a hunch that when I do, I'll find that it's someone I know."

Lloyd laughed. "Well, while in theory transactions between a man and his broker are confidential, I'm sure that a man of your investigative talents will do just what you say you will do." He resituated his hat on his head, tilting it jauntily forward. "I think, however, that you'll find that it's all stale news, Headley. After all, there is no law that says a man can't sell as many shares of a company as he wants to sell when he wants to sell them."

"May I quote you on that?" Headley asked with rich sarcasm.

"Good day, Mr. Headley," Lloyd said with a pleasant smile. He had walked a dozen paces before inspiration came to him. Phineas Headley, already walking in the opposite direction, turned when Lloyd called his name.

"I'm willing to talk with you," Lloyd said, "but let's get out of the wind. There's a bar two blocks down."

He set a brisk pace. The lanky newsman lagged slightly behind. The bar had just opened. Only the bartender was there.

"Coffee," Lloyd called out as he guided Headley to a back table. He waited until two freshly brewed, steaming cups of coffee were on the table. "Headley, you've been after me since before Black Friday. Do you have something against me, or do you just like to be near me because I'm so damned good looking?"

Headley laughed. He had a nose for news, and his nostrils were twitching. He decided to be straight with Miles.

"I was after you, Mr. Miles, because I thought you might be a key to the activities of Gould and Fisk."

"But that's no longer true, is it?"

"Well, not entirely. I'm intrigued by yesterday's KC&S debacle." He sipped his coffee. "It smacks of Drew's handiwork."

Lloyd laughed. "Maybe it was Gould. He and Fisk learned from old Dan'l early on, before they took Erie away from him."

"No. No, it wasn't Gould." Headley looked with clear, hard eyes over his coffee cup. "But, as you say, Mr. Miles—"

"Call me Lloyd."

Headley raised one eyebrow. "Things change so rapidly, *Mister* Miles, that I can't keep up with them, so let's keep it simple. As you say, there's no law against buying and selling stock. So you didn't ask me here to talk about the KC&S affair."

"You want to nail Gould and Fisk, don't you?"

"I have no personal animosity for either of them," Headley said. "There are still some answers I'd like regarding the Gold Ring's near corner."

"I think you've been going at it wrong," Lloyd said. "You've been concentrating mostly on me and Jay Gould. Neither of us represents the weak link in the chain."

"I can agree with that." He mused. "Fisk?"

"Indirectly," Lloyd said. "Jim's not stupid, in spite of his clowning." He leaned forward. "But he does have his weaknesses."

"Booze? Women?" Headley snapped his fingers. "That chubby little temptress, Josie Mansfield?"

"You might also ask a few questions of a young gigolo named Ned Stokes. He likes money."

Headley was writing quickly on a wrinkled scrap of paper. "What sort of questions should I ask of this Stokes fellow?"

"You might ask him how much Jim Fisk is willing to pay to keep certain letters from being published."

"Are you giving it to me straight, Miles?" Headley asked.

"A fearless investigative reporter such as yourself should be able to establish whether or not I'm being straight with you without depending on my word alone."

"Yeah, sure. Listen, you're telling me that Fisk's little honey is cheating on him with this Ned Stokes and that the pair of them are blackmailing Fisk?"

"Did I say *that*?" Lloyd asked ingenuously, with raised eyebrows.

"All right, all right. Is that all?"

"Isn't that enough?" Lloyd asked. He grinned. "Well, maybe just another tidbit or two. Why are you still interested in the Gold Ring?"

"Not many people realize it, but what happened both before and on Black Friday is going to become a part of the history of this country. A hundred years from now students of economics will be studying what Gould did to the financial system of the United States. I'd like to be a source for those future scholars."

"You want to write another book?"

"Something like that."

"If you dig too deep, you're going to be walking in quicksand, Headley."

"Well, I've been there before."

"Two congressional committees have already agreed that Jay Gould was the mastermind."

"Yes, that's simple enough. What I want to know is who paid off whom in Washington and in New York City. How much of the profit went into the pockets of William Tweed? I don't think President Grant was an active conspirator; but did he agree to do nothing? If Grant didn't agree to stand by, then how did Gould have the nerve to pour so many millions into the market when he knew as well as anyone that all the government had to do to break his corner was to open the vaults of the Treasury?"

"I can't help you with questions like that," Lloyd said, "except to say that I think U. S. Grant is a great American hero, and I'll fight any man who tries to blacken his name or Mrs. Grant's. Gould put about fifty million into the gold market before Black Friday, and Fisk was not far behind him. Gould started selling without telling Fisk. In fact, Fisk was still buying while Gould was unloading. I can't tell you if Gould split his profit with Fisk. But whether he did or not, down deep, Fisk might resent Jay's going on his own without telling him. If Fisk feels any discontentment, it might be made more volatile because Jim's pride has been wounded by Josie's cuckolding. If someone could convince Jim that his good friend and partner Jay Gould is ready to dump him entirely, shove him out of the Erie . . . Do I have to spell it out any further for you?"

"Nope," Headley said.

"Once again, then, I bid you good day."

"Just one more question, Mr. Miles?"

"Of course. Isn't there always one more?"

"Even a slow-witted newspaperman like me can see that you're not after Jim Fisk by giving me this information. Off the record, why do you want to sting Jay Gould?"

Lloyd grinned, but his lips were tight, the expression more a grimace than something pleasant as he remembered the tone of Gould's voice saying, *"Sit down, Miles. You are not rich enough to be the first to leave."*

"I don't know, really," Lloyd said. "Maybe it's just because Gould is the most stingable son of a bitch I've ever known."

"Mr. Miles, I am not ungrateful."

"I counted on that," Lloyd said.

"But that doesn't mean that I'm not going to write the story of the KC&S affair."

"Write away," Lloyd said. "As old Jim said after he appeared before the Trent committee, nothing is lost save honor." Inside, however, he was furious. He had put Headley on the scent of Josie Mansfield and her young lover for two reasons: first, because of what Jay Gould had said in the sanctuary of his own home; and second, because he was searching for a favor from the newspaperman. He had assumed that when he'd tipped Headley to Jim's personal troubles as a possible entree to more interesting information, the newspaperman would reciprocate by not printing the fact that it was one Lloyd Miles who had manipulated KC&S stock. "But you're a silver-plated bastard, Headley."

"I made no deal in return for information from you," Headley pointed out.

"I did," Lloyd said harshly. "And I don't like it when some simple little bastard backs out on a deal with me."

"See you around," Headley said.

"You can count on that," Lloyd said as he got up and walked away.

CHAPTER 22

Leah Miles was astounded when she realized that it was Christmas. She had spent the month of November visiting Victoria and Tennessee in the pleasant room in the Ludlow Street Jail where the sisters held court for reporters, well-wishers, their lawyers, and the city employees of the jail who had come to look upon them as special guests. It was out of boredom and a wish to get on with things that Victoria used some of her profits from the KC&S scheme to post bond. Then, to the disgust of Leah and others, she promptly repeated her charge against Anthony Comstock and was just as promptly hauled off again to the pleasant room on Ludlow Street.

It was a hectic time for Leah. While she was busy trying to convince Victoria to accept assistance in posting still another bond, George Francis Train, the multimillionaire dandy who had offered to bail the sisters out after their first arrest, gave them another form of support. He selected sensual passages from the King James Bible and printed them under lurid headlines in *The Train Ligue,* his little paper. Anthony Comstock, the self-appointed guardian of public morality, had Train indicted in state courts on the same charge that had been Victoria's downfall, and the millionaire found himself not in a pleasant room in the Ludlow Street Jail but among convicted murderers. Being arrested, it seemed, was exactly what he wanted in order to prove his point that Victoria and Tennessee were the victims of blue-nosed censorship. He refused to post his own bond.

As the weeks passed, and Christmas was come and gone, Train smuggled stories for his periodical out of the jail. Twenty-two felons who awaited hanging on Murderer's Row elected Train their president. Victoria and her running mate, Douglass, lost the election, to the surprise of no one. U. S. Grant had bested the newspaper editor, the eccentric Horace Greeley, handily to earn a second term in the White House.

Leah visited Train as the old year was wearing to an end in the aftermath of a sleeting snowstorm. The grim prison depressed her. Train looked wan and unhealthy. "Mr. Train," she said, "you have proved your point. When a man can be jailed for printing excerpts from the Bible, the system is definitely askew. Please post your bond."

"Are Victoria and Tennessee still imprisoned unjustly?"

"Yes, but—"

"But me no buts," Train said. "I will persevere until this travesty of justice has been made right."

"Please, Mr. Train," she begged. "Think of your health."

"Miss Leah," he said tenderly, "your concern touches me. But I have traveled far and wide, and I have chosen to fight injustice wherever I encounter it. I fought it in the wilderness in Australia when I designed and put into place a supply system for settlers there. I have spoken out to kings—to Louis Napoleon and Eugenie in France, and to the queen of Spain—on injustice. I traveled around the world in eighty days to prove that civilization has come to the entire planet. And now I find that two ladies whom I very much admire can be jailed without real cause and that I myself can be thrown in with murderers because I choose to call attention to Mr. Comstock's duplicity and hypocrisy. No, I will not surrender."

* * *

Meanwhile the participants were keeping the courts busy. At Victoria's instigation Theodore Tilton filed a suit for alienation of affections against Henry Ward Beecher, and the press had a field day. Comstock filed a libel suit against Victoria and Tennessee.

"Good, good," Victoria gloated. "Let him face me and the truth in a court of law!"

To Leah's surprise Henry Ward Beecher's congregation backed their minister all the way, refusing to believe that for over two years he had committed adultery with Elizabeth Tilton. And when Elizabeth Tilton left her husband, saying that she had pursued Beecher and that he had never, never taken advantage of her forwardness, had never done anything "indelicate" with her, Leah despaired.

But Victoria refused to quit. Out of jail again, she began to sell her belongings from the office and from her brownstone on Thirty-eighth Street to pay for her lawyers and for the continued publication of the *Weekly*. To prove once and finally that all men were hypocrites, she began to gather lists of middle-class and upper-class men who frequented places of prostitution.

Fed up with his tenants' notoriety, Victoria's landlord raised the rent and then sued her for nonpayment of debts. Victoria and Tennessee moved into the offices of Woodhull, Claflin, and Company and fought on, managing, somehow, to keep the *Weekly* in print with articles speaking out for the rights of women and Negroes—and for evolution, science, and political and social reform.

The Spencer Grays, an all-black regiment of the New York Militia, named Tennessee their honorary commander. A group of black officers with a smartly uniformed escort of enlisted men called for Tennessee at the office. The building's owner warned both Tennessee and Victoria that he would tolerate no such scandalous incidents on his property. When Tennessee defied him and rode off proudly with the black officers to conduct a review of her honorary command, she came back to the office to find that all the remaining belongings of Woodhull, Claflin, and Company were on the sidewalk in front of the building.

"Honey," Victoria said to Leah, "I don't think I need to tell you that I don't have the money to pay your salary this week."

Leah smiled sadly. As a matter of fact, there'd been no money to pay her salary for three months.

"We're going to have to stop publication," Victoria said. "At least temporarily."

"Oh, Victoria—"

"Don't worry," Victoria said. "The world hasn't heard the last of us."

Lloyd was at home when Leah, carrying her personal belongings from the office, arrived. He came to put his arm around her. "You know that I offered to help," he said.

"I know. Victoria is so proud." She hugged him. "But I know where the bond money came from. Thank you."

"Purely business, that," he said. "I gave Victoria a stock-market tip in exchange for brokerage services and then handled her purchases while she was in jail."

"The *Weekly* won't be published anymore."

"Don't count Victoria out, not yet," Lloyd said.

"No, Lloyd. They've beaten her. All of the Congregational churches in the country came out backing Beecher."

"The suit hasn't come to court yet," Lloyd said.

"But when it does," Leah said sadly, "the verdict will be in Beecher's favor. Poor Mr. Tilton doesn't have a chance."

"Well, that's all behind you now, dear," Lloyd said. "I'm glad you're out of a job. I haven't seen enough of you lately, and there's something I want to show you."

He took her in a carriage to upper Fifth Avenue and told the driver to go slowly as they passed the flamboyantly Gothic, block-long town house of Cornelius Vanderbilt.

"Leah," Lloyd said, "they don't invite us into their closed circle. We don't winter in Asheville, and we don't have a summer house at Newport or Bar Harbor—at least not yet. They call me a parvenu. Some of them don't know the meaning of the word and can't pronounce it, much less spell it. Instead they say that I'm a Johnny-come-lately. So be it. I say to hell with their little circle. Let them keep on kissing each other's asses—" He grinned sheepishly. "Sorry."

She shrugged. "If women are to be equal and have the right to vote, I suppose we'll have to adjust ourselves to being treated equally in other ways. Why should you have to speak differently just because you're with me?"

"Because you're my little sister," he said. He told the driver to stop. An older structure just two blocks from the Vanderbilt house was being demolished. "They can keep us out of their drawing rooms, but they can't tell me where to build my home—not as long as I have the money to buy the property and to build the house." He grinned at her. "Like the neighborhood?"

She felt a surge of pride for him. She knew what it meant to him to be able to buy property and build in the same neighborhood with the richest men in the world. "If you like it, Lloyd, it's just fine with me."

"Good for you." He put his arm around her and told the driver to move on. "You've got a lot of shopping to do."

"Oh, no."

"There's a place nearby that deals in European antiques," he said. "I think I'd like an Empire reception and entertaining area. What do you think?"

"Your wish, sir, is my command."

CHAPTER 23

Jay Gould called Lloyd Miles into his office. Lloyd had just
accepted delivery on the first of several suits he'd ordered
from one of the city's finest tailors. Gould chuckled when
he saw his assistant in the sartorial splendor of perfectly
fitting virgin Shetland wool, Irish linen, and silk cravat and
vest.

"I get the impression, Miles, that you won't be with us
much longer," Gould said.

Lloyd expressed surprise, then smiled. "Well, it's an un-
certain world, Jay."

Gould's consumption had been especially bothersome
during the night. He felt frail, depleted. He was reminded
of a time not long past, when he and Jim had been young
and unknown . . . when old Dan'l Drew first named them
to the Erie board to aid him in still another head-to-head
battle with Vanderbilt. The newspapers had misspelled
Jim's name, calling him Mr. Fish or Mr. Fiske. And it had
been simply "one J. Gould." Had it actually been so recent? And now there was another sharp-eyed, fidgety, ambitious young fellow who reminded Jay very much of himself only a few years before.

"I'm never going to put you on the board, Miles," Gould said musingly.

"I hate stuffy meetings," Lloyd responded.

Gould thought, *Ah, so I am right. He is ready to spread his wings and fly away.* Aloud he said, "Since you are, as of now, still working for us—" He smiled. "You are, aren't you?"

"At your service, sir," Lloyd said with a little bow.

"There are some very special people coming in today on the White Star Line. Four o'clock is the expected first-class-passenger release time. I had planned to meet them myself, but—" As if in explanation a fit of coughing caused him to reach for his handkerchief.

"Four o'clock," Lloyd said. "I'll be there."

"Englishmen," Gould said after recovering from the coughing fit. But he was pale and weak. He handed Lloyd a list of names headed by Lord Brian, duke of Ravendale. The others were peers of lesser rank but with equally grand titles—an earl, two marquesses.

"The redcoats are coming," Lloyd said.

"Be nice to them, Miles," Gould reminded. "As I said, these are very special people."

"Aha," Lloyd said. Very special people, to Gould, were those who had more money than good sense. "Anything here that you might care to share with your number-one assistant?"

Gould laughed. "I understand you're doing well enough on your own."

"Oh, so-so," Lloyd said with a shrug.

"These are *mine,* Miles," Gould warned. "Your duty ceases after you make apologies for me, inform them to meet me here in the office tomorrow in time for lunch, and get them settled in their hotel."

"I hear and obey," Miles said.

After checking the movement of prices at the stock exchange Lloyd gave his broker a few orders—nothing major, just some profit taking on shares that had done well. He started for the docks in plenty of time. A raging fire in a

four-story building blocked a major intersection and cost
him half an hour in travel time. He had allowed for some
delay, but then the rear wheel fell off the hansom cab and
the vehicle lurched to one side, dragging its axle on the
cobblestones; the driver fell on his head and was knocked
unconscious. Until help arrived, Lloyd stayed to lift the
driver's head onto a seat pad from inside the disabled cab,
then to calm the frightened horses. When medical assistance finally came, he checked his watch, swore, and waved
down an empty hansom cab.

Lloyd was over an hour late. The steerage passengers
had been released from the White Star liner. Hordes of
Slavic faces peered out from bundling masses of shawls,
scarves, and scabrous coat collars. He pushed his way
through the crowds; heard soft, frightened voices speaking
in a variety of languages; and saw, at last, a well-dressed
man of his own age standing beside the gangway tapping
the dock impatiently with the ivory tip of a silver-embossed
cane.

"Sir," Lloyd asked, "are you with the Ravendale party?"

"I am Ravendale." His accent was, of course, British
upper-class. His frock coat was a silvery pearl, his vest a
checkerboard of gay colors. "And you, sir?"

"Lloyd Miles." He held out his hand. After looking at it
suspiciously, Ravendale took it and held it limply for a
moment. "Well, sir, if we can round up the rest of your
party I'll escort you to your hotel."

"Oh, they've already gone on to the hotel," Ravendale
said. "I waited only to see just what sort of fellow this Jay
Gould is to keep us waiting so long." He shouldered his
cane and used it to tip his top hat forward a bit. "And now
I see that our Mr. Gould doesn't even have the decency to
meet us in person."

"He's unwell," Lloyd said.

"Sorry."

"I'm to extend his apologies, to which I add mine. If you
care to hear the reasons for my lateness, I'll be happy to
relate them."

"Right now," Ravendale said, "I think I could do with

something more than mildly alcoholic. While I'm drinking, you may feel free to make your excuses."

Lloyd had never cared for members of the English peerage—not that he had encountered that many of them. He had been introduced to a couple here and there and had always felt an urge to ask them why they didn't remove the corncob from a certain unmentionable orifice and try to be a little bit human. His first impression of Lord Brian, duke of Ravendale, did not improve his opinion of highborn Britishers. The man was slim and pleasant looking. In fact, although Lloyd didn't consider himself to be the ultimate authority, he suspected that women would find Ravendale to be handsome. He was two inches taller than Lloyd, and he wore Savile Row tailoring as if he'd been the original model for it. His long face was dominated by sandy-red eyebrows over slate-gray eyes, an aristocratic nose, and a wide, affable mouth that, Lloyd was to learn, smiled easily.

There was very little talk as the two men rode to the Grand Central Hotel. Lloyd sent Ravendale ahead into the lounge while he saw to it that the Englishman's luggage was taken up to his room. Then he met Ravendale seated at the bar, a tall whiskey tilted to his mouth.

"There you are," Ravendale said. "What will it be?"

"Whisky-soda," Lloyd said, taking the next stool. Then he quickly related the reasons for his lateness at the docks and apologized again.

"Apology accepted," Ravendale drawled. "Ah, now I feel slightly more human. So, Mr. Lloyd Miles, what are we going to do for the rest of the evening?"

"I haven't the slightest idea what you're going to do," Lloyd said. "But I'm going home."

Ravendale laughed. "That's quite inhospitable of you. Here I am, a stranger in a strange land, and you're going to leave me to my own devices?"

The twinkle in Ravendale's eyes struck a sympathetic chord in Lloyd. "The entertainment is pretty good in the hotel dining room," he said. "And the bar stays open late." He winked at Ravendale. "And if you feel the need for company, just talk to one of the bell-hoppers."

Ravendale raised both eyebrows. "I'm to socialize with the bell-hoppers?" Lloyd laughed.

"Oh," Ravendale said, touching his temple with his forefinger. "I see. The bell-hopper can provide—"

"Exactly," Lloyd said.

"Not my cup of tea, actually," Ravendale said. "But thank you for the information."

Lloyd finished his drink, then stood. "Jay Gould's office, eleven-thirty," he said. "Will you tell the others?"

"Certainly," Ravendale said. "Must you go?"

Lloyd considered the matter. Leah was accustomed to having him miss the evening meal on occasion. And he was curious about Jay Gould's business with the Englishmen. "Finish your drink and come along," he said.

Ravendale gulped the rest of the whiskey.

"Do you want to go to your room before I show you the town?"

"Not if you'll find me a public pissoir within, say, the next thirty seconds," Ravendale said.

Over dinner at a fine restaurant Lloyd learned with surprising ease why the four Englishmen had crossed an ocean to see Jay Gould. "My companions fancy owning an American railroad," Ravendale said. "And I understand that Mr. Gould owns a small one."

"Well," Lloyd said, spreading his hands, "small to middling if you're talking about the Erie."

"Yes, that's it."

There was one thing of which Lloyd was certain: Jay Gould had no intention of giving up the controlling interest in his prime money-generating machine, the Erie Railroad. Lloyd could only assume that Jay had something smart in mind—perhaps something like watered stock—for the peers from across the sea. Jay was apparently looking for new fields to conquer or, to be more accurate, more pockets to pick. When Vanderbilt came to the rescue of the stock exchange, he had used money from England. Had that given Gould an idea?

"Just what is Mr. Gould offering, if you don't mind my asking?"

Ravendale shrugged. "I don't really understand these things. Something about a split?"

"A stock split?"

"Yes, I think that's it."

"And he's offering you and your friends a chance to buy stock before the split."

"Correct," Ravendale said around a bite of roasted duckling. "At a price just slightly above the market, since the stock is coming from his private holdings."

"And you're inclined to accept this offer?"

"Oh, not I, old boy," Ravendale said, laughing. "I'm just along for the ride. Old Bertie is the one who really wants to own part of an American railroad, and he asked me if I wouldn't come along with him, since Piggy and Peter are such dismal company. Bertie will never forgive me for not asking him along with us tonight, you know."

Lloyd chuckled. Old Bertie and Piggy and Peter were about to be sheared like sheep. He was curious as to why Ravendale wasn't going along as well, but he let the matter rest there.

After dinner he took Ravendale into Jim Fisk's private box at the opera house. Ravendale sipped from a sterling hip flask during the performance and applauded heartily each time the dancing girls came onstage.

"Good Lord, Lloyd," he whispered, pointing to a well-developed girl in the chorus line. "Cast an eye on that healthy little damsel."

"Would you like to meet her?"

"Oh, I say!"

The "healthy little damsel" was called Twinkles Thomas. For Lloyd she had a friend named Elviny. Elviny was called Viney. Lloyd naturally assumed that that was because Viney was a shortened form of her name. Later that night, in the sitting room of the duke of Ravendale's suite in the Grand Central Hotel, with the duke and Twinkles hidden away behind a closed and locked bedroom door, Lloyd found another possible reason for the dancer's nickname:

she clung to him with astonishing fervor and strength as she whispered his name at crucial moments.

Breakfast was served in the suite. Viney and Twinkles were bright and cheerful. Ravendale smelled of stale whiskey, had a terrific headache, and was cross until he had consumed two cups of strong tea and put away four eggs with ham steak, buttered toast, and a waffle on the side.

"I say," he ventured brightly, looking first at Twinkles and then at Viney. "I say, Lloyd, didn't we draw a fine pair of queens?"

"Aw, go on," Viney said.

"In truth," Ravendale insisted. "Jewels of equal beauty. I would be hard put to choose between you, were I offered the chance."

"Who's *not* offering?" Viney asked with a beaming smile.

"Brian, you have to be in Gould's office in an hour," Lloyd reminded gently.

"Oh, damn," Ravendale said. "Really?"

Lloyd grinned. "Well, if you're not interested in Mr. Gould's generous offer . . ."

"Not in the least, old boy," Ravendale confessed cheerfully. "I say, ladies, I do hope that you're not expected anywhere."

"Can't say as I am," Twinkles said, her eyes sparkling.

"Me neither," Viney said.

"I'm sorry to state," Lloyd said, "that I am a working-man and must leave you."

"Too bad," Ravendale sympathized.

" 'Bye, honey," Viney said. "I think the prince here needs a massage to help rid him of his headache."

"Oh, my, yes," Ravendale agreed, winking as Lloyd headed toward the door.

Lloyd found the other Englishmen in the hotel dining room. He introduced himself and, since Brian had not had the opportunity to inform his friends of the day's arrangements, told them the time of their appointment in Gould's office. Lloyd arrived first and explained to Gould that he had three out of four of the Englishmen coming; the duke of Ravendale had other concerns.

"Just as well," Gould said.

"He indicated that he had no interest in an American investment," Lloyd said, hoping for some enlightenment from Gould as to his plans.

Gould laughed. "Not unless someone loaned him the money," he said.

Lloyd waited.

"The man's penniless and in debt," Gould explained. "Gambled away all the family's liquid assets within a year of his father's death. Now he's in danger of losing the ducal estates. Ravendale has been living off his friends for years." He laughed. "And if the word gets around that this titled ass, this wastrel, this internationally known swell of dissipation, is in New York, the elite of our fair city will fall over themselves to invite him to dinner. They'll spend thousands entertaining him, and he won't be able to ask anyone out to dinner because he couldn't afford to pick up the tab. But, by God, he has a title, and that is enough to admit him to any company."

Lloyd was bemused. Did he perceive bitterness in Gould's voice? Did Gould, too, feel resentment at being excluded from the highest echelons of New York society? Was his well-known scorn for social gatherings merely a cover for his not being invited by the true leaders of society?

Gould waved one hand in dismissal of the subject. "Three out of four will do nicely, Miles."

"Anything else, Mr. Gould?" Lloyd asked.

"No. I won't need you anymore."

With the germ of an idea in mind Lloyd hurried to a bookstore and asked for a book about the English peerage. Dukes came first, followed in order of importance by marquesses, earls, viscounts, and barons. Brian, duke of Ravendale, was a man of royal blood who was invited to tea with the queen. He possessed something that mere money could never buy.

Or could it?

He found Ravendale sprawled on the bed in his suite, shamelessly naked and snoring loudly.

"I say, old boy," Lloyd minced with fine sarcasm, "your bum is showing."

Ravendale groaned, reached for a sheet, tugged it over him. "Lloyd?"

"No, it's the devil coming to punish you for your sins."

Ravendale opened one red-rimmed eye. "Oh," he moaned. He grinned, winced when the movement made his head hurt, and said, "Whatever the punishment, the game was well worth it. Do you know why they call that one Viney?"

"I want to talk with you," Lloyd said. "Have a quick bath and get dressed. I'll be down in the lounge."

"Have mercy," Ravendale groaned.

"And don't take too damned long, old boy," Lloyd said.

Ravendale looked fresh, youthfully innocent, and he was ravenously hungry when he joined Lloyd in the lounge. One would never have suspected that Ravendale had spent most of the day sporting and drinking with two chorus girls from Jim Fisk's opera house. Lloyd and Brian had lunch in the dining room. Lloyd noted that the duke made no offer either to pick up the tab or sign the check to have it charged to his room.

"What shall we do tonight, my friend?" Ravendale asked cheerily. "More of the same?"

"I'm afraid not," Lloyd said. "There's someone I want you to meet."

"Someone as charming as our two queens from the opera house?"

"More so, but in an entirely different way. My sister."

"Oh, dear," Brian said. "Then I suppose I must be on my good behavior."

"I'd appreciate it."

Lloyd had notified Leah by messenger that they would be going out to dinner with a business associate. She was dressed in purple velvet, and Lloyd's latest gift, a large emerald, dangled from her throat. Her soft, abundant hair was swept high. When Lloyd ushered Ravendale into the apartment and made the introductions, Ravendale's eyes widened. He was quite stunned upon seeing Leah.

"Oh, dear," Leah said. "Shall I bow, make a curtsy, or what?"

"My dear lady," Ravendale said, "none of the above." He extended his hand, took hers, and brushed his lips in the air above. "I am so pleased. I feared you would look like your brother."

"Here now," Lloyd protested. "There's a definite family resemblance."

"Ah, but on her the family resemblance is so different, and *vive la différence.*"

"You're going to turn my head hopelessly," Leah warned.

Ravendale took her arm and escorted her to the waiting cab, then sat beside her facing Lloyd. The destination was Delmonico's.

Lloyd had brought home several young men obviously for Leah's inspection over the years, but he'd never brought one, she thought, as handsome or well-spoken as Brian Ravendale. As they ate, sampled wine, and then as she danced with Brian, Leah began to think that one day when the duke decided to take a wife, some English girl was going to be very, very lucky.

"Brian," she told him as they walked back to the table to rejoin Lloyd after a lovely waltz, "you dance so beautifully that you made even me seem graceful."

"If so," he said, "it was only because I was floating on your beauty."

"Oh, my," she said.

He held her chair. She arranged her bustle and her skirts. "Lloyd," she said, "this man is indescribably charming."

"Have a care, Englishman," Lloyd said. "The girl is my sister."

"I can't understand it," Ravendale said to Leah. "Are you sure that he was not adopted?"

Leah could not remember having spent a more pleasant evening. She accepted Ravendale's compliments, however pleasant, as mere word play, and not once did she have romantic feelings toward him. But, oh, my, he was a lovely dancer, and he was so fine to look at. She protested when Lloyd told her it was time to go, and she actually became angry when she realized that she was to be dumped at home while Lloyd and Brian went out again.

"Be a good girl," Lloyd told her, whispering into her ear, "and I'll buy you something nice."

"You're heartless, making me come home so early."

"You need your beauty sleep," he said, not making matters any better.

It was time for Lloyd and Brian to pick up Twinkles and Viney at the opera house. On the way there Lloyd asked abruptly, "Ravendale, how much money would it take to pull you out of your hole and put you into a position where the estates would support themselves?" In the long silence that ensued, Lloyd thought that he had grossly overstepped his bounds and that the duke wasn't going to answer.

"In American dollars?" Ravendale finally asked.

"That's the only language I speak."

"And quite well." Ravendale nodded, his lips twisting. 'I've asked about you, Mr. Lloyd Miles. People are calling you the Young Lion of Wall Street. I'm told that that's a comparison to the master, the Old Lion, Cornelius Vanderbilt, and is, therefore, quite a compliment."

"I have not yet begun to roar," Lloyd said. Oh, damn, he was pleased. His broker had said the same thing, but Lloyd had assumed that the man was merely indulging in good business practice and buttering up a client.

"One million, perhaps two . . ." Ravendale estimated.

"Well, that's quite a spread."

"Let's allow room for error, shall we? Four million."

"How long would it take you to gamble it away?"

"My dear boy," Ravendale protested, holding out his

hands, palms toward Lloyd. "I am cured of that affliction. Never again. I swear it before heaven."

"Let's talk more about it later," Lloyd said as the cab drew up at the stage-door entrance to the opera house.

Ravendale took Lloyd's arm. "My friend," he said, "you have touched on a subject that gnaws at me. You hint that you might have some solution for my very, very distressing financial situation, and then you say that we'll talk about it later? My God, *please.*"

"Four million," Lloyd offered. "I think we could call it a dowry."

"Ah. I see," Ravendale said in a soft voice.

"Think about it."

"I have," Ravendale said quickly. "My dear brother-in-law-to-be, I will, one day, find a way to thank you both for your financial aid and for introducing me to your charming and utterly beautiful sister."

Lloyd put his hand atop Ravendale's, where it lay on his arm, squeezed hard, then squeezed harder until Ravendale looked at him in puzzlement. "Number one, I will look at your books and give suggestions as to how to solidify your financial position. I have no intention of throwing four million dollars onto the gaming table at Monte Carlo or down the neck of a whiskey bottle. Number two, my sister will be made happy."

"I see no problems there," Ravendale agreed. He used his right hand to pry Lloyd's hand away. His slate-gray eyes held Lloyd's in a level gaze.

Lloyd laughed. "Good. Now, brother-in-law, I think we have two queens awaiting us."

CHAPTER 24

On a pleasant spring day Lloyd Miles was in his broker's office, watching the tape, when he was approached by a young messenger boy. Lloyd flipped the boy a quarter and took the message. It was from Jim Fisk:

Miles, I'd consider it a great favor if you'd come and have a talk with me in my room at the Grand Central Hotel.

Lloyd had taken his leave of the Erie Railroad and Jay Gould some weeks before. His own trading now occupied most of his waking hours. In addition, through a meticulous study of charts of prices and earnings, quarterly reports, news items, stock-market gossip, and intuition, he had discovered a small tool company in West Virginia that was overcapitalized to the tune of almost two million dollars, and he was in the process of buying control.

His first inclination was to ignore Fisk's request, but curiosity got the better of him. The street was awash with rumors about the man who had once been called the Barnum of Wall Street, the Prince of Erie, and other names not so flattering.

At the hotel Fisk was wearing the imitation naval uniform he loved so well. Some of the brass was tarnished,

and Jim had gained weight, so the pants bulged dangerously close to splitting a seam. "Thank you for coming,
Miles," Jim said. "Drink?"

"Little early," Lloyd said. "Guess I'm getting old. I've
cut out all booze before sundown."

"Good for you," Jim said, pouring a drink for himself.

"So, Jim, what's the problem?" Lloyd asked.

"I thought maybe you could go talk to Jay for me,
Miles," Jim said.

"But I quit the Erie a month or so ago," Lloyd said.

"Yeah, but you always got along good with Jay. Sort of
like you were two of a kind." He raised one hand defensively. "Now, don't get me wrong—I mean that as a compliment. You've both got good heads on you. So since you
two always hit it off, I thought maybe you could ask Jay to
see me, tell him all I want to do is talk. I just want to know
why, that's all."

"Why what?" Lloyd asked in resignation as he sat down.

"You haven't heard that he's deserted me? Pushed me
out of Erie?" He drank deeply from his glass.

"No. I knew it was coming, but I hadn't heard."

"He didn't even tell me face-to-face that he was going to
dump me." Jim was on the verge of tears. "After all the
things we've been through together, Miles. Almost landing
in jail . . . having to hide out in New Jersey . . . being
threatened with lynching after Black Friday. And then he
just pushes me out and won't even tell me why."

"Would it make you feel better to have him tell you that
you're drinking too much and that people are calling you a
fool because of Josie?"

"Boy, you sure know how to put it bluntly," Jim said.

"That's more politely than you'd get it from Jay."

Fisk put his head in his hands. "Did you know that
they're threatening to take me into court?"

"Who?"

"Josie Mansfield and Ned Stokes."

Lloyd barked a laugh. "*They're* going to take you into
court? Hell, man, you're the one with a grievance! You
should have them arrested for blackmail."

"They've been talking with that newspaperman Phineas Headley," Jim said. "That son of a bitch is trying to black-mail me too."

"Headley?"

"Not for money. He says that if I'll tell him the whole story about the gold thing, he won't print that Ned Stokes is grazing in Jim Fisk's pasture." He looked up, his eyes red. "And now Jay's pushed me out of the Erie. Will you go have a talk with him, Miles?"

"Jim, it wouldn't do any good. The thing for you to do is pick yourself up, kick Ned Stokes in the ass, toss Josie out on hers, and then get on about your business. You still have the ship line, don't you?"

"Last time I looked," Jim said, then drained the last swallow of whiskey.

"All right, come out of it, then. Be a man. Hell, you're not the first fellow who's had a pair of horns put on his head by a wench. Let people laugh. They'll have their little moment of amusement, and then they'll forget all about it. You'll be able to get back to doing what you do best—making money."

"You think so, Miles? You think I oughta tell 'em that I'm not going to give them any more money?"

"Damned right I do."

Fisk stood up and sucked in his stomach. "Then that's exactly what I'm going to do," he declared. "Let 'em tell the world what they know." He chuckled and sounded like the old Jim. "Hell, maybe they know something that might just make Jay eat his liver a little bit—what do you think?"

"Could be," Lloyd said.

"Miles, I'm damned glad you came over here. Listen, stick around for a few minutes. Josie's on her way over here right now to collect the latest installment." He banged his forehead with his palm. "Goddamn, to think I've been stupid enough to pay those two bastards."

Lloyd stayed for the same reason he'd come to the hotel, curiosity. Within fifteen minutes Josie Mansfield entered the room. A magnificent fur that had been given to her by

Jim was draped over her shoulders, and her plush body was shown to good effect in a light brown dress.

"I thought you'd be alone, Jim," she said.

"Well, honey," Jim said, "maybe I wanted a witness."

"A witness?" Josie asked innocently. "To what, honey?"

"To the fact that I'm telling you that you've had your last dime from old Jim, 'honey,' " Fisk said. "And you can tell your pretty boy Stokes that if I ever see his face again, I'm going to do my very best to see to it that his nose protrudes from the nape of his neck."

Josie's plump, pretty face clouded. "Jim, honey, don't do something you'll be sorry for later."

"This is something I should have done a long time ago," Jim grated. He moved with surprising swiftness for a bulky man and jerked the fur coat off her shoulders.

"Give me my coat!" she whined, her mouth crinkling in anguish.

"Let Stokes buy you another one," Jim said. "Now, get your ass out of here, 'honey,' before I forget I'm a gentleman and plant a size-twelve boot dead center in your ample charms."

"Ned's gonna be real mad," Josie warned.

Jim roared with laughter. "Well, dog my cats," he said. "So Ned's gonna be real mad. Now, ain't that just too goddamned bad."

"Jim, please give me my coat," Josie said in a coaxing voice. "Please, honey?"

"Go to hell," Jim said.

"Well, you'll regret this," Josie said, sounding like a peeved little girl. "You're gonna be real sorry." Then she turned on her heel and slammed the door behind her.

Jim stood with his head hanging for a long time. At last he looked at Miles. "I loved that little girl," he whimpered. There were big tears in his eyes. "She's the warmest, softest woman I've ever known."

"They're all soft and warm, Jim," Lloyd said.

"Yeah, I guess you're right." He brightened. "Well, Miles, let me get into something not quite so conspicuous, and I'll buy you the finest dinner this hotel has to offer."

"Some other time," Lloyd said, rising. "I need to get home. My sister has company for dinner." He smiled, thinking of how smoothly things were going between Leah and Ravendale. The Englishman had stayed on after his friends went back to their country. He was following Lloyd's instructions by being slow and easy in his courtship of Leah.

"Yeah, well, if you have to go . . ." Jim said.

"Keep your chin up," Lloyd said as he left the suite.

He walked quickly down the ornate corridor, pleased to be away from Fisk. He had managed to escape without making any promises about seeing Gould on Fisk's behalf.

As Lloyd strode down the corridor, he saw Phineas Headley. The journalist was standing beside Josie Mansfield at the top of a grand staircase, which climbed in elegant grace from the lobby to the mezzanine. As Lloyd approached, Josie ran down the stairs. Headley, seeing Lloyd, smiled and nodded. "Mr. Miles."

"Headley."

"I've been hoping to run into you," the writer said, pulling a sheaf of papers from his coat pocket. "There's something here I want you to read before I print it."

Lloyd took the papers and scanned them quickly, then looked up. He did not bother to hide his anger.

"Had to go all the way to Kansas, Mr. Miles," Headley said, "to find the young man you sent into Kansas City with the false story saying that the KC&S had obtained right-of-way through the Indian nations." He shook his head slowly. "They're not too fond of you out there, Mr. Miles. They say you gutted the KC&S, that it will take it a decade to recover, if it ever does."

"Headley, this is all past history," Miles said.

"Well, I'm going to write a book about how easy it is for men like you and Gould to rape the market," Headley said, "and how it affects the common people. The KC&S had to lay off two dozen men, Miles. Does that make you feel proud?"

Lloyd had regained control of his temper. He smiled icily, his eyes hard. Given a choice, he would choose not to have it known that he'd planted the story about the railroad's fictitious right-of-way; but it didn't really matter. There were those who compared him to Vanderbilt and to Jay Gould, and both Vanderbilt and Gould seemed to be impervious to negative press attention. He tipped his hat and turned away. From behind him he heard Jim Fisk call out, "Hey, Miles!" He turned.

"Speak of the devil," Headley drawled. He hurried to meet Fisk. "Mr. Fisk, I've just had a chat with Josie Mansfield. She says she's going to spill everything. Would you care to comment on just what it is she might tell the public?"

Jim laughed and bellowed, "Well, you little cocksucker, she might tell the world that I'm hung like a stud hoss, for all I know."

"Come on, Jim," Headley said, falling in beside Fisk. "It's going to hit the fan now. What did you do to her up there in your rooms? She was madder than hell, and I think she meant it when she said that she was going to give me the whole story just as soon as she'd told Ned Stokes what you did to her."

Fisk had reached the top of the broad flight of carpeted stairs. Miles was two or three steps below him.

Headley kept pace as Fisk caught up with Miles. "Lloyd," Jim said, "someone left the door open, and the maggots are crawling in."

"Jim, here's your last chance to make it easy on yourself," Headley said. "Wouldn't you rather I have both sides of the story instead of printing it the way Josie's going to tell it?"

"Print it any way you goddamned please," Jim fumed. "I don't give a big rat's a—" He stopped talking, halted. At the foot of the stairs a disheveled young man was pointing a gun toward him.

As Lloyd saw the gun, saw the man's fingers tightening, in a flash of certainty he knew that the man at the foot of the stairs was Ned Stokes and that Stokes was going to shoot Fisk.

Lloyd yelled and moved at the same time, seizing Phineas Headley by the arm and jerking him in front of Fisk just as the revolver in Stokes's hand spouted flame and black smoke. He heard the thump of the bullet into Headley's flesh, like the sound of a ripe melon being dropped onto stone. Headley was falling. Down below, two burly bystanders were running toward Ned Stokes.

As Fisk bellowed a wordless cry of fear, the pistol flamed again. Lloyd felt the passage of the ball and heard once again a melon drop onto stone. This time Fisk sank slowly. At the foot of the stairs the two big men were pinning Ned Stokes's arms. But the revolver spoke yet again, and a crystal chandelier shattered.

One glance at Phineas Headley told Lloyd that the writer had been struck in a vital spot. Blood was oozing from his mouth, and his eyes moved slowly. "You—you—" he muttered, the words coming out with blood. "You—did —it to me."

"Well, Headley," Lloyd said evenly, "can you think of anyone who deserved it more?" He knelt and withdrew the sheaf of papers from Headley's coat pocket.

Headley's throat constricted, and he uttered a gargling sound. His legs pounded a little rhythm on the carpeted stairs as Lloyd turned his attention to Jim Fisk. Fisk's eyes were open.

"The son of a bitch shot me," Fisk said in wonderment. "He wasn't content with screwing my girl and stealing my dough—he had to go and shoot me."

"Take it easy," Lloyd soothed. "We'll have a doctor here in a minute."

"Am I hit bad, Miles?"

"No," Lloyd said. There was blood on the front of Fisk's white shirt, but with Jim's bulk it was difficult to ascertain exactly where the bullet had entered.

Jim Fisk died the next day. Lloyd did not go to the funeral, which was held several days later. He was told that Josie Mansfield was there in black, her dress a bit baggy because she hadn't eaten since the shooting and Ned

Stokes's imprisonment for murder. The front sections of the newspapers were full of stories about Fisk and Josie and Ned Stokes and, to a much lesser degree, Phineas Headley.

CHAPTER 25

When the newspapers blazened the dramatic demise of the Barnum of Wall Street, Adam came out of his office to call Philip's attention to the death of Phineas Headley, an event described briefly in the long and detailed accounts of Jim Fisk's troubled relationship with Josie Mansfield and of the confrontation with Ned Stokes on the great staircase in the lobby of the Grand Central Hotel.

"Poor old Headley," Philip said. "In the right place for a story once too often."

"Read a bit further," Adam requested.

Philip read aloud. " 'An eyewitness praised the heroic attempt by one Mr. Lloyd Miles, a Wall Street trader, to save Headley from the murderer's deadly accurate aim. When Miles realized the intentions of the killer, at risk to his own life he tried to jerk Headley away from the line of fire. Unfortunately, he was a second too late, for the first ball fired by the assassin struck Headley's heart, killing him almost instantly.' "

"Quite interesting, isn't it," Adam mused, "that our old friend Miles should be with Headley and Fisk at such a time?"

"I think it's understandable," Julia remarked. "Miles works for the Erie Railroad."

"Make that past tense, my dear," Adam corrected. "Ditto for Jim Fisk. Miles left the Erie over a month ago. And even as Jim Fisk walked down the carpeted stairs to meet his fate, his 'friend' and former partner, Jay Gould, was cleaning away the last traces of big Jim from Erie. Fisk had been booted off the board of directors and deprived of all official standing with the company."

"That *is* interesting," Julia agreed. "But what does it mean?"

"I don't know yet," Adam admitted as he scooted out of the room. "But I intend to find out."

For the next two months Adam Grey was preoccupied with an important research project. He made his need for privacy clear to everyone in the office. He left the office several times, transported in his wheelchair by the strong young man whom Philip retained for that purpose. A flow of telegrams from Adam's office went to New York, and at least twice a day Western Union boys delivered responses.

"Is he more pale than usual?" Philip asked Julia when Adam left the office on an errand having to do with his project.

"Perhaps," she said, "but he's full of energy. Whatever it is he's researching, it is stimulating to him."

"Well, we don't want him overdoing it," Philip said.

As if in response to Philip's concern Adam didn't come to work the following Monday. Julia reported that he was feeling tired and had decided to take a couple of days to rest.

The office seemed unnaturally quiet without the occasional sound of the wheels of Adam's dolly rumbling across the wide floorboards. Each morning when Philip asked Julia about Adam, her report was encouraging—he was puttering around the garden, catching up on planting and pruning that he'd let slide. He was in good spirits and seemed as well as could be expected. On Wednesday Julia said that she thought Adam was feeling better. "He's ready to come back to the office," she told Philip.

"Tell him to take off the rest of the week," he said. "There's not much going on anyway."

That afternoon Philip had a lunch engagement with Maryland's senior senator, a man who shared Philip's concerns regarding the unpredictable swings of the gold and stock markets. There was a small core of lawmakers who felt that some controls should be placed on the way business was transacted. Philip and the senator agreed that because of the Gold Ring the nation had come frighteningly close to a financial panic similar to past cataclysms that had resulted in lasting depressions. The two men discussed possibilities over lunch, then parted after having arrived at the conclusion that it was not yet time to suggest controls. The President and the majority of the members of Congress believed that natural forces—supply and demand —were controls enough, that laissez-faire was a sacred creed in the Industrial Age.

Philip decided to walk back to the office. It was a lovely day, just warm enough to remind one that spring was inevitable, but still cool enough to be invigorating. Now and then he'd recognize a pedestrian, tip his hat, and smile. Sparrows were building nests in any available nook. Fat pigeons strutted on the lawns and cooed in contentment. He reached the intersection with Pennsylvania Avenue, halted to let a heavy coal wagon rumble past, stepped down off the curb, and felt a sudden sense of foreboding that brought him up short in midstride. He looked around. There was street traffic, but nothing that posed an immediate threat. He stepped back onto the curb, removed his hat, and ran his fingers through his hair. The feeling persisted that something was dreadfully wrong. It was unlike anything he'd ever experienced. He could not shake off a sense of dread, a nagging, adrenal unease.

Well, he decided, something he'd eaten had disagreed with him. He stepped out into the street and, although he had had no previous intention of doing so, waved down a cab and gave the driver the address of the Grey house.

* * *

Adam Grey had died alone and in great agony. He had left organic evidence of his terminal struggle from the back steps, where his dolly lay overturned, to the bedroom, where he lay crumpled on the floor in a puddle of his own excreta.

The smell of death drifted out through the open windows to greet Philip Trent as he walked through spring's first flowers. The feeling of appalling wrongness was replaced by crushing sorrow. When he saw the overturned dolly at the back door, Philip ran across the garden, careful not to crush Adam's plantings. Bloody vomitus soiled the stoop. Adam had dragged his legless body through it, leaving a slimy trail on the floor.

Philip gagged at the stench as he stood in the doorway between kitchen and bedroom. He knew without looking closely at the pathetic little bundle on the floor beside the bed that Adam was dead. He'd smelled the results of death too many times on the battlefield. When the brain ceases to function, all muscles relax; the bladder and the bowels empty themselves. And before death Adam had vomited again, so the smell of raw blood mixed with the other stench.

Philip would never remember exactly what he did next. He knew that Julia must not be allowed to see how Adam's body had betrayed him, how the terrible stomach wounds that he had suffered on the sands before Fort Fisher had at last erupted, perforating his intestines and bringing on a painful, slow death. She could not be allowed to realize how Adam had fought a hopeless last battle against his wounds, trying to get to his bed to die with some dignity.

Philip remembered standing in the doorway gagging, weeping, and the next thing he knew he was swabbing the back stoop carefully after rinsing the vomitus and blood away into the grass that, in summer, would grow luxuriantly up to the steps. All traces of Adam's shame had been washed away. The soiled clothing was burning on the trash heap at the back of the rear garden.

Clouds had moved over the city from the southeast, bringing the promise of rain. The winds that came before the rains swept the last traces of the odor of death from the little house before Julia arrived at the end of the workday to find Philip seated grimly on the front stoop.

Her eyes widened in fright, and then squinted in pain. "Adam?" She turned in at the gate, and hurried up the walk through the fine rain. Philip halted her as she started to run past him into the sitting room. Cool, misty rain swirled around them on a gusting wind.

"Julia," he said. "Ah, Julia—"

When she started to twist from his grasp, he immediately removed his hands from her arms. She walked slowly across the sitting room and paused in the bedroom doorway. Adam lay in their marital bed, his eyes closed, his hands folded on his breast, his hair brushed neatly. She walked to the bedside and touched his cold face. She did not weep.

Unseasonable cold returned after the rains. Philip, Gus, Julia, and old Miss Mercy were bundled into overcoats as they stood in the new national cemetery at Arlington. A bugler played the sweetly sad melody called "Taps."

Afterwards, they went to Julia's house. Then, toward nightfall, Miss Mercy insisted upon staying with the young widow. Gus and Philip walked through the poor neighborhood to a major avenue where they were able to hail a cab. Gus broke the long silence after they were seated and the vehicle was bouncing along the rutted street.

"The war lasted longer for him than for most."

Miss Mercy stayed with Julia through the weekend. Philip and Gus visited on Sunday afternoon and found the two women seated in the front room, both knitting busily. Julia's eyes were red. She looked pale in her black mourning dress.

"She won't be in this week," Miss Mercy told Philip in the office on Monday morning.

"Was she all right when you left her?" Philip asked.

"Putting up a brave front, poor child," Miss Mercy said.

"Wouldn't you think that the best thing for her would be to get back to work as soon as possible?"

"Told her that myself," Miss Mercy replied. "And Lord knows she'll need the money."

"She doesn't have to worry about money," Philip said. "Tell her that when you see her tonight."

The week passed slowly. At Miss Mercy's advice Philip stayed away from the cottage on the edge of the shanty-town at Washington's outskirts. "She needs a little while for herself," Miss Mercy said, "without any pressure. If you show up, she'll be reminded that she should be coming to work."

Another Monday came and went, and still there was no word from Julia. Tuesday . . . Wednesday . . . When he asked Miss Mercy about Julia, the old woman just shook her head.

"It's like trying to talk to a fence post," she said.

Spring had fully returned when Philip walked by Adam's flowers to knock on the front door on Wednesday evening just before dark. Julia, looking worn and ashen, in the same black dress she'd been wearing when he last saw her, opened the door. "Oh, Philip."

"May I come in?"

"Yes, of course," she said, stepping back into the gloomy house.

He lit a lamp. In the orange glow he could see that she had lost weight. "Have you been eating?"

"I just don't seem to be hungry," she replied.

"You sit right there," he told her.

The kitchen cupboard was almost barren of food. A loaf of bread decorated with blue mold spots lay uncovered on the counter. A slab of cheese was wrapped tightly and looked edible, and there were some eggs in a basket. He kindled a fire in the wood cookstove, then stoked it until the iron top began to be uncomfortable to his touch. He broke six eggs into a pan, shaved in some cheese, and added salt and pepper. After cutting away the mold and the outer crust of the bread, he set the salvaged material to warm to softness in the oven. There was a partial bottle of wine—he'd brought it himself on a happier occasion.

She obeyed meekly when he ordered her into the kitchen. After taking one tentative bite she ate hungrily. He lifted his glass, nodded toward hers, and she sipped wine.

"That's it, young lady," he said approvingly when she had finished her portion of the eggs. "We miss you. We just can't have you sitting out here all alone, not eating right, not seeing anyone—"

"I'm all right," she said softly.

"I'll have Miss Mercy provide a breakfast snack for you at the office tomorrow morning."

"Thank you." She rose and started to clear the table.

"No, no," he said, leaping up to take the plate from her hand. His fingers, touching hers, generated a sharp jolt of electricity. Her eyes went wide, and she turned away quickly.

"Sit down," he ordered. "I'll clean up, and then I'll bring you another glass of wine."

There wasn't much cleaning up to do—the pan, a spatula, a knife, two plates, two forks. He went into the sitting room with a glass of wine in each hand. "That's the end of it," he said.

"It was Adam's favorite," she said.

"Yes, I remember."

"He was so fond of you, Philip," she said, "and so proud to be able to help you in your work."

"I miss him terribly," Philip confided. "During the day I often look up, thinking that I hear those little wheels rumbling along the floor."

She burst into tears and leapt to her feet.

"Oh, damn," he said, cursing himself. He caught her at the door of the bedroom. "Julia, I'm an idiot. Forgive me."

She turned. Her vibrant face was distorted with grief. "No, it's right that we remember him. Please remember him."

He put a light pressure on her shoulders, and she clung to him. Her weeping was uninhibited, the gulping, gasping, racking sobs of a woman consumed by anguish. He patted her back lightly. Her sobs lessened. He felt the wetness of her tears through his shirt, but mostly he felt the lovely contour of her, the warmth of her, and he berated himself for experiencing a sensual pleasure in the midst of her mourning. She gulped back a sob and pushed away.

"Oh, my," she said.

"First time you've had a good cry?"

"Ummm."

"It might be a good idea if you would lie down."

"I am exhausted," she admitted.

He steered her to the bed. She sat on the edge. He knelt, unbuckled her shoes and pulled them off, then lifted her legs and swung them onto the bed. She was sniffing, wiping tears from her cheek. He gave her his handkerchief, then fluffed the pillow. A light quilt was folded neatly at the foot of the bed. She lay back, and he pulled it up to cover her legs. "Are you all right?"

"Yes, thank you."

He sat in the one chair in the bedroom. A glow of light from the lamp in the sitting room outlined her reclining form. She seemed so small, so vulnerable.

"Julia, you will come back to work tomorrow?"

"Yes."

"Whatever we can do, Miss Mercy and I—"

"I know."

"Well, we want you back with us."

"All right."

He watched her in silence. She turned her face away and wept quietly. He could tell only because of the heaving of her chest. He sat there for a long, long time. She gave a deep sigh, turned onto her side, pulled the quilt up to her shoulders, and after a while her breathing became deep and rhythmic. He tiptoed to the kitchen, locked the back door, and blew out the lamp. He decided to leave the lamp burning in the sitting room but rolled the wick down low so that there was only a feeble glow. Before leaving he tiptoed back to the bedroom and stood beside the bed.

"Good night, dear Julia," he whispered so softly that it could not possibly have awakened her.

She turned quickly, in a panic, and seized his hands. "Don't go! Not just yet."

Her hands were fire in his.

"I don't want to be alone," she whispered. "I can't stand the thought of being alone."

"I'll stay," he said, trying to disengage his hands from hers. She clung tightly.

"I just don't want to be alone anymore." Her voice was choked, and she was pulling on him, tugging at his hands.

He sat on the edge of the bed. "I'll stay. Go to sleep."

"Thank you."

He held one of her hands between his. She lay on her back. He could feel the contour of her thigh through the quilt. "I have terrible dreams," she said sleepily. "I dream about abhorrent things. Adam used to have nightmares. Did he ever tell you that?"

"No, but I don't doubt it. Most men who fought in the war relive it now and then in dreams."

"Do you?"

"Not so much recently. For a long time after I first came home I would dream that I was back in the Reb hospital in North Carolina, with both my legs hurting like fury. There'd be a dozen ghoulish doctors standing around with bone saws, ready to take my legs."

"They took Adam's."

"Yes. Try to sleep now, Julia. I'll borrow a pillow and the quilt and lie down on the couch in the sitting room. You get under the blankets. It's turning cool outside."

"Your sleeping here is scandalous," she said.

"Shocking," he agreed as he went into the front room.

He pulled off his shoes, coat, and vest. The quilt he'd taken from the bedroom provided enough warmth. He heard Julia stirring. She went into the kitchen, and he heard the door to the attached intimate room close, then open after a short time. He heard the rustle of material as she undressed in the dark bedroom, and finally the creak of the bed.

"Philip?"

"Yes."

"You don't have to stay. I'm all right now."

"Then I'll stay until you're asleep. Good night."

"Good night. And thank you."

He put his hands behind his head and studied the patterns of moonlight coming in the windows. In the silence he could hear every small movement she made.

He dozed and was awakened by her cry. He leapt to his feet and rushed into the bedroom. She was moaning, thrashing. She had thrown off the covers, and in the moonlight he saw a length of bare leg where her nightgown had ridden up. Once again she cried out.

"Julia." He put his hand on her shoulder. "Julia?"

She went stiff, rolled quickly onto her back, made a sound like a sob, and sat up to cling to him, her arms around his waist, her face pressed against his stomach.

"You were having a bad dream," he said.

"Oh, damn, damn, damn," she was whispering.

He pushed her back onto the pillow and was reaching for the blanket when she put her hand in his belt and pulled him toward her with surprising strength. He was off balance and managed to catch himself before falling directly atop her. But her arms went around his neck and tugged, and his mouth contacted hers, and a jolt of lightning transformed him instantly. He had never felt such ravaging desire. Julia, squirming under his weight, tugging at his clothing, moaned with a sweet, almost painful passion.

The urgency that had been building in him since first meeting Julia Grey overwhelmed him. Soon her nightdress lay in a heap on the floor, with his clothing atop it. They came together as naturally and as effortlessly as if they were lovers of long standing, and after the first fury of desire was satisfied, they remained entwined, in silence. Then, for a while Julia wept softly while Philip stroked her back and made soothing sounds in her ear. Her hips began to undulate, urging Philip once again into the exquisite pleasure and extended appreciation of her small, taut body.

In the chill hours after midnight he rose and dressed.

She was sleeping, or so he thought. He started toward the front door.

"Philip?"

He turned.

"Don't blame yourself. I am equally at fault."

Her words stabbed him in the heart. "Forgive me," he said.

"Of course."

He went back to sit on the edge of the bed. She shrank away from him and clutched the cover to her chin.

"I will, of course, leave Washington," she said.

He opened his mouth to protest.

"Oh, damn," she said bitterly, tears flowing, "I forgot so soon. I was so damned eager to betray his memory."

"Julia . . ." But he could think of nothing to say, for his guilt was as keenly painful as hers. He reached for her hand. She tried to pull away, but he held on tightly. "What in the hell would you do if you left Washington?" He put his fingers to her mouth to prevent her answering. "You have a duty."

"I had a duty to honor my husband's memory—at least for more than a few days," she said acidly.

"Julia, it happened. I think you were as helpless as I to prevent it. It happened, and it's over. You have a job, and I need you. I'm not going to let you go running off somewhere just because I let my emotions get away from me. I want you to come back to work. I promise you that what has happened here tonight will never happen again."

"I can't."

"Mrs. Grey," he said, releasing her hand, "of course you can. I think Adam would want you to. I know he wouldn't want you to go off by yourself, away from your friends." He forced a laugh. "And besides, if you left me, I'd have to hire someone to be chaperone for Miss Mercy in the office. I might get some old battle-ax."

"How could I face you every day, knowing—"

"Damn it, Julia, please—"

She was silent for a long time. "Whether or not I see you, I will know what I did."

"Yes."

"All right," she agreed. "Will you please go now, Mr. Trent?"

And so came the long days, the endless weeks, the worst days of Philip Trent's life. Julia called him Congressman or Mr. Trent. He called her Mrs. Grey. At last Miss Mercy pulled him aside and said, "She's fading away, Mr. Trent. She's failing just like Adam did."

But there was nothing he could do. He had promised. He had promised her and himself and the memory of a man who had been his true friend. Never again could he take her into his arms, never again whisper the words of longing and love, never again know the sweet, small feel and the deep, ripe goodness of her. He had violated all rules of honor, had intruded into a widow's mourning to ravish her on the same bed where he had bathed, dressed, and laid out Adam Grey's dead body.

CHAPTER 26

The courtship of Leah Miles became grist for the daily mill that ground out sometimes accurate news and often inaccurate gossip for the hungry curiosity of what Lloyd Miles liked to call the "uninformed electorate." The situation made Leah extremely uncomfortable. Brian, however, tolerated the press. In fact, he laughed and joked with reporters and made no special effort to avoid them when he escorted Leah to the opera house or to dinner. Questions were shouted at them as they climbed down from a carriage, or emerged from a theater, or tried to find just a hint of privacy in a restaurant:

"Can we expect wedding bells soon, Duke?"

"Miss Miles, how does it feel almost to be a part of the royal family?"

"Duke Ravendale, how does the royal family feel about your courting an American commoner?"

After one particularly bothersome intrusion by newsmen, Leah asked, "Good heavens, Brian, how can you stand it?"

"Their interest is unavoidable," he replied. "There are two ways to explain it, my dear. One is delicate, the other not so. We could say that a flower will attract bees. That would be a fitting simile for you. Or one can say that a heap of offal attracts flies, which is, I daresay, quite applicable to the press but not very flattering to you and me."

Leah could not bring herself to think of living with Brian, although he was a charming man. During the whirlwind of his attentions to her, he abstained from heavy drinking and smoked only by her permission. Since she'd grown up with Lloyd, a habitual cigar smoker, she objected to Brian's smoking only when they were in a closed carriage. Ravendale was soon familiar with her preferences, not only in that matter but in many others. She liked just one glass of white wine in the evening. She was particularly fond of oysters and made pleased sounds over a box of fine chocolates.

As for Lord Brian, duke of Ravendale, he seemed to be content just being in Leah's company. When the whirlwind reached its maximum intensity and the courtship culminated in a splendidly formal, if not too romantic, proposal of marriage, Leah's face flushed with pleasure. Her reaction was not based in any burning desire for Brian, nor because of a towering passion. But it was exceedingly pleasant to be the center of a man's life, and she did not want to become the maiden aunt of any children Lloyd might one day sire.

To Lloyd's grim satisfaction the invitations that had come with regularity to Ravendale began to be worded differently after the duke's engagement to Leah was announced. Now they read: *The duke of Ravendale and his fiancée, Miss Leah Miles, are invited . . ."*

The invitations, however, did not include the brother of the bride-to-be.

There was an elegant sort of excitement for Leah as she prepared for the wedding. Lloyd, serving as "father" of the bride, insisted that no expense be spared, although he told both Leah and Brian that he would not allow the wedding to be a society circus. The guest list was to be deliberately small. To Ravendale's chagrin Lloyd took a pen and cut the duke's list of suggested guests from almost one hundred to five.

When Ravendale protested, Lloyd told him, "My dear fellow and friend, it has been made quite clear to me that I am not welcome in the homes of those people whom I crossed off your list. Since my money is paying for this wedding, I will humor the whims of all those who do not care to associate with me by leaving them uninvited."

Since severing his connections with Jay Gould and the Erie Railroad, Lloyd had become a loner. He was obsessed with increasing his fortune, and his efforts resulted in gratifying success. He added a few names to the guest list. Most of those he invited were young comers, not wealthy in the definition of Gould or the Rockefellers. Some were invited out of a cold, calculated design to give Lloyd an opportunity for closer contact with men who might possibly be useful to him in the future.

Lloyd laughed with delight when his sister insisted on inviting not only Victoria and Tennessee but Colonel James Blood, William Pearl Andrews, George Francis Train, Theodore Tilton, and assorted controversial and sometimes quarrelsome figures from the women's suffrage movement. Since the press was ecstatically calling the wedding "the affair of the season" he was wryly pleased to accede to Leah's wishes; flaunting the notorious sisters and their cohorts at a press event from which New York's finest had been excluded provided another way of spitting in the eye of "society."

The presence of Victoria, Tennessee, and Theodore Tilton assured massive press coverage, for after 112 days of scandal Tilton's suit against Henry Ward Beecher had just been concluded with no decision because of a hung jury. Furthermore, Victoria and her younger sister, although impoverished, were still vocal and very much in demand by the newspeople.

Leah became the duchess of Ravendale on a steamy summer morning. It was dreadfully hot in the church. Lloyd perspired freely, soaking his newly tailored formal attire and wishing the ceremony to be over. The rites were Episcopalian, and the words intoned by the dignified minister were solemn and beautiful. When groom kissed bride, it was the first time their lips had met.

The catered reception was held in a lavishly decorated hall, which was not at all crowded. A full orchestra played. A few of those business acquaintances invited by Lloyd had not appeared, thus assuring that their names were moved in Lloyd's mind from one list to another.

Perhaps it was the smallness of the gathering that allowed for casual cheerfulness. Or perhaps it was the glowing vivacity of Victoria and the playful flirtatiousness of Tennessee, who insisted on kissing the groom. (Brian made no protest.) When the plump and pretty Tennessee lifted herself onto her tiptoes and pressed a wet, lengthy kiss onto the aristocratic mouth, which was, at first, unresponsive, there was general laughter.

"Now, Tennie!" Leah cried out jokingly. "That man is mine! You'll have to find your own."

"My darling Leah," Victoria said, "I've been thinking the same thing. I believe, my dear, that you've started a trend that will be followed by not a few others."

Even Lloyd enjoyed himself. He danced with Tennessee and then Victoria. Victoria told him that it had been a lovely wedding, a grand reception.

"How are things with you?" he asked.

"Oh, you know. . . ." she said vaguely.

"I heard that Cornelius Vanderbilt's new wife has insisted that he cut Tennie out of his will," Lloyd said.

"That was inevitable," Victoria confirmed. "It was a disappointment to hear of it, naturally, but not entirely unexpected."

"Look, Victoria," Lloyd said, "I'm not as rich as the old boy was, but I'm not exactly poor, either. What do you need? Tell me. You know I've always been willing to help."

"You're a darling boy," Victoria said. "But we'll manage."

"Do you think that by accepting help from me, you'll be

obligated?" Lloyd asked. "I don't think I've been *too* guilty of pushing myself on either you or your sister."

"But I am obligated to you, Lloyd," she said with a smile. "When you sent the KC&S deal our way, it was the last significant income we had. It got us out of jail." She reached up and kissed him. "No, darling boy, I don't mind being obligated to you." She thrust her pelvis toward him warmly. "And you can push yourself *into* me any time both of us feel the urge. It's just that—hell, I don't know." She looked away, and there was sadness in her eyes. "Anyhow, we fought a good fight."

"Never a dull moment," Lloyd agreed.

"Maybe Leah has the right idea," Victoria said. "Find a man who can afford to provide the little necessities—diamonds, country homes, first-class travel—and get the hell out of the United States."

Lloyd laughed, not only because of the irony of Victoria's thinking that Leah's diamonds had been paid for by Ravendale but because marrying a titled Englishman didn't sound like the best solution to Victoria's current problems.

There was the cutting of the cake and the tossing of the bridal bouquet, then the bride and groom were off for a quick honeymoon to Niagara Falls, where the weather would be, Ravendale had been told, delightfully cool. The Claflin contingent left shortly afterward. The reception thinned down to a few hard-core drinkers who lingered around the bar. Lloyd realized that he was hungry. He fixed himself a plate and carried it to a secluded table in a corner, away from the bar and the bored orchestra. He applied himself to eating with as much concentration as he directed toward the making of money and did not notice the *click-clack* of feminine footsteps approaching. He raised his eyes from his plate, to see well-formed female hips in a gaily ruffled gown, a pert young bosom, and at last the face of Abby Kershaw.

"May I join you?" She had a plate of food in her hand.

"Be my guest."

"Which I am not, since I was not invited," she said, sitting across from him.

"Do you want something to drink?"

"Yes, thank you."

Lloyd snapped his fingers for a waiter. The servants were gathered in a group near the orchestra. No one heard his summons until he stood up and bellowed, "Service, goddamn it!"

"Yes, you are a man of direct actions," Abby said wryly.

Two young men scurried to the table. Abby ordered champagne.

"Get me some coffee," Lloyd said, "and be damned sure it's hot."

"Am I forgiven for crashing your reception?" Abby asked.

"Does it matter?" he asked coldly.

"You do hate me, don't you?" she asked.

"Hate you?" He shook his head. "No."

"I've been pretty rough on you, haven't I?"

He didn't answer. "All right, Abby, why are you here? If it's just to prove that you can attend the reception without being invited, fine. If I had known you wanted so badly to come, I'd have sent you an invitation."

"Really?"

"Why not?"

"I was told what Jay Gould said to you that night. And that my father laughed at you."

Lloyd nodded. "That was long ago, small stuff."

"Not so small that you didn't ruin my father in revenge," she said frankly.

He looked at her, his face expressionless.

"And you did it deliberately, didn't you?"

"I was just doing a deal."

"All right," she said.

He took a bite of turkey, but he was no longer hungry. The meat seemed to expand as he chewed it. Abby ate daintily and sipped champagne between bites. He pushed his plate away and studied her. Her long lashes were dramatically dark. Her black hair glowed with reflected blue highlights. When she looked up at him, her green eyes held the depths of the oceans. It both appalled and amazed him that he was, in spite of everything, still totally captivated by her. He waited until she had finished and had dabbed her lips with a linen napkin.

"Wait here," he said, rising. She nodded. He went to find the caterer. "I'm leaving," he told the man. "You can throw the drunks out anytime you're ready."

"We have forty-five minutes of the contracted time remaining," the caterer pointed out.

"It's up to you," Lloyd responded, then he went back to the table. "Let's go," he said, reaching for Abby's hand.

She made no protest. His carriage was waiting. He gave the address of his home. It would be empty, since Leah and Brian were on their way to Niagara Falls. She asked no questions. At the apartment he showed her to Leah's room, with its private bath. "I'm soaked," he said. "I want to get out of this monkey suit and have a quick bath. You can freshen up in here."

When he came out of his room in shirtsleeves she was sitting on a wine-colored love seat. He took both her hands, lifted her, put his arms around her, and found her mouth. To that moment his actions had been purely a mechanical exercise of power. He had bought a husband and a title for Leah; now he would buy something for himself. It would be up to Abby whether this was to be a temporary arrangement for sex or a permanent liaison.

"You are so damned sure of yourself," Abby said when he broke the kiss.

He put his hands on her firm young breasts. "I didn't come looking for you, darlin'. You came to me."

It was no longer a cold, calculated thing for him. Her soft lips had heated him. His passion had been building since their ride from the reception; but now there was in him a longing for something he'd never known—not just for her body, but for a kind word, a certain look of love or compassion or understanding in her oceanic green eyes. His heart was pounding as he stroked the warm roundness of her breasts.

"I think you misunderstand why I'm here," she said, her expression softening.

"It doesn't matter," he said. He turned her, found the tiny pearl buttons that held the green gown, and undressed her slowly. His desire grew to an overwhelming tenderness and need, which forced him to silence and rendered him weak as her lacy underthings joined the dress on the floor. He turned her to face him. She was more curvaceous than Rosanna, much slimmer than Tennessee, and more elegantly shapely than Victoria. Her skin, from her flushing cheeks to her large black pubic bush, was the tone of aged silk and, as his hands worshiped her, as smooth.

He carried her to his bed and could not take his eyes from her as he undressed, although her eyes remained closed. She did not open them during all the time that he claimed her with fingertips, with lips, and with searching, eager tongue. She looked at him only when, with a gasp, he completed his possession of her, then clung to her, motionless for a moment.

And then her green eyes smiled at him knowingly as she lifted her hips and said, "Now, Lloyd Miles, now I have *you.*"

"You are so smooth," he marveled, as he rested his head on one hand and caressed her stomach with the other. "So soft and so smooth." He kissed her. Her lips were bruised from hours of lovemaking. She moaned softly but made no attempt to pull away. "Hurt?" he asked.

"A nice hurt," she whispered.

"I didn't think it would be so . . ." He searched for a word. "*Wonderful* is too weak to describe it."

"Try again," she urged.

"Fabulous. Amazing."

"Amazing? How?"

"I've never known anything so totally complete."

"And you've known a lot of women," she said, a hint of censure in her voice.

He pulled back and smiled, but his eyes were hard. "Let me say, my dear, that I have never deflowered a virgin."

Her face darkened. "Would you have liked it better if I

had screamed a bit? If I'd had a bit of chicken blood secreted to smear on the inside of my thighs?"

He laughed. "No, my dear. Odd though it may seem, in
this activity as in others, I value experience."

"You are a son of a bitch at all times, aren't you?"

"At least I'm consistent. I don't fuck people I wouldn't
invite to a party."

She laughed. "But you didn't invite me, you ass. Is that
consistency?"

He chuckled. "Got me."

"It was my father who called you a goy and a parvenu,
not I," she pointed out.

"Are you saying, darlin', that if I'm worthy enough to
take you to bed that I'm good enough to marry you?"

She smiled and reached for him, to pull his head down
and to press it against her warm, moist breasts. "What do
you think?"

He ran his tongue around an erect nipple. "Can we talk
about it later?"

"Much later," she said, tugging his body into position.

Much later he asked, "Now what about marriage?"

"Is that what you truly want, Lloyd?"

"What do you think?"

She sat up and crossed her legs. Her luxuriant black bush
glistened with moisture. The room was hot. A drop of perspiration rolled from one taut breast down her stomach.
"The truth is, I believe that it served my father right to lose
everything. He's always been an ethnocentric, arrogant son
of a bitch, and he needed a lesson in humility. But he is my
father, and my mother deserves more than to be kicked out
of the home in which she's lived since she was a child. It
was her family's home, not my father's, and he's going to
lose it—and everything else."

"Unless?" Lloyd asked.

"Unless he stumbles upon just over two million dollars
within the next few weeks."

Lloyd roared in laughter.

She looked at him in consternation. "Is it that amusing?"

"I was just thinking," he said, gasping for breath, "that

yours is going to be the most expensive piece of ass that I've ever had."

She reached for him and rubbed her hard breasts against his chest. "But the best," she intoned. "The smoothest, the most amazing, the most fabulous."

"And the price is two million dollars?"

"Two and a quarter," she said, moving to brush her lips over his nipples.

His hands slid to the small of her back and caressed the lovely outflow of hip. "Most expensive—"

"Yes, you've said that already."

"Anything involved other than pure business?" he asked.

"We fit nicely together," she said. "You'll get your money's worth."

"And what if I lost my head and said, Abby, I love you?"

"Please," she said, "let's keep it simple."

"If that's the way you want it," he agreed. "How is it to be? Do we sneak off and do the deed quietly?"

"Heavens no," she said, pushing him away. "A girl only gets married for the first time once."

"Already planning a second time?"

"Stop it," she said.

"All right." But he couldn't resist another jab. "Does Papa pay for the wedding out of the two million?"

"Two and a quarter," she reminded. "No. A wedding is not in the budget."

"Great," he said.

"Papa doesn't know yet." She unfolded her long, luscious legs, got off the bed, and stretched, pushing her breasts out. "I guess I'd better go home and tell him that I've arranged an unsecured, nonrepayable loan for two and a quarter million dollars and a wedding for his only daughter."

"Want me to go with you?"

"Good Lord no," she said. "He's going to want to kill you on sight."

"An impulse that, I believe, two and a quarter million dollars will dull nicely," Lloyd remarked.

* * *

It was not yet dark when Abby left the Miles home. Lloyd had a bath, devoured some fruit and cheese, then went over his accounts to see just how badly he was going to be dented after having purchased both a husband for Leah and a wife for himself. The bulging surface of his financial holdings did show a small concavity after deducting the high cost of matrimony; but dividends to be paid on his blue chips would go a long way toward repairing the damage. And once he'd milked a healthy little steel company down in Pennsylvania of its assets, he wouldn't miss the millions that he was going to write out to the duke and to Psaleh Kershaw.

He was trying to digest the quarterly report of a rather interesting bank in mid-New York State when a loud pounding sounded on the door. He gathered his lounging robe around him and answered the unceasing rapping. The first thing he saw was the black and deadly eye of the muzzle of a large revolver. Then he looked up into Psaleh Kershaw's face.

The older man pushed past Lloyd while keeping the gun's muzzle pointed at him. "I'm going to shoot you," Kershaw threatened.

"That's killing the goose that lays the golden egg," Lloyd pointed out, sounding a lot calmer than he felt.

"First you bankrupt me with your filthy railroad scheme—"

"Oh, come on, Kershaw. What did you have in mind for the KC&S? Were you going to say 'Bless you, KC&S, keep that lovely three million in overcapitalization and buy gold spittoons for the carriages?' "

"—and then you have the gall to ask my daughter to marry you."

"Kershaw, put that foolish gun away and sit down," Lloyd said. He turned his back and expected to feel the mule kick of a ball entering his cringing flesh. But he made it safely into the study and sat down.

To Lloyd's surprise Kershaw began to sob, and he lowered the revolver muzzle to point down to the floor.

"You have taken everything from me," Kershaw whined.

Lloyd rose, walked to his desk, and scribbled a check, which he handed to Kershaw. "I think you'll find that the amount is the one that Abby and I agreed on," he said. "Two and a quarter million."

Kershaw, weeping, sat down weakly and set the revolver beside him. "So you think you have won, Miles," he said, pulling out a handkerchief.

"Let's say that we're both winners," Lloyd suggested. "When you're my father-in-law I'm sure that I can steer you into a few good things."

Kershaw shook his head as he loudly blew his nose.

"Look, old man," Lloyd said, "you laughed at me. You insulted and humiliated me. Did you think I'd just take it and say, oh, thank you, you wonderful member of the elite, thank you for noticing me, even if it was to laugh at my expense? You laughed at me, and you were foolish and greedy enough to take the bait. But I'm not a vindictive man. I'm willing to let the past rest. If that check doesn't make good your losses, then give me a figure that will. We can work it out. And if you don't have any liquidity to invest in a little deal I've got going, I'll lend you another million or so. *Lend,* not give this time. It won't be a huge money-maker like the KC&S, but there'll be a sweet little profit."

"That's big of you, Miles," Kershaw said, drying his eyes with the handkerchief. He rose and pocketed the check. "But don't think it's all settled and done between you and me."

"Don't threaten me, Kershaw," Lloyd warned.

Kershaw laughed. "Oh, I won't, Miles. I'm too old to go head-to-head with you. But I wonder if you won't be caught unaware by another instrument of Kershaw's revenge. I wonder, Miles, if you're not on the verge of taking a viper into your cozy little bed."

He was gone, leaving his last words hanging, their meaning obvious to Lloyd. He shook his head. Hell, he'd made a business deal with Abby, just as he'd made a business deal with the duke and with Psaleh Kershaw. Abby was a product of the business world, and a good businesswoman honored her commitments.

The Kershaw name was an old one, and it was engraved on the unprinted but very real roster of the Four Hundred. Since there were no Vanderbilts or Rockefellers or Astors getting married that season, Lloyd's marriage to Abby got almost as much coverage as the alliance of Lloyd's sister with the British royal family.

Leah and Brian postponed their departure for England so that Leah could be matron of honor. Lloyd assumed financial responsibilities customarily reserved for the father of the bride. Because Abby planned everything from the ceremony to the reception, the expenses passed those of Leah's wedding, and then doubled. Not the least among them was the amount paid to the lone rabbi they could find who was willing to join Abby and a non-Jew in matrimony.

It was an impressive ceremony. The names of those in attendance rang little bells in the ears of the society reporters who gathered around like fruit flies. At the opulent reception a servant at the door cried out the roll call of the rich and powerful. Oddly enough, Lloyd did not resent the fact that people who had never given him the time of day now fawned over him.

"Oh, Mr. Miles, you and Abby must join us for our end-of-summer celebration at our Newport cottage."

"You'll be getting an invitation to our charity ball, Mr. Miles. I do hope you and Abby will attend."

Lloyd was a man who believed in doing whatever was required to attain his goals, and he had set out to become a member of the elite not only financially but socially. If that meant marrying into it, then so be it. He had bought and paid for it fair and square.

When the rabbi said, "You may kiss the bride," Lloyd lifted the veil to see tears flowing freely down Mrs. Lloyd Miles's cheeks, and he was touched.

"Oh, my dear," he said, as he kissed her fondly and tenderly, certain that the tears expressed sentiment toward the ceremony and thus for him.

In actuality, as Abby repeated the words of her vows by rote, as she felt her freedom slipping away, she was reliving the night before. In her bedroom in her parents' mansion she lifted and heaved under the ministrations of the young man she would have married had he not been as impoverished as the Kershaws. As her tears came, she remembered with deep sadness the words she had exchanged with her lover, now superimposed over those of the rabbi.

"Don't do this, Abby. Don't do it. You know that I love you."

"I could say the same, but it would be pointless. The reality is that I will marry Lloyd Miles."

Heaving into her, thrusting so deeply that she winced, her lover said, "I love you. I can't live without you."

"You won't have to."

"I don't understand."

"Not at first, and not for a while; but I will come to you, my darling."

"From him, Abby! You'd come to me from his bed?"

"Would you rather I not come at all?"

"No, darling. Come to me."

"You may kiss the bride."

Abby Kershaw Miles did not find Lloyd's lips on hers to be unpleasant. Nor was the wedding night offensive. On the contrary, Lloyd had the skill to lift her into physical heights. That, at least, would be worthwhile in her union with him, and she would take advantage of it to the fullest. She would give him full measure for his money, and if she took pleasure in his sexual abilities in return, that was an unexpected bonus.

CHAPTER 27

Leah, the new duchess of Ravendale, surrendered her long despised maidenhood to a man of some experience in a little hotel in northern New York State. Ravendale's skill and innate gentleness made it painless, if not ecstatic. Ravendale, accustomed to being able to play upon the body of a woman as if she were a finely tuned instrument and he a skilled musician, had almost given up. He was thinking that, by God, he'd come all the way to America to marry a frigid woman, the sort that one heard so much about in England. He was almost prepared to hear Leah confirm distastefully that she was doing her connubial duty.

But then, on an evening of rain and thunder, something happened to her. Suddenly she tensed and clung to him and began to make puppy sounds in her throat. She was blushing furiously as she lifted in answering rhythm to his movements and then melted into him in such a lovely and endearing way that he felt a quick surge of tenderness for her. In a short time she was again clinging to him shyly, kissing him tenderly, and quite obviously asking for a repeat performance.

"Gad," he teased, groaning, "I have created a monster."

She hit him lightly on the chest.

"But such a lovely and savory monster," he said.

So it was that Leah discovered that she had a sensuous nature, after all.

Unfortunately the prelude to love that had begun to grow in her was to be crushed when, back in New York, she discovered the terms of her marriage. It came about by accident. She was packing, looking forward with pleasant anticipation to sailing for England. Her excitement was tinged by sadness at the thought of leaving Lloyd. Leah was looking for an oil-painted miniature of her mother when she remembered that Lloyd had wanted to see the portrait not long after they had moved into the new New York mansion. Ordinarily she would never have gone into his desk. And most certainly she would not have read any of his private papers.

The miniature was propped up against the small drawers under the rolltop. Beside it was a drawer with a label printed in large letters: RAVENDALE LIABILITIES. Leah's eyes were drawn to it, and then she slid the drawer open to find a sheet of paper with columns of figures and explanations scrawled in Lloyd's hand. Most of the liabilities column had *Paid, check number* —— written beside it.

Lloyd has paid Brian's bills? she wondered, flabbergasted. *To the amount of over a million dollars?* She lifted the first page and saw more figures, then looked down at the total: three million nine hundred thousand paid to Lord Brian, Duke of Ravendale.

Three million nine hundred thousand dollars had purchased a husband for Leah Miles. She could draw no other conclusion.

She was seated numbly in the parlor, a wineglass in hand, her head spinning, when Brian and Lloyd came in together.

"Hello, Sister," Lloyd said. "Abby hasn't come in yet?"

"No," Leah replied dully.

"Hello, darling," Brian said, approaching to kiss her on the cheek.

She pulled away. "Don't," she said.

Brian laughed. Lloyd and he had visited a bar on the way

from Lloyd's office, where they had concluded their financial arrangements, and he thought Leah was reacting to the smell of brandy on his breath. "Come to think of it . . ." he said, leaning forward to sniff her breath, which held the aroma of wine.

"I am not surprised that you put so little value on your family name," Leah seethed, "but I had thought that you valued yourself higher than three million nine hundred thousand."

"Whoops," Brian said, pulling back and turning quickly to look at Lloyd.

"Actually, sis," Lloyd said, with the cold smile that was his negotiating expression, "he jacked up the price on me. He told me at first that it would require only one or two million to make it possible for him to give you a good home and a good living."

"Oh, you bastards," Leah said.

Lloyd stepped close to her, took the wineglass from her hand, and picked up the bottle. "How much of this have you had?"

"Not enough," she said, reaching for the glass. Lloyd slapped her ringingly on the cheek.

"I say!" Ravendale yelled.

"And that's enough of that," Lloyd said to Leah. "I will hear no more drivel about a family name or of the personal worth of the man who is your husband. Do I make myself clear?"

"Quite clear," Leah fumed. "Would you like to hit me on the other cheek just to reemphasize how little you have valued me?"

"That's enough, Leah!"

Ravendale inserted himself between brother and sister. "Brother-in-law," he said, "perhaps when you were caring for Leah, you had the right to chastise her. That is no longer the situation."

"Well, by God, it walks, it talks, it makes sounds like a man." Lloyd stepped back, grinning nastily.

"I say, Miles—" Ravendale protested.

"You leave him alone!" Leah shouted. She leapt forward

to thrust herself between Ravendale and her brother. "Insult me if you like, but keep your filthy mouth off him."

"But I bought him for you," Lloyd drawled. "He accepted pay to marry you, and now you want to protect him?"

Leah's face burned bright red. Ravendale put his hands on her shoulders. "Come away, Leah," he said gently. "Come away. It's all right. We've just had too much to drink, all of us."

She allowed herself to be pulled into what had been her bedroom. Ravendale turned her to face him. "Is it all that bad, my dear girl?"

"He sold me," she whispered, tears welling in her eyes.

"Would you believe me if I said that I would have asked you to marry me even if your brother had not been rich?"

"Not in a million years," she shot back.

"Ah, you know me too well in just this short time," he said. "It is true, my dear, that I was in horrendous financial difficulties. It is also true that I accepted money from your brother with the understanding that it would never be repaid. But I am more than a bought-and-paid-for husband, my darling. I have grown quite fond of you—"

"You don't have to make pretty speeches," she grated, jerking away from him. "I understand the situation now. You sold yourself to save your estates. And Lloyd bought a title for me." She turned to face him. "If you can live with it, I suppose I shall learn to do so."

"Stout lass," Ravendale said. He moved toward her swiftly and drew her into his arms. "We'll just have to make the best of it. And the first thing that is absolutely necessary for us is to get out of your brother's home. Two newly married couples in the same abode is one couple too many. Don't you agree?"

"Oh, I'm a dutiful wife," she said bitterly. "Your wish is my command, dear husband. But I don't think I care to sleep in a hotel tonight, if you don't mind."

"As you wish," he agreed.

"You go ahead into the study. I have some things to do here."

After he left the bedroom, she waited until she had heard the study door close. Then she left the mansion. At that moment the destruction of her spirit was as nearly complete as it was possible to be and still leave her with the will to live. It had begun when Lloyd gave her the ultimatum to break off her engagement to Philip Trent. The process of her subversion had continued through her aborted romance with the late Harold Berman and had climaxed with her ascent to the role of duchess.

Victoria and Tennessee, with assorted members of their here-now-gone-later family, had taken a flat in a roach-ridden tenement near the Bowery. The sordid surroundings did not diminish Victoria's dignity. She admitted Leah, who blurted out her tale of unhappiness to the Claflin sisters. They came to enfold her in a big, warm hug.

"Pshaw," Tennie soothed, "how typical that is of men! And you're actually letting it bother you?"

"I think it was rather nice of your brother to see to it that you'd be financially comfortable after marriage," Victoria declared.

"After all," Tennie said lightly, "he's only a husband. And you know how *they* come and go."

"A liberated woman such as you," Victoria said, "should have no difficulty taking the situation in hand. Simply set the rules, dear, and if he doesn't abide by them, you make his life so miserable that he will come to rein quickly."

With tears on her face Leah burst into sudden laughter. "You two are impossible," she said.

"You'll have to admit that Vee makes sense," Tennie said in all seriousness. "You're so *lucky,* Leah! You enjoy social standing; your brother sees to it that you'll always have enough money; you have a handsome husband." She leaned close and whispered. "Is he good in bed? I'll bet he is—he has that look about him."

Leah was smothering her helpless giggles behind her handkerchief.

"Did you enjoy it the first time?" Tennie asked. "Lord,

when I did it the first time, I was so young that I was really small, you see, and we had to work and work—"

"Tennie!" Leah protested.

"My dear," Tennie said with a superior look down her nose, "you are no longer the bashful virgin, you know." She pouted prettily. "But if I'm shocking you—"

Leah giggled again, her face going red as she said, "I didn't enjoy it the first time, Tennie."

"Too bad," Tennie said.

Leah shook a hand limply from the wrist and confided, "But the third time, ohhhhhh."

Gales of feminine laughter and a feeling of warmth resulted.

"In all seriousness, Leah, I think we go badly wrong when we expect *everything* from life. Life, as I see it, is a system that demands give and take. Take the pleasures, the good things, then give without regret when things go wrong. I expect that your duke is a man of honor. All right: he arranged a commercial transaction with your brother. So what? Not too many years ago—and even now in many parts of the world—some man could have purchased you for a few sheep or a couple of horses. This is the very sort of thing we're fighting against, Leah, but sometimes we have to be patient and make compromises. Think of the good you can do as a duchess for our cause."

"I hadn't thought of that," Leah admitted.

"And," Victoria said, "don't give up on Brian—not just yet. My bet is that he'll be a good and attentive husband if you'll give him half the chance."

"And if you don't want him," Tennie teased, "I'll take him on lease with an option to buy."

Leah's tears were forgotten. The sisters had a knack for making her forget her troubles, and as she began to take a new view of her situation, an idea came to her. "Hello," she said, as inspiration struck. "I've got it! If you think that I've done so well, then you are coming with me to England. Both of you."

Tennie laughed. "Darling girl, there's nothing we would enjoy more. But at this moment we would have to do business on the street—a level to which we have not quite fallen—to finance a cab ride to the docks, much less ship fare to England."

"No problem," Leah said. "I have a rich brother, remember? And if Lloyd and Brian balk at the idea, I have some money of my own."

"And just what will we do in England?" Tennie asked. She lifted her skirt and showed a quick flash of ankle and calf. "Or do Englishmen pay higher prices on the street than New Yorkers?"

"We will follow Leah's example," Victoria said, a look of intense concentration on her face.

"Oh?" Tennie asked, then her face blossomed into a smile.

"The duchess," Leah said, "will introduce the fascinating sisters to English society."

"And to selected unmarried men," Victoria added.

Tennie lifted her skirts again and did an exaggerated curtsy. "I say, Your Bloomin' Ladyship, 'ow's yer fuzz today?"

"Fuzzy and warm, Your Bloody Grace," Victoria said, returning the curtsy with a bit more dignity.

"You'll go, then?" Leah asked excitedly.

"Best offer I've had since that ten dollars I made the easy way in Cincinnati," Tennie answered.

Leah thought that Brian was asleep when she crept into her bedroom. She'd had a brandy or two with the sisters, and her head was still light from it. She undressed quietly, washed, then slipped on a thin lawn nightdress, since the night was a warm one. As she settled onto her back, Brian rolled over to face her.

"Leah, I'm sorry you had to learn about the agreement between your brother and me so soon," he said.

"It's all right," she said. "I've come to grips with it." She didn't tell him about the advice she'd received from the sisters. She considered it to be good counsel, and she had determined to make the best of the marriage, for, after due consideration, it was preferable to being a spinster.

"I think you were beginning to like me," Brian said.

"Yes, I was."

"But not now?"

She sighed. "Brian, it's late."

He put his hand on her waist and moved it upward. She cringed but caught herself, remembering Tennie's girlish giggles and the advice to "get as much of that as possible." She reached out and touched his face.

"My dear," he whispered. His lips were warm, tender. She thought at first that she would feel no response to his caress, but she was wrong.

Later, pleasantly sated, she lay in his arms. His quickened breathing slowed.

"My dear Leah," he said, "I have something to say to you. Will you listen and give me the benefit of the doubt?"

"Of course."

"I ran a bit amok when my father died, as you have probably heard. I'm not proud of it. When I met you and your brother, I was seriously considering not completing the voyage home."

"You thought of staying in America?"

"I thought of leaving the ship, alone, in mid-Atlantic," he said.

She shuddered and put her arms around him.

"I didn't think that I could face the disgrace of seeing my family's home seized for debt," he said, "or of losing everything that my ancestors had established. I will always be grateful to your brother for two things, and one of them is more important to me than the other. The one of lesser importance is his generosity in bailing me out of my self-dug financial hole. The other?"

She waited.

"Do you want to know?"

"Yes," she whispered.

"For giving you to me," he said.

"Oh, Brian, I would like to believe you. But can I?"

He laughed. "Perhaps not now, but I think that you will in time."

* * *

Although Lloyd knew that he was going to miss Leah, he, like Brian, was eager to have only one newly married couple in his home. Because of Leah and Brian's plans to leave for England, Lloyd and Abby had postponed their own honeymoon trip. The first days of their marriage had been spent, therefore, with Leah and Brian in and out of the mansion. Since Abby was not at all stingy with her favors and Lloyd had quickly developed an insatiable appetite for Abby-in-the-nude, the lack of privacy proved a hardship.

Lloyd had always been a sensuous man. He was in his prime, healthy, and endowed with an intense appreciation for a well-formed female body. Because of Abby's obvious enjoyment of sex and her pleasing response to his overtures, he found himself in the sometimes uncomfortable position of becoming dependent on her. Although he would have denied that he was in love with her, he acted like a man in love, whispering endearing things to her during the warm, sticky lovemakings of the night.

"I want to thank you," he told her one night after she had clung and clung and moaned her pleasure.

"Thank *you*," she said, chuckling. "Alone I couldn't have managed anything half that pleasurable."

"I'd better not find you wasting any of it by yourself," he said.

"Well, you just stay on the job then, fella."

"What I want to thank you for, Abby, is for not making me feel like a rapist."

"If you want to, I'll fight a little bit next time—but not too much."

"No, I'm talking about that first day. I want to beg your forgiveness for that. I knew why you'd sought me out—to ask me to aid your father. I took advantage of that. I was going to have you if it cost me millions, and even if it was only going to be one time."

"My gosh," she said, "do you suppose there are others like you? If I could earn a couple of million a throw—"

He shook her with sudden anger. "Don't talk like that! Don't ever talk like that!"

"Why, Lloyd, are you jealous?"

"It's just that . . ." He paused.

"That what?"

"That I'm damned jealous," he confessed, laughing.

"Not really. You told me that you were glad I had experience." She licked his mouth, wetting his lips, his nose, his cheek. "Wouldn't you like for me to tell you about my experiences? When I was sixteen—"

He was torn between a puerile curiosity and a flaming anger at the thought of some gangling, awkward boy with his hands on Abby. "Shut up," he said.

"All right. Sorry." She kissed him. "I'm all yours. I'm your wife. All yours." She lay on her back, her hands under her head. His breathing became regular. "Until, husband, the little itch that I'm beginning to feel becomes more powerful," she whispered under her breath, and the thought of the tearful young man she'd bedded on the eve of her wedding sent bolts of fresh, delicious desire downward from the pit of her stomach.

Abby Kershaw Miles found Thaddeus Harcourt, Jr., her ex-lover, at his post in his father's bank on Sixth Avenue. She waited until there were no clients at his stall, then presented herself. He went pale. "Hello, lover," she whispered.

"Abby!"

"It's time," she told him.

Thad flushed and licked his lips.

"Are you due for your lunch hour?"

He glanced at the big clock. "In ten minutes."

"I'll wait outside," she said. "Be thinking about a place where we can be alone."

"Yes," he said.

There was a dingy, cheap hotel not far from the bank. The desk clerk asked no questions. Abby's young man was forty-five minutes late getting back to work. Among the several things that Abby Miles accomplished during the extended lunch—during which there was no lunch eaten—was to make a date for an evening visit to Thad's apartment that very night. She did not bother to return home. She spent the afternoon doing some shopping and arranged to have purchases delivered.

She was waiting in the apartment building's foyer when Thaddeus came home from work. For weeks her needs had been satisfied by Lloyd, but she had discovered, in the grimy hotel room, that it was difficult to get too much of a very good thing.

"I can't stay long," she said.

But resolution and prudence faded before lust, and it was after ten o'clock when she dismounted from a cab and ran up the steps to the Miles mansion. All three of them were waiting for her—or so it seemed to Abby—in the sitting room.

"Where have you been?" Lloyd asked, leaping to his feet. "We've been sick with concern."

"I went shopping and ran into some old friends, and we got to talking," she explained.

"Who?" Lloyd demanded.

"Darling," she said, "I'm very tired. Let me just freshen up a bit, and then I'll tell you all about my exciting day."

He had missed her so much. It had taken only a short while for Lloyd to become accustomed to having Abby waiting for him when he came home from the office. He followed her into the bedroom and, without bothering to close the door, reached for her, to nuzzle her neck.

"Please, Lloyd," she said, pulling away. "I'm so sticky and grimy. I must have my bath."

Lloyd's words were soft. "I don't care about that. I was worried about you."

"Oh, come on," Abby said impatiently. "Keep your hands off me. I told you I was hot and dirty."

"Just how goddamned dirty are you?" Lloyd demanded. There was a smell of cigar smoke about her, and a faint hint of perspiration mixed with her perfume. He put his hands to her breasts. She slapped him and pulled away.

She was, he decided, acting damned suspicious. He seized her, threw her down on the bed, and ran his hand up under her skirt.

"Stop it, you bastard," she said vehemently.

"I want to know just how dirty you are, you little bitch," Lloyd said, overcoming her struggles.

Then he knew. He knew the feel of it, the smell of it when, his heart pounding and pain lancing through him, he withdrew his hand and looked at the sheen of moisture on his fingertips.

Brian took Leah's hand and pulled her close. She wanted to be away from the sound of the angry voices coming clearly to them from the bedroom; but she was helpless to overcome a perverse curiosity.

"Are you satisfied?" Abby asked, and Leah could only imagine the intent of the question.

"Whore," Lloyd snarled, and there was the sound of flesh impacting flesh.

Abby screamed a curse, and for a moment there were the sounds of violence, things being thrown and broken, and another blow. "All right," Abby said, her voice cold and calm. "So you're stronger than I am, you bastard."

"Who was it?" Lloyd demanded.

"Mr. Miles," Abby said, in a dead, cold monotone, "when you bought me, you bought a ticket to dinners and balls in the homes of the Vanderbilts and the Rockefellers. You paid for what I have gladly given you and will continue to give you because that was a part of the agreement. But you did not buy my soul, nor did you buy a part of my life that will forever be closed to you."

"Who was it?" Lloyd demanded again. "Tell me! I'll kill him!"

"Now, wouldn't that be smart?" Abby asked acidly. Then the tone of her voice changed. "Come here," she coaxed.

In the study Brian rose and pulled Leah to her feet. "Let's get out of here," he said.

As she went out the door Leah heard, "Come here,

baby, it's all right. It's nothing. Mama's got so much that you won't even miss a little bit now and then."

Lloyd pulled away from her in horror. She rolled off the bed and began to undress slowly, suggestively. "Don't be angry, my sweet boy," she purred as she bared her young pointed breasts. She dropped the rest of her clothing and stepped out of it. "Take your clothes off," she whispered, then knelt in front of him. "Please?"

Her hands worked as she whispered of her desire for him.

Almost sobbing, he was pulling at his clothes. "God-damn you to hell," he said as he fell atop her.

She had not even bathed.

"Let me tell you about it," she whispered, her lips brushing his.

"Shut up, Abby. Shut up, shut up."

"But he was so strong, baby," she whispered, "and he wanted me soooo badly, and—"

Lloyd moaned in protest, but he could not stop her any more than he could stop his own frantic plungings. Her vivid account retarded his urgency, dammed it behind a conflict of emotions that, when his passion exploded, left him drained of strength.

Abby pushed him from atop her. She stood tall, perfectly formed, and well used beside the bed for a moment. Her ocean-green eyes belied the little smile on her lips. As she turned away she said under her breath, too softly for him to hear clearly, "That, goy, is installment number one of your payment to the Kershaws."

CHAPTER 28

At a quarter past the noon hour on 18 September 1873, the millennium came, Valhalla was overcome, and Gibraltar was conquered. The man who had made millions by selling government bonds to finance Mr. Lincoln's war closed the doors of Jay Cooke and Company. Before the end of the day thirty-seven banks and brokerage houses in New York City followed suit. Trading was suspended on the New York Stock Exchange. The debacle that Cornelius Vanderbilt had almost single-handedly prevented after Black Friday, although delayed, had begun.

Panic.

Within forty-eight hours construction was halted on Jay Cooke's Northern Pacific Railroad—the cause of his downfall—and on railroads in six states. Sawmills in the forests of Michigan began to lay off men.

Thousands of frantic depositors milled around in a pelting rain, wanting to get inside the doors of their banks to claim their money before institutions such as New York's First National followed other houses of finance from coast to coast into insolvency. It was as if the structure of greed, based on expansion—the new Industrial Revolution that had been triggered by the Civil War—and on the inflation caused by Mr. Lincoln's greenbacks, was pouring down from the sky itself in the form of chill, driving rain.

President Grant and his secretary of the Treasury, quicker to move than they had been during Jay Gould's gold corner, rushed to New York and summoned financial leaders to a suite of rooms in a Fifth Avenue hotel.

Grant had a special handshake and a clap on the back for the ex–staff major Lloyd Miles before the emergency conference began. "What do you think can be done, Miles?" Grant asked while they had a moment of privacy.

"Well, General, not a hell of a lot," Lloyd answered. "When the water stops running out of two-thirds of the stock being offered on the market, there are going to be a lot of unhappy bastards. I remember what the commodore said once: 'Building railroads from nowhere to nowhere is not a legitimate business.' And I'm afraid that, among other things, that is what's been going on."

One of the unhappy bastards was Daniel Drew. Drew's twilight years had been unlucky ones. He'd taken one beating after the other in his Erie war with Jay Gould and Jim Fisk; when the Panic of '73 got him firmly in its grasp, he added up his liabilities to over a million dollars. His watered stock was worthless. His net worth was listed in bankruptcy court as: Watch and chain, $150; sealskin coat, $150; other clothing, $100; Bibles and hymnbooks, $130.

The mixture of ecstasy and agony that was the life of Lloyd Miles with his elegant wife seemed to sharpen his business wits. He had started selling months before Jay Cooke's downfall signaled the beginning of the worst depression since 1857. He went liquid, mostly in gold, and joined a few other carnivores, Jay Gould among them, in the debris of the nation's financial system to sniff around the ruins for easy prey.

Lloyd was confident that the panic would end one day. Once again the nation would be on the move, and there would be a need for steel. Once again the rails would expand into nowhere and the steel mills would need coke to make rails. Among his unliquidated holdings was a small coke oven in Pennsylvania. It had been a profitable, if minor, operation. Lloyd now put a few million dollars of his gold into coke-coal lands, bought bankrupt ovens at distress prices, then sat back to wait.

In Washington, James Garfield's committee tried to generate a few favorable headlines for itself by investigating the causes for the panic. It soon became clear that no one, not even the most learned economists, really understood why such things occurred. The public, understandably concerned with the lack of work and scarcity of bread, wasn't interested in esoteric economic theory. There were no clear-cut culprits as there had been in the Gold Ring. Washington, like the rest of the nation, eventually settled back into the doldrums.

Gus Trent probably understood as well as any man the reasons for the panic. "Too much debt," he told Julia Grey. They were seated in the reception area of Philip's offices. Julia, thin, wan, dull eyed, leaned on her elbows at her desk.

"A pyramid of debt," Gus continued. "For example, Jay Cooke and all the stockholders sank every penny they had into the Northern Pacific, with no hope of a quick return. Extending a railroad into the plains of the Northwest is a good idea; but before it'll pay a return, towns will have to be laid out and settled and ranches stocked. In short, there'll have to be people there instead of a vast emptiness with settlers' dugouts scattered every fifty miles or so."

"I wonder," Julia said, "if the transcontinental could have been built if the federal subsidies had been as closely monitored as they were on the Northern Pacific."

Gus shrugged. "Sure wouldn't have been as much incentive for the builders. And in trying to bleed out a quick profit—the way they did with the holding companies double billing the government—the contractors might have bankrupted the Pacific railroads just the way Cooke bled the Northern Pacific dry."

He leaned back and lit a cigar. "Only a few people saw it coming. Some smart Englishman must have realized that there wasn't going to be enough money to allow the Northern Pacific to operate until the population grew large enough to make it profitable. He pulled out his investment, and a lot of other foreigners followed suit. After some of the tricks that have been pulled on the Europeans by men such as Drew, Vanderbilt, and Gould, they're leery of investing money in the United States anyhow. And at the time, interest rates were higher in Europe than here; it only took a little bit of a scare to cause European capital to take an ocean cruise back home. But the long and the short of it is that a loaf of bread can be worth only so much, even in inflated greenback dollars. Prices were getting out of control. I don't care how well you bake a loaf of bread; if you price it too high for the people to buy, you're not going to do much business. And if you don't sell what you bake, then you shut down first one oven and then the others—and with each shutdown someone else is out of a job, and there's even less money to buy your high-priced bread."

"It's all too complicated for me," Julia said.

"Get your hat, then," Gus said. "I'm going to treat you to a lunch. You look as if you need a square meal."

"I'd better not, Gus," she said. "Philip isn't back, and Miss Mercy is home sick today."

"Philip has a key to the offices," Gus said. He went to the brass hat rack near the door, took down Julia's bonnet, and plunked it on her head.

She laughed. "It's backward," she said.

"A good-looking woman looks good any way she wears her hat," Gus said. He took her arm and escorted her, still protesting, out the door.

"Let me lock it," she said.

"Hell, there's nothing in there worth stealing," Gus said. "And if someone does steal it, it's government property and tax dollars will be used to replace it. That'll stimulate the economy."

"Mr. Trent," she said as she secured the door, "you're impossible."

Gus took Julia in a cab to his favorite restaurant, then ordered enough food to feed two stevedores. He hovered over her, demanding that she try this and that, urging her on until she had eaten a good meal.

"Julia, I've been watching you these last months," Gus said, "and I've seen you fade like an autumn sunset."

She put a hand to her hair, which had lost its sheen. "That bad?"

"If I didn't know better, I'd think that you were consumptive," he said.

"No, thank God."

"Girl, I'm going to talk to you like a Dutch uncle—or something." He leaned forward and took one of her small, pale hands in his. "Do you know what I've been wanting for the last decade or so?"

She shook her head.

"A grandchild," he confided. "Doesn't matter to me whether it's a boy or a girl. I just want a grandchild to bounce on my knees and to tell tall tales to when he gets old enough to laugh at his foolish old granddaddy."

"I don't see what that has to do with me," Julia said weakly, although she knew exactly what Gus was driving at.

"It has everything in the world to do with you," he said. "I'm going to tell you something else: I once made a promise to a man who knew he was dying. Now I feel guilty about accepting that promise, because of the way things have been with you and my son. But I think the time is right for me to fulfill that promise to that dying man."

She had taken a long breath and was holding it.

"Yes, I'm talking about Adam," Gus said. "As you know, Adam and I got to be very good friends during that last year he was alive." He paused, wondering how blunt he should be. Adam had lost more than his legs at Fort Fisher; he had lost his male organs. Gus squeezed her hand. "For example, I know why you didn't have any children."

She blushed furiously. "He told you that?"

"He told me that, among other things," Gus replied. "Are you ready for this, Julia?"

"I don't know," she said in a tight voice. "I don't think so."

"Well, ready or not, I'm going to tell you, and I know

you're too much the lady to start bawling or something right here before God and everybody. Adam knew that you and Philip were . . ." He paused and rubbed his chin. "Now, I want to say this right. Whatever I say, and whatever it makes you think—"

She swallowed, then whispered desperately, "I heard Adam talking to you shortly before—before he died. He thought—" She could go no further.

"He thought what?"

"Not here, Gus. Let's go. I can't talk here."

"All right," he agreed.

He took her to the river where he'd once walked with Leah Miles. "What did Adam think?" he pressed when they were well away from other strollers.

"I heard him say it. He thought that Philip and I were . . ."

"Were *what*, Julia? If you believe that Adam thought you and my son were having an affair, then you interpreted it all wrong. Adam knew that you and Philip admired each other and were physically attracted, perhaps—but it was an attraction that both of you were too loyal, too honorable, to allow to come to fruition. And Adam knew that." He scratched his chin. "I know you heard us talking that night at your house. Here's exactly what Adam was saying: He was afraid you and Philip would be too devoted to his memory to admit that you could love each other." He took her arm and pulled her to a stop. Tears swam in her eyes.

"I saw your attitude change toward Philip after that night," Gus continued. "But it got even worse after Adam died. You've really turned the chill on. You call my son Mr. Trent and run out of the room if you're left alone with him. By Gawd, you're still feeling guilty because you think Adam suspected that something was going on between you and Philip. Is that it?"

"Mr. Trent, I loved my husband," she said defiantly.

"Don't you 'Mr. Trent' me, young lady. Nobody could feel that guilty just because she was *suspected* of a little hanky-panky." He looked out across the river for a moment, then turned to face her. "Did my son talk you into doing something while Adam was alive? Is that why you're both being so dad-blamed honorable and acting like Adam was a saint instead of just one hell of a good man?"

"No," she said, but she was unable to meet his eyes.

He shook her. "Don't lie to me. Don't you lie to me."

"I'm not lying," she cried, "nothing happened while—"

"Go on," he said sternly.

"Nothing," she said. "Nothing happened."

"Nothing happened while what? While he was alive? Do you mean that something happened afterward? I see. And you two think you've sullied the memory of husband and friend. What terrible thing happened, Julia? Did you share a kiss, maybe two?"

She jerked away. Angry, he seized her and turned her, then put his face close to hers. "Julia, I want a grandchild. I wouldn't mind having a little girl who looks like you. I'm not going to let you deprive me of that. Now, you tell me what happened!"

"If I tell you, will you leave me alone?" she asked, her voice rising and falling with her sobs.

"No, but you're going to tell me."

"More. Much more," she cried. "And so soon—so soon . . ."

"Just once?" He was beginning to feel more hopeful. If there had been enough fire there to put them in bed together soon after Adam's death, there should still be some embers.

She nodded and, shaking with sobs, hid her face in her hands.

He put his arms around her and hugged her close, cushioning her head on his chest. "Honey, if everyone who gave in to that temptation had to burn in hell, the devil would have to start an expansion program. Now, I want you to stop crying and listen to me, because I'm going to fulfill my promise to Adam and tell you what he wanted for you after his death. I should have done it months ago instead of waiting to see if you and Philip would develop enough sense to stop hitting yourselves over the head; but Adam wanted your relationship to grow naturally, without his interference or mine."

Gus led Julia to a bench on the side of the river. In the slow water near the bank a pair of wood ducks were swimming. The gleaming white head markings of the male flashed in the sun as he put himself protectively between his hen and the intruders.

"Adam didn't think he'd been much of a husband to you, Julia," he said. "He thought he was being selfish to stay alive, hanging on to you."

"Oh, no," she cried out.

"He felt positive that if he seemed to be pushing you into Philip's arms, or if he made you feel that his shade would be standing beside you two at the altar, offering to give the bride away . . ."

She burst into tears. Gus waited until they had subsided a bit.

"He put it to me plainly," Gus said. "He said he wanted you to marry Philip, and he hoped you wouldn't wait too long in doing it. It bothered Adam greatly that he was unable to accumulate enough money to sustain you after his death. But Philip, he knew, could take good care of you. And, Julia, he truly liked Philip. If Adam's looking down from wherever he is, I'd guess that he's a bit angry with you and a little disappointed in my son. Adam said that he considered a week to be a suitable period of mourning after his death."

She was silent for a long time. She took a deep, shuddering breath and asked, "Have you told Philip any of this?"

"No, I don't know whether or not he'd believe me." He chuckled. "He knows how badly I want a grandchild. I thought maybe you'd be able to figure out a way to let him know."

For the first time in months she felt alive. There was new color in her face as Gus and she walked back toward Philip's office. He was there. He greeted them by saying, "Hello, Dad. Mrs. Grey."

"Hello, Mr. Trent," Julia said, but there was something

in her voice that made Philip do a double take. "I was just thinking," she went on, "that it's been a long time since we had one of those argumentative dinners that Adam used to enjoy so much. I would like it very much if Gus and you would join me tonight for corned beef and cabbage. I'll ask you to bring a good red wine, if you don't mind. We'll sit around and solve all the world's problems afterward."

"Fine," Gus said. "That's just fine." He winked at Julia. "I'll meet you there about six, Philip. I've got some things to do."

Both Gus and Julia knew that he was going to be late—that, in fact, he wouldn't show up at all.

EPILOGUE

Leah Miles was only the first of the many bartered brides. Among those who were to follow her example were Consuelo Vanderbilt, duchess of Marlborough; Eugenie Zimmerman, duchess of Manchester; May Geolet, with both Astor and Vanderbilt blood, duchess of Roxburghe; Anna Gould, Jay Gould's daughter, princess de Sagon; and Alice Thaw, countess of Yarmouth.

Brian Ravendale, it seemed, had needed only a stabilizing force to set his life straight. Leah's common sense and the love she came to feel for him were exactly what he needed. Lloyd Miles gave his brother-in-law stock tips from New York so that the original dowry, which was not squandered, grew nicely.

Thanks to the good auspices of the duke and duchess of Ravendale, two attractive and interesting American sisters were in great demand in London society. Leah sent her brother a newspaper clipping wherein Victoria Woodhull Martin vehemently denied that she had ever, ever advocated free love.

"Victoria's husband," Leah wrote to her brother, "is not of the peerage. He is a dignified man of means, a banker named John Biddulph Martin. His lack of a title, as you can imagine, is played upon quite often by Lady Tennie C., wife of the viscount Francis Cook."

Later, in a separate mailing, Leah sent Lloyd a copy of a paper in which Mrs. Victoria Claflin Martin proved conclusively that she was descended from King Robert III of Scotland and from Alexander Hamilton, product of the dukes of Hamilton.

In Washington, Mrs. Julia Trent, wife of one of the most influential Republican members of the House of Representatives, was sorting through the papers of her first husband, Adam Grey. She found a file labeled: *Miles, Lloyd*. The contents, she saw quickly, would interest Philip, for the last research project that Adam had conducted detailed how Lloyd Miles had watered the stock of the Kansas City and Southwest Railroad, then gutted the little company and its unsuspecting investors in order to make himself a profit of millions.

In his almost unreadable scrawl Adam had written, "So long as such blatant stock manipulation is allowable by law, so long as unscrupulous barons such as Lloyd Miles are allowed to fleece those of lesser means and astuteness, this country will face crises like that of Black Friday and the near panic that followed."

"Not to mention the panic of this year," Julia said to herself.

"Reminder," Adam had written. "Suggest to P. that his committee investigate ways of outlawing uncontrolled printing of stock, such as was the practice of Daniel Drew when he was in control of the Erie, and such as in the coup engineered by Lloyd Miles with the KC&S.

"It might also be a good idea to seek ways by the enactment of laws by Congress to require more margin in the trading of gold and stocks. As long as it is possible for a trader to control unlimited quantities of gold with a very small amount of cash, there will be the danger of another Black Friday.

"Actually, although I am, of course, a Republican—this is not, nor has it ever been, a democracy—and believe in economic freedom along with all other freedoms, after making this study I am convinced that the spectacle of grown men standing in the middle of a room screaming buy-and-sell orders at one another represents the most abysmal stupidity of the capitalistic system. The way the gold market and the stock market operate leaves more than ample opportunity for the manipulations of scoundrels such as Jay Gould and Lloyd Miles. As long as men are fearful, avaricious, and conduct vital financial affairs by screaming back and forth, important trends that affect the welfare of our nation will occur as the result of the unilateral decisions of men like Gould and Miles and by the sheep who follow them.

"The financial well-being of this country should not depend on the whims, fears, and ignorances of a relatively small group of men who, operating in the heart of New York's financial district, are isolated from the ebb and flow of the natural laws of supply and demand in the country at large. In their odd world, the worth of a business is determined not necessarily by its efficiency nor by the amount of profit that it makes, but by rumor, innuendo, deliberate lie, and manipulation. If we are ever going to be free of the threat of a recurrence of the devastating panic of 1857 we must find a way to bring sanity to this business of buying and selling gold and stocks and bonds."

There was one final sentence scribbled at the bottom of the last sheet of paper: "Note to P: don't ask me how to do it. That's your job."

Julia questioningly looked at Philip, who had come to stand behind her and read over her shoulder. He nodded. "I've been telling myself the same thing—only not quite so cogently—since Black Friday and especially after what has happened on the stock exchange this year. I think Adam has laid out an agenda for us." He mused. "I think the Trent committee could serve as the instrument to begin a study of possible controls on the markets. I'll talk to the Speaker. And James Garfield."

"The Speaker is all for it," Julia said. "I was talking to his secretary just this morning. As far as Garfield is concerned, I think he'd just want to steal your thunder and take over with the banking committee."

Philip held up his hand. "All right," he said with resignation, "since it seems that my staff members have it all arranged, I think I'll go into my office and take a nap."

It was their old joke. She followed him in, pushed aside the papers he had picked up, and sat in his lap, having just a bit of trouble fitting behind the desk because her stomach was protruding with Gus Trent's first grandchild.

"It's almost quitting time," she said. "Why don't we both go home and take a nap?"

He knew that she was not talking about sleeping.

THE ROBBER BARONS—Book Three
PRIDE AND FORTUNE
by Gerald Canfield

Lloyd Miles buys a small railroad, then spreads the lie that he has a right-of-way through Indian lands. But labor unrest ruins his plan to sell the line at inflated prices. Lloyd's influence brings federal troops into Pittsburgh to subdue the strikers. There he falls in love with young Eda O'Day. His marriage to Abby is in ruins; she adores Thaddeus Harcourt, a small-time New York banker. For revenge Lloyd secretly uses Thad's bank to advance his own underhanded schemes. Abby is sexually assaulted by a gang of New York thugs—a cure, Lloyd hopes, for her promiscuity.

In Washington the outcome of the presidential election is in doubt. Congressman Philip Trent is appointed to find a solution with Southern states. He brings his wife, Julia, to Virginia to reconcile with her estranged family. She and her uncle fight over ownership of Julia's father's land. The task of ending the bitter feud rests solely with Philip's father and Julia's cigar-smoking cousin, Georgia Beth.

In Pittsburgh Eda's father is killed in a riot. Eda learns Lloyd's identity and banishes him. The strikers' defeat means Lloyd's success. But a congressional investigation is fast closing in on him. Can Lloyd outwit Philip again, or is this the end for the financier?

Read *PRIDE AND FORTUNE*, coming next year wherever Dell Books are sold.